Sittin' On A Goldmine Productions, L.L.C.

info@sittinonagoldmine.co

www.sittinonagoldmine.co

ISBN: 978-1-952739-49-1

PARANORMAL COZY MYSTERY

Fries & Alibis

TRIXIE SILVERTALE

Sittin' On A Goldmine
Productions L.L.C.

CHAPTER 1

I WAKE UP with a pounding headache and a dry, sticky tongue. Rolling over, I'm confronted with an unpleasant odor. Oof! My sheets are way past due for a wash.

Flashes of last night's bachelorette party peek through the curtain of fog draped over my brain. A red and pink streamer tickles my forehead with fresh whispers of regret. I yank it from my hair and roll onto my feet.

The room swirls and I cradle my head as more images bubble to the surface. Did I dance on the bar at the Flicka Shack?

No. I think that was Elisa.

But I'm certain that I, the one and only Mitzy Moon, grabbed the mic from Fat Carol and screeched out an endless rendition of "My Heart Will Go On."

I wish I could say this sequence of events is a rare occurrence. No such luck. Over the years of struggling to survive in foster care I built a wall around my emotions. Now I prefer to drown them —or eat them. I exhale stale air and urge my grey matter to make a plan.

Today my To Do list will be short:

1. Take aspirin and drink two gallons of water.
2. Do as little as possible at work.
3. Apologize to Fat Carol.

Don't look at me like that—she calls herself Fat Carol. She's not even fat; she thinks it's ironic. Don't get me started.

4. Wish that I could afford to call in sick, collapse onto my sofa, and binge-watch . . . anything.

As the hydration seeps into my cells, a few more choice moments float up from the murky depths. I should probably head over to the free clinic and get a Z-pak to ward off whatever slimy creatures crawled out of Shady Ben's mouth and onto my tongue while I was licking his tonsils!

By the way, welcome to my life.

This is it: Parties. Booze. Regrets. There's a

whole sad little orphan backstory—but I'm getting ahead of myself.

I could also thrill you with tales of my amazing career at the coffee shop *du jour*, but I don't think you can handle that much excitement in one day.

Yes, I need to get a life—or at least start crowd-funding for one.

KNOCK. KNOCK. KNOCK.

Insistent, but not threatening. It's probably Jennifer stopping by on her morning run to fill me in on the dirty details of my nocturnal escapades.

Lucky for me I'm still wearing my skinny jeans and *Supernatural* T-shirt from last night. No need to wrap up in a nasty sheet.

Not that Jenn stays sober; she just has a relentless Insta. Hooray. Because there's nothing quite as wonderful as a public, online portal cataloging the breadth of my poor judgment.

Stepping over more than one insect carcass, I make my way toward the pounding assault on my aching head.

Before the door opens I hit her with a zinger. "So, what manner of atrocity did I commit, Jenn?"

As the wizened old man hunched in my hallway pulls into focus, my jaw falls slack like a broken ventriloquist dummy. "I was expecting someone else," I stammer.

"That makes two of us," he snipes. His bulbous

nose twitches and he harrumphs into his thick grey mustache with what I assume is disdain.

Ouch.

He balances an ancient leather briefcase against the wall and rummages through the contents. His gnarled hand grasps a bulging manila envelope. He sticks the corner between his teeth—the color of the pouch blending unfortunately with the shade of his chompers. He closes the briefcase with two sharp clicks and clears his throat. Three times. His saggy cheeks flap unceremoniously.

"I'm looking for Mizithra Achelois Moon." A gust of pipe smoke and denture cream wafts toward me on the tail of his inquest.

I stare in surprise, flavored with a pinch of gut-churning horror. The last time someone came to the door and slaughtered the pronunciation of my full, legal name they followed up by informing my babysitter that a commuter train had killed my mother.

The old man shifts his pear-shape back on his heels and strains to see the number dangling from one screw on the door next to my slowly nodding head.

"Do I have the wrong apartment?" He huffs and wags his balding head.

"I'm Mitzy." I can't bring myself to say the whole name. My late mother was the only one who called me Mizithra. It happens to be the name of a Greek cheese, and also the thing that brought her and my since-vanished father together twenty-two years ago.

Theirs had been a classic "meet cute." She was shopping at some over-priced hipster grocery store and my rumored-to-be irresistible father had reached for the same ball of mizithra cheese that my mom had grabbed. Their hands touched. Cut to her apartment. Their naughty places touched. He never called. She kept the baby.

Maybe she named me after the cheese in some strange hope that he would return and they would share a laugh. That never happened. And now she's gone too. So, it's Mitzy. Just Mitzy, okay?

Oh, crap. The old shriveled guy has been talking the whole time I took a trip down memory lane. I missed literally everything he just said. Nod and smile, my mother always said.

So I do.

He hands me the large envelope, says, "I'm sorry for your loss," and shuffles away.

Since I've lost pretty much everything, I shrug and tear open the envelope as I kick the door shut with my UN-pedicured heel.

Cash.

A key.

Documents.

Did I mention the cash?

Pushing aside yesterday's empty takeout container, I upend the envelope onto my dining-room TV tray and stare.

I don't deal with much cash in my world, but I'd have to say this particular pile of hundreds looks like a crap ton of money. I could count it, but I don't want to ruin the illusion of wealth by discovering an actual dollar amount.

I touch the crisp bills. They feel real. I'll have to sneak one to work and make a mark on it with that magic authentication pen, just to make sure it's a real "Benjamin."

Yuck. Visions of Shady Ben's hands on my body slither into my consciousness.

I need a shower.

Touching the bills one more time, I gasp and race to throw my deadbolt and chain the front door. Now that I'm rich some low-life might try to rob me.

As I turn to stumble toward a *Silkwood*-style erasure of last night's transgressions, the shiny golden key seems to call to me.

I pick up the key and feel the heft of it in my hand. The brass is cool to the touch, and the angled barrel displays the scars of age and use. It's definitely larger than any key I've ever seen—and it's not flat. It's sort of a triangle-ish thing with teeth on all three sides.

Weird.

I can't seem to put the key down, so I hold it in my right hand while I shuffle through the loose papers with my left.

Does that say "Last Will and Testament?"

I drop the key.

My eyes race over the words, and with each sentence my hands shake a little more.

My grandmother, a woman I've never met, is dead. But the thing that is flipping my beanie is that this is my disappearing dad's mother. She's dead and she left me her bookshop in some podunk town clinging to the shores of some Great Lake I've never heard of . . .

The cash is meant to help me settle my affairs—if only—and relocate to said podunk town. This stranger thinks (thought) that I would abandon my life to run some small-town bookstore?

I make no effort to stifle my laughter as I drop the papers and walk toward the bathroom, shaking my head.

The steam swirls around me while I scrub the shampoo into my cigarette-smoke-scented white-blonde hair. Another gift from slumming it with Shady Ben. Seems like the second time this month I ended up pity-kissing a rando in the smoke pit at a bar/party.

SPUTTER.

SILENCE.

"No. No. No. Please do not do this right now." I twist the turny knobs in the shower, rub the tile like a magic lamp, and pray to the shower gods to give me enough water to rinse the flipping shampoo out of my ey—

DELUGE.

Ice-cold water thunders out of the showerhead and blasts all sound and feeling from my world. I'm so shocked I can neither speak nor move. I gasp and suck in air as if that can counter the freezing fluid. Fortunately, I've played through this scene a few times and I know the water could stop again at any moment, so I bite the inside of my cheek to keep from screaming and thrust my head under the icy spray.

The water indeed ceases to grace me with its presence roughly sixty seconds later. Close enough.

Wrapping a towel around my shivering body, I run to the kitchenette to make some hot coffee.

No coffee.

That sounds about right.

I promised myself I'd stop at the Qwik Mart after the party last night and grab a few things.

Clearly that did not happen.

On the bright side, I didn't wake up in Shady Ben's shifty bed!

Time to get dressed and run down to that coffee shop where I work and see if I can get a pre-shift cup of wake-up juice.

CHAPTER 2

Don't worry, I put all the lovely cash inside a nearly empty box of waffles in my freezer-ette and taped the key under my toilet tank. I actually stuck the key under the tank with a wad of freshly chewed gum. You didn't believe I had tape, did you?

Now that I'm rich I have to be more careful. Plus, if life in the foster system has taught me anything, that weird old dude will be back this afternoon to say "gotcha" or "oops" and take it all back.

Pushing open the door of Hot Kafka, I inhale the rich scent of waking up.

Dang it! I forgot to clean the whipped-cream stain off my uniform. Maybe I can slip into the bathroom before anyone sees me.

"Namaste, Mitzy!" Prayer hands and a blessed

head nod approach as the soundtrack of singing bowls reaches a crescendo.

Fan-flipping-tastic. The SUPERvisor is already on me. "Hey, Dean." If I still had long hair I could sweep it in front of my face and hide the stain as I run to the bathroom. However, two weeks ago, after I lost a drunken karaoke bet, I ended up with a cross between a Cardi B. pixie and a Betty White curl-bob. I refer to this as the "Bad Bet." Not my finest moment.

"Hey Mitzy, where ya headed?" He tilts his head with what I'm sure he thinks is concern.

Dean miraculously crosses the entire Saltillo-tile floor in seconds and now stands inches from my person.

"Just a quick trip to the restroom before my shift, Dean." I try to scoot past.

"Well that's the thing, Mitzy. Your shift started at 9:45 and it's already 10:00, and well, I'd just be super-pumped if you would take care of your personal business at home and show up on time and ready to work." Huge smile.

And there it is. SUPERvisor Dean is always super-pumped about something. I live for his life lessons. "Copy that, Dean. I'll just—"

"Oh boy, Mitzy. Is that a stain on your uniform? It's darkening your whole aura." Huge smile downgrades to miniscule grin as he gestures toward my Macbeth-sized spot.

I swat his unwelcome paw away from my boob area. "I'll just clean it up right quick and be ready to go."

"Well, gee whiz, Mitzy, I'm gonna have to get you a new shirt and dock that from your pay. I'm super-sorry about that, but we have to put our best face forward at the Hot Kafka. Our customers expect a certain vibe." He finishes with an emphatic nod and an attaboy fist pump.

I'm pretty sure our customers expect coffee without spit in it. I mean, if they wanted fancy coffee served by people in clean uniforms they'd march down the street to the chain store with the mood lighting and free Wi-Fi. Of course, I don't say any of this to Dean. I nod and smile.

As I watch Dean's peppy step take him to the Kokopelli-embellished stockroom door something dawns on me. Hey, wait one darn tootin' minute. I'm rich. I don't need this ridiculous job or this insanely positive SUPERvisor. I follow Dean into the stockroom and make my announcement. "I quit."

"Oh, hey now, Mitzy. Don't get your chakras out of alignment." He raises his hands like this is a robbery. "You'll be back in the black in no time. I'll only charge you my cost for the new uniform shirt. How's that sound?"

I'm sorry about this next part. Please skip ahead and pretend you don't see me do this. "Ya know what, Dean? Here's how it sounds!" I take off the stained shirt, throw it in his shocked face, and strut out of Hot Kafka into the unforgiving Arizona sun.

Too bad I didn't remember that I was wearing my skanky, greyish, holey bra BEFORE I made my statement. The strut would've been so much more impressive in a red lacey push-up thingy.

Instead I run home with my arms crossed over my chest, sweat trickling down my back, and a little muffin topping my skinny jeans.

Slamming my apartment door behind, I throw the deadbolt home.

Just when I finally learned the name of the place, too . . . so long, Hot Kafka. "We could've been Franz." I choke on my own pun as a loud and threatening knock assaults my door.

I hold my breath.

"I seen ya run in there, ya trollop."

That is Mr. Coleman. My landlord. Did you already guess that my rent is late—again?

"I'll be back in the morning with an eviction notice. Ya hear me?"

THUMP!

I jump as his fist connects with the door in one last frustrated punch.

A sudden need to explore lakes comes over me. I believe they were purported to be "great?"

So long Sedona!

I pack my stuff in a crummy ripped duffle bag and an old rucksack. In the movies there's always a framed picture that gets lovingly tucked in the top, but none of my pre-tragedy childhood trinkets survived the foster care system. And now I tend to move frequently; so keeping the load light is essential.

I put the cash in my boots, underwear, bra, and a bit in my wallet. Not exactly sure what to do with the key and not super committed to drug-mule-style hiding.

I have a collection of keys I "borrowed" from the homes where I was placed from eleven until I aged out, but this strange key feels different. This key was given to me. This key was a gift from an actual relative.

I opt for a chain.

I slip the "jewelry" under my shirt and wait for the cover of darkness. Now that I've got money, I don't want to waste any of my little pile of wealth on back rent. I mostly want to make a clean getaway and see what my key opens. It feels like a morbid game show.

"Mitzy Moon! Your long-lost grandmother is dead! Let's see what you've won!"

CHAPTER 3

I DON'T THINK this loud, smelly bus could possibly make any more stops! I mean, why in the wide world does a bus need to stop at an empty bench in a town with the same population as I have fingers?

No one boards. I'm as shocked as you are.

We lurch forward, and I force myself to breathe as shallowly as possible. The odor of diesel fumes, unwashed humanity, and day-old turkey sub—with a soupçon of stale cigarette smoke—is not something I want seeping into the depths of my lung tissue.

I wish I'd made some hatch marks on the bus seat to count the passing days, but it's more than two and less than a million. Finally, the sign for Pin Cherry Harbor welcomes me and promises an end to this *Groundhog Day* of a bus ride.

It's not a green and white metal sign like most

places. No ma'am, this town has a bespoke sign carved from wood and hand-painted with bunches of what can only be pin cherries in each corner.

The bus lurches to a stop with a screech of the brakes and a puff of exhaust. I step off, choke on the engine's haze, and walk to the sidewalk.

I immediately regret my decision to risk a cross-country migration.

No parade. No welcome wagon.

A typical relocation with all the familiar acid reflux and floating detachment.

I look up and down the street that seems to have fallen out of an old black-and-white movie. Nothing too appealing: Rex's Drugstore, a boarded up Montgomery Wards, an unnamed hardware store. But when my eyes fall on Myrtle's Diner the color floods in like a frame from Dorothy's Oz, and I feel the call of the fry.

My stomach growls as I cross the street. When I open the door the smells of grease and goodness hit me almost as hard as the seven sets of eyeballs.

I nod and slip into the nearest booth.

A server who bears the nametag "Tally" swoops in.

"Just passin' through, eh?" She nods, and her freshly dyed, flaming-red topknot reminds me of a cherry adorning a rather old sundae.

I could say "yes," place my order, and go about

my business, but . . . "No ma'am, I think I might stay. I'd like a cheeseburger, well done, with a side of fries. I'll take a bottle of hot sauce with that if you've got it. Oh, and a soda."

Tally's pen does not move. It hovers above the order pad like a super-slo-mo space shuttle docking.

"That's it for me," I add with a tip of my head and a slightly raised eyebrow above my folksy grin.

Tally mumbles something incoherent and hustles back to the kitchen as fast as her elderly legs can take her.

I swivel my head to scan the place for a possible "Myrtle."

All eyes, seven pairs, stare unblinkingly at me.

Including Tally and the cook, who both peer through the red Formica trim of the "orders-up" window.

I give another nod, turn back to my booth, and search diligently for nothing in my rucksack.

The silence reminds me of a country song where everyone can hear a pin drop, or an old saloon after the gun-slinging outlaw walks through the swinging doors. That's me. I guess there's a new sheriff in town and if they don't like it—

The front door of the diner whips open and the actual strong-jawed, clean-cut sheriff bursts through. Uniform freshly laundered. Check. Blonde hair neatly slicked back. Check.

Do I love a man in uniform? Check!

"This the gal here?" The broad-shouldered sheriff gestures toward me and scans the patrons.

I don't turn around, but I think it's safe to assume they all nod.

"Hey there, Miss. We have a strict policy on vagrants in Pin Cherry Harbor. So, I'll just get Tally to pack up your food to go and I'll give you a lift outta town. Sound good?"

I could pull out the will and maybe even brandish the key. Of course, I go another direction entirely. I stand up real slow, like it pains me to have to do it. I look down at the black and white linoleum squares, take a deep breath and look up at the sheriff. When I catch sight of his dreamy blue eyes my heart snaps out a few extra beats and I forget the smart-alec line I want to say. Instead I go with, "Aren't you a tall drink of water." To be fair, he's at least six-foot plus two or three inches.

He blushes profusely. The color only adds to his charm.

I smile wickedly as I remember my line. "I wasn't expecting such a formal welcome, Officer, but I appreciate you takin' time out of your busy day to make me feel so special." I step closer.

He sucks in a breath and tries to step back. I say "tries" because he catches the heel of one of his steel-toed boots on the toe of the other, stumbles, flails, and snags my arm as he falls backward.

Now, I'm no waif, but I'm smaller than him. So, he continues to tumble and I, of course, land smack dab on top of him.

A collective gasp rises from the diner.

I instantly make matters worse by saying, "Well, welcome to Pin Cherry yourself, Sheriff."

His angled jaw flexes and his muscular chest rises and falls rapidly beneath me. As his face shifts to a shade of red that surely puts the town's namesake to shame, I roll clear and offer him a hand.

He shakes his head vigorously, releasing the slicked-back hair so that it falls over his eye in an unintentionally sexy manner. He gets to his feet under his own power.

I notice his thumb depress the button on his radio—twice. In case you're not familiar, this is called "keying" your radio. As a film school dropout, I can tell you how we used to do this on the film set when we needed to respond to something that came over the headset but couldn't answer verbally because the cameras were rolling. I'm pretty sure I just saw the sheriff signal for help.

Tally attempts to hand me a Styrofoam container.

I wave it away and finally brandish the key. "I'll take that for here, Tally." I turn to show everyone the key. "And then I'll be opening up my bookstore if anyone needs a new summer read." My heart thumps rapidly in complete opposition to my false bravado.

A voice crackles over the radio. "Sheriff, you're needed urgently at headquarters."

Didn't I tell you?

Sheriff Too Hot To Handle scrapes his hair back into place, mumbles something under his breath, and practically runs out the door.

I grin stupidly and stare a little too long at his exit.

If one of my student films had been this riveting I never would've abandoned film school.

Tally returns with an honest-to-goodness plate, silverware, my soda, and a bottle of Tabasco that looks older than me.

I ease back into the booth and eat my burger like I got all the time in the world. The remaining customers trickle out—each one sliding me a hard side-eye as they pass.

Once the place clears of customers the cook saunters out and slips into the other side of my booth. His worn dungarees make a short squeak against the red vinyl.

He sizes me up, and I wonder if my bus-applied makeup and dry-shampooed hair will pass muster.

I size him up right back. He's old. Not creepy-crumbly old, but the kind of face that has a story tucked in every crease and eyes that still hold a little fire in their coffee-dark depths. His grey hair is buzzed short, but covers his head in a utilitarian fashion.

I nod.

He nods.

"I've got money," I say with a bit more indignation than I intend.

"I figured as much." His voice is rough as a Brillo Pad, but as comforting as a favorite chair. "So Myrtle left you her bookshop, eh?"

"Mmhmm," I say. I hope we're talking about the same Myrtle. It's especially confusing because I'm fairly certain I'm sitting in Myrtle's Diner, and it seems unlikely that there could be two Myrtles in town.

"You don't look much like her." He tilts his head. "Maybe around the eyes. She had those mischievous grey peepers." His gaze drifts off and a soft smile plays across his lips.

"Did you know my grandmother?"

"I figure I knew her better than you." He clenches his jaw.

"Fair enough."

"You got the gift, too?" His gaze narrows and he shifts in his seat.

I have no idea what he's talking about. Is the

bookstore the gift? And what does he mean by "too?" Is there some other person who inherited the shop? I swallow all those questions and go with, "I'm not sure what you mean?"

"Myrtle had visions. She called 'em premonitions. You get any of those?" He lifts his chin and waits.

And I thought Sedona was full of nutters. "Uh, nope. No visions here."

"Why'd you come?" He leans back and places both hands against the edge of the table.

Aw what the heck. I got nothing to lose, right? "My mother died when I was eleven, I never knew my father, and life in general has not worked out so great for me. I figured I might as well see what Pin Cherry Harbor has to offer."

He nods real slow and fixes me with a surprisingly gentle stare. "Burgers are on the house as long as you're in town." His eyes glisten as he whispers, "She would've wanted that." He slaps the silver-flecked white table once, nods, and returns to the kitchen.

I walk to the counter and peer through the orders-up window. "You never answered my question. How well did you know my grandmother?"

He works his jaw back and forth and I can see he's working hard to stuff his emotions back down where they belong. "Name's Odell."

That name rings a bell. I remember reading it on the bus when I was reviewing the will. It said, *To Odell Johnson, who has always had my heart, I leave my share of Myrtle's Diner.* I smile knowingly and repeat my question. "So, how well did you know my grandmother?"

"I'll answer that one on our second date." A sly smile tugs at the corner of his mouth and crinkles his cheek.

"Fair enough." I walk toward the door and toss over my shoulder, "I don't suppose you can point me toward the bookshop, can you?"

He chuckles, and a metal spatula scrapes across the grill before he answers, "Down Main Street, to your left. Can't miss it."

If I had a quarter for every time someone had given me "can't miss it" directions, I'd be a— Oh, that's right. I am.

CHAPTER 4

WELL, I'LL BE a monkey's uncle! You actually can't miss it. Right on the corner of Main and First. I lean back and shade my eyes against the mid-morning sun. "Wow!" I look around to see if anyone heard my exclamation, but the streets are devoid of walkers, and the old truck sputtering down the road can't hear a thing.

I walk down the side of the massive three-story brick building and run my hand along the rough red-brown surface. I catch my breath as I come face to face with the "great lake" mentioned in the documents, which provided much-needed entertainment on the bus. "Wow!" I say again.

I've never seen this much water in my entire life. The sheer volume is obscene. A flash flood in the desert during the brief monsoon season is a dripping faucet compared to this lush, liquid paradise. The sun sparkles off the water, birds swoop and dive overhead, the cool breeze flutters my hair, and—

"Hey there, you gonna open up or not?"

I swallow my awe and turn to see one of the pairs of eyes from the diner posted up outside my bookshop. I guess I'm gonna open.

I slip the chain with the key over my head as I walk toward my first customer. "I'm Mitzy. What's your name?" The woman looks about fifty or sixty. I'm not that great at guessing people's ages. Her black denim pants, Styx T-shirt, and biker boots say fifty-ish, but her severe grey pixie and lined face whisper an older tale.

"I didn't come for chit-chat, girlie. Are ya opening or not?"

So much for Midwestern charm.

The eight-foot solid wood door that bars my entry to the bookshop is a work of art. I don't have time to inspect the careful craftsmanship that adorns the massive piece with delicate and detailed carving—there is too much sighing and foot tapping behind me. I run my fingers along the edge opposite the hefty iron hinges and locate the cleverly concealed opening that contains the "plug." Yes, I did learn how to pick locks from a delinquent older foster brother. But even he couldn't have popped this cherry. His gross term, not mine. I slide my triangular key into the lock and turn. I don't hear a click so much as I "feel" the lock open. I actually think I felt the whole store awaken. And I realize that sounds as weird as it—well, sounds.

I pull the heavy, ornate door open and have to physically arm-bar the patron from entering before me. It's my shop. I want to be the first to walk in.

No Chit-chat exhales loudly.

I feel around on the left and right for the light switches. Nothing. Goose egg. Nada.

"Oh for cryin' out loud," exclaims No Chit-chat as she bustles past me and disappears into the store.

I gaze around in the dust-filtered window-light and breathe in the scent of worlds. I imagine a short film that will take place within—

LIGHTS.

A massive chandelier flashes to life above me and I gasp.

I crane my neck to take in the impossibly voluminous space. The building did not look anywhere near this large from the outside. There are three stories of bookshelves. All the way from the richly carpeted floor to the gleaming tin-plated ceiling.

A balcony curves from one side of the second floor to the other, passing through a lovely loft/mezzanine in the back.

I drop my bags to the floor and hop-step over

the "No Admittance" chain, run up the wrought-iron circular staircase to the open-plan second floor, and take in the mesmerizing view back toward the rows of slumped-glass windows. Dust floating in the air seems to ride on a gentle breeze down to the bookcases in their thick, stoic rows on the first floor.

"You need me to run to the bank and get the drawer money?"

Oh crap, I completely forgot about my customer. I hurry down the stairs, trip a little, catch myself on the railing, stumble over my bags, and skitter to a halt in front of No Chit-chat. "Why would I need drawer money? And why would I send you to get it if I did, Mrs.—?"

"Nope. No 'Mrs.' Never wrapped that noose around my neck. Everybody calls me 'Twiggy.'"

Twiggy. Hmmm. Now that would be the perfect name for Fat Carol. "All right. Can I help you find something today, Twiggy?"

"You can't even find the lights, doll. And to answer one of your many earlier questions, you need drawer money to put in the cash register." She puts up a finger, capped by a close-clipped nail, to shush me and continues, "You send me to get it 'cuz I been workin' part-time for your Grams during high season since she had this old brewery converted into a bookstore."

I glance around the utterly empty bookshop

and nod and smile. "Well, how is it that you have access to my grandmother's—rather—my bank account?"

"Are you always this thick, or did you hit your head when you tackled the sheriff?"

I clench my jaw to prevent a stream of unladylike phrases from spilling out of my beautiful mouth. "Humor me," I manage to say.

"Tilly's been the teller at the bank practically since the money came by stagecoach. She knows me. She knew your Grams. I walk in, ask for the drawer money, and she hands it over." Twiggy shakes her head like she's ashamed of me. "If I went in there and ask Tilly for $10,000 in small bills she'd laugh and call the sheriff. Understand?"

I barely understand a single word, but I'm not going to give her the satisfaction. I'll refer you to a corollary to the first rule of foster care: never show weakness. "I understand that the only thing standing between me and an empty bank account is a sheriff who can't manage to stand on his own two feet. Oh, and apparently Tilly simultaneously works at the bank and the diner." I give her a "take that" smirk.

Twiggy looks heavenward and invokes my grandmother. "Myrtle Isadora Johnson Linder Duncan Willamet Rogers, if I didn't think so highly of you I'd run this scrawny idiot out of town before sunset."

All I heard was that she thinks I'm skinny. Nice. Oh, that and the fact that my grandmother had at least five husbands . . .

"Tally works at the diner. Tilly works at the bank. They're sisters. Folks say their parents named each of the kids after the town where he or she was conceived. Now I'm not saying it's an appropriate system, but the oldest sister got made in Tillamook, Wisconsin, and goes by Tilly. The youngest got made in Tallahassee, Florida, and goes by Tally, and the brother in the middle got cooked up in Toledo, Ohio, and goes by—"

"Toley," I blurt.

"What the heck kinda name is Toley? No, wiseacre, he goes by Ledo."

I don't believe her for one second. I don't think she liked me stealing her punch line, so she made up the bit about the brother. Regardless, apparently this ornery spinster is my employee, and since I know less than nothing about this place I better make nice. "I'll make a note of those names. Now, would you please walk on over to the bank and get the drawer money. And maybe you can show me around the shop when you get back. Okay?"

Twiggy strides toward the front door and calls back, "Sure enough. I'll show you around the museum and the apartment, too. I s'pose you'll need a place to stay—if you're stayin'." Just before the door closes she adds, "Don't mess with Pyewacket. He ain't a fan of strangers, you know."

The massive door bangs shut behind her, and I make a mental note to get some kind of spring or shock for the unwieldy thing. It's strangely out of place in the brewery-turned-bookshop. The door is intricately decorated with symbols and figures that whisper of faraway places—perhaps my grandmother was a traveler. My gaze returns to the shelves and shelves of books. Reading was my escape from the pain and loss that followed my mother's death. Books contained the only true friends I'd ever known. I smile broadly and close my eyes. I can almost feel the dust in the air, but I inhale deeply regardless of the atoms of paper I'm surely taking in. As I breathe in the energy flowing through the room, there's a noise like someone scratching on metal.

I pop open my eyes and walk toward the sound. There must be a side or rear door. I wander into the back room where Twiggy disappeared earlier and the volume increases.

An illuminated "Exit" sign spills red light into the dim space. As I near the door the scraping becomes clearer. It is definitely an animal. My heart skips a beat. What if my grandmother left me a puppy? I slowly push open the door so I don't hit the hopefully adorable puppy.

Imagine my shock and disappointment when instead of a cuddly bundle of cuteness, I discover a dog-sized alley cat that appears to be half bobcat and half demon! Oh, and it has something nasty in its pointy-toothed mouth. Great! I was hoping to come face to face with a dead mouse today.

I wave my arms to shoo the cat away, but she—or maybe he—I didn't check under the hood, so let's go with "it." It drops the dead thing on the step and squirts past me into the bookstore in a blur of tan fur and tufted ears that almost knocks me off my feet.

Pyewacket, I assume. Nice to make your acquaintance.

Before my brain can send the "give chase" signal, I inexplicably bend down to get a closer look at the leavings.

"Son of a—" I won't repeat what I actually say. In fact, I won't even tell you what's lying on the step. I run into the bookstore screaming unrepeatables at the cat, who I'm now sure is Pyewacket, while I search for a spoon (ew) or tweezers (yuck) or a dustpan. All I can find are chopsticks.

I demand that the cat get out of my bookshop, and to my great surprise, as I open the side door the demon-spawn feline rockets into the alley.

I pick up the "thing" on the step with the chopsticks and fiercely fight my gag reflex as I shuffle-run toward the dumpster at the end of the alley.

My fingers are shaking.

The thing is slipping.

I am less than a foot from the finish line and my arm is poised to dump and run.

A car turns down the alley.

BWAAP. BWAAP.

Two quick hoots from a siren. Hooray.

Red and blue lights swirl on and off, filling the alleyway with an unwelcome, and wholly misleading, party-like atmosphere.

I slowly turn toward the intrusion.

"I thought that was you," he says.

Sheriff Too Hot To Handle is back for seconds.

"Freeze."

Did he just pull a gun on me?

"Don't take another step." He inches closer. "And drop the— Is that an eyeball?"

Clearly the sheriff is not as thoughtful as me. I'm sorry you had to hear it that way.

I nod and smile. What else can I do?

"Drop the eyeball," he repeats. "And step away from the body."

CHAPTER 5

Wait, what? Did he say "body?"

In the confusion, I fail to follow orders and instead turn to see the alleged body. At that exact moment the freaktastic feline Pyewacket leaps out of the dumpster.

Our local jumpy lawman pulls his trigger.

He misses psycho-kitty, but the bullet ricochets off the dumpster and—you guessed it—grazes my shoulder. I scream, drop the icky thing and the chopsticks, and fall on my rump in the alley.

Luckily, Twiggy sees my entire catastrophic embarrassment and delivers exactly what I need most. An earsplitting cackle.

I grab my shoulder and shout, "He shot me! You shot me, you crazy hick cop!" Warm crimson fluid oozes between my fingers, and the alley seems to spin like a merry-go-round.

"Did she call you a hiccup?" Twiggy says to the sheriff through peals of laughter.

All of a sudden her jocularity comes to an abrupt halt. "Is that a body?" Her voice is an octave higher and the laughter noticeably absent.

"I caught her red-handed. Right here, plain as day, trying to dispose of the body." He picks up his radio and calls in something about a 187, some other numbers, and an afterthought about an injured perp.

From rich to perp in less than a week. This must be how Willie Nelson felt. I know I'll probably rot in a cell in this one-horse town, but when Sheriff Too Hot To Handle walks toward me and pulls out his handcuffs, all I can think is how good it feels to be guilty.

"Stand up real slow—um, what's your name?"

I stand. "What's yours, Sheriff? I can't keep calling you Too Hot To Handle." I smile and wobble unsteadily.

He flushes handsomely and his strong jaw twitches as though he's stifling a chuckle. "Name?" he repeats in his "all business" voice.

"Mine's Mitzy Moon, Officer." I hold out one wrist.

"I'll need both hands for the cuffs, Miss Moon."

"I thought you'd never ask." I wink, but as soon as I remove my right hand from my injured left shoulder the blood flows, the stinging resumes, and I faint.

Regaining consciousness in the ambulance, my eyes struggle to focus. The sheriff angles over me with concern, and just a few strands of enticingly out-of-place hair fall over his eye and beg to be touched.

The paramedic shines a bright penlight in each of my eyes and announces, "She's coming around, Harper."

The man named "Harper" leans in.

I smile up at the intense blue-grey eyes and whisper, "What's your first name, Harper?"

The sheriff exhales, leans back, and replies, "It's Erick. But you can call me Sheriff Harper."

I attempt to lift my right arm to give him a proper handshake, and that's when I feel the handcuff clamping my wrist to the gurney.

"Mitzy Moon, you're under arrest for the murder of Cal Duncan. You have the right to remain silent. Anything . . . "

My ears ring just like the victims in the aftermath of a concussion grenade in a B-movie. Murder? I thought throwing my uniform shirt at SUPERvisor Dean was daring and reckless. I've never murdered anything in my life. Except possibly a molten-chocolate lava cake.

As the ambulance comes to an abrupt halt and the paramedic jumps out to slide the gurney to the ground, I get a bright idea. "I want to speak to my lawyer."

"I'll call him for you while they stitch you up. What's his name?" Sheriff Harper pulls out his pen and notepad.

I smile sheepishly. "No idea. I thought I'd call the guy who delivered—" That's the exact moment I remember that I have wads of cash stuffed into my undergarments. Oops.

"Do you mean Silas Willoughby? Your grandmother's attorney?"

"Mmhmm." I nod and smile. "I'd like to speak to him before I see the doctor."

The sheriff gives me a highly suspicious look and lowers his notepad. "Are you refusing medical treatment?" He puts a hand on the gurney. "Hold up, medic," he says to the attendant.

"Not so much refusing as postponing."

"Take her into One," the doctor commands.

He continues to hold the gurney and replies, "She's refusing treatment, Doc."

Boy that Sheriff Harper is a real stickler.

"Jump off the gurney and have a seat in the waiting room, Miss. You'll change your mind when the wound starts bleeding again." The doctor tosses me an exasperated eye roll. "And it will start bleeding again." She hustles off to attend to other matters before I can reply.

Sheriff Harper unlocks one side of the handcuffs from the gurney and locks it around his own wrist.

A tingle of anticipation slides down my spine. You have my attention.

"Dispatch, can you send Deputy Paulsen down to County? I've got a babysitting job for her."

Rude.

"Oh, and get Willoughby on the horn. Tell him Isadora's granddaughter is being charged with the murder of Cal Duncan."

"10-4, Sheriff."

"You can't possibly believe I murdered anyone." I stare at the sheriff in shock. "I'd be covered in blood spatter, for one thing, and—"

He points at my shirt.

"That's my blood. From when you shot me!" I shake my head and chew the inside of my cheek. "This is entrapment. You framed me."

"Do you want to head over to the station for questioning?" He raises an eyebrow.

Butterflies in my tummy take note of his sexy arched brow and intense stare and flutter mercilessly. "What about my arm?" I gulp some air and command my stomach to behave.

"You refused medical treatment."

"I didn't. I asked for my attorney."

"Then we can't discuss the case." He shakes his head in exasperation and smiles. "You can't have it both ways, Miss Moon."

Before I can enjoy his satisfied grin, our intense flirtation is interrupted.

"Sorry it took me so long, Sheriff. That Johan Olafsson was driving his tractor right down Main Street again." The short, squat deputy sizes me up. "This the killer?"

"Alleged killer," I interject.

"She's got a mouth on her, eh? Want me to quiet her down, Sheriff?" She rocks back and forth on her tiny feet in a way that reminds me of one of those punching bags with all the sand in the bottom. The kind that kids knock down but the character keeps rolling back up.

I don't like the ilk of this deputy—not one bit.

"There's no need for that, Paulsen." He transfers the other half of my handcuffs from his inviting wrist to the ample deputy's limb. "Take her into the waiting area and keep your eyes peeled for Willoughby."

"Figures she'd lawyer up. The guilty always

do." She snarls her lip up and jerks toward me like a playground bully.

I don't flinch. One of the first things I learned in foster care was to stand my ground with bullies. I still got the crap beat out of me pretty regularly, but at least I went down fighting.

Paulsen tugs me along behind her as though I'm a bad puppy and directs me, rather roughly, into a dusty-rose vinyl-covered chair.

"Gimme a holler on the squawk box when Silas arrives." Sheriff Harper tips his chin and leaves me to stew with my babysitter.

She nods and picks at her teeth with a toothpick that seems to materialize out of thin air.

Now that my tasty distraction has exited, I notice the antiseptic odor and the chill in the air. I don't like hospitals. Never have. I reach to pull the edge of my shirt down with the handcuffed wrist.

Paulsen instantly yanks her hand. "Give me a reason, scumbag." She massages the handle of her gun and narrows her gaze.

Seems like now would be the wrong time to mention how badly I need to pee.

CHAPTER 6

You KNOW THAT scene in the movie when the music swells and the hero rushes in with a dramatic flourish to save the day? This is nothing like that.

"Over here, Silas." Deputy Paulsen lifts her pudgy hand from her gun for a moment and gives a quick two-finger wave.

Silas Willoughby shuffles down the linoleum corridor with absolutely no sense of urgency. His wrinkled brown suit, mystery-sauce-stained tie, and dilapidated briefcase mumble of a forgotten era. Picture present day Nick Cage in a remake of *Death of a Salesman*.

"Mizithra." He nods.

"Silas." I shrug my wounded arm and nod my head toward the injury, while fluttering the fingers on the handcuffed wrist.

He straightens, harrumphs into his mustache, and seems to gain six inches in height. "Deputy Paulsen, remove the restraints from my client. She is a business owner in the community and not a flight risk."

To my utter stupefaction, Deputy Paulsen works her fat little hand into her snug polyester pocket, pulls out her key, and unlocks the handcuffs.

I rub my wrist and stare at Silas with my mouth hanging open.

He extends a hand, which I gladly take. As he gently pulls me to my feet he places his other hand over my gunshot wound and murmurs something under his breath.

"I don't believe you'll require any sutures, Mizithra. Allow me to convey you to the bookshop, so you have a moment to freshen up before our visitation with Sheriff Harper."

I nod but can't seem to find the mental capacity to smile. I'm too busy staring at my shoulder. There's nothing more than a scratch. The stinging is gone, and the wound is no longer bleeding.

Mr. Willoughby drives me back to the bookstore in his mint condition 1908 Model T. The seats show some wear and the steering wheel has two smooth indentations that cradle his hands, but other than that the vehicle looks like it rolled off the assembly line yesterday.

He parks on the street and I slide out of the car. As I walk up to the door I look at the sign. "Bell, Book & Candle Bookshop." I honestly don't remember seeing that sign this morning. Maybe I did hit my head when I tumbled all over Sheriff Too Hot To Handle—I mean, Erick.

"The key, Mizithra."

"Oh, right." I fumble around under my shirt and extract the key, which has snagged on a one hundred dollar bill from my bra. "Oops." I tug the bill loose and shove it back into my "B" cup.

Mr. Willoughby shakes his head twice before his shoulders return to their normal curve of disappointment.

I put the key in, but there's no "open" sound or feeling. I tug the handle and the door opens. "I left Twiggy in charge," I offer with a shrug.

"You powder your nose and I'll wait in the stacks." He walks into the rows of bookshelves at the front of the shop.

I wander around and try to locate my bags.

An additional instruction floats over the shelves. "Do try to find something other than skinny jeans."

The way he enunciates "skinny jeans" makes them sound like poisonous snakes.

"I put your stuff in the apartment," announces Twiggy.

"And that would be . . . ?"

"Up the stairs, through the Rare Books Loft, tilt the candle next to the copy of *Saducismus Triumphatus* and you're in."

"Maybe you could show me?"

She doesn't respond.

"I have blood all over my hands. I wouldn't want to get that on the candle or the *Saducismus*."

A heavy sigh followed by clomping footfalls herald the approach of Twiggy.

"This way, Your Highness." We twist our way upstairs and through the rows of carefully aligned oak reading tables, each with a lovely brass lamp topped by a thick, green glass shade.

Despite my irritation with Twiggy's curt manner, the secret door does not fail to impress.

"Thanks."

Twiggy exhales and stomps back down the staircase.

I run my hand along the edge of the bookcase door and grin maniacally. My grandmother, who some people in town call Myrtle and others call Isadora, is—was . . . I wish I could've known her. I think she would get me, and vice versa.

After I complete a quick treasure hunt and pull all the hundreds out of my clothes, boots, and undergarments, I stuff the bills under the mattress. I don't know. I'm spitballing at this point.

I whip off my shirt, wash the blood from my hands and arm, and slip on a clean T-shirt. I glance down at the shirt. A cat spilling a cup of coffee with the tagline, "I Do What I Want."

Not quite the right message for an interrogation.

Pulling that one off, I dig through my crap duffle bag for an attitude-free shirt. The best I can find is a blue shirt with images of cassette tapes, huge old cellular phones, CDs, pagers, and other "dead tech." It doesn't have a tagline and it's all I've got. I hope no one gets the joke.

I exit the apartment and tilt the candle back to level. The secret bookcase door slides shut. Sweet! I pitter-patter down the steps.

Silas Willoughby glances up. His face says "not pleased" in at least five languages.

I shrug.

"Do you have identification?"

"Yep." I pat my back pocket. "It's in my pocket," I hastily add, in case he thinks I think my rear end is identification.

"Of course it is," he mumbles as he shuffles out the front door.

CHAPTER 7

The sheriff's station looks exactly like I imagine it should. A touch of Sheriff Valenti from Roswell with a heaping helping of Sheriff Andy Taylor from Mayberry.

Sheriff Harper walks out from his office.

Oh my, I need to add a slice of sex on toast to that description. "Hi, Erick."

"I asked you to call me Sheriff Harper, Miss Moon." While his words say "no," his grin says "maybe."

Silas steps on my witty reply. "Sheriff Harper, you cannot possibly believe that my client would take the life of Cal Duncan. She's hardly been in town long enough to make the man's acquaintance. What possible motive would she have to dispatch a perfect stranger?"

"Silas, you know as well as I do that Cal is this woman's grandfather. I wouldn't call that a perfect stranger."

Once again, I find my jaw flapping in the breeze. A grandfather! A week ago I was a poor orphan and now—now, I'm still an orphan. My relatives are dropping like flies. I guess I'm not poor, though. However, I am being accused of murder . . .

"Follow me, Miss Moon."

Sheriff Harper walks toward the back of the station and I eagerly follow. I make no effort to keep my eyes above the waist. If this is the last fine man I'm going to see before they send me up the river, I don't want to miss a thing.

He pulls out my chair and takes the one opposite.

"Miss Moon, what were you doing in that alley this morning?"

I open my mouth, but Silas places a firm hand on my arm. "You are not required to answer, Mizithra."

I ignore the odd heat of his fingers on my skin. "I'm happy to answer, and let's agree that you'll call me Mitzy from now on."

A pained exhale escapes Mr. Willoughby's person. His hand drops to his side. "As you wish, Mitzy."

"Well, Erick, I was disposing of the thing that

Pyewacket dropped on my back step. I barely looked at it, and I never saw a body until you pulled up and shot me."

"By 'thing' are you referring to the eyeball?"

I gag a little. "Yes."

"When did you arrive in Pin Cherry Harbor?"

"About five minutes before you walked in the diner and pulled me into that horizontal embrace." I nod with a hint of "game on."

"Can anyone confirm that, Miss Moon?"

"There were at least seven people in the diner. I'm sure one of them saw what happened."

He doesn't take the bait.

"What I'm asking, Miss Moon, is if anyone can confirm that you arrived in Pin Cherry this morning?"

Touché, Erick. Touché.

"I'm sure my client can produce her bus ticket, Sheriff. I assume that will suffice?" Silas pushes his chair back.

I straighten up and smile. Yeah. That should suffice. I could get used to having a lawyer.

"We're waiting on the medical examiner to confirm time of death, but if Miss Moon can verify her arrival as of this morning, I feel confident once we check her alibi we can clear her of the charges. I'm no expert, but that body—"

I hastily put up a hand. "Please don't finish that sentence, Erick."

He tilts his head and nods. "It's Sheriff Harper, Miss Moon."

"Come along, Mitzy." Silas wiggles my chair impatiently.

I stand and nod my farewell.

"Don't leave town, Miss Moon."

"I wouldn't dream of it, Erick." I get a little flush of tingles every time I say his name.

"Deputy Paulsen will have some papers for you to sign, Silas." He reaches out and shakes my lawyer's hand. "Thanks for comin' in."

Deputy Paulsen glares at me and picks her teeth with her pinky fingernail. "Sheriff tell you to stick close?"

I frown. "I own the bookshop. I'm not planning on going anywhere."

"That's right," she adds with a nod.

Silas ignores her completely, reads through the document on the proffered clipboard, and signs with an impressive flourish.

I lean in and admire his work. "Nice signature. You study calligraphy?"

"A person's name is a thing of beauty. A unique talisman. It deserves to be honored, Mitzy."

The tone with which he utters my nickname is

not lost on me. I shrug sheepishly and walk out of the station.

On the short ride back to the bookshop Silas doesn't volunteer any information about Cal Duncan, so I inquire, "Was Cal really my grandfather?"

Silas nods.

"Well, if Odell Johnson was her first husband then Cal Duncan—" I quickly review the order of her many surnames "—must've been her third. Right?"

He nods again.

"What's going on? What aren't you telling me?"

He takes a deep breath, lets it out slowly, and swallows. "It's not my place to say."

Can you believe this guy? It's been a heckuva day and I'm in no mood for games. "Everyone else is dead, Silas. It has to be your place. I've already been accused of murdering my own grandfather today. How much worse can things get?"

His shoulders stoop under some invisible weight and his jaw muscles tense. "Everyone else is not dead."

My mind goes into a tailspin. Thoughts are whirring around fast and furious. Holy crap! I have a sister or maybe a brother. I've always thought I would be a cool big sis—

"Your father is alive."

CHAPTER 8

Did I faint? I pinch myself. Ow! Apparently I did not faint. Another movie classic fails to deliver. My father is alive. Why has no one mentioned this since I arrived in Pin Cherry Harbor? Clearly everyone knows who my father is—everyone except me. Don't worry, I ask the obvious question. "Who's my father?"

"I can inform you his name is Jacob Duncan, but I'm afraid I can't say another word without acquiring his express permission." Silas squares his shoulders and turns off the sputtering engine.

"What? Has he refused to have anything to do with me? Is he ashamed of me? Is that why he ditched my mom after he knocked her up?" At least seventeen more questions zip around inside my head, but Silas refuses to answer me or even make eye contact, so whatever the reason that my dad won't acknowledge me—it must be pretty rotten.

I step out of the car and slam the tiny Model T door within an inch of its life. "Never mind. I didn't need him when my mom died. I didn't need him when they carted me off to foster care. I didn't need him when I ran away at seventeen and made it on my own." I choke back tears and shout at Silas and the rest of Pin Cherry, "I sure as heck don't need him now that I'm rich."

Silas makes no move to comfort me. Not that I expect him to, but I do see him flinch. Somehow that small victory satisfies me. I run inside the bookshop, up the stairs, and into my secret apartment.

As the bookcase slides shut behind me the tears flood down my cheeks.

I flop face down on the bed and punch my fist into a pillow until my arm shakes with fatigue. The tears are thick and the snot is thicker. This is a solid, ugly cry.

REOW! HISS!

I may have peed myself a little. My tears instantly cease as I whip around to locate the source of the commotion. "How did you get in here, Pyewacket?"

"Ree-ooow!" His back arches in an unfriendly pose.

"If that's meant to be an answer, I've got nothin',
buddy."

"Oh, you'll understand his every sound before you know it."

I'm sorry to say I definitely pee myself this time. I spin around to confront this new intruder and my eyes nearly pop out of my head. The blood drains from my face and I'm sure I must be white as a—

"Were you going to say ghost, honey?"

The apparition floating in the middle of my apartment chuckles and clutches her many strands of pearls in amusement.

Now I faint.

A warm, rough tongue licks my cheek, but before I can get too excited sharp pointy teeth bite my earlobe. "Ow!" I swat at the carnivorous Pyewacket, but his cat-like—oh, that seems redundant—his reflexes easily put him out of reach before I can connect.

"Don't take it out on Pye. He just wants you to wake up so we can get acquainted. All caracal are intuitive, but his gift has always seemed abnormally strong. He's been quite protective of me ever since I won him in an off-the-books Scrabble game. His previous owner was a nasty piece of work. Poor little Pye was half-starved when I tucked him in my Marc Jacobs bag. I raised him from a cub, you know."

I sit up nice and slow. I scoot away from the swirling-misty ghost woman and press my back up against the solid wood frame of the four-poster bed.

"Mitzy, darling, I'm so sorry I didn't have the pleasure of meeting you in the flesh. Obviously you're in the flesh, but I'm a little, shall we say, insubstantial?"

Her laughter fills the room with love, and my terrified heart swells in spite of the primal fear. "Grams?"

"Who else?" She spins around and curtsies.

"You look so young. Silas said you were sixty-five when you passed."

"A lady never tells her age." Another chorus of chuckles. "One of the perks of being newly dead. I get to pick my 'look', and I went with circa thirty-five-year-old Isadora. Those early years with Cal and the baby were some of my best. And being buried in a vintage Marchesa didn't hurt!" She swishes back and forth to show off her burgundy silk-and-tulle ball gown.

"Is this real?" I press my hand against the floor and search the room for a clock. I'm fresh out of "Inception" tops so I'm not sure how to prove I'm not inside my own dream.

"If this is a dream, Mitzy, I don't ever want to wake up. You're exactly as beautiful and amazing as I knew you would be."

"You said 'the baby.' Do you mean my dad? Jacob?"

"Ah yes, that's why I'm here." Her mood darkens for a moment and she mumbles, "Silas and his rules."

"Silas said he wouldn't tell me anything without Jacob's permission."

"Well, Jacob is going to have a hard time enforcing his rules beyond the veil!" She crosses her arms and shakes her head.

"Silas said—"

"Silas can kiss my ample behind! That man never took proper advantage of me when he had the chance, and I'm not going to let him interfere with my afterlife."

And there it is. I just figured out where I get my trollop gene. Gram Gram is a little skanky!

"Easy honey, there's a thick line between 'empowered woman of means' and 'skank.'" She raises an eyebrow and nods.

"Can you read minds? Is that a ghost thing?"

She chews her perfectly drawn coral lip for a second. "I don't think it's mind reading. It just is. It seems like everything is energy, and now I'm connected to that energy in a different way. I'd say it feels more like there's no boundary between your thoughts and my thoughts. Does that make sense, dear?"

"Kinda." I shrug. Who am I to say what makes sense? I'm talking to a ghost.

She smiles and swirls closer. "Let me tell you about Jacob."

I grin and hug my knees to my chest.

She covers everything from his first tooth to his first day at college, before a dark cloud seeps into her energy. "When he dropped out of college and spent all his time with that Navy reject Darrin MacIntyre . . . " She presses her hand to her heart. "That's when Cal cut Jacob out of the will. How was he to know what would happen?"

"What? What happened?"

"Well, I hate to admit it, but Cal and I spoiled your father something fierce. So when the easy money stopped and Cal offered him an honest job, your father continued to take advantage of Cal's generosity. Eventually, he was fired and that's when things took a turn— He and that good-for-nothing Darrin cooked up a dangerous scheme."

"Like a pyramid scheme? Like multi-level marketing?" I lean forward.

"I wish, dear. No, I'm afraid they decided to rob one of those big box stores on Black Friday."

"Did they get caught?"

"Oh, that's not the half of it." She sighed and flickered. "The robbery went sideways and the store manager got shot. Now, I still don't believe Jacob did it, but that Darrin testified against him and your father went to prison for murder and armed robbery."

"*Holy Foley*! No wonder Silas didn't want to tell me."

"Don't blame Silas, dear. When your father found out about you he swore every member of the family to silence. He thought your mom was doing a great job raising you and he didn't want his mistakes to screw up your life."

"But she died when I was eleven and—"

"He told us nothing would be worse for you than having a convict for a father. Putting you in my will was my final rebellion. I never agreed with him, but I felt some kind of obligation while I was alive. He'd had such a hard life in prison."

"Had? Is he out of prison? Where is he? I want to meet him!" I get to my feet and pace. Part of me wants to meet him, at least. The other part kind of wants to yell at him and pound my fists against his chest—in the rain—like a Nicholas Sparks movie.

"Slow down, dear. Silas will get permission from Jacob, and then you can go and meet him. Last I heard he was down south somewhere. Seems like it might have been Chicago or Minneapolis."

My shoulders droop. "I can't leave town."

"Nonsense, dear. Twiggy and Pye can hold down the fort for a couple days."

"No, it's not that I don't *want* to leave town. I *can't*. I'm a suspect in Cal's murder."

Isadora's smile fades and her eyes fill with sadness and loss, or perhaps it's shock. The ghost of grandmothers past disapparates and Pyewacket hisses menacingly.

And . . . scene.

CHAPTER 9

I'M NOT CERTAIN if Grams left because of my implication in Cal's murder or if she received a summons from the other side, but either way I'm not waiting for anyone's permission on anything. I've made up my mind. I'm going to talk to my father.

Bounding down the stairs two at a time, I blindly trip over the chain at the bottom.

As I'm untangling myself and checking to make sure I didn't split open my skull, the dulcet tones of Twiggy's cackle reach my ears.

"You aren't exactly coordinated, eh? Seems like I've seen you on your hind end more than your feet today." Additional chuckles punctuate her observation.

"What's this stupid chain up for anyway? I don't care if people go up and down the stairs." I reach for the hook, but Twiggy's strong hand beats me to the clasp.

"You'll care if someone walks off with a book worth two hundred thousand dollars. Then you'll care." She does not remove her hand from the chain.

"You can't be serious!" I glance up the circular staircase and shake my head in disbelief.

"I realize you don't know me that well, doll, but I don't 'kid.'" Twiggy tilts her helmet of grey hair and crosses her arms over her square torso.

"If they're all so valuable, why aren't they in a museum or something?"

She makes a sweeping gesture to indicate the bookshop. "Behold 'something.' Once a month your Grams opens up the Rare Books Loft and every one of those little green-glass desk lamps shines on a rare tome that someone made reservations to view—months in advance."

"Do they pay for the reservation?" Little cash-register bells ding in my head.

"Naw. She only allows scholarly research, not looky-loos."

So much for my fleeting plans to take over the world with my rare-books money. "Hey, I need to do some research. Do we have old newspapers in here?"

"It's a bookshop not a library." Twiggy rolls her dark-brown eyes.

"I want to look into my dad's case. Grams seems pretty certain he's innocent and—"

Twiggy takes a big step back and stares at me like my head's on upside down. "I thought you never met Isadora? And who told you about your dad?"

Oops. I didn't think this through. I can't exactly tell her I've been chatting with my dead grandmother's ghost . . . First I'm a suspect in a murder and now I'm talking to dead people? I mean, this woman already thinks I'm uncoordinated and mildly incompetent. Do I want her assuming I'm a full on wack job?

"Is it the gift? She never thought it was hereditary. Your dad never . . . She wound up believing it was something she learned from the books."

Twiggy's rambling doesn't seem to be directed at me, but she sounds like she might be able to handle the truth. When in doubt . . .

I take a deep breath and launch into my tale. "I'm not sure how to explain this, Twiggy. I don't want you to think I'm insane or seeing things, but my grandmother's ghost appeared to me up in the apartment and told me all about the robbery and the murder charges." I swallow and wait.

Twiggy smacks the heels of her hands together as though I just gave her the answer to a riddle she'd been working on for months. "I knew it! If anyone could find a way back it would be Isadora. I bet you ten to one that Silas had something to do with this. He spends entirely too much time in that Rare Books Loft." She nods and paces in a circle. "I'd say I can't believe it, but I can. I absolutely can!"

This is going far better than I could've imagined.

Twiggy stops suddenly and glances left and right. "Is she here right now?"

I scrunch up my face and look down at the ground. "She sort of beamed out when I mentioned that I was accused of Cal's murder."

"Oh, hells bells, doll. You broke her heart. Cal was still alive when she crossed over. If she's trapped on our side she might not know . . . " Twiggy wanders off, mumbling under her breath and gesticulating randomly.

I take a step, but before I utter a word Twiggy calls out, "I'll get your dad's old case files. I used to have a little thing with the records tech, and I think he's still got the hots for me."

"Thanks," I shout. As the elaborate front door bangs shut, I chuckle and try to reconcile two things: 1. Someone has the "hots" for Twiggy; and

2. That someone is a "he." I mean, you get what I'm saying, right? No judgment. I just thought she was playing softball for the other team.

I wander through the stacks as I review my new life in Pin Cherry Harbor. I own a bookshop that houses some insanely valuable books. I have a bank account with a seemingly substantial amount of money in it. To borrow Twiggy's phrase, I think I have "the hots" for Sheriff Erick. I can eat burgers and fries for free whenever I want, thanks to my grandmother's storied past. I'm caretaker to a dangerous and mildly psychotic wildcat. And—will wonders never cease—I'm not an orphan.

That last one hits me hard. My disappearing dad is alive and he knows I exist. He should've gotten in touch with me. He should've acted like an adult and faced up to his responsibilities, but I'll discuss that with him face to face. Grams seems pretty certain he didn't murder anyone, but what if he did? Do I want a relationship with a homicidal convict? I've managed to take care of myself without him for twenty-one years . . .

A sharp scratch at the back door interrupts my self-evaluation. I grasp the handle and pause. "Pyewacket, if you are currently holding parts of any human in your mouth I demand that you drop them this instant." That should do it. I ease the door open.

Pyewacket snakes through the crack and zips past me. He's four-legged lightning with a little tilt in his sideways gallop. Maybe he was hit by a car before Grams rescued him?

Through the cracked door, the movement by the dumpster is clearly visible. Yellow crime-scene tape blocks off the back half of the alley, and a lone investigator places found items in evidence bags.

I close the door before she sees me.

Now where's that cat? I walk toward the front of the store, but I don't see or hear anything. "Pye, oh dear sweet Pye. Where are you?" I hope the fur-demon can't detect the sarcasm in my tone.

Something hits my head. I clutch my chest, jump, and squeak in fear.

"Ree-ow." Soft but condescending.

I wait a tick for my heart rate to return to normal and then I stoop to pick up . . . "What is this?" I turn the glossy black button over in my hand. Four holes. A large debossed anchor with a rope wrapped around it marks the surface. Not mine. I walk toward the trash bin.

Before I can toss the useless button out, Pyewacket leaps to the floor and his claws snag my pant leg. I stumble and drop the fastener.

"Reeeee-ow." A warning.

I might actually detect a slight variation in the meows. Grams said I would learn to understand him. Let's test my theory. I pick up the black button and move toward the wastebasket.

THWACK!

Pye hits me hard with a right paw. He got a chunk of ankle flesh with that one. "Okay, okay. I'll keep your trash souvenir." I slip the button in my pocket and roll my eyes. What a freaky cat.

The front door opens and there's a definite surge of excitement at the prospect of my first customer.

The surge heats up a notch as Sheriff Erick saunters toward me.

"I'm sure it goes without saying, Miss Moon, but you'll have to make other arrangements for the bookshop's waste disposal until we complete our investigation."

"Couldn't you have sent my good friend Deputy Paulsen over to deliver that message?" I tilt my head and try to look enticing.

"She's . . . I sent her . . . She's on official business." He steps closer to me and reaches toward my face.

My heart thuds. Is this happening? I want it to happen, but I assumed it would take weeks or even months to get him to see me as more than a "perp." I lean into my hope.

A strange look enters his tantalizing blue eyes.

My eyelids softly lower.

"Is that gum?"

My traitorous eyelids pop open.

He picks something off my forehead and rolls it between his fingers.

My face is most assuredly a blotchy shade of unbecoming crimson.

His full lips part in a bemused chuckle. "Yep. That's some Big Red if I'm not mistaken."

You don't say. I hope he's referring to the gum and not my befuddled countenance.

"I'd ask how you got chewing gum on your forehead, but I'm not sure I want to know." He walks his sexy behind over to the cash register and tosses the ABC gum in the trash can that he obviously knows exists. Seems like everyone in this town knows more about this bookshop than me.

"Nobody knows more than me, honey."

"*Great Gatsby*!" I did not see Grams fade in, and her wicked giggle makes me wonder how much of my indignation she witnessed.

Sheriff Erick tilts his head and raises an eyebrow. "You must really like books, Moon."

I nod emphatically. "Mmhmm." On the plus side, he's dropped the honorific, "Miss."

"I'll leave you to it then." He turns.

My gaze uncontrollably drops. He makes polyester—

He looks back.

Busted. I glance up and swallow.

Grams giggles into her ring-ensconced hand.

"I'll let you know when we've finished in the alley."

I nod and smile.

He leaves.

I exhale.

Grams whispers, "You've got it bad, dear. And I should know."

Ignoring the jab, I launch into an apology. "I'm so sorry about Cal, Grams. I didn't mean to drop that bomb on you. I thought you already knew. I thought you were back to tell me who killed him or something."

She presses her hand to her heart and takes a deep breath. "Cal was a wonderful man and a well-meaning father. I'm sorry you didn't get to meet him."

"Do you know what happened?"

"Near as I can tell, that's not how things work in between. I seem to be tethered to the bookshop, and I think you and Pye are the only one's who can see me."

"Pyewacket can see ghosts?" That cat is too much.

"He can sense me. Let's test out the visual angle."

Grams drifts toward the sleeping Pyewacket

and floats up to the top of the bookcase where the hellcat naps. She brushes her fingers through his whiskers below the scars bisecting his left eyebrow.

Pye instantly leaps into arched, Halloween-cat pose.

"It's only me, sweet kitty." Grams rubs her hand through the air along Pye's curved spine.

He moves the black tufts on his ears and flicks his short club of a tail. His large golden eyes search the air.

"I'd say 'sense' but not 'see.' Would you agree, Mitzy?"

"Agreed." I plop onto an over-stuffed ottoman at the end of a thick oak bookcase. "Grams?"

"Yes, dear."

"I'm going to look into dad's case. If you think he's innocent—"

"Now, don't misrepresent me. I never said he was innocent. I said I don't think he committed the murder. But I think you best focus your efforts on proving your own innocence before you worry about Jacob's misdeeds."

"You can't seriously think that Erick believes I killed Cal? Can you?"

"Oh, it's Erick is it?" Grams wiggles her shoulders and flashes her eyebrows up and down suggestively.

"Be serious, Grams."

"All right. Being accused of murder is serious, dear. Look what happened to your father. Cal was an important man in these parts, and Sheriff Harper will be under a lot of pressure to wrap this case up real quick and tidy. Everyone gives him a long leash because he's a war hero, but he'll have to charge someone—soon. Suspicion in a small town goes a long ways."

That can't be a thing. There's no way I'm going to jail for murder just because my dad—

"It absolutely is a 'thing.' And I suggest we put our heads together and see if we can't crack this thing before Sheriff Erick knows what hit him." Grams rubs her palms together eagerly.

"All I know is that I definitely did not kill Cal. Other than that I don't know where to start. I've never solved a murder, you know." I cross my arms and sigh.

"We've all seen an episode or two of *Murder She Wrote*, haven't we?" says Grams, encouragingly.

Oh, if we're counting television shows and movies as experience then I'm pretty sure I have a doctorate in criminology.

"That's the spirit!"

I jump. "It still freaks me out a little that you can hear my thoughts. So, new rule: If I don't say it out loud you don't get to respond. Got it?"

"I'll do my best, dear. But you have to understand it's rather all muddled together." She puts a hand to her mouth and squints her eyes. "I'll try to watch and see if your lips are moving. If your lips are moving then it's fair game."

"Fair enough." I shrug. "So where do we start?"

"You should have a notepad. Detectives always write notes."

I wiggle my smartphone. "I forgot to pay my bill, so I don't have any service. The notepad app still works, though."

"I like improvisation, Mitzy."

"What am I writing?"

"Let's make a list of all the suspects and then you can go question them!"

Boy, she's one gung-ho ghost!

"I'm just—"

"Lips didn't move, Grams. Lips did not move." I wag my finger and she covers her mouth with her hand. "Besides, people aren't going to let me question them. I'm a civilian. I can't force them to talk to me."

"Sweetheart, haven't you heard the saying 'You get more flies with honey'? You don't have to make anyone do anything. You're simply a grieving granddaughter who wants to learn as much as she can about her dearly departed grandfather." Grams' eyes twinkle.

"Oh, you're a sneaky Gram Gram."

Our raucous laughter disturbs the reclining Pyewacket.

My heart feels fuller than it has in ten years.

CHAPTER 10

The front door of the bookshop bangs open. Grams vanishes.

A shout dissolves into the books. "A little help?"

Sounds like the honey-voiced Twiggy has returned. "On my way."

Twiggy balances a box on her right hip and juts her thumb toward the rusty white International parked with one tire up on the curb. "The rest are in there."

"I hope you didn't have to do anything unsavory." I chuckle.

"As a matter of fact, I have to go to bingo next Tuesday night. But I told him I'd bring a friend for his friend, so that makes us even."

I stop with a box half out of the SUV. "Am I the friend you're bringing?"

"The one and only." Twiggy pulls her foot off the huge door and it slams shut before I can get there. Great. I'm in town one day and some bingo-hall mafiosa is already pimping me out.

Three trips later, we have all the boxes inside.

"I'm not so sure about bingo, but thanks for getting these files, Twiggy. We should take them up to the apartment. I don't want anyone to find out I'm looking into my dad's case."

Twiggy nods in agreement and walks into the back room.

I guess when I said "we" she heard "not Twiggy." I unhook the chain across the stairs in protest and make five trips up and down the circular staircase. Despite the irritation with my employee, I can't help but grin when I tilt the candle and watch the secret door open into MY apartment. The glorious smell of books is less within the private rooms, but there's still the lovely feeling of being wrapped inside the pages of adventures.

I line all the boxes up and rest my hands on my hips. I'll need thumbtacks and string. I've watched *Elementary*. I know I'm going to need a visual representation of the connections between the suspects in the case. I'm not an idiot.

I run down the stairs—and trip over the blasted chain, which the helpful Twiggy has resecured.

Is that a muffled chuckle? Do I hear a chuckle? I

jump up and storm into the back room. "Did you hook the chain?"

"Did you unhook it?"

Is this a Mexican standoff? Actually, no. If my movie knowledge serves me, a Mexican standoff requires three people—one of whom must be Salma Hayek. I choose not to take the bait. "I need thumbtacks and string, or possibly yarn."

"You got it, boss." Twiggy rolls her chair back to the desk and continues typing information into the computer.

"Do we have any?"

"Any what?" Clickety-clack go the keys.

"Tacks and string?"

"I put 'em on the weekly order."

I don't believe her, but even if I did . . . "I need them today. Actually now would be great."

"Rex's." She does not stop typing.

It's like she's speaking in a code and I don't have the decoder ring. "Excuse me?"

"If you can't wait for the order, you'll have to toddle on down to Rex's and see if she's got what you want."

"Rex is a she?"

Twiggy slowly turns her chair like a villain in a Bond film. "What is it with you?"

I shrug and gesture for her to answer my query.

"Rex was a man. A man that owned a five and

dime in Pin Cherry Harbor. When that man up and died of natural causes seven and a half years ago, his wife took over the store. She runs Rex's Drugstore located at 414 Main Street." She rotates back to the screen, shaking her head in bewilderment.

I'm not proud to admit that I make an inappropriate gesture to the back of her smug little grey head before I leave.

Grams gives a "tsk, tsk" at me as I walk out. "Lips didn't move," I growl through my clenched teeth.

The crisp early-evening air on Main Street blows my frustration away and I take a deep cleansing breath. Not like a crystal-crunching, aura-scrubbing cleansing breath—just a nice deep breath of fresh air.

My stomach growls when I pass Myrtle's Diner. Tacks and string can wait. Mama needs some fries. I push open the door. Once again, all eyes turn.

"Hey, Mitzy. Have a seat. I'll throw your burger down."

I nod and smile. Seriously, a huge self-satisfied, face-splitting grin. I'm a regular. "Thanks, Odell."

"Cheese?"

"I'm feeling Swiss."

"I've got American."

Oh Icarus, you flew too high. "American will be divine."

Divine? Did I just refer to cheese as divine? I glance around the diner and don't see any faces I recognize. Good, no witnesses.

The rasp of polyester against vinyl precedes the appearance of a short, squat figure sliding out of a booth. Spoke too soon.

"Glad to see you haven't tried to make a run for it." Deputy Paulsen rests one hand on her pistol. "I've got my eye on you. Stay close." She wipes the grease from the corner of her mouth with the back of her hand.

"Geez," I mumble, as the front door swings shut.

"Ah, don't mind Pauly. She's had a bee in her bonnet ever since Sheriff Harper won the election, again."

Oooh, small town gossip!

"They still lookin' at you for Cal's murder?"

Oooh, small town gossip. See what I did there?

"Erick says he's waiting for time of death from the medical examiner, but Silas took a copy of my bus ticket down to the station, so I expect to be cleared soon."

I'm aware of the looks and murmurs from the four-top in the corner, but apparently this is how things are done in a small town. "So, the deputy's name is Polly Paulsen?"

"Yep, but on account of her dad wantin' a boy so bad he spelled it like the apostle Paul, and then threw the 'y' on there to give it a girlie flair."

"So it's Pauly Paulsen? I'd change my name."

Odell catches my eye through the orders-up window and a mischievous grin spreads across his face. "That right, Mizithra?"

Sic burn, old man. Sic burn. I shake my head and Odell delivers my food. "No server on the night shift?"

"If you mean a waitress, I manage all right most nights. Tally's daughter comes in on weekends for the rush."

I glance around at the sprinkling of patrons. "Mmhmm."

As I devour the burger, I have to admit that the hot, melty cheese actually is divine. I finish off the perfectly golden fries and lean back.

"Made short work of that." Odell tosses his observation across the diner without judgment.

"What can I say? I worked up an appetite today." I grab my dishes and slide them into the bin under the counter. Call it instinct or years of food-service employment. There's always a bin under the counter.

"Thanks, Mitzy."

"My compliments to the chef."

I walk out and make a hard right toward Rex's. The self-satisfied smile evaporates when the door does not budge under my efforts.

"They close at four, dear."

A woman who bears a striking resemblance to Tally, but with a backcombed monstrosity of grey hair rather than a tightly wrapped bun of flaming red, taps her watch as she walks past.

"Tilly?" I blurt.

She stops and spins on her pink kitten heels. "Do I know you, dear?"

I extend my hand as I say, "I'm Mitzy Moon. Isadora's granddaughter. I inherited the bookshop." That last one turns the lights on.

"Oh, of course. Twiggy mentioned something about being under new management. She's such a hoot."

Is she, though? "I guess that makes me the new management," I reply with a friendly wink.

"Come on by tomorrow and we'll get you all set up with a new passbook and your own box of checks."

Oh, how extravagant. I wonder what checks do? "Well, thank you kindly, Tilly—Tally—Tilly." I blush profusely. "Sorry about that. I'll see you tomorrow, Tilly."

The click-scrape of her kitten heels on the uneven cement sidewalk fades as she turns the corner.

A cold, late-summer wind blows down Main Street, pulling the damp chill from the massive body of water and spreading it over the town. I hug my arms around my middle.

I'm suddenly too aware of being alone on the street. I duck my head and jog back to the bookshop.

String or no string. It's time I learn something about Jacob Duncan.

CHAPTER 11

I HOIST OPEN the massive front door and come face to face with Twiggy.

"You need me to come in tomorrow?" She turns and slides by me.

It's an undeniable fact that I could use a more thorough tour of the bookshop. However, I have no idea if I can afford a paid guide. "Do I pay you?"

"Your Grams and I had an understanding."

"I assumed. Do you want to have an understanding with me?"

She nods.

"I'm meeting with Tilly tomorrow. Once I get a handle on the bank account, I'll see what I can offer you."

"Accounts. Bank accounts," Twiggy corrects.

I swallow my retort. "Like I said, after my

meeting with Tilly." I try a new tactic. "Can I meet you at Myrtle's for lunch?" The moment of surprise on her face pleases me.

"I gotta eat." She shrugs and walks off down the street. Not the street that runs beside the shop, which is Main, but the one in front of Bell, Book & Candle, which is—

Stepping off the curb, I search for a street sign because I can't remember the address of my own bookstore. "First Avenue." Makes perfect sense. It is the first "avenue" on this end of town. There's the enormous lake, my bookshop, and this street is the first intersection on Main. Not terribly creative, but accurate.

I walk into my bookshop and twist the locks into position on the large door.

Twiggy must shut off the lights as part of her closing procedure. I fumble for my phone in the eerie, semi-dark store. The bookcases feel oppressive in the low light, and I make a mental note to hire an electrician to pull some wire and place a light switch right next to the front entrance.

I deftly step over the chain and make my way to the candle handle. I chuckle as I reach for the device.

"Oh good, you're finally back."

I make another mental note to purchase adult diapers to staunch the flow of ghost-related pants accidents I've been having. "Grams, you've got to come up with a more subtle entrance strategy."

"Sorry, dear. I started to go a little coffin-crazy once you left. Twiggy can't see or hear me, and I can't leave the bookshop. I was anxious. Maybe over anxious."

I walk into the apartment and the lights automatically switch on with a slow ramp up to full power. I place my hands on my hips. "Now why didn't you put one of these do-hickeys at the front door?"

"Doesn't make sense to have the lights flicking off and on every time someone walks in the front door!"

I shake my head and put on my onesie reindeer pajamas. "Time to reopen this old case."

Off comes the lid of file box number one.

Choking on the dust, I grab a cloth from the bathroom and wipe down all the boxes before returning to the first time capsule.

"Good idea, dear."

It's nice to have a cheering section—even for the mundane.

Grams smiles and begins a reply to my unspoken thought. "I—"

I point to my lips, which did not move, and Grams nods. We're establishing ground rules. Which seems important in any inter-species communication. Oh, and I've decided ghosts are a different species.

The first evidence box contains police reports and witness statements. I learn that the robbery took place right after closing and that Jacob and Darrin came in through an unsecured employee entrance on the loading dock.

The statements are all from employees of the box store. None contain details about the shooting. After a cursory review, I deduce that my father, Darrin, and the store manager were the only people in the room containing the safe and later the corpse.

I make a pile of witness statements. I place the security guard statement on top of that pile. He's the only one who noticed any kind of detail. The other statements were just the emotional accusations of traumatized employees.

It's unclear whether the other employees knew a robbery was in progress prior to the gunshot. Each statement seems quite fuzzy up to the point of the sound of a gun.

"Do you think he did it, dear?"

The hairs on the back of my neck stand at attention. "I forgot you were here, Grams."

"I was doing my best not to jump into your internal debate. Weren't there any security cameras in the room where the safe was?"

I pick up the police report and scan through it a

second time. "Says here that the camera was disabled by gunshot. Also says the perps took the tape and smashed the security equipment."

"Make a note on your phone thingy."

I swipe open the app and stare at Grams. "Do you think they took the tape before or after?" I type a quick note.

"If it was before, wouldn't the guard have tried to stop them?"

I make another note and move toward file box number two.

By the time I lift the lid off box number five, sunlight paints grey streaks across my ceiling. "What time is it?"

"How would I know, honey? Time has no meaning on this side."

I press a button on my phone and yawn. It's 5:13 a.m. "I better get a few hours sleep before I open the shop."

"I'll wait over here." Grams floats to a beautiful scalloped-back chair in the corner and hovers near the puffy seat.

"Can you 'fade out' or something? It's unnerving to have you floating in a corner watching me."

"Of course, dear."

I wonder if she's genuinely gone or just in "low power" mode so I can't see her. I swear there's a chuckle coming from somewhere. Oh well, too tired to care.

I flop onto the four-poster bed and snuggle into the heavenly mattress, Egyptian cotton sheets, and sumptuous down comforter.

Dreamland holds no rest for me. The robbery plays out from every angle in my nightmares. I watch my father fire the gun over and over.

When Pyewacket jumps onto the bed, compressing my chest and shocking me instantly awake, I actually feel relief. My time under the comforter hasn't delivered any rest.

I rub the sleep from my eyes and absently scratch my fingers between Pye's ears. He's suspiciously docile. Is that purring? It sounds like a small lawnmower. Choosing caution, I pull my hand back. "What are you up to, you wicked kitten?"

"He's hungry." Grams swirls closer.

"Holy Hera!" I don't think I peed this time, but a ghost greeting first thing in the morning is definitely unsettling. My heart is certainly pumping blood with all its might now. Rise and shiver, I say.

I blink, yawn, and scrape a hand through my haystack of a hairdo. "I have to feed him? I thought he was a free agent. Don't bobcats kill mice or something?"

"Pyewacket is a caracal and he can certainly take care of himself, dear. However, he needs a human to open the box of Fruity Puffs and pour them into his bowl."

"Come again?" I look at the fiendish feline and try to reconcile him munching on kids cereal. "Fruity Puffs?"

"It's his little treat. I spoiled him." Grams floats her hand along his back.

Pye responds with an unsettlingly loud purr.

"And now that spoiling falls to me, I suppose?"

"Would you?"

I chuckle and shake my head.

Downstairs in the back room I locate the cereal. Pye threads himself around my legs in an insistent, and dangerously unbalancing, figure eight. As soon as the Fruity Puffs hit the bowl he attacks. The way he powers through the sugary treats you'd think . . . you'd think he was a spoiled child.

I bend to scratch his ears.

He emits a deep, throaty growl and a needle-clad paw swipes toward my hand.

I jump back. "Easy, tiger. I'll make a note to keep my hands to myself during Fruity Puffs feeding time."

Grams giggles. "He takes it very seriously, the little cuddle bug."

That's not the term I would've used.

A sharp knock at the front of the store interrupts our tender family moment.

I shuffle toward the door and twist the locks open.

The early morning sun wraps an enticing glow around the broad shoulders of Sheriff Erick. I steady myself on the door. "Well, good morning to you." I grin lasciviously.

"Mitzy Moon, I'm here to take you in." Sheriff Harper reaches toward me with the handcuffs.

For the first time since I laid eyes on him, I step away. "Hold on a minute, Erick. Haven't we already played this game? My lawyer supplied you with the bus ticket. There's no way I was here when Cal was killed."

He drops his hand and shakes his head. He looks genuinely sorry for what he's about to say. "I called Silas before I headed over. The ME puts time of death between 1000 and 1100 hours yesterday." He shifts his weight from one foot to the other. "The bus comes through town at 0930 and yesterday it came early, 0900 hours."

"You're serious?" I put my hands on my— Oh crap! I'm still wearing my reindeer onesie. "Can I at least change?"

Sheriff Erick shakes his head. "Sorry, but I've got to take you in. If it's any consolation, you make a cute reindeer."

A healthy glow floods my cheeks.

"You'll give her a minute to make herself presentable, Sheriff Harper." Silas places a friendly but firm hand on the sheriff's arm.

I didn't even see my lawyer arrive, but I'm grateful for the chance to put on some jeans.

"Make it quick," the sheriff says.

I manage to negotiate the chain and race into the apartment. "Grams? Grams? Are you here?"

"I don't like the look of this, dear. What will you do?"

I shrug as I wiggle into my least ripped pair of skinny jeans and the only button-down shirt I own. "I'll tell Silas to send Twiggy over," I call as I rush down the stairs.

"Is there someone else in there?" Sheriff Harper's hand moves toward his holstered weapon as he peers around me.

Think fast. Think fast. "Just Pyewacket. I didn't want him to worry." I catch Silas's eye and he nods his approval.

"I'll be sure Twiggy sees to the cat," Silas adds in support of my story.

I hold out both wrists and take no pleasure as Erick clicks the handcuffs into place.

CHAPTER 12

I RUB AT the ink on my thumb. Fingerprinted. Booked. The humiliation. I lean back against the concrete wall of the holding cell and hug my knees to my chest. Is this how it felt for my dad?

I'm sure he was upset to be accused of a crime he didn't commit. But he committed part of the crime. Everyone seems to agree that he was in on the robbery. What went wrong?

With nothing but time on my hands, I close my eyes and call up the images of the witness statements. Every single witness claimed to have heard two gunshots.

Everyone except the security guard. He claimed he heard three.

The medical examiner's report stated the victim died instantly. A single gunshot.

If the first shot was the one that took out the camera then the guard must've arrived before the manager was—

Who fired the third shot? Who destroyed the security equipment and took the tape? Why didn't anyone else hear the third shot?

I scan through the police report in my mind's eye and recall no mention of a third bullet being recovered.

"Thought you might be hungry."

The sight of Odell's concerned face and the paper sack, which I pray holds a burger and fries, nearly brings tears to my eyes. "Starving. How'd you know?"

"Paulsen comes in for breakfast every morning. You'd a thought she'd found the Lindbergh baby." Odell shakes his head and worry creases his brow.

I gently tug the bag from his hand and add, "I didn't do it."

"Only a fool'd think you did." He makes to spit on the ground but thinks better of it. "I don't like the smell of this thing, you hear me?"

I nod and shove another handful of fries into my mouth.

"Odell? What are you doing in here?" Sheriff Harper sidles up to the holding cell and looks from my benefactor to me. "She's not allowed to have visitors."

"Gotta feed your prisoners, Sheriff. This ain't a gulag." Odell ignores the sheriff and grabs the bars of my cell. "Same thing for dinner?"

Mouth full, I nod emphatically.

"Odell, I'm warning you . . . " Sheriff Harper tilts his head in earnest.

Odell waves him off and walks out of the station, as though the sheriff just announced the sky is purple and he's not having it.

"Silas said he had something to take care of, but he asked me to let you know he'd be back this afternoon." Sheriff Harper gives me an uncomfortable nod and turns.

"Erick?" I use a soft tone and let my voice crack a little.

He exhales and looks over his shoulder at the cell.

"How did the ME determine time of death?"

"Miss Moon, I'll be sure to give your lawyer a copy of the report. He can pass along the details. In the meantime, I'll ask you again to refer to me as Sheriff Harper. First degree murder is no joke."

He walks out and I lick the salt off my fingers. Murder. Like father like daughter. What an unfortunate family legacy.

The sound of a key in the cell door wakes me. I look around in momentary confusion. My all-night investigation into my father's case must've caught up to me. I rub my face and work to bring my visitor into focus. "Hey, Silas."

"You have been released on $100,000 bail." He extends a hand to help me up. "I'll return you to the bookshop. Your arraignment will be held a week from tomorrow."

I take his hand and follow him mutely out of the holding cell. I can't believe this is happening to me. This over-eager sheriff in this backwater town is actually going to accuse— "Did you say $100,000?"

"I did." Silas holds the door for me as we exit to the street.

"I don't have that kind of money. Did you post my bail? I can't repay you. I mean, I don't plan—"

"Isadora's estate is more than capable of posting bail. Now, it behooves me to remind you that you mustn't leave town. But if you're anything like your grandmother, I'll assume you're all fight and no flight."

The shock of the money is sure to be distorting my face, but the truth of his assumption pushes a smile through. "I'm a fighter. If Erick isn't going to look for any other suspects, I'll just have to do it for him."

"You may require these."

Silas lays a key ring in my hand.

I rub the emblem. "I have a Mercedes?"

"Indeed. I thought you might be in need of

transport to and from the questioning of witnesses." He smiles and gives a little wink.

"I'll have a list of suspects by supper. Can you get me their addresses?"

"Twiggy is a resourceful woman. Folks tend to experience a degree of intimidation in her presence. Take her along as you see fit." Silas opens the door of the Model T and I slide in with a fresh sense of purpose.

Looks like I'm working two cases at once. At this rate, I'll have to hang an addendum sign in the front window: "Bell, Book & Candle Bookshop and Detective Services."

CHAPTER 13

Back at the bookstore, Grams is swirling mad while Pye chases something through the stacks. If it's a mouse, I don't want to know.

Twiggy walks out of the back room and, for a split second, I swear there's concern on her face. Whatever it was is quickly replaced with cool indifference.

"Oh, you're back."

"Apparently."

"Silas give you the keys?"

"He did."

She nods and walks away.

Grams impatiently announces, "I have two names for that list, dear. Start writing or tapping. There's no time to lose."

Once I retreat to the safety of the apartment, I

whip out my phone and prepare to take dictation. "Whenever you're ready, Grams."

"Top of the list has to be Cal's gold-digging third wife, Kitty Zimmerman-Duncan. And write down her boyfriend, too."

I pause and raise an eyebrow. "She has a boyfriend?"

"She's thirty years younger than Cal, pumped full of collagen, Botox, and a set of—"

"Grams!"

"What can I say? I never liked her. Too fake. From her misappropriated British colloquialisms to her Jessica Rabbit hair . . . I thought Cal could do better."

Not my place to say, but it sounds like my Grams may be more than a little jealous.

"Well, it's—"

I point to my lips.

Grams crosses her arms and swirls angrily around the apartment.

"I've written 'The trollop's boyfriend' on the list, if that makes you feel better."

"Thank you. It does."

I chew the inside of my cheek. "That's not a very long list."

"Truth is, dear, Cal and I drifted apart these past few years. I don't know who he was doing business with or which folks were in his new social circle." Grams places a hand over her heart and sighs.

"That's all right. I'll see if I can meet with Kitty and maybe she'll let something useful slip."

"Yes. One day at a time. That's all any of us can manage."

I get a strong AA vibe from that comment, but I let it lie. Too late. I try to stuff the thought down, but I catch Grams looking at me with a pained expression. The kind of regret I've had on many a morning after. I smile and nod.

She does the same.

It's probably best if I change the subject. "Silas mentioned that I might take Twiggy along on the interrogations."

"Oh, not on this one, honey. Kitty has a golden stick so far up her—"

"Grams!"

She giggles uncontrollably. "I guess my roots are showing."

"Do you come from a long line of street fighters?" I chuckle.

"As a matter of fact, I played a little roller derby before I met Odell. There were actually a few contenders before Odell—truth be told." A mischievous grin plays across her ghostly lips.

"The truth will have to be told at a later date, Grams. Where can I find Kitty?"

She looks down her nose at me and scrunches her face like there's a bad smell in the air. "You won't get within fifty yards of her looking like something Pye dragged in."

I walk toward my duffle.

"Unless you're hiding the Queer Eye guys in that bag, dear, you're going to need to borrow something from my closet."

I can't picture myself wearing some sixty-five-year-old lady's clothes. I roll my eyes.

Grams swirls toward the closet. "Oh, ye of little faith."

I open the door and the lights pop on with flair. My jaw drops. "Holy crap, Grams!"

She chuckles with satisfaction as I step into a closet right out of *Sex and the City* meets *Confessions of a Shopaholic*.

Just to be clear, I love clothes. The fact that I wear ripped skinny jeans and snarky T-shirts is my protest to poverty, not a fashion choice. I walk reverently through the closet and my fingers dance across the fabrics. Yes, I said fabrics. I'm on Project Runway now.

"You'll want the aquamarine tea-length dress with the Valentino T-straps. Kitty's got a thing for Valentinos."

I pull the padded hanger supporting the lovely

frock and check the tag. "Matthew Christopher? Must've been one special occasion."

"I married Cal in that dress."

I turn and see little apparition tears rolling down Grams' cheeks.

"I can't possibly wear this, Grams."

"I want you to, dear. I'll never get to wear it again . . . He always said I looked like an angel fallen from heaven in it."

I hold the dress in front of me and gaze into the full-length mirror. "Oh brother. I better start with a shower."

Grams chuckles. "And they say wisdom is wasted on the young."

I won't bore you with the particulars, but let's agree that it is the single most enjoyable, all-hot-water-no-surprises shower of my life.

I sit down at the marble-topped vanity and stare at my freshly scrubbed reflection. I get a flash of my mother's face and I smile wistfully. Memories of sitting on the Formica counter in the bathroom of our studio apartment watching her "put on her face" drift softly into my consciousness. She would explain each step to me as though she were a warrior preparing for battle.

"This is called foundation and it covers up any weak spots or imperfections so I look ready to conquer the world."

I miss the sound of her voice.

"The blush gives me a little color so they can't tell I'm running on four hours' sleep."

I remember she worked at least two jobs, but maybe it was three. Time erases so much.

"This cinnamon mocha lip tint gives me a confident smile, but keeps it professional."

Her smile could lift the clouds from any bad day.

"A gentle application of smoky shadow gives my eyes depth and intelligence. Not that I'm not intelligent, this just confirms their suspicions."

I know that my smarts absolutely came from her.

"Always give the eyebrows a light nudge with a pencil, so you look like you mean business."

Then she would apply a little mascara to my lashes before she coated her own and finish by saying, "Dark lashes give you a finished look. Serious but mysterious." And she would kiss the tip of my nose, every single morning until—

I twist the mascara wand back into the tube and blink back the tears that are threatening to fall.

"I would've loved your mother, Mitzy."

A wave of self-conscious heat flushes my skin. I whip the towel off my head and fluff my white-blonde locks. "What am I going to do with this?"

Grams swirls around and chews on her thumbnail. "This will be tricky, since I can't physically move anything around. But if you can follow instructions, I'm sure we can brush you into debutante status in no time."

"I'm game for anything."

Ghost cosmetology school is in session.

I've never spent this much time on my hair in my life. Prior to the "Bad Bet" haircut after my karaoke humiliation, I was a high-pony or messy-bun girl every day.

The application of "product" and the judicious use of a blow dryer and styling wand create a sleek, socialite look. "I'm a knockout, Grams."

"Give me a little credit, dear. I did have five husbands and an undisclosed number of 'special friends.'"

"Grams! I'm shocked by what I'm hearing."

"Don't get all high and mighty with me, Mitzy. You talk in your sleep, and this Shady Ben you mumble about sounds like he was a *very* special friend."

"Ouch." Who knew ghosts could be so nosy and merciless.

"All right, off you go."

"Where exactly am I going?"

Grams freeze-frames for a split second before answering. "I think I heard you say it's Thursday. Is it the first Thursday of the month?"

I take a quick look at my phone. “Yup.”

“Oh, she’ll be at the mansion hosting the Duncan Club monthly luncheon.”

“Maybe I should go another time.” I tug at the gorgeous dress and wiggle my toes in the Valentinos.

“Nonsense. We didn’t get you all gussied up for nothin’. You get in that fancy Mercedes and you walk into that luncheon like you own the place. After all, your pedigree is far better than hers. You’re a Duncan by blood, dear.”

Ooooh, I have a pedigree.

CHAPTER 14

As I drive out to the mansion, I can't help but think about how much I *don't* miss my old life. My pattern of over-socializing and drinking to dull the pain of my disappointments and loneliness wasn't as fulfilling as I thought. I haven't had a drink since I arrived in this tiny town in almost-Canada, and I've been too busy to miss anything. My short flash of personal reflection is interrupted when I spy my landmark ahead on the right.

A large granite stone bears what I can only assume is the Duncan family crest with a large "D" in the center. I turn, pass through the massive wrought-iron gates, and continue down the drive. And it is a drive, not a driveway. I can't even see the house as I curve gently through the thick birch trees. The blur of black-and-white peeling bark is a little mesmerizing.

It's impossible to resist playing a moment of what-if as I fantasize about growing up this wealthy.

The drive straightens and I am struck by the sheer size of the mansion. It sits on the shore of the great lake that graces the entire region with its presence, but this massive home actually rivals the body of water.

It's easy to see my younger self running through the trees and skipping stones across the lake.

The slate slabs of the driveway curve widely to the left, allowing room for fifteen to twenty cars to park in front of the three divided two-car garages. Two soaring gables sit astride a magnificent entrance, and light spills through massive windows. The entire home is faced in split rock, and at least three chimneys poke through the steeply sloped roof. A terraced patio hugs the side of the home and works its way toward the surging waves.

My daydream evaporates like mist over the water. I need to focus and get my game face on.

I drive past the fifteen cars lining the drive. I park the Mercedes, pop the door, and step out.

Before I walk into who knows what kind of society luncheon, I take a minute to admire my wheels. A 1957 silver Mercedes 300SL coupe with those sexy, gullwing doors. I whistle softly under my breath, slip the key into my vintage beaded handbag, and swallow. "Game on, Moon."

My heels click magnificently against the stone, and the deep resonant gong of the doorbell does not disappoint. I'm not surprised when an aptly dressed maid opens the massive wooden double-doors.

"May I help you?" Her eyes take in my attire and find it acceptable.

"I certainly hope so. I'm looking for Kitty." I thought about using the "Mrs. Zimmerman-Duncan" option, but I thought "Kitty" might make it seem more like we were loosely acquainted.

"The ladies' club meets in the Fireplace Room." She turns and walks soundlessly across the hardwood floor.

I follow, painfully aware of the clunking of my heels.

She stops, gives a little bow, and gestures me into the space.

I almost ask her to point out the hostess. No need. If Jessica Rabbit came to life and traded her sultry voice for a cheap, imitation faux British accent . . . I give you, Kitty Zimmerman-Duncan.

I choose to "mix" a bit before I introduce myself to the hostess. Maybe I'll overhear something useful.

"I'm gutted, I tell you, gutted. He was my

world." Kitty dabs a finger under her unwet eye while several orbiters murmur their concern.

"Have they found the killer?" A short brunette, who is clearly playing out of her league, asks the indelicate question.

"They arrested someone straightaway, which was brilliant, but Pauly told me the woman is already out on bail."

So Deputy Paulsen has a direct line to Kitty. Good to know.

"Do you need any help with the arrangements, love?"

This older woman looks to have quite a pedigree, and I take note of the massive yellow diamond on her left hand.

"Oh, Chantelle, I super love that you would make such an offer. That's just brilliant. I think I have everything sorted. Thank you so much." Kitty's hand presses against her double-Ds, and her face struggles to make an expression. I'm guessing the Botox interferes.

As I'm about to make another pass through the gaggle—it happens.

"Do I see a new face? Oh, the Duncan Club adores new members. How brills!"

I'm caught like a deer in headlights. I fumble with a smile and debate whether a curtsy is required.

She extends a shockingly pedicured hand weighed down by several carats of blue diamonds. "I'm Kitty Zimmerman-Duncan. Welcome to my humble home."

I hope she doesn't see me gag as I take the bejeweled limb and delicately shake. I don't know what possesses me but for some reason I say, "Mizithra Moon, darling. So good to meet."

The name has the desired effect.

Her eyes widen and she takes in my attire, all the way down to the Valentinos.

"Are those? Oh they are! Oh brilliant!" She pulls me into her inner circle and whispers, "I've never met a pair of Valentinos I didn't love. I'd kill for those." I believe that eye twitch was meant to be a wink, but again, the Botox must prevent many of her simple facial functions.

"Is there somewhere we can chat in private?" I whisper and give an actual wink.

She ushers me up three separate sets of stairs, two steps each, and through some curved glass doors.

This showy wine cellar is bigger than my old apartment. Geez! I swallow the disgust and return to the mission at hand.

"What is it, love? If the dues are a bit too much to pay in one go, I'm happy to let it slide for a month or two. Our little secret." She pats my hand and steals another glance at my shoes.

"Actually, it's about Cal." Wait for it . . .

She presses the diamond-weighted hand to the double-Ds and gasps. "Oh, the pain is still so fresh."

I'm not getting any sincerity from that, but it could be the lack of emotion on her plastic face. I break my news. "He was my grandfather, and I'm so upset that I didn't get a chance to meet him." I hope my pained expression carries more authenticity.

She steps back and narrows her gaze. "Are you – Are you Jacob's kid?"

Now that was decidedly un-British. I detect a hint of angry New Yorker. I place a hand over my mouth and nod.

To her credit, she recovers rapidly. "Oh you poor dear. I'll ask Svenka to make you some tea. Chantelle can run the meeting. We'll slip up to the study and the two of us can have a dash of girl chat. What do you say?"

"That would be divine." What is it lately with me and that word? Granted, a chat is more divine than cheese, but get a grip, Mitzy.

Kitty slips out of the wine cellar and signals to the maid. They exchange hushed words.

A strange shiver ripples across my skin. Is this the scene in a James Bond film where two enormous goons walk in, drag me off screen, and then we cut to them tying me to a platform above a shark tank?

The maid, Svenka, leans to the right and sizes me up with an overly plucked raised eyebrow before scurrying off to do her mistress's bidding.

Looks like I'll be spared the unnecessarily complicated death scene, this time.

Kitty returns, all smiles, and escorts me up to the study—coffered ceiling and all. She takes a seat on one of the curvaceous leather chaises and gestures for me to take the other.

I admire the drama of the piece, but I don't know how to sit on it. I'm sure it would provide a fabulous place to lie back and nap, but it's tricky to find a lady-like purchase on the undulating surface. I opt for a prim perch on the edge of the large curve and smile at Kitty.

"When did you arrive in Pin Cherry, Mizithra?"

I almost correct her, but luckily I remember that I chose the proper version of my name to accompany my ridiculous hairdo and frock. "Unfortunately, I arrived too late." I'm the one running this interrogation. I can't let her take over. "How long had you known my grandfather?"

"Oh, we first met almost fifteen years ago in Aspen. Cal loved to ski."

"Did you live in Colorado?" If I were a gold-digger, I would guess the slopes of a high-end Aspen ski resort would be prime real estate.

"I lived there seasonally."

Translation, she worked for the ski resort or for some local establishment. "Oh, how fun. Was it love at first sight?"

She hesitated before pasting on a huge, wrinkle-free smile. "I can't speak for Cal, but I thought he was brilliant fun the moment I met him."

"How sweet." I swallow my nausea. "Did he propose right away?"

She twists her huge diamond ring and shifts her position on the chaise. "He wanted me to meet his friends, and— Anyway, I came back to Pin Cherry Harbor with him and we were engaged that spring."

"Did you start the Duncan Club?"

She stiffens and eyes me suspiciously. "Not that you would know, but his second wife, Isadora, started the Club."

"Oh, I didn't know." Grams failed to mention that nugget. "What does the Club do?"

"Well, I'm not sure what Isadora had planned, but when I took over I wanted the Club to provide exclusive social opportunities to Pin Cherry's deserving women."

By deserving, I assume she means the wealthy

and the social climbers. “Do you have events other than the luncheons?”

Her whole face lights up. “Oh yes. We have three fundraisers each year. The Halloween Masquerade was Cal’s favorite. It was always the most successful. We held it at the old Wells Iron Ore Refinery. The huge building was the perfect place for a haunted ball.”

“Sounds wonderful. I wish I could’ve seen it.” I almost convince myself of my interest with that line.

“Oh, you’ll have to come this year—if you’re still in town. It’ll be brilliant.” She pats her hands together eagerly. “Cal would’ve wanted it to continue.”

I’m not sure if she’s trying to convince herself or me. “When was the last time you saw my grandfather?”

“Monday morning, I suppose.” She brushes the pleat of her skirt and smiles.

“I thought he died on Wednesday? You didn’t see him on Tuesday or Wednesday?”

She stands and paces to the study’s large bay window. “The stress of the trauma is making me lose track of time. I guess Wednesday at breakfast would’ve been our last moment together.” She presses hand to ample chest. “I’m sorry. I still get so emotional.”

I bustle over and pat her shoulder. "I'm so sorry to put you through all this. I'll leave you to your grief, Kitty. I didn't mean to stir up the pain."

She nods and bites her collagen-stuffed lip.

"I'll see myself out."

She turns as I leave and says, "Thank you for your understanding, Mizithra. So many people have misjudged my relationship with Cal. I loved him for so much more than his money."

Her words, not mine. "Of course you did, dear." I nod and smile.

CHAPTER 15

GRAMS IS FIT to be tied by the time I return to the shop.

"What's gotten into you?" I ask.

"I never thought I would be treated more unfairly in death than in life!" She swirls up to the high ceiling and floats down in a slow spiral of self-pity.

I look around the massive bookshop and spin the Mercedes keys around my finger. I'm having a tiny bit of trouble seeing where life treated her poorly. "I'm not sure I understand."

"They won't tell me anything about Cal. I'm his wife! I should have rights, dear. Even if this is the afterlife, I should still have rights." More swirling.

It may be the wrong time to point out that she

was not technically his wife when he died. Instead I change the subject. "You were spot on about Kitty."

If a ghost can change from out of order to Vegas neon in the blink of an eye, that's how I would describe the switch that flipped in Grams. "Tell me everything," she purrs.

I relay the sequence of events as best I can, despite the incessant interruptions.

"Good call using Mizithra, dear. Anything that sounds even remotely hoity-toity blows that girl's skirt up."

"Do you think it's odd that she's planning to hold the Halloween Masquerade without Cal?"

"Why is that odd?" Grams shrugs.

"Kitty, said it was always Cal's favorite. I thought maybe it would be rude to have it without him."

"Halloween, Cal's favorite? That doesn't sound right. That man hated costumes of any kind. He wouldn't even wear matching sweaters for the family Christmas photos."

I whip out my phone and make a note of that. "There was one other thing . . . " My voice drifts off as I type up my concern.

"And?" Grams hovers anxiously.

"Oh, I didn't realize I stopped talking." I put the phone down. "She said the last time she saw Cal was Monday morning. When I mentioned he was killed on Wednesday, she claimed PTSD and said she must've had breakfast with him on Wednesday."

Grams darkens. "Where was he for two days?"

"Maybe nowhere, Grams. Maybe Kitty was confused and she did see him Wednesday. I just thought it was worth mentioning."

She gestures to the phone. "You made a note?"

I nod.

"Good. Who's our next suspect?"

"The only thing she mentioned was some iron ore refinery. Do you know who owns that old place?"

"It used to belong to the Wells family, but I heard the bank foreclosed on it . . . " Grams drifts toward the floor. "Tilly would know."

Tilly! "Oh crap! I was supposed to meet with Tilly today—and meet Twiggy for lunch." I turn and run out the front door and down Main Street.

I grab the door of Myrtle's Diner and pause to catch my breath. I pull the door open, spy Twiggy, and blurt my breathless apology. "So . . . sorry."

A whistle from the kitchen grabs my attention.

"Who do we have here?" says Odell with a chuckle.

"No idea," adds Twiggy. "I hope you have some filet mignon back there, Odell."

I look down at my designer gown and shoes.

Crap. "All right, get it out of your system." I walk to the table and take a seat in the booth opposite the cackling Twiggy. "I'll have my usual, Odell."

"Right away, M'lady." He barely completes the gibe before his guffaws join the fray.

I take a deep breath and raise my finger to let them both have a taste of my fancy rage—

"Miss Moon?" Sheriff Harper stands in the middle of the diner, looking like he's just seen a ghost.

Ah, what the hell. I stand and place one hand at my boned-and-stayed waist. "Erick."

"You look . . . That's a real—" He swallows several times and looks around the near-empty diner as the color creeps across his cheeks. "Were you out at the Duncan place this morning?"

"I was." Clearly he already knows the answer to this pop quiz. I have the urge to reach over and muss his hair. I love it when those long bangs hang—

"I'll have to ask you to stay clear of this case, Miss Moon." He squares his shoulders.

My heart flutters. "Your *case*, is it? Does that mean you might actually be looking at someone besides me as a suspect in my grandfather's murder?"

"I'm not at liberty to discuss the case, Miss Moon."

I decide to press my advantage. I swish closer to the sheriff. Close enough for the layers of my tulle skirt to brush against his polyester pants. It looks sexier than it sounds. "We both know I didn't kill him, Erick. Why don't you share your news with me and I'll share mine."

He carefully scoots back and his boots squeak against the flooring. "What news?"

"My step-gramma was feeling chatty this morning." I smile in what I hope looks like a cat-that-got-the-canary kind of grin.

He shakes his head in defeat. "It'll be in the official report soon enough. The ME recanted the initial time of death."

I lean toward the lovely specimen of manhood. "Go on."

"I'm afraid I can't say any more. The new time of death could be critical to uncovering additional suspects."

I can't seem to stop myself from putting a hand on his arm. Goodness, that bicep is exactly as firm as I imagined.

"Excuse me, Miss Moon." He flushes pure magenta and tugs his arm.

I tighten my grasp. "Would it interest you to know that Kitty said the last time she saw Cal was Monday morning?"

His eyes widen and his pupils dilate. I hope I'm

the reason for the dilation, but my celebration is short lived.

He pulls free and hustles out of the diner before I can say another word.

Twiggy gives me a slow clap. "Looks like you've got 'em on the run."

I turn back to the booth and look around in confusion. Gosh darn it, that man makes me lose all sense of time.

"Your burger's comin' out in a minute, Mitzy. You want a bib or something?"

I toy with a witty comeback, but when I remember the pride in Isadora's eyes as I slipped into this piece of her history, I choose propriety. "Yes, maybe a couple."

Covered in clean dishtowels and fortified with fries, I remember why I'm meeting Twiggy. "I didn't get a chance to stop by the bank." I gesture to my getup.

"I figured," she responds.

"I'll be heading over there after lunch and then I can meet you at the bookshop to discuss your pay." I shove the last fry in my mouth and lick the salt off my fingers.

Twiggy looks me up and down. "Talk about making a silk purse out of a sow's ear."

I stop with my pinky finger half in half out of my mouth. What can I say? She's right. I shrug.

"Before you turn yourself inside out"—Twiggy slides out of the booth—"your Grams never paid me. We were best friends." She walks past me and calls back. "You and I—we're good."

The door swishes open and closed. I look at Odell and he salutes me with his metal spatula. "That's a tough nut to crack, that one. Good for you."

I'm not sure what I did to earn Twiggy's loyalty, but I'm in no position to refuse allies. I thank Odell for the delicious food and stroll over to the bank.

I bask in the effect of my luscious outfit on the public at large.

Tilly rushes to my side when I enter the bank. "Good afternoon. How can I help you, Miss."

"Hi, Tilly. You told me to stop by to get something called 'checks.'" I smile broadly.

She's obviously taken aback. "Miss Moon? Oh my stars, I didn't recognize you in that—" She stops herself and blinks rapidly. "Well, don't you just look divine?"

Looks like I'm not the only one who defaults to that word under pressure.

She walks back to her meager brown desk and beckons me to follow.

I press my advantage while she's discombobulated. "Tilly, are you familiar with the Wells Iron Ore Refinery?"

"Of course. They were the largest employer in the region during the boom years." She doesn't look up from her paper shuffling but takes a form and loads it into a typewriter.

I lose my train of thought as I stare in fascination at the device I have only read about in old books.

"Why do you ask?"

Oh, right. I'm supposed to be gathering information. "When did the refinery go into receivership?" I hope that's the right word . . .

"Receivership?"

Crap. Wrong word.

"Oh, no dear. The bank doesn't own that property. Finnegan settled the loan almost two years ago." She cranks the little knob and feeds the form through the typewriter.

"Finnegan?"

"Yes, Finnegan Wells. He's the great-grandson and current owner."

"But I thought the refinery was abandoned. How could he afford to pay off the debt if the iron ore business dried up?"

Tilly looks up from her forms. "I'm sure I have no idea, dear. What's your sudden interest in iron ore?"

Oops. Pushed too hard. "No interest. Just making conversation."

She pinches her lips together and raises an eyebrow.

"Do you need me to sign anything? Oh, Twiggy mentioned that there's more than one account. Do you have statements for me?"

She gets up without a word and returns with two thick files. "We keep the records in the vault. I'll have the clerk make copies for you."

"You don't have electronic records?"

"How's that, dear?"

I slowly scan across the tidy wooden desks in the bank. I don't see any computers. What if I slipped through some kind of time portal when I stepped off that bus? Maybe I did fall into an old black-and-white movie. No computers? I open my vintage handbag in a panic. I touch my smartphone and breathe a sigh of relief. Okay, technology does exist—just not in this bank. "How do you keep track of deposits and withdrawals?"

Tilly looks at me as though I have a tentacle growing out of my neck. "That's what the passbook is for, Miss Moon." She slides three small books the size of passports across the desk and lays a form in front of me. "Sign at the bottom. Press firmly. You have to get through three copies."

I sign the top page and lift it up to sign the next page. There on the yellow sheet my signature already exists. "What is this?" I lift the yellow sheet and my signature already exists on the pink sheet, too. "How did—?"

Tilly looks at me for a moment. "It's called NCR paper. The carbon is built into each sheet so the signature transfers through. That's why I told you to press firmly." She smiles and shakes her head in amusement.

I stare at the paper as though it possesses magical powers.

"You get the pink copy. The white copy goes in your permanent file, and the yellow copy stays at the teller window in case you need to make a withdrawal and forget your passbook."

I don't have a clue what any of those words mean. I take the pink sheet and the three little books and walk out of the time machine in a daze.

CHAPTER 16

The Bell, Book & Candle is as "not busy" as usual when I return. Twiggy carefully shelves books and Pyewacket is nowhere to be found.

"Grams? Grams?"

"Don't look at me," volunteers Twiggy. "I can't see her."

I negotiate the chain in my heels and teeter up the stairs to the apartment. I drop the paperwork on the bed and unbuckle the tiny T-straps on the Valentinos. As my feet sink into the thick area rug I let out a sigh.

"Don't complain, honey. I know ten women who would kill to wear those shoes for five minutes."

"Grams!" I smile and rub my poor tootsies. "Trust me, if I'd only had to wear them for five minutes I wouldn't be complaining." I wiggle out of the dress and eagerly slip back into skinny jeans and a snarky tee. However, when I look in the mirror I have to admit that I miss the knockout a little.

Grams shoots ahead of me into the closet. "You can't hang that up in here, Mitzy."

I look at the dress and then at Grams. "I'm not sure what you're saying. Where am I meant to hang it?"

"Darling, you wore it for hours. You have to take it and have it properly cleaned."

"Like a dry cleaners?" Girls with skinny jean and T-shirt wardrobes don't get much dry-cleaner action.

"Exactly. Take it down to Harbor Cleaners on 3rd Avenue. Tanya knows how I like it."

"Now?"

"Now."

Copy that, as they say in the film business. I slip on my kicks and march down the street to see Tanya about my fancy ghost gramma's couture cleaning needs. There's a sentence I never expected to utter in my life.

Shockingly, there's a man in line in front of me at the cleaners. It's the first time I've had to wait for anything in Pin Cherry and the experience intrigues. He's mid forties, fit for his age, with a surprising amount of thick black hair. I imagine he's a hot property in these parts.

A woman returns from the back. That must be Tanya. Her movement stirs the atmosphere and a fresh wave of chemically impregnated air wafts over me. Ew.

"I'm sorry, Finnegan, I wasn't able to get the stains out completely. I'm not sure what kind of wine it was, but it really dug in."

He nods and hands her a credit card. I notice a ring on his right hand. The symbol looks familiar, but I can't place it.

Tanya pulls a small device out from under the counter and lays the credit card in it. She places a slip of paper over the card and—

This can't be happening! I'm witnessing someone use one of those old credit card slidy machines from the eighties. It's like I'm visiting a pioneer village attraction where people still make their own candles and brooms. It's fascinating.

"See something you like?"

I might have leaned in a little more than I intended. The man's voice is too friendly and far too suggestive. I'd like to say something about how he's old enough to be my father, but if this is Finnegan Wells—and according to the slidy-device slip it is—I'd like to ask him a few questions. "I'm new in town. What's your favorite place for pie?" I may or may not have winked as I said this.

He smirks and looks me up and down. "I'll get a booth at Myrtle's on Main. Do you know the place?"

"I'm sure I can find it . . ." I pause for his name.

"Wells, Finnegan Wells."

"I'll be there in five, Finnegan." One more wink. Why not? You get more flies with honey, right?

He walks out and looks over his shoulder to stare at my rear end.

Yuck. I hope that's not what I look like when I'm lusting over Erick.

"How can I help you, Miss?"

"Hi, Tanya. My grams said you'd know what to do with this dress. It holds a special place in her heart and requires some TLC."

She looks at me like I'm crazy. "The dress I recognize, but have we met?"

Right. In her world my grandmother is dead. "Haven't had the pleasure, but my grams, God rest her, always said you were the best."

A relieved smile spreads across her face. "Any stains?"

"I don't think so. I only wore it for a couple hours. I tried to be careful."

She examines the dress with a shrewd eye and

peers at me over the half moons of her bifocals. "You've certainly done better than him. He brings that shirt in and tells me there's a wine stain." She shakes her head in disdain. "Forty years I've been in the business. I know a wine stain when I see one."

"I'm sure you do." I nod supportively. "What do you think it was?"

"I'll tell you what I know. That was blood if I'm a day."

I don't follow her analogy, but I go with it. "Blood? Why would he say it was wine?"

"Your guess is as good as mine. I suppose his girlfriend doesn't want him fighting anymore."

"Who could blame her?" Imagine that! He's got a girlfriend and he just invited me to pie. "Maybe I shouldn't meet him for pie, eh?"

Tanya laughs. "I wouldn't want to call down that woman's diamond-studded wrath." Her eyes go wide.

She clearly said something she regrets. I don't have enough information to know what, but I make a mental note to add an actual note to my phone as soon as I can. "When can I pick up the dress?"

"Monday okay for you?"

"Perfect. Thanks, Tanya."

I turn to leave.

"What name do I put it under? Isadora's account was closed when she passed, bless her."

"Mitzy Moon." I derive a secret pleasure from watching her lips mouth the name silently. Word does travel fast in a small town. Now she has a face to put with the rumor.

I hustle over to the diner and pray that I can catch Odell's eye before he blurts out a greeting.

Taking the slow and careful approach, I peer in the corner of the window. Finnegan is holding court with Tally, his back to the door. I can't see Odell. I take a deep breath and hope for the best.

I push open the door slowly and search the orders-up window for some sign of life.

Tally takes no notice of me.

Odell's face pops into the window and he raises his spatula.

I put a warning finger across my lips and shake my head. I nod toward the outspoken Finnegan.

Odell winks. "Tally, I need your expertise."

Tally nods to Finnegan, giggles at something he says, and sashays into the back.

I rush over and put a hand on Finnegan's shoulder. "I hope I didn't keep you waiting."

He tilts his head and grins up at me. The white of his teeth nearly blinds. I'm not sure if it's overwhitening or grossly mismatched veneers. Upon closer inspection, I also notice the too-even blackness of his monochromatic hair.

He stands and purposely brushes up against me as he gestures for me to take a seat in the booth.

"What do you recommend?" I dare to steal a glance toward the kitchen.

Odell and Tally have their heads together and she's whispering furtively.

"They have the best pin cherry pie in Birch County." He catches my eye across the table and winks. "I always have the pie."

"Oh, how quaint." I nearly gag on my own reply.

Tally approaches the table and struggles to avoid my eye. "What can I getcha?"

My companion stares at Tally with a look that I will dub "the buffet." This accurately describes how his eyes move up and down a woman's body as though he's starving and she's a multi-course smorgasbord for the pillaging. Oh, and let me add—yuck.

"I'll have the pin cherry pie, as usual, Tally. And don't skimp on the ice cream." He winks.

The wink is as over-reaching as if he had smacked her on the ass.

She looks down at the table and says, "And for you, ma'am?"

I giggle and say, "When in Rome."

Finnegan chuckles and winks.

Tally stares at me and shrugs.

"I'll have the pie and ice cream, too." I pretend to struggle to read her nametag. "Tally," I manage.

She grins and practically runs back to the kitchen.

Finnegan leans across the table and whispers in what must pass for sexy in his one-track mind, "Tell me about yourself." He punctuates the phrases with a little snap of his teeth.

Is it possible that he smells of scotch at two in the afternoon? I lean toward him in spite of my disgust and purr right back. "I'd rather hear what a powerful man like you does in a tiny little town like Pin Cherry." I try to lick my lip in a sexy way, but the bile rising in my throat nearly chokes me.

He doesn't notice.

"Big fish. Little pond." He leans back and props his arm across the back of the bench seat. "My family just about owns this town. The Wells men ran the iron ore business around here since before this town was even incorporated."

I would love to point out that the iron ore business dried up two or three decades ago, but more flies with honey . . . "Do you still run a refinery, or operate any of those big machines?" I bat my eyelashes to distract from my hideous delivery.

"We don't mine any ore these days. I'm more of a local entrepreneur and philanthropist." He spins the massive signet ring on his right hand.

If memory serves, every unemployed loser on reality TV refers to himself as an "entrepreneur." "How fascinating," I gush. "What sort of philandering do you do?"

He grins.

He thinks I don't know what I said. That pleases me deeply.

"Probably the biggest event I sponsor is the massive annual Halloween Masquerade. We convert the refinery into a mind-blowing haunted ball and raise a small fortune for charity."

"How exciting." I'm running out of exclamations of praise. "You said 'we.' Who can you trust to help you organize such an important event?" I cross my fingers under the table.

"Oh, no one plans a fundraiser like Kitty Zimmerman." His eyes glaze over for a moment and it seems he's enjoying a private mental picture.

"Don't you mean Zimmerman-Duncan?" I try to maintain an absolute innocence in my tone.

"Of course, of course." He looks at me with a hint of suspicion and perhaps concern. "Do you know Kitty?"

"We only just met today at the Duncan Club ladies' luncheon." I search my mental thesaurus for a word I can utter without choking. "She's stunning."

He leans back and smirks. "She's something, isn't she?"

"Mmhmm." I can't wait to tell Grams that I uncovered "the trollop's boyfriend." Check. Time to push a little harder. "So what charity?"

His eyes snap into sharp focus. "Beg your pardon?"

"I was wondering which charity you and Mrs. Zimmerman-Duncan support with all the money you raise?" I watch as his beady eyes dart left and right. I can almost smell the smoke wafting from the little gears in his cretinous mind as they whir toward disaster.

He shifts and the vinyl bench seat creaks under his sweaty backside. "I didn't catch your name?" His fake smile strains.

"Oh, it's Mitzy. Mitzy Moon." Once again I derive a sick pleasure from watching his lips mutely form the syllables of my name.

Tally sets down two slices of glistening red pin cherry pie with mountains of creamy vanilla deliciousness melting over the flaky pastry.

Finnegan's entire demeanor shifts from lascivious predator to threatened wild animal. "I don't appreciate being played." He slides out of the booth in a huff.

Tally scurries away.

I shrug and slide a slice of pie in for closer inspection. “Thanks for the recommendation. The pie looks delicious.”

He leans down and his voice comes out as a scotch-tainted growl. “No one makes a fool of Finnegan Wells.”

I raise a forkful of pie as though it is a glass of champagne. “Duly noted.” I shove the whole bite in my mouth and let the ice cream dribble down my lips.

He glowers.

I wipe the drip with my thumb and suck the ice cream off. “See ya ’round, Finnegan.” I flutter my remaining fingers in a “toodles” kind of wave.

He storms out.

I exhale, thank every foster care bully that toughened my hide, and fight to gain control of my racing heart.

Tally gasps.

Odell utters a low whistle. “It was like watching Myrtle come back to life.”

I can’t wait to get back to the bookshop and tell Grams all the good news. Including the bit about Odell’s lovely compliment.

CHAPTER 17

When I get back to the bookshop the front door is locked, so I fish out my key and let myself into the store.

I don't know if I'll ever get used to the eerie silence, but the booktopian smell gives me an unexpected dose of comfort. When I close the door and twist the locks, I actually feel "home." I haven't felt that sensation since my mom passed. Venturing north to explore the "great lakes" has turned out pretty okay.

I cautiously make my way through the darkness into the stacks and close my eyes. Today was a rollercoaster, but having this place to come back to gives me a solid feeling I've never known. Tomorrow, before anyone can show up and arrest me, I'm going to walk along that narrow balcony edging the second floor and climb to the top of that teetering ladder. It's time for me to know more about this bookshop than anyone else. I'm going to start with the first book on the top shelf in the north corner and work my way through every precious tome in MY store.

Opening my eyes, I stretch out an arm to either side. The spines of books that could take me to other realms tickle the tips of my fingers and I sigh with satisfaction. No matter how tough things got, and whether the ends met or not, my mother always made sure I had a book to read.

A small flicker of light swirls toward me and expands. "How was that, dear?" She fades in and smiles.

"I didn't even pee a little, Grams. I think that's the one. That's the entrance I prefer."

Her melodious laughter sweeps over me and drifts into the stacks. She politely leaves my previous private thoughts untouched.

I pull out my phone and use the blue glow to guide my feet up to the apartment. "You aren't going to believe what happened at the cleaners."

She floats over to the bed, and the way she hovers it almost looks like we're having a sleepover. She appears to lie on her tummy, ankles crossed, with her chin resting in her hand. "Tell me everything," she gushes. A vision enveloped in Marchesa.

Inhaling sharply, I cover my mouth, and tears flood from my eyes.

Grams instantly whirls to my side. "What is it? Did someone hurt you?"

I imagine I can almost feel her ethereal hand rubbing my back. "It's nothing bad, Grams. I don't know what came over me. I looked at you on the bed with that attentive smile and—"

"Oh, honey." She wipes her cheeks. "I hate that I can't hold you, but I'm so glad I'm trapped in this bookstore."

We both laugh through our tears.

"I never had family like this—not since Mom, well, you know."

She nods.

"I didn't realize how lonely I was until I came to Pin Cherry Harbor. Aside from the arrest for murder, this has been the best few days of my life."

"That murder charge will never stick, dear." She flicks away the idea and claps her hands together. "All right, enough touchy-feely sharing. What happened at the cleaners?"

I tell her about Finnegan Wells' bloodstained shirt.

"Make a note." She points to my phone.

Next, I mention Tanya's comment about diamond-studded wrath.

"Kitty?"

"It has to be, right?"

"I told you there was a boyfriend." Grams is positively glowing. "Didn't I tell you?"

"You did." I finish with the pie-related events at Myrtle's Diner.

"Odell always was quick on the uptake. Smart as a whip, that man." She smiles and her energy grows calm, as she seems to drift through her memories. "I'll never forget the day we opened that diner."

I must ask the burning question. "Why did you switch from Myrtle to Isadora?"

"When things ended with Odell, I truly felt like a part of my life and my heart were gone forever. Myrtle was the wide-eyed girl who fell head over heels for a young hero. When the drinking drove the wedge between us—"

"Odell's an alcoholic?" He seems so clear-eyed and steady.

Grams turns away and a long silence hangs between us. "Not Odell, dear. Not Odell."

"Oh."

She looks into my eyes and nods. "Oh, indeed. My second marriage was a non-stop party. When the car accident took Max from me and left me with a limp and one kidney, the light finally came on. I dropped 'Myrtle' and all her mistakes. Isadora got sober, went to meetings, and formed a stable relationship with a responsible man—Cal."

"I had no idea."

"Of course you didn't. Water under the bridge, dear." Grams gives me that Midwestern stiff-upper-lip look.

"Now I understand why you left Odell the diner in your will."

"He never remarried, you know." Grams touches a tiny silver band on her left hand.

Never one to get too comfortable with raw emotion, I launch into the *coup de grâce* of my meeting with Finnegan. "Anyway, he mentioned that same Halloween ball and how much money they raise for charity. But, get this, when I asked him the name of the charity he got all bajiggity with me."

"I have no idea what that means, honey."

"Oh, right. He became defensive, and said, 'No one makes a fool of Finnegan Wells.' Then he gave me a threatening glare and stormed out."

Grams fans herself and breathes a sigh of relief. "What did you do?"

"I ate the pie. I'm not an idiot."

She laughs so hard ghost snot comes out her nose.

My chest swells with pride.

I'm too exhausted to go through my dad's case files, so I treat myself to another ridiculously perfect hot shower and collapse into bed.

CHAPTER 18

Pyewacket's rough tongue attempts to lick my eye open. I toy with the idea of ignoring him, but the recent memory of his pointy teeth on my earlobe causes me to roll out of bed.

I stumble to the bathroom and Pye rubs against my legs, nearly knocking me off my unsteady feet. "Let me wake up, son."

Shockingly, Pye immediately ceases his assault. His tufted ears twitch and he leaps to the top of an antique armoire near the secret door. His head tilts and a dangerous look sharpens his gaze.

Wood scrapes against wood as the bookcase slides open.

I step back into the bathroom and peek around the beveled molding.

The door is completely open, but no one enters.

A disembodied voice utters a stern warning. "Robin Pyewacket Goodfellow, if you deign to lay one claw upon my head I'll turn you into a mouse."

Pye hisses.

Silas enters. "Pardon the unannounced early morning call, Mitzy. I have much to discuss."

I stare. Clearly I need coffee, but did I just witness Silas and Pye having an actual conversation? I mean, Pye seemed to know who was coming, and Silas expected the attack. I rub my eyes and yawn loudly.

"Lovely," murmurs Silas. "May I escort you to breakfast at the diner?"

"Gimme two minutes."

"Please, take five." Silas gently lowers himself onto the scalloped-back chair and Pye appears directly under the ready fingers of the attorney. The tufted ears relax and the gnarled fingers scratch. They have the comfortable air of old friends.

I shake my head and close the bathroom door. A splash of water, a rinse of mouthwash, and skinny jeans swapped for my leggings. I'm ready to eat.

I cross the room and Silas leans back and squints. "What's this now?" He gestures to my tee.

I look down and shrug. "It claims that abstinence is only 99.99% effective." I point to the graphic. "It's the Virgin Mary and baby Jesus. Get it?"

Silas cocks his head to one side, and a flash of amusement touches his milky-blue eyes. "I do. That is quite humorous."

He could've simply laughed, but I suppose stating the fact of something's hilarity is another way to go. "Ready for breakfast?"

"Indeed." He rises from the chair.

"Hi-ssss." Pyewacket launches through the open bookcase and down the stairs.

"I better give him his Fruity Puffs. I'd hate to see what those claws could do if he gets impatient."

"Lifetimes of indulgence. He'll never learn." Silas shakes his head.

I hurry after the wildcat.

When I come out the front door of the bookshop, Silas is working levers and sliding the gearshift in the Model T, but there are no sounds of its sputtering engine. I lean in and suggest, "How 'bout we walk the two blocks?"

Silas mumbles something, ostensibly to the car, and exits his vehicle. "Very well."

There's only one booth left in the bustling diner and Odell doesn't notice us when we enter. My goodness, this must be the weekend rush—but it's Friday.

Silas leads the way to the booth and Tally arrives before I can slide in.

"You best get your orders in right quick. Those

three tables just sat down, but I can slide yours in ahead of them if you know what you want." Her bright red bun bobs anxiously.

"Bring us two specials and some black coffee." Silas nods his dismissal.

"I might not want the special, Silas. And I take cream."

"We'll need to address your trust issues," he mumbles.

I take offense, but keep it to myself. "Why is this place so busy on a Friday?"

"It's opening day of the Pin Cherry Festival. I hope you've asked Twiggy to assist you at the bookshop."

What makes him think I would've asked Twiggy to assist me during a festival whose existence I only just uncovered? I let it lie and move on to neutral territory. "You said we had a lot to discuss. Did you get a copy of the medical examiner's report?"

He nods. "The amended report."

"New time of death?"

"Originally, based on decomposition and insect activity, they claimed Wednesday morning between 10:00 and 11:00. However, after the forensic pathologist reviewed the tissue samples sent to the county crime lab—"

I lean forward.

"—the corrected time of death is Monday night between 8:00 and 9:00 p.m."

I lean back and slap a hand on the table. "Kitty said she hadn't seen him since Monday."

Silas places two fingers on my hand. "Decorum, Mitzy."

"Is our local ME a hack?"

"Not in the least. However, at county they discovered a strange striation in the cells that indicated the body had been frozen immediately after the murder. The extreme temperature slowed decomposition and gave a false time of death."

I glance around and catch several people as they look away. I lean in and lower my voice. "There's no way I'm a suspect now, right?"

"Unfortunately, no one on the bus remembers you, and the ticket alone isn't an airtight alibi. However, I do think Sheriff Harper is finally pursuing other avenues."

"Like the avenue of how the skanky widow and her boyfriend knocked off my grandfather for his money?" I tap my pointer finger on the table —lightly.

"Evidence points toward Kitty. What's this about a boyfriend?"

I whisper, "I think there's something going on between her and Finnegan Wells." I suddenly recognize the symbol from Finnegan's ostentatious signet ring. "Plus, he was wearing a ring with the Duncan family crest on it."

Silas steeples his fingers and his eyes travel to a place I can't follow. "Interesting. Quite interesting."

"What? Did I solve the murder?"

Tally gasps at the word and clatters our plates onto the table. "I'll—um—coffee." She scurries off.

I look at the plate in front of Silas and see an egg-white omelette with green peppers and cheese. No toast. No potatoes. My heart sinks as I shift my gaze to my own plate. I have a pile of fluffy scrambled eggs with chorizo and jalapeños, two slices of sourdough toast, and a golden-brown mound of home fries. "How did we both get the special?" I point to our two completely different breakfasts.

"That is what is special. Odell always knows what you want."

I grin like a fool and look toward the kitchen. Odell gives me an amused nod before he jumps back into filling orders.

Tally places two steaming mugs of java on the table and slides a little melamine bowl filled with individual creamers toward me. "Thank you." I pour a good deal of thick, rich cream into my coffee and slide the bowl toward Silas. He waves it off and continues with his report.

"The business I had to attend to involved a conclave with Cal's lawyer. There were some matters between his estate and Isadora's that needed settling. She mentioned that Cal had come to see her Monday morning and requested some drastic changes to his will. The alterations would have left Kitty with a mere fraction of what she'd been promised."

"Whom was he leaving everything to? I mean, Grams died before him so—"

"He was moving Jacob into the primary position and you as the contingent."

"Me? Why me? I thought he and my dad were estranged. I don't understand."

"Nor do I, Mitzy, but this information regarding Finnegan Wells intrigues." Silas scrunches up his large nose.

"Did I mention the Halloween Masquerade?" I ask. "He said that they, he and Kitty, raised a small fortune for charity every year, but when I asked the name of the charity he got all bajig—I mean, irritated and left." Silas tilts his head and I add, "Plus, Tilly said the loan on the iron ore refinery had been paid off."

A slow smile pushes up Silas's sagging cheeks. "You are far more than a barista, Miss Moon. Far more."

CHAPTER 19

I WALK BACK to the bookshop alone. I may be slipping down the suspect list for Cal's murder, but that fails to lift my spirits. Silas promised to set up a meeting with my father and that prospect has me on edge.

I stop and stare at the line forming in front of Bell, Book & Candle. I definitely need Twiggy. Crap! I don't even have her number—or a phone with service. I'm rich now. I should definitely handle my cell-phone inadequacy.

I cross the street slowly, tossing around various delay tactics, when a familiar cackle reaches my ears.

"Right on top of the poor sheriff. I'm telling you—"

"You certainly are." I interrupt Twiggy's recounting of my crash landing on Erick at the diner and shove my special key in the lock.

Murmurs and snickers close in around me. This is not the day I had planned. I pull open the large door and Twiggy and her acolytes stream through without so much as a glance at their benefactor—or a thank you. I give a little harrumph and march to the back room.

Twiggy holds up a bank pouch and nods. "I took the liberty of grabbing the drawer money. I knew you'd be swamped with the Pinners."

I want to wallow for a few more minutes, but she's actually pretty thoughtful. "What are Pinners, dare I ask?"

"Out-of-towners that come up once a year for the Pin Cherry Festival." She shakes her head.

"This is the first I'm hearing of the Pin Cherry Festival," I say with more bite than I intend.

"Easy, doll. I'm sure there's still time to put your name in the hat for Princess of the Pin Cherry Festival, if that's what's got you so wound up."

"You know what?" I don't bother to finish the thought. I grab Pye's box of Fruity Puffs and march up to the apartment without another word.

Once inside my hideout, I sputter all kinds of snappy retorts.

"Since your lips are moving, I'm gonna jump in."

I shove a handful of cereal into my mouth and crunch loudly.

"Didn't you just come from breakfast?"

"I stress eat when I'm not stress drinking. Don't judge."

Grams puts her hands up in surrender. "Two things, dear: Pyewacket's wrath will be merciless if there are no Fruity Puffs for tomorrow's breakfast."

I remove my hand from the box and search the high places for furry retribution.

"And Twiggy will bend over backward for you if you show her a little respect."

"She was entertaining a crowd with stories of my misfortune."

"Are you saying landing on top of Erick Harper was unfortunate?" Grams winks.

I giggle and blush. "Hardly."

We both laugh.

"I was hoping to spend the day going over Dad's case files. I didn't know there was a princess pageant and a cherry jubilee!"

"You're too funny, Mitzy." Grams floats toward the settee and repeats, "Cherry jubilee. Delightful." She settles into a reclining hover. "Just run down and let Twiggy know how much you need her help and that you have to review the case. Piece of cake, dear."

"Is there a bakery in town?"

Grams looks at me as though I've lost it.

"You said cake, and I thought 'yes' and now I want cake."

"Take the Fruity Puffs downstairs and clear your schedule. We need to—"

"Cal was changing his will," I blurt.

Grams shoots up toward the ceiling. "Cereal. Schedule. Case." She ticks off the list on her bejeweled fingers and hurtles toward me. "No time to lose, Mitzy. No time to lose."

The sight of Ghost-ma barreling directly at me lights a fire beneath my feet. I hustle back downstairs.

Grams was right, of course. Twiggy is more than happy to take the reins for the day and that leaves me free to delve into my father's history and find the real killer.

By the way, I've pre-decided he's not guilty. But there's a method to my madness. People always say that if you only have a hammer you'll always find nails. I'm paraphrasing. So, it stands to reason that if I assume innocence I'll find the proof. I know, pure genius. Right?

The bookcase barely slides closed before Grams swoops in with questions. "Did you say Cal was changing his will? Why on earth would he do that? Do you think he knew about Kitty and Finnegan?"

I wave my hand wildly to get her attention. "I

only know what Silas told me. He met with Cal's attorney to settle some business between your estate and Cal's and the attorney said she met with Cal on Monday to discuss the changes. Of course, Cal never returned to sign the new documents."

"What were the changes, exactly?"

"Silas said Cal was giving pretty much everything to Jacob and then me as something called a contingent."

"To Jacob? You must've misheard, dear. Cal disowned Jacob after the murder conviction. He never would've put him in the will . . . unless . . . "

"Unless what? Unless what, Grams?"

"You better dig into those files, honey. And you better search Cal's office tonight to see if he left any clues that would tell us what changed his mind about Jacob."

My eyes widen. "Search Cal's office? I'm sure it was just an end-of-life, no-regrets kind of thing. You know, like you putting me in your will in spite of my dad's edict."

"Sweetie, I knew I was dying. I had time to put my affairs in order. Cal was murdered. There has to be another reason he wanted to leave things to his son, to Jacob."

"Good point," I concede. "But I'm no cat burglar, or any kind of burglar. There's no way I can break into Cal's office tonight."

Grams swooshes past me and hovers above the vanity. "Oh, you don't have to break in, Mitzy dear. I have a key in the secret compartment of my jewelry box."

Secret doors. Secret compartments. My Grams could be mistaken for a shady character.

"I beg—"

I point to my lips and shake my head.

"Fine. Let's see if you can find the compartment without my help."

I sit down at the marble-top vanity and pick up the tiger-maple jewelry box. I carefully inspect all sides and the bottom. I open the lid and then slide the latch to the left. A thin drawer pops out the right side.

Grams gasps. "How did you know?"

I force myself to think of anything besides how I discovered the trick. I don't want her to have the satisfaction of hearing my thoughts.

A ring in the top compartment catches my attention. I slip it out from between the smooth rolls of purple velvet for a closer look.

Grams silently moves closer.

I hold the ring toward her. "I like this one. It has a cool dome-y shape."

Her reply is barely a whisper. "It's a cabochon."

I lean in and ask, "I heard something about a Shaun."

She clears her throat. "Cabochon. That's what the shape of the stone is called. It's just an old mood ring I picked up at a pawn shop in the seventies."

"What's a mood ring?" I ask as I run my finger along the twisted gold rope surrounding the stone.

"Why don't you put it on?"

Something in her voice makes my pulse race. I slip the band on the ring finger of my left hand and twist it back and forth.

She continues her explanation. "The stone changes color depending on your mood. I can't remember them all now, but purple meant that you were feeling romantic, and I think brown or grey meant your were nervous. Some rings had pink, but—"

I hold up the hand bearing the ring and look at my grandmother.

She stops in midsentence. "What is it, dear?"

"What does black thunderstorm tornado mean?" I swallow hard.

She zooms in. "What?" She tries to touch the ring but her ghostly fingers pass right through my hand. "Darn it! What do you see?"

I pull my hand back toward me and stare into the ring.

The room disappears. Everything is black. Energy is swirling around me like flashes of lightning. I call out to Grams, but no one answers.

I feel a powerful need for alcohol. I feel intense love for my son. I feel a desire for power—and knowledge. I feel sorrow over my divorce. I miss Max.

My head is spinning. These aren't my feelings. "Grams! Help me!"

I collapse.

When I open my eyes Grams is hovering above my body, calling my name. I can't hear her voice, but I can see the panic in her ghostly face.

"Take off the ring," she cries.

I hear that! I whip the possessed ring off my finger and drop it on the floor. I push myself to a seated position and take several shaky breaths. "What the heck happened?"

"Did you have a vision?"

I shake my head. "That's a pretty random question, Grams." I exhale and tell her about the blackness and the feelings.

"Maybe it's hereditary," she mumbles.

"What's hereditary?"

"I used to get visions and premonitions—when I was alive. But it seems like you might be clairsentient."

"Who's Claire?" I hold a hand against my left temple. "I'm so dizzy."

"It's not a who, it's a what. Clairsentient means that you can feel other people's emotions, and you get messages through them. Sometimes you can even feel things beyond the veil."

I tilt my head and look at my grandmother like she's lost her mind. "So, you're saying I can feel dead people?"

She nods. "Maybe."

Apparently, my clever *Sixth Sense* reference is lost on her. "What's happening to me?"

"I honestly don't know, dear. We can talk to Silas about it tomorrow. For now, I think it's best to get a drink of water and distract yourself with the case."

I open my mouth to protest, but then an odd thought tumbles in. "Grams, why would I want to talk to Silas about this?"

She turns away and, if I didn't know better, I'd say she's acting a little cagey. "Oh, you know, he reads all those books in the loft. He has a wealth of arcane knowledge."

I'm too woozy to battle Ghost-ma. I walk to the bathroom and slurp some water from the faucet.

"Honestly, Mitzy." Grams shakes her head.

"I'd never make it all the way down those swirly stairs to get a cup." I wipe the dripping water with the back of my hand. "Now, where were we before I had my episode." I attempt to chuckle, but it makes my head throb.

"You were getting the key to Cal's office." Grams helpfully points toward the jewelry box.

I look suspiciously at the Pandora's box, but I'm anxious to shift my focus to something I understand. "Which key is it, and why do you have a key to Cal's office?"

"It's the brass key that says 'Do Not Duplicate.'" She snickers. "It doesn't say anything about 'Do Not Keep.'"

"And the why?"

"Oh, he gave me a key when we were married. I must've forgotten to return it after the divorce." Her innocent ghost eyes widen.

"Mmhmm. Thing is, Grams, I can't imagine that the key still works thirty years later." I turn the key over in my hand. "He may have even moved his offices."

"Never." She shakes her head. "Cal Duncan's family has owned the Midwest Union Railway since his great-great-great-grandfather drove the first spike through the rail where the tracks begin down by the docks. The president and chief engineer's office has always been in the top floor of the Pin Cherry Harbor station. And Cal never changes something unless he has a real good reason. If it ain't broke, don't fix it was his favorite motto."

"Then he must've had a real good reason to change his will," I mumble.

"Exactly," Grams says, emphatically. "So, you'll search his office tonight?"

I rub the letters etched into the key and surmise that breaking and entering should carry a lighter sentence than murder. Plus, technically it's not "breaking" if I have a key, right?

Grams confirms my thoughts with a nod.

"All right. Let's put that on the back burner for now and dive into Dad's case."

"10-4," says Grams.

I chuckle and hunker down next to the stack of witness statements. There's still nothing useful here. I go back to the list of evidence. "It says Dad had a 9mm in his possession at the time of the arrest and Darrin had a .45. I'm no expert, Grams, but I can't imagine that ballistics could confuse those two rounds. They pulled a 9mm slug out of the victim."

"Jacob didn't do it. A mother knows."

I'm not sure how to respond, so I continue with my summary. "And a 9mm slug from the damaged security camera in that room." I lie back on the floor and look through my hovering grandmother. "All the witness statements claim to have heard two shots. Two 9mm slugs. Dad had a 9mm. I'm not seeing the magic bullet, Grams."

"Read the police report out loud. I always used to read my screenplays aloud when something wasn't working."

I sit up and stare, dumbfounded, at the ghost. "You wrote screenplays?"

"Oh, dozens. I never got to make a film, though. Such a shame. All that talent and the world will never have the pleasure." She sighed.

"I went to film school, you know."

She shakes her head. "I didn't. Would I have seen any of your films?"

I shrug. "I dropped out and only worked on a few short films and commercials before selling my soul to the exciting world of coffee."

"All our experiences make us who we are, dear. The choices you made brought you to me." Grams smiles warmly.

I always looked at my life as a series of regrets, but if things had turned out differently . . . I may not have been so eager to escape my life in Arizona and venture off to great lakes and mysterious harbors. I basically failed "up." That's called the Peter Principal.

A stifled chuckle escapes from my ghostly matriarch.

I playfully shoo her away. "Enough personal reflection. We need something to investigate." I pace in front of the open file boxes and wait for lightning to strike.

"You said both of the recovered bullets were 9mm, right?"

I nod and continue to wear a path in the plush Persian rug. "The rifling!"

"I thought you said it was a 9mm not a rifle, dear."

"Think about every cop show you've ever watched, Grams. They always prove that a bullet was fired from a specific gun by doing a rifling test." I crouch down and sift through the reports in box number three. "That makes no sense . . . "

Grams swoops down. "What? What is it? You're not giving me anything!"

I drop the report and stare through Grams. "The ballistics report says that the bullet recovered from the camera matched the lands and grooves on Dad's gun."

"Well, he always said he was the one who shot out the security camera."

"Right. The problem is the bullet they recovered from the victim didn't match."

"Was there a third gun? You said Darrin had a .45."

"No, it's not that. The other slug was smooth. There was no rifling at all."

"Is that possible?"

"I'm not an actual detective, Grams." I stand and resume my path. "Who do we know that knows stuff about guns?"

"Sheriff Erick?" She snickers.

I like that she's calling him Erick too. "Who do we know that won't arrest us for having boxes of evidence 'borrowed' from the records tech at the sheriff's station?"

"Of course, dear." Grams swirls around and I wait. I barely know anyone in Pin Cherry. I certainly don't have a list of everyone's hobbies.

Grams seems to be thinking out loud. "Cal had some hunting gear, but that 9mm that Jacob stole was his only handgun."

"What about Odell? He kinda looks prior military."

"Yes! Good eye, dear! Odell did a short stint in the Army before we married. He was an Army chef. That's how we got the idea to open the—"

"Grams, focus." I snap my fingers and interrupt her reverie.

"Odell is our best bet. Maybe you can grab some lunch and ask him a few questions."

"Lunch? Wow, I totally lost track of time." As if to scold me, my stomach growls audibly.

"Run along, Mitzy. I'll be here when you get back."

CHAPTER 20

THE DINER IS PACKED with Pinners and I'm forced to take a seat at the counter. The round, red-vinyl-covered stool scrapes a little as I spin to face the kitchen.

Odell looks up, gives me a knowing nod punctuated by promising a sizzle.

Tally slides a soda, or rather a pop—the local term—in front of me and keeps walking.

The woman has stamina. My best guess is that she's in her sixties and she never slows down. I take a sip of my soda and snippets of conversations waft into my consciousness.

"Kitty always has the best party of the festival."

"Such a shame about her husband."

"I heard some vagrant murdered him in an alley."

"You don't say!"

The Duncan-blooded part of me wants to make a scene and tell them all to shove their gossip where the sun don't shine, but the curious part of me hopes to overhear something useful.

Tally sets my plate down and winks.

I look up and catch Odell's eye. "I need to talk to you," I shout.

"I'll take my break when you finish. So, in about two minutes?" He chuckles and throws down another batch of burgers.

He's not wrong. I devour the juicy burger and french-fried pieces of perfection in roughly two minutes.

"Tally, kitchen's on a break," he calls above the din of the busy restaurant.

I bus my dishes and follow Odell out the back door. This has to be the cleanest alley I've ever seen.

"What's on your mind, Mitzy?" He pulls out a beat up cigarette and puts it in his mouth.

I wait for him to light it.

He does not.

"What's going on there?" I point to the unlit smoke.

"Oh, I quit fifteen years ago."

I raise an eyebrow and gesture for him to continue.

"I carry one around in my pocket and put it in my mouth when I take my breaks. Reminds me what it took to give it up—how far I've come—that sorta thing."

"Doesn't it make it harder?"

"You'd think, but I've always liked to prove to myself that I'm stronger than average."

"That why you joined the Army?"

He grins. "Who told you that?"

I clearly can't tell him the truth. "Just a lucky guess." I point to the haircut.

He rubs a hand over his grey buzz cut and nods. "What can I do ya for?"

I chuckle. "How folksy."

He nods. "Not that I don't enjoy your company, but . . . " He pokes his thumb back toward the busy diner.

"I'll get to the point. I have a gun-related question and someone said you'd be the person to ask."

"Boy, seems like your lucky day," he teases.

"I'm looking into my dad's old case—no one knows except Twiggy—and I found something odd."

"Shoot." He chuckles.

"They recovered two bullets from the crime scene. Both 9mm. The one they pulled from the destroyed camera had rifling that matched my dad's gun."

He nods. Seems like everyone knows the details of this small-town murder.

"The wackadoo thing is that the one from the victim's wound was smooth."

"Perfectly smooth?" Odell tilts his head.

"That's how the report makes it sound. No rifling, but it was—well, it was cause of death for the store manager, so it had to be fired."

"Boy, that never came out in the trial."

"Really? Do you think the cops suppressed it?"

"I doubt it was intentional. Two 9mm bullets. One perp with a 9mm gun. I s'pose they figured if one matched that was close enough. They were under a lot of pressure to convict quick." Odell shook his head. "Small towns never like scandals."

"Do you know what would've caused it?"

Odell slips the raggedy cigarette back in his shirt pocket and shakes his head. "I've got some Army buddies who know a little too much about guns. I'll ask around."

"But don't say anything about my dad's case," I caution.

He points to his grey hair and says, "I wasn't born yesterday, kid."

"Thanks, Odell. Grams said—" I freeze and my eyes dart around like pinballs.

He leans back and narrows his gaze.

I have no idea how to cover that slip. I figure a

good old-fashioned ramble and run is my only option. "I better get back to the bookshop. It's so busy." I continue to stammer nonsense as I yank open the back door and escape through the diner.

I practically sprint, emphasis on practically, back to Bell, Book & Candle. Grams is waiting right inside the main entrance and I start babbling as soon as I see her, utterly oblivious to the stares and whispers.

"I'm sorry, Miss Moon, you'll have to repeat that. I didn't quite hear you." Twiggy walks toward me and levels a concerned stare.

I slap a hand over my mouth and hop over the "No Admittance" chain before she, or I, can say another word.

Grams surges through the bookcase and is swirling anxiously in the bedroom by the time I make my way through the secret door—human-style.

"Sorry about that, dear. I didn't think you'd start talking the minute you saw me."

"My fault. I was all flustered because I slipped up with Odell. I couldn't stop myself from blurting as soon as I walked in the bookstore." I smack myself in the forehead. "Stupid."

She ignores my self-deprecation. "What do you mean 'slipped up?' What did you say to Odell?"

"He was super helpful and said he'd ask some

Army buddies about the weird bullet. I kinda blurted 'Grams said' before I could stop myself."

"Did he hear you?"

"Oh he heard. He heard." I pace from the four-poster to the secret door.

"Water under the bridge. We can't cry over spilt milk."

Laughter grips me. "A bird in the hand . . . a stitch in time . . . " I laugh so hard tears come to my eyes.

"Well, I never." Grams crosses her arms and shoots up to the ceiling.

"I thought we were just shouting out proverbs." I wipe the happy tears from my eyes and catch my breath. "Regardless, it will be a day or two until we hear back from Odell. Where does that leave us?"

"Don't you mean irregardless?"

I take a deep breath and prepare to launch into my well-rehearsed speech on this pet peeve, when Grams zips down to the Persian rug, laughing all the way.

"Well played. Well played." I like this comfortable banter with my Ghost-ma.

She chuckles in spite of our no-mind-reading rule. "To answer the question you asked out loud, it leaves us with a pressing need to search Cal's office. Are you able to do that tonight?"

Before I can answer, Twiggy's disembodied voice interrupts.

"Mr. Willoughby is here, Mitzy."

I look at Grams. "What the heck is that? Can she hear everything we're saying?"

"It's an intercom, dear. Over there next to the bookcase." She floats toward the secret door. "See this fancy scrollwork? It covers the speakers, and these mother-of-pearl inlaid buttons are the way to respond. The one on the left lets you talk and the one on the right is the 'call' button to ring the back room. The middle rings the museum."

That reminds me that I haven't seen the museum yet. Maybe tomorrow. I push the button on the left. "Can you send him up to the apartment?"

"You have to take your finger off to hear her reply," Grams prompts.

"—his way, doll," is all I catch, but I get the gist.

"Does Silas know about you?"

Grams looks at me and shrugs. "Does he know about you?"

"We're not talking about me."

Grams lifts a finger to protest.

I silence her with a shake of my head. "I'm not ready to talk about the incident. Is that clear?"

She nods obediently.

"Now, back to my question. Does he know

you're hanging around the bookshop like some kind of afterlife mascot?"

"Oh, that." She hesitates and doesn't make eye contact. "Let's see if he picks up on anything."

"And if he doesn't?"

"What are you getting at, honey?" She looks pensive.

"Do I tell Silas that the ghost of my dearly departed grandmother hangs out with me in the apartment?"

"It's not hanging out, Mitzy. I'm trapped in between. I can't leave the bookshop for some reason. I'm just making the best of things."

I open my mouth to take offense at that last bit, but the bookcase slides open and Silas fixes me with a disappointed look.

"Good morning, Mitzy."

He makes no effort to hide his distaste for my preferred name. "Hey, Silas. What brings you up to the clubhouse?"

He glances at the papers strewn about the floor. "Any progress?"

I bring him up to speed on my suspicions as Grams swirls closer.

Silas stiffens and steps past me. "I feel a chill. Do you have a window open?"

I raise an eyebrow in her direction and she

snickers. “Maybe it’s a sense and not see thing, like Pyewacket.”

“Maybe,” I reply.

Silas looks at me as though I’m daft. “Maybe? Are you reporting that you are unable to recall if you raised a sash?” He looks down the row of casements. “They appear to be secure.”

Grams swirls closer.

Silas shivers. “Do you feel it right now?”

He pulls a pair of round spectacles out of his coat pocket and holds them in his right hand. He murmurs something I can’t quite make out and hooks the curved brass bows behind his ears. As he peers through the taffy-tinted lenses, a slow smile spreads across his lined face. “Ah, Isadora. I had hoped it was you.”

My face goes slack. I can’t help but wonder what just happened!

“Silas is an alchemist, dear.”

I gaze back and forth between my Ghost-ma and my lawyer-turned-wizard and can’t find a single syllable.

“Can you communicate with her?” asks Silas.

I close my mouth, swallow, and—

“Mitzy, he can see me now, but he can’t hear me. Maybe it will take some time . . . I don’t know how this works. You have to bring him up to speed.”

I continue to search my brain for word bits.

"Sweetie, Silas is the one who uncovered the information in one of my wonderful books. He's studied the rare books since I began collecting them and he convinced me I could find a way to wedge myself between the worlds and have a chance to meet you."

I manage to force out a single word, "Yes."

He smiles up at Grams, and she presses her hands to her ghost-chest in a pantomime of gratitude.

I find my voice. "Are you a wizard?"

Silas chuckles and coughs. "I'm an alchemist. It's the study of mystic and scientific transmutation of matter. Some people confuse it with wizardry. Some might even be inclined to label me a warlock; however, I would protest such nonsense."

A memory leaps forward. "That day in the hospital! When you touched my gunshot wound and I stopped bleeding . . . Was that magic?"

"It's not magic, Mitzy. Through the knowledge I've gathered, I'm able to make permanent changes to the state of matter." He smiles warmly.

"Sounds like magic to me."

Grams floats between us. "It's not magic, dear. I'd say it's more philosophical than spells and potions."

"It sounds like magic to me, Grams."

Silas's sagging cheeks perk up. "You can truly

communicate. Magnificent!" He claps his hands together and nods. "We did it, Isadora."

A happy glistening of tears wets the corners of his eyes, and despite my confusion, I can't stop myself. I hug Silas tightly. "Thank you. Thank you for giving me a chance to know my grandmother."

He stiffens uncomfortably, clears his throat, and steps away. "You're quite welcome. Now, I came on business." He takes off the round spectacles and slips them back in his pocket. "I've arranged a meeting with your father."

"Oh." Now that he's scheduled something, I'm not entirely sure I'm ready to meet dear old Dad. I'm looking into the case, and I hope he's not guilty, but what if he is?

"You know your father didn't do this, Mitzy. You have to meet him and hear his side." Grams flickers in and out. The powerful emotions must be draining her or something.

She has a point. I'm pretty certain my dad didn't commit the murder, and I've lost everyone else in my life. What have I got left to lose? "I'd like to hear his version of events."

Silas nods.

"When do we meet?"

"How about breakfast tomorrow at that dining establishment you prefer?"

"Myrtle's Diner? That seems too public. I might cry or yell or—"

Silas offers another option. "How about in the museum, after breakfast? Perhaps 10:00?"

"All right. I'll see you both tomorrow."

Silas puts on his spectacles, smiles at Grams, and says, "That gown and that age suit you, Isadora. Until tomorrow."

She waves.

As the door closes behind him, I fire off a few inquisitions. "Um, why didn't you tell me about Silas and the alchemy? Why didn't you mention you planned to stick around after death? And how on earth did you and Silas come up with this crazy plan?"

After hours of question and answer regarding rare books, magic, alchemy, and the afterlife, I'm temporarily out of queries. I reserve the right to re-open the investigation at any time.

Grams agrees to my terms.

Back to the business of my current investigation.

"Tell me again how this thirty-year-old key to a penthouse office is going to work?"

Grams explains the layout of the train station/office complex for Midwest Union Railway and how easy it will be for me to gain access to Cal's office.

"Now, I haven't been there in years, dear, but they never had any security or anything. Pin Cherry is a safe town."

Except for Cal's murder, I guess.

We agree to disagree on the relative safety of the town and enter the holy closet to select the proper attire for prowling. I vote for all black, but Grams wisely points out that I don't want to look like a burglar.

In the end, we agree on a charcoal-grey Donna Karan pantsuit with a lilac blouse.

"You'll look like you belong there. If anyone is there after hours, they won't think twice about a business woman with a key to the place." Grams nearly pats herself on the back.

"If anyone is there after hours, I'm going to rip out of there like a cat with its tail on fire."

Pyewacket gives a soft hiss from his perch atop the antique mahogany armoire.

"Oh Mitzy, so dramatic." Grams rolls her eyes.

I plug my phone in. I've seen enough movies to know that a fully charged battery is essential for spy photography. "Do you have a thumb drive, Grams?"

"Is that a gardening tool?"

I chuckle. "It's to save files from a hard drive."

"You've lost me, honey. Just take pictures."

My spy kit is shy a few nifty gadgets, but I resign myself to reality and wait for sunset.

CHAPTER 21

THE NARROW STREETS around the train station are utterly deserted. I drive by several times to make sure there are no cars in the parking lot.

It seems the only folks out at this time of night are a few die-hard locals at the dive bar, Final Destination, down by the docks.

Once I satisfy my nerves, I park my rather obvious silver gull-wing Mercedes two blocks over and walk back to the Midwest Union Railway building.

I slide the key in the lock in the back door and whisper a prayer as I apply pressure to the key.

CLICK!

No way. Grams will never let me forget this. I carefully open the door and tiptoe down the hallway, searching for the steps up to Cal's office.

I get turned around a couple times, but eventually find the stairwell Grams described and gain access to the office with my handy master key.

The room is impressive. Enclosed in thick, gleaming glass, Cal's office looks over the entire train station. The converted building houses office space, conference rooms, a break room, and part of the original terminal has been preserved as a display housing a shining steam engine.

I close the door and lock it. Again, I've seen the movies.

I reach for my phone and panic. I pat myself up one side and down the other and stifle a scream. I left my flipping phone on the charger!

New plan. If I find something important —take it.

I choose a methodical search pattern. Framed photos. Bookcase. Desk. Trash.

I make my way around the Viking statue in the corner and move to the photos hanging on the one section of wall that is not glass. The light from the few after-hours fixtures in the station cast enough illumination for me to make out the faces. Two family photos from my father's early years. I chuckle at the likeness of the Isadora in the photos to her current form. She does indeed look similar to the ghost that haunts my bookshop. The third image is a hunting-trophy shot with Cal, a moose, and another man I don't recognize. The fourth picture is much older. Cal looks about twenty, and he and three buddies are all bunched together for the camera. They each have a cigarette hanging from the corners of their mouths and they are all in military uniforms. Army, I'm guessing. Before I turn away, something grabs my eye. That man next to Cal—

I inhale sharply. I'd recognize that buzz cut anywhere. The hair might be several shades darker, but that man next to Cal is absolutely Odell Johnson.

Funny, Odell never mentioned they served together. I make a mental note to ask Grams if she knew.

The bookcase holds a few small art pieces, several awards, and hardbound volumes that seem to be all for show. In fact, one has a hollowed-out spot for a flask. Nice touch. But a thorough search doesn't turn up any secret messages or hidden keys.

I pass the trash can on my way to the desk. Not to jump out of order, but the waste bin is empty.

The desk has been cleaned and organized. Possibly the sheriff, but more likely a secretary. Cal was apparently too modern to have a paper desk calendar and someone has taken his computer. I go through the drawers.

Nothing of interest in the top drawers. The right file drawer contains a bottle of D'Aincourt Cognac Premier Cru. The matte black bottle with raised metal insignia rests in a custom wooden case.

Grampa Cal's fancy. It's irresistible. I have to take a sip.

It smells like baked pears with cinnamon. The taste of vanilla, nutmeg, and luscious fruit warms my whole tummy. Good gravy! So, this is how the other half lives.

I have one more sip. It's beyond words.

I reluctantly replace the bottle. Didn't Grams say they met at AA? Maybe Kitty drove him back to the bottle? I shrug and continue my search.

The left file drawer contains a few manila folders with notes for supplier meetings and one with receipts.

I sit in my grandfather's cushy, ergonomic leather chair and sift through the slips of paper. Lunches, dinners, fishing trips, hunting lodges, and a—private investigator?

A noise from downstairs startles me. I shove the PI receipt in my bra and put the file folder back in the drawer.

If I hide under the desk and get discovered I'll look guilty. If I walk around the room like I own the place—

I move toward the books on the shelf when the beam of a flashlight hits me right between the eyes.

"Don't move. I'm going to need to see some identification."

Great. Sheriff Erick.

He fumbles with the handle. "Miss, I'm going to need you to unlock this door, or I'll be forced to break it down."

I saw the thickness of the door and I'm certain he has no chance, despite his burly shoulders and powerful legs. However, I also know that he's a little trigger-happy, and I don't want another accidental bullet wound. No point in testing the breadth of Silas's skills.

"Don't shoot, Erick. I'm opening the door."

"Miss Moon? I didn't recognize you."

I open the door.

He holsters his gun and stares at me.

I choose to take this as progress.

"How did you get inside that locked room?"

He doesn't know I have a key. Time to think fast. "I came up earlier to get a feel for the kind of man my grandfather might've been. I guess the secretary didn't see me sitting in here in the dark. She just locked me in. I'm awfully lucky you showed up. I could've been stuck in here until day shift." I pat him gratefully on the back as I slip past and head to the stairs.

"Just a minute, Miss Moon."

I stop, but don't turn.

"The door unlocks from the inside."

Darn! He's got me there. "I must've forgotten with all the emotion of being in my grandfather's office and knowing I'll never have the chance to meet him. I wasn't thinking straight." There, that sounds like a solid girlie reason.

"You wouldn't be poking around in Cal's murder case would you?"

"Me? I just own a little bookshop. Before that, I was a barista. Hardly sounds like the pedigree of a crack detective." I start down the steps.

He hurries to catch up, and the scent of his nearness gives me a little infarction.

"If you happened to stumble across something you'd let me know, wouldn't you, Moon?"

The sound of my name on his lips . . . "Have you hit a dead end in the case?" I reach the bottom of the stairs and turn. "You don't still suspect me, do you?" I reach out and adjust the nameplate above his badge.

"Is that alcohol on your breath? Have you been drinking?"

Oops. "My grandfather had some lovely cognac is his—office. I just drank a toast to his memory." It's best not to mention the bottle was in the desk. I don't want him to think I was snooping.

"I see." He looks me up and down.

I shiver and smile. "You didn't answer my question, Erick. Am I still a suspect?"

He swallows twice and looks everywhere except at me. "You're not our primary suspect, but we haven't found evidence that knocks you completely off the list."

"There's a list? Whose company am I keeping, Erick?"

"I can't discuss an ongoing investigation."

"Swallow once for yes." I lean toward him. "Is Kitty on the list?"

He swallows and steps back.

"How about Finnegan?"

He swallows again. "Let's clear out of the train station, Miss Moon." He steers me out by my elbow.

I step out to the parking lot and chew the inside of my cheek. Maybe he'll drive off and I can walk to my cleverly concealed car without his notice.

"Assuming you only had the one drink, can I give you a ride to your car?"

My eyes widen.

"I observed it parked over on Chokecherry Lane. This is the third building I cleared."

Awww, he was worried about me. "Like I said, lucky you found me."

He chuckles and opens the passenger door of the patrol car.

At least I'm sitting in front this time. That's progress, too.

CHAPTER 22

I QUIETLY LET myself into the bookshop and make my way without the aid of light. I wish I had my phone.

I am gaining some familiarity with the place, and I'm rather proud that I've made it to within sight of the chained staircase without—

CRASH!

A tumble of books hurtles to the ground behind me and I scream.

Grams appears out of nowhere. "What is it? Is someone after you?"

I hold a hand to my heaving chest and thudding heart. I gasp for breath and reply, "No idea. I don't see—"

A single sound pierces the night. "Reow."

Of course. The demon cat, out for some late night fun. "That cat tried to kill me."

A ghostly snicker tinkles though the darkness.

"It's not funny. I could have a weak heart. Those frights could be deadly." I stomp off to the back room and flood the bookshop with light. "Now, let's see what kind of mess he's made this time."

Grams ghost-pets the purring CAT-astrophe while I clean up.

I put a few books back on the shelf before I recognize the pattern. "What are you doing with all these books about guns in your bookshop? A US Army technical manual?" I slide it into place. "Or *The Theory and Design of Ammunition*?"

"I don't recall adding those to the collection, dear. Sometimes Twiggy picks things up at estate sales. You'd have to ask her."

I look from the book in my hand to the pesky fur-covered terror. Did he knock these down on purpose? I shake my head, but keep the ammunition book all the same. "I'll take this upstairs for a little light reading."

Pyewacket purrs loudly and bounds up the steps ahead of me.

"That's a good kitty," coos Grams.

"Please don't encourage the tan terror."

A phantom throat clearing cuts the silence

when I drop the Donna Karan suit on the floor, but I choose to ignore it. Instead, I climb into the heavenly bed, click on a bedside lamp, and open the weaponry treatise.

Soon the tantalizing lull of dreamland—

A furry torpedo knocks me awake and possibly fractures my floating rib.

The riveting text on bullets, sub-projectiles, and grains per pound times the acceleration of gravity had lulled me into a lovely sleep. I was right in the middle of a magnificent dream starring Sheriff Erick when kitty-bomb attacked.

"Anything?" Grams floats next to the bed.

"I can't keep my eyes open." I lay the book on the bedside table and snuggle in for the night.

Pye kneads his claws into my shoulder.

"Shove off." I give him a tentative push. I want him off, but I don't want to draw his wrath. "I'll keep reading in the morning with a strong cup of coffee and—some Fruity Puffs, if you don't let me sleep."

Pyewacket growls softly, but parades to the end of the bed and curls up like an angel.

Cut to—angel falls from heaven, directly onto my chest, and I wake up gasping for air.

"I'm up. I'm up." I push the comforter and Pyewacket off my scared-to-life body and stumble to the bathroom.

"Are you up already?" Grams calls from a modest distance.

"Yes, apparently I couldn't wait to jump back into that enthralling book." I gesture toward the manual on the nightstand and see Pye stretched across my pillow with one insistent paw resting on the spine.

As soon as I make eye contact his tufted ears twitch and his hefty paw slides.

The book thunks to the floor.

"I said I'm going to read it!" I throw my hands up.

"He needs his breakfast, dear. And you need some coffee." Grams swooshes through the wall as she mumbles, "Not a morning person."

"I heard that!" I open the bookcase and Pyewacket rockets past, knocking me sideways.

I pour a bowl of Fruity Puffs for him and one for myself.

Pyewacket gives me an "if looks could kill" stare.

"Just this once, Pye. I haven't had time to get to the market."

He ignores me and eats.

I push "brew" on the coffeemaker and munch the cereal while I wait for my go-go juice.

Steaming mug in hand, I climb back up to the apartment.

Two cups of coffee and one argument with Pyewacket later, I've actually found something. "This sounds promising . . . "

"Do tell, dear."

"There's a thing called a sabot. It's made out of plastic and can hold a bullet inside the barrel."

"Isn't that where all bullets go, honey?"

I drop the book on the bed and sigh. "I'm not explaining it right. If I understand all this technical mumbo jumbo, it means that you could shoot a small bullet out of a bigger gun."

"And?" Grams circles her hand impatiently.

"Well, technically, Darrin could've placed a 9mm bullet in one of these sabot thingies that fit into his .45-caliber gun. That would explain the lack of rifling on the second 9mm bullet."

"What about the third shot?"

"Maybe there wasn't a third shot. I keep reading Darrin's statement and it seems like the mysterious third shot was how he explained the gunpowder residue on his hands. But the police never found a third bullet or the missing security tape."

"If there was no third shot—if Darrin fired the shot that killed—"

It's hard to watch a poltergeist cry. "This is good news, Grams. This means it's actually possible that Dad didn't kill the store manager."

"That's why I'm crying, dear. We turned our

backs on him. We let him rot in jail." The tears turn into full-blown weeping. "What kind of mother must I be?"

"Grams, you can't blame yourself. The police didn't even figure out what Darrin did."

Pyewacket adds his mournful call to the keening.

After years of hiding my pain from taunting foster siblings, I don't "do" emotion too well and I can't imagine how to begin comforting a ghost. I slip into black skinny jeans and a "Hot Mess No Stress" tee with a stack of syrupy pancakes pictured.

The mourning duo doesn't acknowledge my exit. Fine by me.

I hustle down to the station.

"Is the sheriff in?"

"Whom may I say is asking?"

Wow. This clerk has to be the only person in town who doesn't know me. "Tell him Mitzy Moon has urgent news."

Her eyes widen and one eyebrow does a comical arch.

Now that is the reaction I've come to expect.

She picks up the phone and delivers my message.

Sheriff Erick rounds the corner, looks down at my T-shirt, grins, and shakes his head.

I shrug and follow him back to his office.

“What’s the urgent news, Moon?” His smile is warm and his gaze lingers.

I toy with the idea of saying I had a dream about him, but I need him to be cooperative and I want to engender some good will. I’ll save that little gem for later. “I promised I’d share any information with you and I’m here to keep up my end of the bargain.”

Surprise tainted with suspicion paints his handsome face.

“I think Darrin MacIntyre killed that store manager.”

Erick leans forward and confusion floods his expression. “I thought you were here about Cal’s case?”

“Not today.” I smile innocently.

“Well, the protests of a long-lost daughter are expected, but that case was decided many years ago. In fact, your dad’s already out of prison. Why would you point the finger at Darrin now?”

Anger rises faster than I can tamp it down. “Are you saying that it’s all right for my father to serve a fifteen-year prison sentence for a crime he didn’t commit just because he’s out now?”

Sheriff Erick leans back.

“Are you saying that my dad should carry the label ‘murderer’ around for the rest of his life when there’s a better-than-average chance he’s innocent?” I take a deep breath and power up for more.

Erick stands and puts his hands up. "Easy, Erin Brockovich. Why don't you tell me why you think he's innocent and we'll take it from there."

I look down to see that I'm standing and waving my hands like a nut job. Deep breath. One more for good measure. I lower my arms and sit. "Are you aware the bullet that was recovered from the victim didn't have rifling."

He narrows his gaze. "Where did you get that information?"

"Did you know or not?" I sidestep his question.

"I wasn't on the force back then. Rookies hear rumors, but I never saw any evidence to support that claim." He leans forward. "Have you?"

"Let's assume I have." Feint and parry. "If that were the case, is it possible that Darrin MacIntyre fired the kill shot from his .45 by using a sabot to jacket the 9mm bullet?"

He shifts his sexy jaw back and forth. "Where are you getting your info, Moon?"

"Oh, Pyewacket got me a book on guns and ammo." *Touro!* I swish my imaginary bullfighter's cape. I slip by without answering another query.

I can see by the look on his face that what I've proposed regarding the use of the sabot is possible. That's enough. I stand and smile. "Thank you for your time, Sheriff."

He opens his mouth, but I twist on a dime and rush out like a hipster to an artisanal cheese shoppe.

I'm tempted to stop at the diner for a proper breakfast, but a flash of nervous tummy hits me and I hurry back to the apartment.

I'm going to meet my father in less than two hours. I should probably shower.

I peel off my tee before the bookcase closes.

"What's the hurry?"

"I'm freaking out about meeting him."

"Jacob? Oh, he'll love you, dear. Don't worry about a thing."

"I'm freaking. It's what I do."

"Where'd you go?" Grams pats under her puffy eyes. "Pye and I didn't see you leave."

"I ran my theory past Erick. He wouldn't answer, but I could see by the look on his face that it's possible."

Grams disappears into the closet. "I'll find you something lovely to wear."

Why argue. I unhook my bra with one hand while I twist the hot water on with the other.

A slightly sweaty, crumpled piece of paper falls to the bathmat.

I pick it up and smooth it out on the counter. Oh yeah, in the flying book fiasco, I forgot all about the PI.

Grams bursts through the wall from the closet. "What PI?"

I grab a towel to cover myself. "Grams, rule number two: no phase-shifting into the bathroom without an express verbal invitation."

She giggles. "Number two, in the bathroom. You're a stitch, Mitzy."

She vanishes back through the wall, still giggling.

I'd close the door, but what's the point?

I slip under the glorious spray of water. Hot, steamy showers will never get old.

I wrap a thick cottony towel around myself and sit down at the vanity to attempt a replication of the makeup I applied for the ladies' luncheon.

"You look lovely, dear."

I go for a more casual version of the sleek hairdo that Grams had supervised, but I use product and a blow dryer all by myself.

"Come and see what I've picked out."

Grams heads through the wall and I walk around, like a civilized person.

"Where is it?"

"I can't actually move anything, honey. I'll point and you grab. These boots." A pair of knee-high, black-leather riding boots

I nod approvingly.

"And I thought this sweater with your own

jeans." She points to a chic black-and-grey-striped cashmere boyfriend sweater.

I touch the soft knit and purr appreciatively. "This will look great with skinny jeans."

"I thought you'd like to pair it with something of your own. To feel grounded in yourself."

"Kinda woo woo, Grams."

"I was just trying it out. Seemed like something you kids would say."

"Not this kid." I put on the outfit and look at myself in the full-length mirror. "Do you think he'll like me?"

"How could he not, dear? You're his daughter." She brushes a tear from her cheek.

"You should've been buried with a handkerchief, Grams."

"Oh, Mitzy." She laughs. "You're too much."

I walk to the secret door and turn to look up at Grams. "Ready?"

"You want me to come?"

"Can you?"

"I actually haven't tried to go into the museum. I'll be there if I can."

"All right. But don't say anything. I'm crazy nervous already. If I start talking to ghosts in front of him . . . Just be there for moral support."

"You got it."

I walk out into the Rare Books Loft and the

bookshop actually has customers milling around on the first floor.

"It's on the third shelf at the end of the self-help stack." Twiggy's knowledgeable yet impatient voice drifts up to my ears.

Good to know that's being handled. Now I need to figure out how to get into the museum.

Grams floats down to my side and winks. "Follow me," she says.

I guess her thought-hearing comes in handy in a crowded room.

Near the double-stacked rows of windows at the front, there's a grey metal door marked "Employees Only." Man, I have got to get familiar with this place.

Grams fades through the door and pops just her head back toward me. "Looks like I can access the museum." She slips out of view.

I depress the metal push-bar and follow.

A new world. The smell of ink, metal, and history.

The space is only half the size of the bookshop, but it has an entire second floor rather than balconies and a mezzanine. The ground floor houses large equipment in a variety of historical displays. "Is that an actual Gutenberg press?"

"I'll give you a full tour later, dear. I hear Silas."

I turn to face the door I just passed through.

There's a scrape as the metal bar is pushed. The door swings open— My chest constricts. I can't breathe. Beads of sweat pop out on my forehead.

"Breathe, dear. Focus on me and breathe." Grams hovers between the opening door and me.

My heart races, but I manage to gulp down some air.

Silas walks through first. His balding head, thick grey mustache, saggy cheeks, and baggy brown suit give me a strange sense of calm.

The man behind him is tall and handsome. His close-cropped, ice-blonde hair is the exact hue of my own, and his piercing grey eyes lock onto me with intense worry.

"Mizithra?"

Years of emotions agitate in my gut like a washer on spin cycle. Longing. Hate. Anxiety. Fear. Disappointment. Loss. Abandonment. Love. "Dad!" I lose all sense of modesty as I close the distance between us, and despite the fact that I promised myself I would not cry, I sob into his blue cotton shirt.

His strong arms engulf me and I feel safe, safer than I've ever felt in my life. I wish my mom could've felt this safe.

"Thank you for agreeing to see me." His raspy voice is barely a whisper.

His voice is thick with emotion. He actually

thought I might not agree to see him? This poor man. I squeeze my arms around him. "I can't believe you're real."

I swipe the flood of tears from my face and assume that my careful application of makeup is caput. But I don't care, because my dad is alive. I'm not an orphan.

He leans back and looks down at me with so much love I might melt. His voice catches a little as he says, "I can't believe you're here. What have you been doing since you got to Pin Cherry?"

Before I can reply, Grams swirls in and blurts, "Tell him about the sawb-oh thing and how we think he's innocent—and that wicked Darrin—"

I wave my hands. "Give me a second, Grams. My world is spinning for the third or fourth time this week. I'll tell him everything in a minute. Gimme a second to process."

Silas grins. "Isadora never had the gift of patience. I see that hasn't changed."

I look at my dad and my shoulders sag. We just met and I'm hearing voices. He'll probably disown me on the spot.

"Silas brought me up to speed on the way over. I'm not sure if I believe in ghosts, but if anyone could find a loophole in death, it would be my mother." He glances around the room and announces to the air in general, "I'm sorry I wasn't at the funeral, Mom. I didn't think the town would take too kindly to my return."

"Tell him I love him. And tell him we know he's innocent."

"She says she loves you." I shrug self-consciously. "And I'm not sure if Silas mentioned it or not, but we've been looking into your case and we think we can prove that you didn't commit the murder."

Jacob shoves his hands in the pockets of his faded jeans. "I guess we're jumping right into it then." He takes a deep breath and walks to the front windows.

"We've lost too much time already," I offer quietly.

He nods and stares into the distance. His fingers wipe absently at the dust on the sill and he exhales.

I want to ask a million questions about the time he spent with my mother, if he loved her, and if he ever thought of me, but the best way to give him a fresh start is to clear his name. I plow ahead. "Darrin shot the guy, right?"

Jacob laughs, but it's a bitter, humorless sound. "I stopped saying that after my first nickel in lockup."

I walk over and put my hand on my dad's arm. "Look, I'm not going to pretend I understand what it's like to serve a sentence for something you didn't do, but I got accused of murder about an hour after I arrived in this town. You lost fifteen years of your life. You want to give up the rest of it, or are you gonna fight?"

He has to pull himself back from a faraway place. It takes a moment for his eyes to fully focus on me. "Who accused you of murder? Whose murder?"

"Sheriff Er—Harper arrested me for Cal's murder."

Jacob shoots Silas a worried look. "Why didn't you tell me about this?"

Silas shrugs. "She's been all but eliminated. He's moved on to questioning Kitty and Finnegan Wells."

"Kitty," grumbles Jacob.

"Do you know anything about the interrogations? Did they admit to the fake fundraising?" I walk toward Silas as I fire questions.

"I delved into the 'charity' that benefits from the Halloween Masquerade philanthropy and your suspicions were correct. It funnels through several convoluted pipes, but in the end it lands in Finnegan's pockets."

"And what about the affair? Is he seeing Kitty?"

"Apparently, she vehemently denied it, but phone records provided evidence of a suspiciously high number of calls between the two." Silas shakes his head.

Grams swishes down and gives me a sanctimonious grin. "I told you it was the trollop."

"So, they did it? Did Cal find out about the affair? Is that why he was changing his will?" I slap my hands together. "Of course, Kitty must've found out about the will and convinced Finnegan to kill Cal before he could make the changes official."

Jacob raises his hand like a schoolboy. "May I ask a question?"

I don't want to pause, but I gesture for my father to speak.

"Who said Cal was changing the will?"

Silas steps into the fray. "I spoke to your father's lawyer earlier this week. It seems Cal was leaving the bulk of his estate to you."

"Me?" The color drains from Jacob's face and he looks left and right. "Me? He hasn't spoken to me since the gavel fell and they carted me off to prison. What on earth would possess him to put me in his will?"

Before any of us can speculate, the metal "Employees Only" door opens and two anything but employees walk through.

Deputy Paulsen already has her weapon trained on my dad. "Don't move, convict."

"Sheriff, what's this about?" My father's face reddens with anger.

I chime in with, "Erick, what's going on?"

Sheriff Harper pulls out his cuffs. "This is standard procedure when dealing with ex-cons. Everyone keep calm. Kitty Zimmerman-Duncan claims she was having an affair with Jacob Duncan. Obviously we have to follow every lead in a murder investigation." He walks toward my dad. "I'm not putting you under arrest, I'm—"

"Arrest? You think I killed my own father?" Jacob looks like a trapped animal.

His eyes snap to the door and I sense his need to escape.

I feel it in my gut, just like when I had my episode with the mood ring. I rush forward.

"Freeze, scumbag." Deputy Paulsen points her gun straight at my heart.

"Dad, don't worry. We know you're innocent. We'll find the proof. Please don't do anything stupid."

He shakes his head. "Seems like the only stupid thing I did was come back to this backwoods piece of—"

"Dad, don't make it worse." Despite the firearm zeroed in on my torso, I reach out and place a hand on the sheriff's arm. "Erick, it's only questioning. Can you please skip the handcuffs? He'll cooperate." My eyes plead with the sheriff. "You'll cooperate, right Dad?"

"Sure, for you. I'd do anything for you." His voice is barely a whisper.

The knot in my stomach fades.

Jacob's shoulders relax.

Erick slips the cuffs back in the holder on his belt. "Don't make me regret this, Jacob." He takes him by the arm and they walk out.

Silas follows and adds, "Please note that my client is represented by council, Sheriff."

Deputy Paulsen brings up the rear and mumbles a familiar refrain, "The guilty always lawyer up."

CHAPTER 23

Silas drives off to meet my father at the station, but I decide to walk. I have a stop to make.

I push open the door of the diner and the lunch crowd is packed in like sardines. Every seat is full, and Tally's daughter delivers food while Tally takes orders. My timing isn't great.

I slip back into the kitchen and the smell of burgers instigates a loud growl from my stomach.

"Should I throw one down for ya?" asks Odell.

"No thanks. I've gotta get over to the station."

He looks up and raises an eyebrow.

"Long story. I'll be back for lunch after the rush."

He returns to flipping burgers and drops the basket into the fryer. Popping, snapping, and bubbling welcome the raw potatoes into the oil.

I push the hair back from my forehead. Geez, it's hot back here. I guess I'd have a buzz cut too if I had to work over a grill all day. "How come you never mentioned that you and Cal served together?"

His spatula stops mid-slide. "That's none of your business, kid. Twiggy shouldn't be tellin' tales out of school."

I have no idea what he means. "Twiggy didn't say a thing. I saw a picture of you, Cal, and a couple other guys in uniform. The photo was hanging in Cal's office."

He doesn't look at me. "Why were you poking around in there?"

"Odell, what's going on? Did something happen between you and Cal?"

He plates up a few orders and refills the fry basket for the next batch. "I won't speak ill of the dead, Mitzy. That's all I'm saying on the matter. Your grandmother and Cal are together now." He scrapes his metal spatula across the grill and I barely hear his last comment. "That's how it should be."

He can play coy all he wants. I happen to have direct access to one person in that triangle, and I've never known her to keep quiet. "Thanks, Odell."

"See ya later, Mitzy," he calls through the orders-up window as I leave.

I walk back to the bookshop.

Grams is nowhere to be found. I think as loud as I can while searching the apartment. No response, and no sign of Ghost-ma.

If at first you don't succeed, try, try . . . the best friend.

Twiggy rings up several books for an eager customer, wraps them in gold tissue, and places them in a black paper bag with a gold embossed Bell, Book & Candle logo on the side.

"Thank you. I just love this bookshop." The happy customer takes one more look around before she walks out.

"Twiggy, have you got a minute?"

She scans the stacks before she replies, "They can live without me for a couple minutes."

And modest, too. Once in the back room, I launch straight in. "I saw a picture of Odell and Cal serving in the Army together. I asked Odell about it and he said he wouldn't speak ill of the dead. Can you shed some light?"

"Did you ask Isadora?"

"I can't find her."

Twiggy nods. "Must be something going on, you know, on the other side."

I spare Twiggy the explanation of this in-between place where Grams is trapped and wait for a reply to my question. "Do you know anything?"

"I know everything, doll. If your Grams gets peeved about me telling this story, she better not haunt me. All right?"

"All right." I answer with a confidence I don't possess.

"Your Grams was a USO gal and she and Cal really hit it off."

"But I thought Odell was her first husband?"

"Am I tellin' this story or are you tellin' this story?"

"Please continue," I say with a bow.

"Anyway, the boys got shipped off, and Myrtle promised to wait for Cal. Odell came home first and he looked her up straightaway. Myrtle was a free spirit and a bit of a drinker back then. She had a few too many, woke up next to Odell, and claimed true love."

"I can relate," I mumble.

"They did seem to be in love. She had a bit of money saved and Odell had saved his Army pay, too. They had a quickie wedding, bought the diner, and dove into their new life."

"But they ended up divorced."

"Clearly. Did you want to hear why?" Twiggy takes a stack of bags and ties little gold ribbons on the handles while she talks.

I nod silently.

"Cal returned from his deployment a year later,

and when he came callin' on Myrtle he discovered that his best friend had stabbed him in the back. Things got ugly fast. Myrtle drank while Odell and Cal fought. She divorced Odell and ran away. I lost touch with her during the Linder years—that was the second husband. She traveled the world, partied with the rich and famous, and lived dangerously. When Linder died in a car crash five years later, she got his fortune. The accident shook her up. She got sober and dropped her first name."

"Wow."

"I'll say. When she came back to Pin Cherry as Isadora Linder, Cal pursued her relentlessly. They had a fairytale wedding. Odell and Cal never spoke again."

"But Odell spoke kindly of Grams when I came to town."

"He swears Cal broke them up, and he never blamed your Grams for any of it. He never remarried because he claimed he still loved her, but there was always bad blood between him and Cal."

"How bad?"

"After Isadora died, Silas had to contact you before he could make the details of the will public. But in the meantime, Cal tried to buy up the diner and the bookstore. Tally said he and Odell had a knock-down, drag-out in the diner a few weeks ago."

"Does Erick know about this fight?"

"The whole town probably knows. Why?"

"Well, wouldn't that make Odell a suspect?"

"Odell? He wouldn't shoot anyone."

"Twiggy, he was in the Army."

"Sure, doll, but he was a chef."

"Wait, how do you know Cal was shot?"

"I hear things." Twiggy shrugs.

"Did you happen to hear the caliber of the bullet?"

"Nah, I'm a little deaf in one ear, you know." Twiggy grins and returns to the floor of the bookshop, just in time to help a customer who sounds desperate to locate a first edition of *Captains Courageous*.

I have first editions. This day keeps getting weirder.

Heading toward the stairs, I stop and pretend to browse when a snippet of gossip grabs my interest.

"I heard the owner passed away recently."

"How is it still open?"

"I'm sure it's something with the missing will. I saw Janice at the pie judging, and she said no one knows if there's a new owner. The whole place might shut down."

"What about all these books? Oh my goodness, it breaks my heart."

"Did you hear about the murder in—?"

That's my cue to leave. Maybe I'll put my name in the hat for Pin Cherry Festival Princess. Despite my notoriety as a murder suspect, it sounds like folks need to meet the new owner of Bell, Book & Candle.

I chuckle while I make sure the coast is clear. Good, no one on the mezzanine. I pull the candle handle and slip into the apartment.

I could go through my dad's case files one more time, but it seems pointless. I only have the one lead, and I need to wait for Odell's Army buddies—

The PI! Don't ask me to connect the dots. I run to the bathroom and grab the receipt. It's the weekend, but private investigators probably answer their phones seven days a week. I know I would. That reminds me, I'm definitely going to get my cell service re-activated on Monday.

I scan the apartment for a phone. There's a landline in the back room downstairs, so I thought there would be a line up here.

I don't see anything. I'm about to open the bookcase and look for Twiggy when the fancy scrollwork covering the intercom speaker catches my eye. Hooray!

I press the button on the right.

Nothing.

I press it a little longer.

Nothing.

I press it for longer than necessary.

"Yes, Your Highness?" Twiggy replies.

I don't care for her tone. "I was wondering if there's a phone up here?"

"Do you see a phone?"

This woman knows exactly how to push my buttons. "The lack of visual discovery is the reason for the call."

"Don't get your panties in a bundle, doll. It's in the privacy booth."

"The what now?" I look around the room and nothing stands out.

"Notice that bump-out in the far left corner, beyond the bedside table and the flapper display?"

I stare at the flapper and grin. There must be some juicy stories in my family's past. But I don't see the "bump" that Twiggy mentioned. "No, I don't see anything."

"Trust me, it's there. Anything else?"

I don't reply. How can she ask if there's anything else when she didn't address the first thing? Geez!

I walk to the far corner, past the flapper, and see that the wall comes out in a square. I assumed there was a chimney or some ducting running up the wall of the building.

I press on the wall and to my surprise—not as much surprise as a secret bookcase door or a Ghost-ma—the wall springs open to reveal a well-lit, cozy phone booth.

I step in and it takes me a minute to figure out rotary dialing. Once I solve that mystery, I dial the number on the receipt.

"Hello?"

I expected more. "Um, hi. Is this Jackson Investigations?"

"You called me."

Does he mean yes? Does he mean no? "I did. I was wondering if we could meet?"

"You got a case? I ain't got time for chit-chat."

Maybe this guy is related to Twiggy? At the very least they both went to the same finishing school. "Yeah, I got a case."

"Be at the diner in an hour."

The line goes dead.

I can't meet him at the diner. If Odell is somehow involved . . . I dial the number again. The clickety-swish of the rotary phone is growing on me.

"Hello?"

"Yes, hi. We just spoke and I can't meet you at the diner. Is there someplace else?"

"The pizza place on 87th."

"Wait, wait." I don't know much about Pin Cherry, but I'm fairly certain there's no 87th. "What city are you in?"

"How'd you get this number?"

I look down at the address on the receipt. Craptastic! This guy is in Minneapolis. "I'm calling from Pin Cherry Harbor."

He's unusually slow to respond. "How'd you get this number?" This time there's a menacing growl to the tone.

"Look, I'm Cal Duncan's granddaughter. I'm not sure if you heard what happen—"

"This conversation is over."

DIAL TONE.

That went well.

I step out of the booth and press the wall-door closed.

I'm sure that sheriff trumps PI. Looks like I'll have to share my lead with Erick if I want to get this private eye to talk. Fiddle-farts.

I wipe the smeared mascara from under my eyes and walk to the station.

Maybe I should ask if they have a punch card. Ten punches and I earn a date with the sheriff. Now there's a frequent-felon club I'd gladly join.

CHAPTER 24

The influx of tourons—my clever word for tourist/morons—from down south has pushed the small sheriff's station to its limits. A frantic lady in red has misplaced her handbag or maybe it was stolen; she's not sure. There are four teenagers arguing with a deputy about how the bottle of pin cherry wine got into their car without their knowledge. There's a large man with an impressive handlebar mustache that claims his pin cherry pomade stand was robbed.

I make a beeline for the desk clerk.

"Hi, I'm here to—"

She looks up from her game of Furious Monkeys and recognition flashes across her features, instantly replaced with disdain. "They're in interrogation room one." She points, dismissively. "Down that hall."

"Thank you." Let the record show that at least one of us has manners.

I approach the room and my hand hovers above the tarnished handle. Should I knock? I do.

"Come in," says Erick.

I smile and open the door.

My father looks up and shakes his head.

Silas looks more grim than usual and his shoulders seem to bear an additional burden.

"What's going on?"

The three men exchange a glance that has meaning only to their special trio.

"What?" I repeat.

Sheriff Erick stands and offers me his chair. "Close the door, Moon."

I close the door, but sitting seems like giving up. "I'll stand."

"Suit yourself." Erick returns to the chair.

"Can someone tell me what the heck is bringing down this room?"

Silas for the win. "Miss Moon, the sheriff has far more evidence than we assumed to support Mrs. Zimm—"

"Just call her Kitty," I interject.

"To support Kitty's claim of an affair." Silas pats my father on the shoulder.

"Of course. But the affair was with Finnegan Wells."

"We looked into that, but Mrs.—Kitty came forward with evidence to corroborate her claim that Finnegan was blackmailing her, and that she was actually having an affair with your father."

"She's a liar." I slam my hand down on the table.

"Easy, Moon." Sheriff Erick gives me a stern look.

Luckily I remember why I came to the station. "And the PI can confirm all this?"

The various versions of shock that pop up on the faces of the triumvirate are priceless.

"What private investigator? Hired by who?" Sheriff Erick leans forward.

"By whom," I correct. "I'm sure your thorough investigation included questioning the PI Cal hired. The one certainly hired to tail Kitty." There's a wonderful joke in there, but I must press on. "There are probably pictures of the dirty deeds committed by her and Finnegan that will clear my dad in a second. But I forgot, this town isn't about clearing my dad. Seems like you're all way more interested in suppressing evidence if it facilitates a speedy conviction."

"Mizithra, that's enough." Jacob puts his large, calloused hand on top of mine.

"It's Mitzy, Dad." I pull my hand away. "So, what did the PI have to say, Erick?"

"It's Sheriff Harper, Miss Moon. It sounds like you have some information you failed to share."

I know the words are meant to fill me with guilt and shame, but when I look at the muscles clenching in his rugged jaw I get all warm and gooey instead. I slap the receipt on the table. "I'm sharing it now. I spent my time wisely in Cal's office."

He picks up the slip of paper, reads the imprint, and looks me dead in the eyes.

My knees wobble.

"I could arrest you—"

"Save it for an actual criminal, Sheriff." I take my dad's hand. "Come on. We're walking out of here until the sheriff comes up with something besides the lies of a cheating hussy."

Silas grins briefly and smooths his mustache with a thumb and forefinger before schooling his features back into brooding introspection.

Jacob looks up and smiles. "Thank you, Mitzy."

I pull the door open and hold it for the men as they leave. I look over my shoulder and give Erick a wink. "Oh, and you're welcome." I add a little extra wiggle as I strut out of the station.

Dear lord, baby Jesus, I hope that PI doesn't have pictures of my dad with Kitty!

Silas stops on the sidewalk and turns toward me. "I see potential in you, Mitzy."

But based on his recent revelation, the comment fills me with more trepidation than pride. "As an investigator?"

"As many things." He smiles and leaves us.

Way to vague it up, Silas.

Jacob sighs and says, "I could use a burger."

My eyes snap from the departing alchemist-attorney to my father. "Did you say that out loud or is my stomach reading minds?"

He chuckles and slings an arm around my shoulders. "Come on, let's see if Odell will serve me."

"Or me," I add. My last conversation with Odell didn't exactly end with balloons and streamers.

The lunch rush has cleared out and Tally eyes us nervously as we slide into a booth.

I smile and wave her over.

She approaches slowly. "Hi, Jacob."

"Hi, Tally. It's good to see you're still the brightest pin cherry in town."

She blushes and pulls a pencil from her flame-red bun. "What can I getcha?"

He smiles warmly. "We'll have two cheeseburgers, two cokes, and we'll split an order of fries."

Tally's eyes widen and she looks at me with concern.

"I'll have my own order of fries."

She sighs with relief. "That sounds better."

Jacob chuckles. "Sorry about that. I suppose I have quite a few things to learn about you. I'll make a mental note regarding not sharing fries."

"If there were a cardinal rule, that would be it." I sit back and stare at my father. The complications of Cal's case and the unresolved issues of my dad's old case all swirl haphazardly in my head. But my mouth takes a different route entirely. "Why did you leave Mom?"

"Whew!" He swallows. "You get right to the point, huh?"

"I figure we've lost twenty-one years. Why waste time on small talk?"

"Can't argue with that."

Tally slips the drinks onto the table and hurries away.

"The truth is, Mitzy, your mom and I never were together. It was a weekend fling and we didn't even exchange numbers."

I unroll my bundle of flatware and stare at the fork.

"I didn't find out about you until you were almost five. It was a fluke. I was back in Phoenix on railroad business and I thought about that amazing weekend so many years before and drove up to see the red rocks."

I swallow my hurt and fold the corners of my napkin into the center.

"I went poking around the old haunts I'd explored in Sedona during that college trip—and there you were."

I look up for a second, but the emotion bubbles too close to the surface. My napkin requires immediate attention.

"You and your mother were having ice cream in a place that used to be a sushi bar. I saw your hair—those eyes . . . I knew."

I fold the napkin ferociously and force myself to staunch the waterworks. I can't look at him, but I can't keep it inside. "Why didn't you say something to us? I think she was always waiting for you to come back."

"Maybe or maybe not. Truth is, she had my name and knew where I was from. If she had wanted me in your life she could've tracked me down."

I open my mouth to protest, but maybe he's right. Maybe it was all my childish wish for a father that I projected . . . Too much psychobabble. "Didn't you want me?"

His hand shoots across the table and grabs mine. "I was a disaster. It was right after I got back from that trip that Cal fired me. He'd already cut off my allowance when I dropped out of college, so losing the job was the last straw. I made a stupid plan with Darrin. You know the rest."

"But Mom died. I was all alone."

"I'm not saying I made the right choice, Mitzy. But I couldn't let you find out that your dad was a convicted murderer. You deserved better."

"What changed?"

He tilts his head.

"Why did you agree to meet me now?"

"According to Silas I didn't have a choice. He said either I come with him or he would give you my address. The way he described your, um, tenacity . . . Let's just say I wanted to come quietly and on my own terms."

The food arrives and a tense silence hangs between us as I mow through my fries. I lick the salt off my fingers and stare at my living, breathing father. "Maybe you did make the right choice."

He sets his burger down slowly and looks at me with decades of pain in his eyes.

"Isadora said that everything in my life led me to this point." I chuckle coldly. "I can tell you that my life in Sedona was nothing to brag about. I ran out on three months' back rent and a bunch of other unpaid bills when Silas delivered the money and the will."

"You should pay those bills." He waves the

words away. "Not the point. Please finish what you were saying."

"I don't know what I was saying. All I know is that I'm here. You're here. We're both innocent of murder, and I'm going to prove it."

He smiles broadly and his eyes spill over with pride. "Like I said, there doesn't appear to be any saying 'no' to you."

We share a conspiratorial laugh and finish our burgers.

I turn to wave to Tally and see Odell walking toward the table.

My freshly gobbled burger and fries churn.

My dad grips the edge of the table, and his knuckles whiten as he pushes back into the red vinyl bench seat.

Odell puts up both hands. "I come in peace, Jacob."

My dad relaxes his grip.

I don't care whether he comes in a coat of many colors, I don't like being taken for a ride. "Why didn't you tell me about the fight you had with Cal?"

Odell's gaze snaps to me. "Boy, you don't miss a thing. Not a darn thing."

I purse my lips and stare insistently.

"The truth is always the best defense, kid. I knew it made me look guilty."

"No wonder you were being so nice to me when they threw me in the slammer!"

Jacob leans forward. "What? When?"

I wave him off. "Did you do it?"

Odell's eyes widen and his brow creases. "Murder Cal? You serious, kid?"

"Yes. You have more motive than me. He was trying to take the bookshop, the diner—all your memories of Myrtle. Did you kill him or not?"

"He didn't know about Isadora's will. He assumed she'd been irresponsible, as was her tendency, and thought he'd buy it up 'fore it went on the auction block."

I throw up my hands in frustration. "So?"

"I knew what she'd done—in her will. He was trying to take the bookshop from you, but I couldn't tell him until Silas found you. I'm old, Mitzy. Too old to be slinging burgers in a diner every day. If he was only after the diner, I probably would've taken the money and left town for good. But he was gonna take the bookshop from you."

"But you didn't even know me."

"I knew Myrtle or Isadora, or whatever you wanna call her. I knew how much she regretted never meeting you and how much it meant to her to think that you would get to know her through her bookshop."

Oh, if Odell only knew the half of it.

"I couldn't let him do it." Odell smacks his right fist into his left palm.

"Are you saying you did kill him?" Jacob blurts the accusation and gets to his feet.

"No. No." Odell waves his hands and takes a step back. "I'm saying Myrtle and I rebuilt our relationship when she was ill. I thought if I could keep that bookshop for Mitzy, I could make up for all the ugliness the first time around."

Jacob nods slowly. "My dad could be pretty vindictive."

I look from Odell to Jacob. "Do you believe him, Dad?"

Before Jacob can answer, Odell jumps in. "I'll call Sheriff Harper right now and make a statement if you think it'll make a difference."

I slap my hand on the table. "Since my dad is their latest suspect, I'll take your offer. The more suspects on the list, the better." I point to the phone on the wall behind the counter. "Thanks, Odell. It would mean a lot to Isadora."

Odell hesitates, but he marches over and makes the call.

I pat my dad on the shoulder and we turn to leave.

"Hey, Mitzy," calls Odell.

I glance back.

"My buddy DeVine says that 'bout the only

valid explanation for the absence of rifling on the second bullet woulda been a thing called a sabot."

And that's a Yahtzee for me! A surge of warmth surrounds my heart. "Thanks, Odell."

"Anytime, kid."

Dad and I walk out the door and I turn toward the bookshop.

He pulls away and stands on the sidewalk, chewing the inside of his cheek in an all too familiar way.

"What's up?" I ask.

"This is where we say goodnight, I guess. I'll head back to my hotel and meet you for break—"

"Are you pulling my leg? As far as I'm concerned this day is never going to end. You're coming back to the bookshop and we're having a sleepover."

He laughs. "A sleepover? You sure?"

"Uh, yeah." I look up and down the street. "Where can we get popcorn, Red Vines, ice cream, and possibly pie?"

"Follow me." His arm beckons. "There's a Piggly Wiggly on 4th."

"Is that a store or a livestock barn?"

He laughs so hard he chokes a little.

I pat him on the back and feel happy all over.

CHAPTER 25

Back at the apartment, Dad and I set up camp on the thick Persian rug. He is also sufficiently impressed by the candle handle and the secret phone booth.

I run down to the microwave in the back room and pop two bags of popcorn.

When I return to the apartment, I interrupt a standoff between Pyewacket and Dad.

"Is that thing yours?" asks Dad.

"That is Pyewacket. Grams said he's a caracal. He was her rescue and he's spoiled rotten." I toss a hot bag of popcorn to Jacob and turn my attention to the furry beast. "Pye, Dad's cool. If you don't back down, I will 'forget' to give you Fruity Puffs in the morning."

Pyewacket shakes his hackles down, twitches

his ear tufts, and yawns.

Dad looks at me. “That can’t be the original Pyewacket? But does he talk, too?”

“What?” I chuckle and shake my head.

“Hey, your ghost grandmother haunts this place and apparently communicates with you. Why would it be so strange if that wildcat talked?”

“You got me there.” I shrug. “I have no idea if he’s ‘original’ or not. And if he talks, he doesn’t talk to me, but he seems to understand when I talk to him.” I toss a piece of popped corn toward Pye. His powerful hind legs propel him through the air and he snatches the fluffy white projectile with ease.

“I’d hate to be a sparrow in his line of sight.”

“Or an eyeball,” I mumble.

“What’s that?” Dad leans on the stack of pillows under his arm.

I quickly explain how Cal was discovered in the alley behind the bookshop. I skim over the gory details of Pye’s involvement. I need several Red Vines to calm my stomach.

“What was Cal doing in the alley?”

“Oh, he definitely wasn’t killed in the alley. The ME at county confirmed that he was killed somewhere else. The body was frozen to obscure time of death.” I shiver.

“Someone was definitely trying to set you up.”

Jacob sits up and crunches absently on a handful of popcorn.

"Me? Why would they want to set me up? No one in this town even knows me."

"But they know me."

"Huh?" Pyewacket rubs against me and I scratch between his ears. "So were they framing you?"

"All I know is that I wasn't having an affair with Kitty, and I had no idea that Cal was changing his will. One set of facts makes me look guilty and the other points toward innocence." He munches on another handful of popcorn.

I reach for my bag and discover Pye's head shoved so far into the bag that his tufts are all that's showing. "Pye! You little thief!" I swat at his tan backside.

He shakes the bag off and popcorn flies everywhere.

Jacob laughs so hard his eyes water.

I want to be furious, but the sound of my dad's laughter warms my heart. I chuckle and start to collect the scattered kernels.

"Here, let me help." He grabs a trash can and picks up a handful.

I wave my hands. "Hey, don't throw it away! I plan on eating that." I pass him the popcorn bag.

"Put 'em back in here. I'm not terribly fussy when it comes to my snack foods."

We get the mess under control just as Grams makes an appearance.

She clutches her pearls and dabs at her eyes. "I never thought I'd see this day! Dear, do you think he would like to look at some photo albums?" She swirls nervously above my dad.

"That sounds wonderful, Grams."

Jacob stiffens and his eyes dart left and right. "She's here? Now? Is she by me?"

I laugh a little. "Sorry, Dad. I'm so used to her popping in and out now, I forget to announce her entrances." I point to a spot above and to the left. "She's right there."

He looks over his shoulder and smiles. "Hey, Mom."

She rushes toward him and he shivers.

"I felt something cold. Is that her?" His skin is peppered with goosebumps.

"That's her." I look at my own arms and shrug. "I don't get the chills from her. Never did. I saw her right away, and we could talk. Maybe it's because I can see her?"

"I'm sure that's it, dear." Grams nods her head and floats away from my shivering dad. "Ask him about the albums."

"Oh, right. Grams asked if you'd like to look at photo albums?"

"That sounds great."

"Over here, honey." Grams swooshes over to a built-in bookcase and gestures to a row of volumes.

I grab a couple and return to the floor next to my dad.

The first album is ancient. The pages are black construction paper with tiny red paper corners stuck to the pages. Each black-and-white photo is tucked snuggly into a group of four corner-holders.

Jacob runs his fingers along the page. "I think this is Cal as a baby, but I don't recognize anyone else."

Grams swirls closer.

The hair on my dad's arm stands up.

"Those are Cal's grandparents. And that boy pulling the wagon is Cal's older brother. He was killed in Vietnam." Grams sniffles.

I touch the image of the young boy. "How sad."

Dad looks at me. "What's sad?"

Oh, right. I'm the only one who can hear the ghost. I repeat the story about Cal's older brother.

Jacob touches the picture and shakes his head. "He never talked about it, but it definitely explains his obsession with making the family railroad successful."

We work our way through the album, Grams

giving me the stories and me sharing them with my dad. It's a strange and emotional history lesson.

As the snacks run low and my eyelids grow heavy, I close the fourth album. "I'm beat, Dad. Mind if I grab a few before the sun comes up?"

"Sure," he says. His voice sounds sad.

"Is everything all right?"

He takes my hand in his large strong one and squeezes gently. "I guess part of me is afraid that if I close my eyes, you'll be gone when I open them up. Dreams like this are what kept me sane all those years in prison, but I never thought for a minute it could be real."

I throw my arms around him. "It's real. I'm not an orphan and you're not in prison. It's real, and tomorrow we're going to show this town what happens when you cross the Duncans."

"And Mitzy Moon," says Dad with a chuckle.

CHAPTER 26

After a perfect breakfast at the diner, Jacob and I walk down to the sheriff's station.

The waiting area is nearly empty. Apparently the weekday Pin Cherry Festival activities aren't as well attended as opening weekend.

A swarthy little man with a messy black mustache, five-o-clock shadow at nine in the morning, and a paunch hanging way over his belt, catches my eye.

"You Jackson?"

He looks up. "Who wants to know?"

I smile and cross my arms. "Seems like the conversation isn't over after all."

Jackson scowls at me and leans forward.

I don't like the way he's looking at me.

My dad steps up and adds his prison-tough presence to my side.

Jackson's eyes widen. "You're the son. Jacob Duncan."

I'm not sure if it's a good or bad thing that he recognizes my dad.

"Why did my grandfather hire you?" I ask, hoping to catch him off balance.

The pint-sized PI looks around nervously. "It's not safe. I'm telling you right now, leave it alone."

My dad leans down and growls, "Are you threatening my little girl?"

I never felt so happy to be called a little girl in my entire life.

"It's not me you need to worry about."

"Mr. Jackson, the sheriff will see you now," the Furious-Monkeys-playing clerk announces.

Sheriff Erick takes one look at me and strides into the waiting area. "Moon, I told you to let this go. Leave the investigation to the professionals."

"Oh, is that what you're calling this circus act?" That was so much harsher than I intended. Too late. "If it wasn't for my amateur investigation you never would've found this guy." I point to Jackson and narrow my gaze. "And by the looks of him he's hiding something."

Sheriff Erick steps closer to me.

My skin tingles.

"I'm warning you, Moon."

"Oh, everyone is full of warnings today." I wave it away with a flick of my wrist. "I'll have Silas pick up a copy of Jackson's statement this afternoon."

I hook my arm through my dad's elbow and walk toward the door. I throw one last comment over my shoulder. "And, you're welcome."

Dad heads off to meet with Cal's attorney to see if he can get to the bottom of the will-changing rumor and I wander back to the bookshop.

I learn from the empty establishment and a close inspection of the sign in the window that we're closed on Mondays. I walk upstairs and plunk down next to the file boxes.

Things are still a mess from the sleepover, so I go through my stacks and organize the reports and other documents as I pack the lot back into the cardboard containers. I'll see if Twiggy wants to return them tomorrow.

My hands linger on the security guard's statement. Something is off. Why is he the only witness who claims to have heard the third shot?

Grams drifts down next to me with a pleading look on her face and an overall "depleted" appearance.

"What is it? What's going on?"

She flashes back to technicolor. "I know you didn't say it out loud, dear, but why don't you see if you can track that guard down and ask him yourself?"

I channel Kitty for a second. "Brilliant!"

I brush my teeth, and apply an extra layer of flirty mascara to make my eyelashes pop and some fresh lip tint.

"That should do the trick." Grams winks. "What man could say 'no' to that face?"

"Sheriff Erick, for one," I reply bitterly.

"Oh don't you fret. He'll come around."

"Wish me luck." I grab the keys to the Mercedes and head off toward the larger town to the north, Broken Rock. That town was desperate for the tax revenues and allowed the big box store that Pin Cherry Harbor had refused.

The address on the coffee-stained witness statement is over fifteen years old, but I have to start somewhere.

The drive through Black Cap Trail and Pancake Bay, along the coast of the magnificently massive body of fresh water, loosens some of the knots in my neck.

Most of the bravado I throw down in front of Sheriff Erick is for show. Deep down I'm still a little terrified that my dad or I could wind up taking the rap for Cal's murder.

Near the outskirts of Broken Rock, I speak the address into the map app on my phone. I paid off my past due bill and the exorbitant re-activation fee, but at least I have a phone now.

Look at me, "adulting" like an— Well, you get the idea.

"You have arrived at your destination," announces the helpful phone.

I check the house number against the old police report. Yep, I have arrived.

I scope my makeup in the rearview mirror and press my lips together to even out the color. All right, let's go get the truth.

I open the small gate, close it quietly behind, and make my way up the old, buckled sidewalk. As I mount the steps to the porch, I notice the front door is ajar.

The hairs on the back of my neck jump to attention. This is the part in the movie when the star grabs their gun.

I don't have a gun.

I'm probably seriously overreacting. Maybe the man just didn't latch his door. Maybe I've actually seen too many movies.

There's no stack of decaying newspapers piled up on the porch so it's safe to assume someone who lives in the house has passed through this door in the last twenty-four hours. I recite this invented factoid to calm my frayed nerves.

I ring the doorbell several times. This way if the

guy is home he'll absolutely hear, and if there's an intruder inside, they'll have ample warning and hopefully bolt out the back door.

No one answers.

No one bolts.

It's deadly quiet. Why did I say that?

I push open the solid wooden door and it creaks with appropriate Scooby Doo intensity.

Nice and loud, I shout, "Delivery for Mr. Whitakker. Anyone here?"

Nada. Bupkus.

The plain white blinds in the living room and the complete lack of throw pillows on the lumpy sofa lead me to believe Mr. Whitakker lives alone.

I give one more shout, "Hello? Is any—?"

My throat tightens and cuts off my voice. I freeze with one foot on the stained grey linoleum and one foot on the threadbare brown carpet. There are other feet.

These feet are not standing feet. They're covered by the soles of a man's slippers, and I'm afraid to report that they seem to be attached to a body.

I put my hand over my mouth to capture the inevitable scream.

I step into the kitchen and lean around the cabinet.

I scream into my hand and search the room.

I've never been so grateful for cell service in my

entire life. I run out of the death house, leave the door open, and I dial as I run. Please don't be on a coffee break, Furious Monkeys!

She answers. "Pin Cherry Sheriff's Station. How may I direct your call?"

"I need Sheriff Erick—Harper, right away. It's an emergency." My breath comes in little gasps.

"You should have called 911 if—"

"Put Erick on the line. I've got a dead body here!" Okay, maybe I lost it a little. But I don't "do" dead bodies.

"Sheriff Harper here."

"Erick, it's Mitzy. He's dead. I came to ask him some questions, and the door was open and then a body—there's so much—I mean, it's fresh—"

"Miss Moon? Where are you?"

I recite the address.

"What are you doing in Broken Rock?"

"I wanted to question the security guard. Something just didn't sit right with me—"

"Miss Moon, I need you to get in your car and drive directly back to this station. Can you do that?"

"But the body, and I wanted to know about the third shot—"

"Mitzy, this is serious. There was no third shot. The security guard was the inside guy."

"What? That doesn't make any sense. Does my dad know about this?"

"Mitzy, please get out of that house."

I'm temporarily distracted by the desperate concern in Erick's voice, so I don't let him know that I'm already in my car.

"If you come to the station, I'll let you read Jackson's statement."

I know it's a blatant bribe but— "Deal."

I lock myself inside the Mercedes and drive as fast as my heart is racing. I figure a dead body is the best excuse I'll ever have for speeding.

CHAPTER 27

I RUSH INTO the sheriff's station and am surprised to see my dad in the waiting area. He's lounging in a chair, absently rubbing the sleeve of his light-blue Oxford shirt between his thumb and forefinger.

He looks up and smiles. "Harper asked me to come back in."

"Did he say why?"

"Something to do with the PI's statement. I asked Silas to meet me here, just in case."

Oh boy. This does not sound good. As much as I believe in my dad's innocence, I'm growing increasingly concerned about this private investigator's involvement. What if he killed the security guard? I cross my arms and pinch myself. Get it together, Moon.

Sheriff Harper walks out of his office and looks

from me to my dad. "Good, you're both here. I'll need you to come to my office."

I didn't hear the word arrest. I follow without formal protest.

Jacob is the first to speak. "What's all this about, Harper? What was that PI up to?"

Erick closes his door and motions for us to take the seats in front of his desk.

My nerves are shot and I don't have it in me to argue. I collapse into a stiff brown chair.

Erick shuffles some papers on his desk and sighs. "Looks like Cal hired the PI to look into your old case, Jacob."

"My case? Why?"

"I don't think we'll ever know for sure, but this Mr. Jackson was paid for one thing and one thing only: to find out what actually happened the night of the robbery." Erick moves the same papers around again.

I lean forward and put both hands on the edge of his metal-topped desk. "And?"

"I have to follow a couple leads and verify some of the information—"

"But?" I strum my fingers impatiently.

"But it sounds like Jackson found some evidence that would refute Darrin's testimony."

My father leans back in his chair. The wood

creaks as he squares his shoulders and clenches his jaw. "What kind of evidence?"

"Jackson spoke to the security guard. He had a deal with Darrin to destroy the monitoring equipment and the tape from the day of the robbery. Darrin was supposed to cut him in on thirty percent of the take."

"News to me," my dad grumbles through gritted teeth.

Erick nods and continues, "When Darrin got caught the guard threatened to come forward, but Darrin promised Whitakker an extra $10,000 to keep quiet."

My dad's hands grip his knees, and the only sound in the room is his fingers squeezing across the denim fabric. "Darrin didn't have that kind of money," he growls.

"Not all the stolen cash was recovered. It seems like Darrin had time to stash some of it somewhere and he used it to bribe the guard. He promised him more when he got out." Erick drops the papers on his desk and leans back in his chair. "He made the deal with the district attorney to make sure he got out before you."

"Worked out pretty well for good ol' Darrin. He was sentenced to forty-eight months and got out in thirty-two with time off for good behavior."

I put my hand on top of my dad's tense fingers. "I'm so sorry, Dad."

He shakes off my sympathy.

I sigh and continue questioning Erick. "Who killed Whitakker?" I shudder as the image from the kitchen floor in Broken Rock looms in my memory.

Sheriff Erick sighs. "Jackson claims Whitakker kept the security footage as insurance, and for blackmail. As long as Darrin kept the payments trickling in, the tape was safe. Once Jackson found out about the tape, Cal offered a massive payoff to get his hands on it. Someone wanted to make sure that didn't happen."

My dad's white knuckles crack and his teeth grind. "Darrin."

"That's what we're thinking too." Erick leans back and shakes his head sadly.

I look from Erick to my dad and back. "So, Darrin killed Whitakker."

Jacob's voice cracks as he adds, "And Cal."

"And Cal," I whisper. The wind goes out of my sails. My witty banter vanishes. "What now?"

"We have a statewide BOLO out on Darrin MacIntyre, but something tells me he hasn't left the area." Erick locks eyes with my dad. "What do you think, Jacob?"

"He's gonna finish what he started."

"We'd like to put you in protective custody."

Jacob reaches for my hand. "Both of us?"

"We have no reason to believe Mitzy's in danger."

Jacob stands and the room seems to shrink to half its size. "He dumped a body in the alley behind her bookshop and she just walked out of a murder scene. I'm not leaving her unprotected."

"I understand your concern, Jacob. We're a small force. We feel you're the target. It's unlikely that Darrin is even aware of Mitzy's presence in Pin Cherry, or her connection to you."

My dad's fists ball up tightly.

I jump up and step between them. "Why don't you just stay with me, Dad? We'll have a sleepover, and I'm sure Sheriff Harper can spare a patrol car to keep an eye on the bookshop." I look at Erick with a desperation I can't hide. "Deal?"

He nods. "I can arrange that. We'll find him. Don't worry."

"I hope you find him before I do." Jacob puts a hand on the sheriff's desk and leans down. "I don't mind making good on that murder charge."

I grab my dad's arm and pull him out of the station before he says— Well, it's too late for that, but I don't want Erick to lock him up.

We walk silently back to my car.

"Take me out to Cal's place."

"I don't think we want to stir things up with Kitty. Let's—" My voice cracks as I plead.

"I need to pick something up." He stares straight ahead and his jaw is set.

I don't like the look in his eye or the last thing he said to Erick. "Dad, I don't want you to get a gun. Please don't do what you're thinking."

"Darrin needs to pay for everything he took from me."

I can't stop them. The waterworks burst. "But he could take so much more. Please, Dad, I'm begging you. I just found you. Don't let this revenge take you away from me again."

His eyes soften and he looks at me. "He killed my father, Mitzy."

"And now you want to give him a chance to kill mine?" I sob uncontrollably.

He scoops me into his arms and his chest heaves as he chokes back his own emotion. "All right, you win. Let's have that sleepover."

CHAPTER 28

THE FESTIVE MOOD of our previous sleepover is absent as we walk into the darkened bookshop. I press the flashlight app on my phone and we walk somberly toward the staircase.

The uplifting feeling of bonding has evaporated and the heavy weight of Darrin's betrayal hangs over us like a dark storm cloud.

I unhook the "No Admittance" chain, and Jacob and I circle up the metal staircase.

In the apartment, we straighten pillows and blankets in silence. I can't stand it.

"Dad?"

The eyes that look over at me are dark and empty.

"I can't imagine what you must be feeling right now, but—"

He lifts a hand to stop me. "Darrin was my friend. It's not about the money or the side-deal with the security guard. That was classic Darrin. He always hedged his bets. That slippery side-deal crap is what got him tossed out of the Navy." Dad folds a pillow and punches his large fist into the feathers. "He stole fifteen years of my life."

I nod. "And he stole you away from me." I sit down on the floor and rest my small hand on top of my dad's fist. "But the truth has finally come out. We're together, and the police can take care of Darrin."

He sighs. "I hear what you're saying, Mitzy. My brain agrees, but my broken heart wants revenge. I need to make Darrin pay."

The veins in Jacob's arm pop up as his fist tightens.

I pull away—helpless.

He jumps as goosebumps cover his skin.

"Grams?" I look up.

"Sounds like a good news/bad news situation, dear. What happened?"

I bring her up to speed on the security guard, and Darrin's killing spree.

"Poor Cal. He was trying to make things right with Jacob. He wanted another chance." She floats toward the coffered ceiling. "Poor, poor Cal."

Desperate to shift the mood, I lift up the remaining packet of microwave popcorn and say, "Wanna split this?"

Jacob pulls his mind back from whatever road it had traveled down and smiles. "Sounds good." He snags the pack from my hand and stands. "Microwave is in the back room, right?"

"Correct. Two minutes and twenty seconds should do it."

He chuckles. "Give or take, eh?"

I blush and nod. I'll spare him the story of the burned popcorn, the smoke alarm, and the horrible scent that still lingers in the back room.

Jacob leaves and I turn to Grams. "Can you believe this Darrin jerk? I mean, how did Dad even end up being friends with such a colossal—"

Grams interrupts my tirade. "They were best buddies since sixth grade, or thereabouts. Darrin's family moved into town and the boys hit it off. They played football together. Cal would take them hunting, and they were inseparable."

"But Darrin is evil!" I stand and pace to the window.

"He was always the instigator, but in high school it was fairly harmless things like staying out past curfew and stealing a few beers from the fridge. Darrin didn't go completely off the rails until he got expelled from school."

"College?"

"He never made it. He was caught stealing some test answers their senior year and the school had a zero-tolerance policy. He was expelled." Grams floats toward me.

I chew on a Red Vine and nod my head. "He never got his GED or anything?"

"I can't say for sure, dear. But Darrin was furious about the injustice. Your dad went off to college and Darrin joined the Navy for a spell, but he was dishonorably discharged in no time. Once he was back on the street, he couldn't let go."

I plop down on the settee and reach for another Red Vine. "What do you mean?"

"Simply, that Darrin hounded your father endlessly. He would take him out every weekend, and eventually every night. Your dad always liked to party, so it didn't take much pressure to get him to ignore his studies."

I could relate to the aimless party cycle. "Did Dad drop out or get kicked out?"

"His grades plummeted. Cal cut off his allowance and threatened to stop paying for college. My Jacob loved to rail against authority." She turns away and I assume she's hiding her tears.

"But how did they go from partying to robbery?" I ask.

Grams goes absolutely still. It is strange. It looks like when you press pause on a movie.

"What is it?"

She flickers. "How long has Jacob been gone, dear?"

I shrug.

She vanishes through the wall and comes flying back a few seconds later, like a ghost comet.

"He's here!"

I don't have to ask "who." The fear on her face tells me everything.

I grab my phone to call Erick. It's DEAD! I must've left the stupid flashlight app on.

"The phone booth," says Grams.

I run to the corner and push the wall. The door pops open and I pick up the receiver. "The line is dead," I shout. I have to stop saying that word.

"You've got to go for help, Mitzy." Grams is a fright. She's fading in and out like a signal that's not quite strong enough.

I nod and smile. "Wish me luck."

"Take Pye. He can create a distraction."

Sure, why not place my life in the paws of a psycho-cat.

I open the bookcase door. Pyewacket races past me.

I creep toward the spiral staircase. I don't smell burnt popcorn, so I assume Jacob never made it to the back room.

Pyewacket's low menacing growl chills my

blood.

Before I can shush the cat, the scrape of a metal door slowly opening and closing interrupts. I close my eyes and replay the sound. I remember hearing the click of a push bar before the scrape, not the twist of a handle. They went into the museum.

I hurry down the stairs and feel my way along the stacks toward the "Employees Only" door. There's no time to go for help. It's me or nothing.

I don't know what's on the other side of that door, but if there's any chance I can save my father . . . I depress the push bar as quietly as possible and apply slow steady pressure to the door.

So far so good. The door barely makes a sound.

A furry creature brushes past my leg and through the narrow opening.

I clamp my jaw shut and scream silently. That demon-spawn!

I take a slow breath in through my nose and listen for any clue as to Darrin and Jacob's location.

Grams pops up next to me and sends my heart into a bucking bronco routine. I don't have to worry about Darrin getting his hands on me; Grams and Pye will kill me long before he discovers me.

"Don't even joke about such a thing, Mitzy!"

Oh right, she can hear my thoughts. I'll let it slide for now. *All right, Grams, I'm allowing telepathic communication. Where are they?*

She vanishes from my side.

The crashes, thunks, and groans would indicate a struggle. A couple of thuds. Another groan.

Grams reappears. "He's forcing your father up to the roof. I don't like this one bit."

Neither do I.

"Follow me." Grams swooshes across the floor.

I hurry along and— "Mm— Gr—" I clap one hand over my mouth and press on my bruised hip with the other. *I can't walk through Gutenberg presses, Grams.*

"I'm so sorry, dear. I was worried about Jacob and I forgot about— Never mind. Hurry, Mitzy."

I rub my bone bruise once more and follow her to the back stairs.

The struggle is growing more violent. *They're way ahead of me. Grams, can't you do something? I'll never get there in time.*

"What can I do, honey? I can't talk to your dad and I've tried to move things, but I'm no Patrick Swayze."

There has to be something, Grams. You're made of some kind of energy. I can see you. Pyewacket can sense you—

Where's Pye?

Grams flies up the stairwell.

I creep up as quickly as I can without making a racket.

"Ree-ooow!"

CRASH!

"Son of a—"

I don't recognize that voice. It must be Darrin. Good job, Pye. Extra Fruity Puffs for you!

I rush up the steps.

The sick wallop of fists connecting with flesh echoes down the stairwell.

The thud, thud, thud of a body falling down the steps.

I cross the landing and the body crashes into my leg.

Oh dear Lord, please let that be Jacob.

"Dad?" I whisper.

"Mitzy, get out of here. This is my fight."

I grab his arm and help him to his feet. "Come on, Dad."

"What a special moment." A harsh laugh echoes down the stairwell. "Nobody's going anywhere. Isn't that right, Jake?"

I look up and see the outline of a gun barrel illuminated in the dim stairwell—pointing straight down the stairs. Straight at my head.

"You know what, Jake? I came back to make sure you went back to prison for life, but imagine my surprise when I discovered your long lost baby girl. How about I kill her first—"

"You'll never get away with this, Darrin." I'm

just spitballing now, but this is the point in every movie when the good guy gets the bad guy to talk.

"But I already got away with it." Darrin points the gun at my dad as he taunts me. "Maybe I'll kill him first. Cops are already looking at you for Cal's murder, princess. If you kill Jake too, that oughta convince 'em."

"They know about the sabot, Darrin." I can barely make out his face in the darkness, but the lack of a snappy comeback leads me to believe this is news to him. "And they recovered the tape from Whitakker's place."

His deep, satisfied laugh fills the museum.

My mouth goes dry and my throat feels like it's closing.

"You shoulda quit while you were ahead, girlie." He walks down another step closer to us. "You torpedoed your own lifeboat."

Jacob pushes me behind his tree trunk of a body.

"I made sure ol' Whit told me the location of the tape before I killed him."

I shiver uncontrollably. I mean, I was pretty sure Darrin killed the security guard, but hearing him brag about murdering someone makes me a little sick to my stomach.

"Once I take care of you and your patsy of a daddy, I'll take this handy key" —he jingles a key ring— "and pick up the tape from Whit's safe deposit box. The last bit of evidence that can clear your pops will be gone. He'll die a murderer."

He steps down. "And you'll be that pathetic millennial that committed murder but then got so 'emo' that she offed herself."

"Let her go, Darrin. Your beef is with me."

"Always the hero." Darrin spits on the stairs. "Why do you think I set you up, buddy? Because I knew you were too stupid to figure it out and too weak to fight back."

The museum lights start flashing like a disco.

You go Grams! If that's you . . .

"Prison changes people." Dad shoves me down toward the ground and lunges at Darrin.

"No!" I scream.

Everything flashes before my eyes like a stop-action movie.

The pulsing lights show me bits and pieces.

The gun fires.

Fur flies.

"Reeee-OW!"

Pyewacket's furry form falls slack on the stairs.

Jacob has one arm around Darrin's neck, slowly choking the life out of him, while the other hand struggles to control the gun.

Another bullet fires, narrowly missing my head and embedding in the brick.

The lights stop flickering and stay on.

The welcome sound of heavy-soled boots running across the concrete museum floor races toward me.

"Up here," I scream.

Darrin and my dad tumble down the stairs past the still-unmoving Pye.

Sheriff Erick lunges up the stairs two at a time and pushes me out of the way just as the wrestling duo hits the landing.

"Freeze!"

My dad comes up with the gun and aims it at Darrin's head.

"Dad, no." I'm shaking uncontrollably. "Please, Daddy. Please don't do it." I can't stop the tears.

"Go ahead, Jake. Pull the trigger." Darrin's words are filled with the bravado of a man who knows his life is a heartbeat from ending.

Sheriff Erick moves his aim from Darrin to my dad. "Jacob, drop the gun. Let us handle this now. Don't do something you'll regret."

Deputy Paulsen shoves past me to even things up. "Don't move, scumbag."

I can't believe she's aiming at my dad too! And still pulling cheesy one-liners from eighties cop movies! I wipe my tears and prepare to tackle her.

"Come on, Jake. You know you want to end this

once and for all." Darrin baits my dad. "You know you need to settle this score."

"You might be able to frame me for murder, Darrin, but you can't actually turn me into a killer."

Jacob spins the gun around and hands it to Sheriff Erick, grip first.

Darrin lunges up.

My dad's knee connects with Darrin's face in a bone-splintering crunch.

Darrin cradles his face with both hands. "My nose! He broke my nose!"

Grams appears. "Good job! That's my boy!"

"Step away, Jacob." Erick nods his head toward me. "Both of you, clear out." He moves closer to Darrin. "Darrin MacIntyre, you're under arrest for the murders . . . "

Murders. Plural. That's all I need to hear. I smile through my tears and shove past Deputy Paulsen to hug my dad.

Erick and Deputy Paulsen cuff Darrin and drag him off, to the cheers of my Ghost-ma.

"He's got a key to Whitakker's safe deposit box. Make sure you get that!" I shout to the departing law-enforcement duo.

I squeeze my dad once more, drop my arms, and slowly approach Pyewacket's twisted shape.

I reach out my shaky, grateful hand to touch his brave, motionless body. And I pass out.

CHAPTER 29

Bright sunlight warms my cheek and I stretch my arms. As I luxuriate on the soft mattress beneath me with the cozy comforter over me, for a split second, I believe it was all a horrible dream.

But the image of precious Pyewacket on that staircase—

I sit up and look for my dad. "Grams! Grams! Where is everyone?"

She fades in right next to me and I jump.

"Your phone is fully charged and it's on the bedside table. Silas said to call him as soon as you got out of bed."

"Where's my dad? Did they arrest him?"

"No, dear. Bless his heart. He came in and whispered to these four walls that he was going down to the station to view the tape. I'm sure that was for my benefit, but that was hours ago."

How could I have slept so late? I grab my phone and press. It's after noon. I've been asleep forever.

"You were scared out of your wits, honey. You needed a good—"

I point to my lips. "The crisis has passed, Grams. Standing rules apply."

"Of course."

I call Silas.

"Good afternoon, Mitzy. How are you feeling?"

"Who cares about me? Where's Pye? Can I see the body before he's laid to rest? Is there a pet cemetery in Pin Cherry? We should have a service. Maybe the sheriff will give him some kind of medal."

I do not appreciate my attorney's hearty laugh.

"Actually, Mitzy, we all care about you a great deal. And I'm afraid Pye did take a bullet for you and Jacob."

My eyes well up. I never should've called him a demon spawn. "He's dead? That poor, sweet kitten."

"Not exactly. Robin Pyewacket Goodfellow has certainly given one of his lives, but it appears it was not his ninth. He's heavily sedated at the Pin Cherry Harbor Animal Hospital. You may visit him anytime."

I can't help but cry. That irritating furry fiend saved my stupid life. I sniffle loudly and continue, "What about my dad? Where's he?"

"It would seem that VHS tape players are not as plentiful as they once were. Sheriff Erick has requested one be brought up from the big city. However, Twiggy heard about the dilemma and claims she can acquire one, post haste. Your father and I are enjoying a late repast at the diner and awaiting the arrival of the required tech."

I hang up without replying.

I look down at yesterday's skinny jeans and cashmere sweater. I don't know where the blood came from but it's oogy and I want it off me. I search through the pile of clothes on the floor of the closet and find an acceptably clean pair of jeans. I pull them on and shove my finger in to tuck the pockets down.

I pull out the black button gift from Pyewacket. I turn it over in my hands. And I suddenly know exactly where this button came from—

"Navy peacoat!"

Grams swooshes down. "Where did you get that?"

"The amazing Pye brought it in from the alley. I'll bet you Twiggy's next paycheck that this is a button from Darrin's coat."

"You better give that to the sheriff."

"Right after breakfast. I don't think I can see him on an empty stomach."

"Honestly, Mitzy." Grams rolls her ghost eyes.

I shrug and pull on my boots as I hop through the secret door.

I run down the spiral steps two at a time and . . . flip over the chain at full speed. "Twiggy!"

There's no reply.

Grams hovers next to me. "She came in early, but then she had to run off to get the tape player thingy."

Curses. I check my face for gum or other floor souvenirs and resume my rapid run—now it's more of a limp—to Myrtle's Diner.

I push open the door of the diner. There's my dad—alive and well. The scent of golden, delicious french fries envelopes me. This is my idea of heaven.

My dad is out of the booth before I can take another step. We meet in the middle and hug like we haven't seen each other in twenty-one years.

Tally claps and sniffles.

"Breakfast or lunch?" Odell calls from the back.

I'm pretty sure that's not onions making his eyes water. Boy, I'll never get used to how fast news travels in a small town. "Both," I say with enthusiasm.

Dad puts his arm around my shoulder and we slide into the booth across the table from Silas.

"Any news on Darrin?" I ask as I blindly reach for the steaming mug of coffee Tally set on the table.

"Nothing official, but I believe it would not be premature to say that Darrin MacIntyre will never again experience life outside of a prison cell." Silas nods appreciatively and takes a sip of his coffee.

"As it should be," growls Jacob.

I lift my mug and get a nose full of whipped cream. I pull back and look down in confusion.

Tally smiles from across the restaurant and says, "Half coffee, half hot chocolate, topped with fresh whip. I thought you could use a little pampering."

I smile gratefully as I wipe the whip off my nose and come at the delicious smelling beverage from another angle. After I manage a couple sips, I give a big "thumbs up" to Tally. "Perfection."

She giggles and scurries to the orders-up window.

The rest of our wonderful, celebratory meal is spent discussing who was more awesome in our fight for our lives against Darrin.

As I lick the salt off my fingers, I say, "Obviously, the award goes to Pyewacket, hands down."

"Hands down," Jacob and Silas say in unison.

There's a beep, and Silas pulls his phone out of the pocket of his wrinkled brown suit.

I stare at the cell phone and smirk at my own private joke. For some reason I expected Silas to have a miniature rotary phone in his pocket, or maybe a Morse code thingy.

"Text from Sheriff Harper. Looks like they're ready for us." He slips the phone back in his pocket and slides out of the booth.

Jacob drops several crumpled bills on the table, and Silas lays a crisp twenty next to the pile.

We walk down to the station in anticipatory silence.

Jacob holds the door for Silas and me.

Sheriff Erick waits for us in the—area designated for such a purpose.

"Good afternoon," he says.

"Hey Erick." I grin.

His cheeks flush, but I can't tell if it's from irritation or embarrassment.

"How's Darrin's face?" I couldn't care less about that jerk's broken nose, but I enjoy bringing it up immensely.

Erick shakes his head. "He'll live."

"That's a shame," I retort.

"A real shame," echoes my dad.

The television and VHS player are set up in the station's small conference room.

I look around at the bland wood paneling and the chipped veneer on the table. I bet this room has seen some things. More than its share of donuts at the very least!

Jacob pulls out a faded blue chair for me and we settle in to watch the day his life turned to—crap.

Sheriff Erick dims the lights. "There's no audio."

We stare at the wiggly screen.

"Give it a second for the tracking to adjust," says Erick.

Whatever you say. Like I know anything about tracking.

The image stabilizes and I can see it's a small office. Nothing stands out in the black-and-white image.

The door, which is at the top of our screen, blasts open and a scared little man with thick glasses walks in with his hands up.

The dashing Darrin has a gun shoved in the guy's back.

My dad shift in his seat.

A young, handsome Jacob is next to appear in the pantomime on the screen. The guy in glasses points up at the camera and my dad aims—

The screen goes black.

My dad's shoulders slump. Silas turns to shake his head in our direction.

"There's more," says the sheriff.

The screen comes to life again with footage from a completely different angle. Looks like the store manager wasn't as stupid as Darrin assumed. And the security guard must've planned to blackmail him all along.

The new angle seems to be from a camera on the desk across from the safe.

Darrin shoves the manager down on the ground and holds the gun to the back of his head.

The manager shakes violently with fear.

We can't see the safe open, but we see zippered bank bags being handed up to Darrin.

The bags stop.

Darrin roughs up the manager, shoves him to the side, and looks into the safe.

Suddenly a large hand appears at the bottom of the screen.

It's hard to tell, but from this perspective it looks as though the manager might be reaching for the phone.

Darrin grabs something and the manager gets flung up against the safe.

"Close your eyes." There's no emotion in my dad's words.

I close them immediately.

Next to me, my dad flinches.

"Despicable," murmurs Silas.

"That tape and the evidence we found at Darrin's place will be more than enough to clear you of the murder charge, Jacob."

"Oh, and this." I take the black button bearing the fouled anchor from my pocket and set it on the table. "Pye brought it in from the alley. I swear I wasn't poking around. I didn't even know what it was until my dad mentioned Darrin's dishonorable discharge from the Navy."

Sheriff Erick looks at the button, picks it up, and shakes his head. "I'm not sure if you're lucky, talented, or diabolical."

"Can I be all three?" I smile as innocently as I know how.

My father interrupts our mutual admiration society. "You were saying—about the murder charge?"

Sheriff Harper nods and continues, "The conviction will be expunged from your record."

I turn to hug my dad, but I'm not prepared for the look on his face.

His eyes are red and his jaw is clenched tight.

I swallow hard. I don't know what to say. I can't begin to imagine how hard that must've been for him to watch. "I'm sorry you had to see that, Dad."

"That poor man. Why did he reach for that phone?" Dad slams his fist on the wobbly table. "Darrin was always overreacting."

Silas stands and places a firm hand on my dad's

shoulder. "It's in the past, Jacob. Your anger won't bring that man back."

I watch as my father's shoulders relax and his breathing calms.

I force a smile to my face. "Let's go see if Pyewacket needs some Fruity Puffs."

Jacob nods and follows me out of the station.

"I have no idea where the animal hospital is. Do you?"

Jacob looks down at me and a faraway mist fills his gaze. "I went there once with Cal. He hit a dog out on some back road. I can probably find it."

I fish the Mercedes keys out of my pocket. "My car's parked back by the bookshop."

"Don't tell your Grams you let me drive it." He chuckles as he takes the keys.

"Why not?"

"It was one of the many things that Isadora 'strictly forbade' when I was growing up." He spins the key chain around his finger. "The Mercedes."

I'm not sure I like the way he says that. I'm already hoping I won't regret this.

We arrive at the animal hospital in one piece. However, I'm going to enact Isadora's rules for all future car rides. My dad is what you'd call a "lead foot" and I'm sure he purposely took the longest route possible to the vet.

I take a couple deep breaths to settle my stomach and pop open the gull-wing door.

Dad walks around and offers me a hand. His face-splitting grin unnerves me.

I snatch the keys from his hand. "I'll be driving back."

For a moment he looks like an over-eager puppy. "Are you sure?"

"Positive." I walk into the stark white clinic and approach the über-modern reception desk.

A man with Tally's smile and Tilly's pouf of grey hair jumps to his feet. "Mitzy Moon, as I live and breathe!" He extends a hand.

I roll the dice. "Ledo?"

"Well now, they said you were sharp as a tack!" He grabs my hand and nearly shakes my arm off. "I bet you're here to see that brave kitty."

"Looks like I'm not the only one getting top marks today, Ledo."

Tally's brother's confusion transforms into amusement before my eyes. He swats me on the back and guffaws. "And sassy as a cucumber, too!"

Don't look at me. I had no idea vegetables could be sassy.

Ledo opens the door to a small recovery room. "The bullet grazed his scapula and punctured his lung—but the good news is that it missed the liver."

He sweeps his arm forward and smiles sympathetically. "You can stay as long as you like."

I whisper my thanks as I walk past and enter.

The sight of the large and powerful Pyewacket lying motionless on a tiny bed with tubes coming out of him and needles poking into him compresses my chest.

Jacob slips an arm around me. "It looks much worse than it is, sweetie. This morning the Doc here"—He gestures to Ledo—"told me they have to keep him sedated so he doesn't rip out his stitches."

Doc Ledo smiles reassuringly at us.

I stare at the friendly man who greeted us when we came in. Why is the veterinarian manning the front desk? No time to puzzle that out. I nod and smile.

"When can we take him home?" asks Jacob.

I can't make any words. I just stare at the bandages, and the images of that horrible night in the staircase replay, intercut with footage from that awful security tape.

"He'll have to stay at least until the weekend. We need to make sure there's no seepage."

At the word seepage, my full attention returns to the doctor. *Johnny Mnemonic*, starring Keanu Reeves, is one of my favorite movies of all time. Not a terribly popular choice with painfully poignant film-school students, but I like it. Seepage is one of the worst things that can happen in the movie. I cannot allow Pye to suffer any seepage.

"Can I stay with him?"

The doctor looks at me like I'm a little simple. "You want to stay here? At an animal hospital?"

For some reason the question offends me in my time of grief. I've seen women carry dogs in their purses. I can't be the first person who wanted to stay close to their beloved pet. "Yes. I'd like to stay in this room." I remember that I'm rich. "I'll have a cot brought in."

Jacob chuckles. "Sweetie, this isn't *Keeping up with the—*"

"I'm not leaving Pyewacket." I'm suddenly keenly aware of my attachment to this tan fur ball.

Doc Ledo nods politely. "I'm sure we can arrange something, Mitzy."

"I'm sure you can."

Ledo leaves without another word.

Jacob puts an arm around my shoulders. "Is the money going straight to your head?" He stifles a laugh.

"It might be," I admit as I blush.

He ruffles my hair as though I'm a six-year-old kid. "I don't deserve you."

I desperately attempt to repair my hairdo, before I remember how I rolled out of bed and went directly to breakfast. I must've looked like warmed-over death when Erick saw me. Oh brother!

"I need to follow up with Cal's lawyer. Is it all right if I leave you here?"

"How will you get back? We drove quite a ways to get here." I touch my dad's arm in concern.

He pats my hand. "It's only a couple blocks back to Main Street. I took the long way here."

"I knew it!" I punch him playfully on the arm.

He hugs me. "Can I escort you to the Pin Cherry Festival tonight?"

"Absolutely not." I shake my head and cross my arms. "I'm sitting right here next to Pye until he's released."

Jacob shrugs. "Your loss. Tonight's the pin cherry pie-eating contest. I won three years in a row —back in the day."

"Tragic." I roll my eyes.

He laughs and leaves me in the sterile little room with nothing but the beep of machines to break the silence.

I scratch Pye's head right between his ears. "You are the most irritating mammal in the universe, Pyewacket. And I think I love you."

I swear he purrs.

CHAPTER 30

I SPEND THREE days doting on my four-legged savior. Odell brings me sustenance, and Silas takes messages to Grams.

By Friday evening my dad has had his fill. "I know I'm twenty-one years too late, Mitzy, but I'm pulling the dad card. I'm escorting you to the closing ceremonies of the Pin Cherry Festival tonight and I won't take 'no' for an answer."

I open my mouth to protest.

He crosses his arms and pinches his nose. "And someone has to tell you the truth about how badly you need a shower."

I look down at my "Free Contradictions $1.00" tee and scrunch up my own nose. The truth hurts.

I scratch between Pye's tufted ears, lean over to him, and whisper, "I'll be back tomorrow. Don't do anything stupid—anything else stupid—before I get back."

His left front paw moves.

He's probably swatting a chunk of skin off my ankle in his drug-induced dream. Little adorable demon. I can see exactly why Grams spoiled him rotten. Looks like old Pyewacket has gotten himself another convert—perhaps I should say slave.

I look up at my dad's stubbornly crossed arms and exhale loudly. "All right, I'll go. I'm sure Grams would love to get me into another one of her vintage dresses."

I check out with Doc Ledo and make sure someone will be in the office on Saturday to let me in. Once Pyewacket's welfare has been secured, we drive back to the bookshop.

He gives me a quick hug. "I'll go get cleaned up and be back to pick you up around 6:30. Sound good?"

"What about dinner?" I haven't had anything since Odell's breakfast special was delivered to my bedside vigil.

"There's a large food court at the festival. I'm sure you'll find a variety of fried things to devour."

"Rude." I grin and shake my head. I like food. What can I say? One day when my metabolism slows down . . . I'll worry about that later.

Once I'm safely over the chain and ensconced

in the dream closet, Grams fusses over dress selection.

"No. Red is too on the nose." She swirls down the row again.

"You said that a half hour ago." I sink onto the antique bench in the middle of the small room. "I'm going to shower while you debate with yourself."

She barely acknowledges my exit. "Whatever you say, dear."

I have to wash my hair twice. Truth time, the shower was way overdue.

Back at closet headquarters, Grams has narrowed the selection down to five semi-finalists. I immediately rule out three of the options as too "foofy" for my current mood. I agree to try on the remaining two finalists.

I don't hate the flowy white dress, but I plan to eat at this festival. In the end, Grams and I agree on the black, cherry-sequined dress by Altuzarra. It definitely hits the theme on the head, and the dark background ensures that any drops of pin cherry will be camouflaged.

I attempt to recreate the sleek sophistication of my ladies' luncheon hairdo.

"It's a good effort, honey."

Ghosts! Who knew they were so opinionated.

I grab a pair of black chunky heels with a delicate ankle strap. I need a solid heel to walk around the festival grounds, but the single strap looks great with the embellished ruffle on the dress.

The intercom buzzes.

"Yes?"

My dad's voice comes through the speaker. "Ready?"

"Be right down."

I turn to Grams. "How do I look?"

"Gorgeous, smart. Maybe the sheriff will be there." She chuckles.

"Ha ha. I'm sure a lawman has better things to do than traipse around a fruit festival."

Grams nods fervently. "I'm sure you're right."

Her tone concerns me. I shake it off and hurry across the mezzanine.

As I circle down the staircase my dad lets out a low whistle. "Watch out, Pin Cherry! Mitzy Moon has arrived."

I blush. "Cut it out. You're my dad. You're supposed to be impressed."

He shakes his head. "If you don't spend most of the night dancing, I'll eat a pin cherry pie."

I laugh and hook my arm through his elbow. "That's not much of a compliment since I happen to know you can easily eat a pile of pies if there's a trophy at stake."

We take Dad's 1955 Ford F100 pickup. I take note that he drives his own vehicle at a calm, rational speed. I'm grateful to arrive at the fairgrounds without incident and breathing normally.

Even a big city girl like me has to admit that the festival looks magical. Edison lights hang in front of every booth as far as the eye can see, and the requisite cherry lights adorn hundreds of birch and pine along the border of the grounds.

A riff on "the gazebo" stands in the center of the fair. The six-sided structure is constructed from logs and resembles an old log cabin without walls.

A large, well-lit dance area wraps around the rotunda. I hope my dad is wrong about the dancing. Very wrong.

We make our way through the booths.

"Thanks for talking me into this, Dad. It's pretty fun."

His eyes widen in mock horror. "Just 'pretty fun?' I was thinking this could be my 'not a murderer' celebration. Seems like that should at least get a 'rad,' or whatever you kids are saying these days." The laughter lifts my spirits.

His mood is infectious and I hook my arm through his as I cheer, "Let's get turnt!"

He giggles like a schoolboy as he walks me toward a large pink-and-red canvas tent. "You have to try the deep-fried pin cherry ice cream," says Jacob.

I throw caution to the wind and give in to the dark side of cherry.

Cakes, cookies, relishes, sandwiches, smoothies, donuts . . . By the time I'm sipping my second red Solo Cup of pin cherry wine, I'm a dedicated fan of all things festive.

An older gentleman in a tuxedo with tails, and pin cherries adorning his top hat, steps up to the podium in the log-zebo.

"That's the mayor," whispers Jacob.

"Ladies and gentlemen, honored guests and dedicated residents, I'd like to invite Sheriff Harper to join me at the microphone.

Erick makes his way through the crowd, shaking hands and patting backs like a politician. As he climbs the steps, I nod. "Now there's a dessert I'd like to try."

Dad nudges me. "Mitzy, shhh."

All the color would drain from my face if my cheeks weren't artificially rosy from pin cherry wine. I honestly did not mean to say that out loud. I take a big sip of my wine and promise myself I'll blend in for the rest of the party.

While the sheriff explains the hallmarks of a Pin Cherry Festival Princess my attention wanders. Tilly and Tally stand across from me on the edge of the dance area.

They are cheering and clapping.

I catch their eye and wave.

They respond with frantically over-zealous waves. Then Tally points to the log-zebo.

It looks like she's gesturing for me to go up there. Does she know about my crush on the sheriff?

Jacob nudges me. "I'd get up there if I was you. It's worse if the Pin Cherry Patrol carries you on their shoulders."

Why is he laughing? And then I hear my name.

"Come on, Miss Moon." The sheriff waves me up to the stage. "Let's all give another round of applause to encourage our new Pin Cherry Festival Princess up to the mic."

Now the color truly does drain. Wine or no wine.

My own father gives me a firm push.

The crowd parts.

All sound vanishes from my world. The terror of this moment has me trapped in a slow-motion walk of shame.

Suddenly a cackle of delight breaks through.

The one and only Twiggy hoots and howls from her prime location right next to the steps.

I guess that answers the question of how my name got tossed into the hat for Pin Cherry Princess. Oh, my vengeance will be merciless.

The Pin Cherry Patrol swoops in and, before I can protect what's left of my dignity, I'm hoisted up on the shoulders of four burly high school boys and trucked up to the podium.

After they dump me unceremoniously on the dais, I stumble forward and suffer further embarrassment as Sheriff Erick grabs me around the waist to keep me from falling. Let the record show that he hesitates in removing his arm until well after I'm stabilized.

"Congratulations to Pin Cherry Harbor's newest resident and our new Princess!" The mayor slips a sash over my head to the thunderous cheers of the festivalgoers.

My face must be as red as a cherry.

"And now for the traditional dance. Take her for a spin, Sheriff." The mayor plops my hand into Erick's and shoves us toward the empty dance area.

I pinch myself mercilessly. If I can just wake up . . .

The sheriff leads me down the steps and spins me.

The shock of his dance skill snaps me out of wishing this was all a daydream. I count it a small mercy that I don't land on my backside.

Erick catches my hand in the nick of time and swirls me back into a "leave room for the holy spirit" respectable partners hold. "From murderer to princess in less than two weeks. What does the future hold for the indomitable Miss Moon?" His smile intrigues.

Time to get ahold of this thing. "I guess you'll have to stay tuned, Erick."

He grins and dips me.

The crowd goes wild. And a bunch of couples join in the dancing.

I nearly lose my sash.

He whips me upright and I can't help but notice the tiny beads of sweat on his brow. Oh, he plays the confident man about town, but it would seem that ol' Mitzy Moon still keeps him off balance.

The humble brag has no sooner formed in my mind than Erick catches that darn boot of his and we tumble onto the grass at the edge of the dance arena.

Once again, his Too Hot To Handle body breaks my fall.

Many hands scoop down and help us to our feet.

Lucky for me, Jacob is the first to grab my hand. He scoops an arm around me and shields me with his body. "Well, that was unfortunate." He chuckles.

"I'll say." I brush grass off my dress and smooth my hair. "I was just about to get the upper hand."

My dad laughs. "Come on, slugger. I'll get you a pin cherry brownie to make it all better."

I do not resist.

Silas stands next to the brownie booth and waves as we approach. "Ah, serendipity."

I shrug.

"I have news." He takes an unnecessarily large bite of his brownie.

Jacob gets two more, and the three of us head toward a park bench while Silas continues to chew.

He lifts the chocolate-cherry confection for another mouthful and I put up my hand. "Can we get the news?"

With regret in his eyes, he gently places the bar back on his napkin. "Kitty and Finnegan were arrested today."

I look at Jacob and raise my eyebrows.

He shakes his head.

"Don't keep us in suspense, Silas."

"Of course. Your tip about the fabricated charity led to an entire laundry list of charges. Not the least of which is her affair with Finnegan, which violates the fidelity clause in the pre-nuptial agreement she signed."

"Wait, I thought she said Finnegan was blackmailing her?"

Silas sneaks a small bite of his brownie and nods. "Oh, he was. He was entertaining the affair, commemorated it with photographs, and then blackmailed her when he found out about the pre-nup."

I chuckle. "No honor among thieves, I guess."

"Not that there ever was," my dad mumbles.

"Sorry, Dad."

"No worries. Not your fault." He shoves the rest of his treat into his mouth.

"I'm glad they won't be fleecing the town with another one of their fake Halloween balls." I clap my hands.

"Or inheriting," Silas adds.

My dad stops chewing. "Hmm?"

"Well, that trollop violated the pre-nup. In addition, Cal's attorney is in possession of the handwritten request for the alterations to the existing will, which she feels certain she can have declared valid as a holographic will."

I shake my head in confusion. "If it's a holograph, that means it doesn't actually exist, right?"

Silas shakes his head and his jowls wiggle in a way that my pin-cherry-wine-soaked brain finds hilarious.

He ignores my giggles. "Not with a will, Mitzy. A holographic will is a document written in the testator's own hand that serves as a legal last will and testament." He looks at my face and adds, "The testator in this case is Cal."

I smile and nod.

Jacob wipes the chocolate from the corner of his mouth and stares at Silas. "What does that mean?"

"Since Kitty is in no position to contest the holographic will, it means that you are Cal's rightful heir. As he intended."

Jacob chews the inside of his cheek and puts an arm around my shoulders. "And my daughter?"

"Mitzy will be the contingent beneficiary; again, per Cal's wishes."

I reach up and squeeze my dad's hand. "Does this mean you'll stay in town?"

"I don't know, Mitzy. I'd have to quit my job."

"Oh, sorry. I didn't realize—"

"You didn't let me finish. I'd have to quit my job delivering pizzas."

I look from him to Silas and back.

"Ex-con joke. Probably not the right crowd." He gives me a little hug. "I'll move to Pin Cherry on one—make that two—conditions."

"Which are?" I lean back and narrow my gaze.

"You promise to have breakfast with me every Sunday morning at Myrtle's Diner—"

"Done. What's the second?"

"You allow me the honor of purchasing all of Pyewacket's Fruity Puffs until he or I leave this earth."

Silas chuckles until his hound-dog cheeks turn red.

I hug my dad tightly, but selfishly find myself wishing one of his conditions had included another dance for Sheriff Erick and me.

Squad goals. A girl's gotta have goals.

End of Book 1

~ A NOTE FROM TRIXIE

Wow! Ten months ago I was outlining this book and wondering if anyone would ever get to meet Mitzy. But here we are!

One of the best parts of bringing Mitzy to life was the wonderful feedback from my early readers. Thank you to my alpha readers Angel, Michael, and Andrew. HUGE thanks to my fantastic beta readers who gave me extremely useful and honest feedback: Veronica McIntyre, Renee Arthur, Nadine Peterse-Vrijhof, and Lori Watson. And big hugs to the world's best ARC Team – Trixie's Mystery ARC Detectives!

Thank you to my brilliant editor Philip Newey! Some authors dread edits, but it was a pleasure to work with Philip, and I look forward to many more. Any errors are my own, as my outdated version of

Word insists on showing me only what it likes and when it feels so moved.

Google can give an author all kinds of helpful information, but there is absolutely no substitute for "straight from the horse's mouth." Thanks to my "horses!" John Girard, thank you for answering my inane questions about what it was like to be a correctional officer. Your insights gave the character of Jacob a great deal more authenticity. Morgan, thank you for giving me the straight talk I needed to add some edge to Odell's Army backstory and, of course, your firearms expertise will never go to waste. And finally, thank you to Josh for all the years you begged for a caracal! I was never as brave as Grams, but your passion for them sent me down the "rabbit hole" and once I learned all I could about the little beasts—I knew I had to have one—even if it lives only in my mind.

Now I'm writing book four in the Mitzy Moon Mysteries series, and I think I may just live in Pin Cherry Harbor forever. Mitzy, Grams, and Pyewacket continue to get into trouble in book two, *Tattoos and Clues*. But I'd have to say that book three, *Wings and Broken Things*, is when most readers say the series becomes unputdownable.

I hope you'll continue to hang out with us.

Trixie Silvertale (October 2019)

PARANORMAL COZY MYSTERY

Tattoos & Clues

TRIXIE SILVERTALE

Sittin' On A Goldmine Productions L.L.C.

CHAPTER 1

As I DRIFT between the luscious memory of dreams and the insistent arrival of reality, a large paw thwaps my forehead. A moment too late, I recognize the rough caress of my dearly departed grandmother's fiendish feline.

I roll my head to the left, but the lightning reflexes of the rescued caracal are a step ahead.

His fangs give my tender ear a nip.

My hands press against his tan fur to retaliate with a shove to the floor, but the thick scar behind his scapula fills my heart with forgiveness. He took a bullet for me—and my dad. I guess he can bite my earlobe.

It's still hard to believe how my life changed with the contents of one manila envelope. I went from poor orphaned barista, living in a run-down studio apartment in Sedona, Arizona to wealthy bookshop owner, with a father, in the quaint town of Pin Cherry Harbor. Plus I have this cat . . .

I scratch his head right between his black tufted ears, and his purring shakes the whole bed. "All right, Pyewacket, I'll feed you."

As I rise from the soft, fluffy pillow and push back the cozy down comforter, I can't protect my heart from the shock of what my sleepy grey eyes behold.

Let me assure you I'm not referring to the large caracal that slobbered in my ear.

Nope. Turns out, I'm not alone in my antique four-poster bed.

Next to me, painted in dappled autumn sunlight, lies a man.

This man is handsome. His hair is a tousled mess of buttery brown and his chin whispers of stubble. His T-shirt and jeans adorn my floor. His name is lost.

Pyewacket fixes me with a judgmental stare and casually cleans one of his tufted ears with a dangerously clawed paw.

This guy's name is somewhere in my rum-logged brain. Greg? Larry? Gilligan? Oh, come on, Moon! You certainly didn't bring the Skipper's little buddy home. "Gary!" I did not mean to shout that at the top of my lungs.

The man next to me rockets up and one hand dives beneath his pillow. "What happened?" he stammers in a husky voice.

I play coy. "What do you mean? Are you okay?"

He catches sight of Pye and hastily dives out of the bed. "What the—?"

"That is Pyewacket. He was my—" Before another word passes my lips, I search the air for any sign of my grandmother's strangely absent ghost. She probably didn't leave me a gorgeous three-story bookshop and this swanky apartment for one-night hookups with dockworkers I pick up at the Final Destination dive bar, but I'm still adjusting to small-town life in almost-Canada. "Pye was my late grandmother's cat."

He shakes his head and keeps his stare fixed on the caracal as he backs toward his pile of clothes. "That ain't no cat. That's a lion." Gary dresses faster than any fling in recent memory and looks around the room in confusion. "How the heck did we get in here?"

Pyewacket leaps off the bed with an effortless push of his powerful hind legs and looks toward the secret door.

I still don't sense the otherworldly presence of Grams anywhere. Bonus points for me if I can keep it that way. "Don't worry. I have to feed the cat. I'll show you out."

As I slip out of bed, Pye crouches low and slinks toward the already shaky Gary.

He fumbles around in his pockets and scans the floor.

"Did you lose something?" I ask, nonchalantly.

A low growl emanates from Pyewacket, and Gray backs away as he replies, "Yeah, I can't find my . . . phone." His eyes dart and his fists clench.

Even my pickled brain can pick up on the fact that he's lying. To be clear, it could be my gift of clairsentience functioning despite my hangover, but I barely know what the word means—let alone how the gift technically works.

Glancing down to make sure my bits are covered, I laugh at the phrase on my oversized tee. "I Drink and I Know Things." One thing I clearly don't know is when to stop drinking. I fluff my extra-messy, snow-white hair and shuffle toward the hidden exit.

Gary follows me hesitantly toward the wall, which I know is a secret door from my apartment to the bookshop. Unfortunately, the sexy-but-not-too-bright Gary is confused by the lack of a traditional door—and also terrified that my giant cat is going to eat him.

He looks left and right. "Hey man, joke's over. Let me outta here, okay? Last night was great. You're great. I'll call you—"

Gary is a delicious conundrum. The typical fare of my previous life in Arizona, and a leftover bad habit in a new town. He is hunky, muscular, tall-ish, and jerk-adjacent. I will not let this bad decision escape without amusing myself. "Just say my name and you'll be out in a flash."

The utter blankness of his stare would be comical if it weren't so insulting.

"Courtney?" he whispers.

"Not even close," I mumble as I walk toward my fully stocked walk-in closet.

He shouts a series of equally incorrect names at my back.

I enter the closet, jump at the glowering stare of my hovering Grams, and grab what I need.

"We'll be discussing this later, young lady," Isadora announces as she crosses her bejeweled limbs over her vintage Marchesa silk-and-tulle burial gown.

Fortunately, I'm the only one who is tuned into her ghostly frequency.

I return to the main room to find that Pye has my "rando" cornered and there are little beads of perspiration on Gary's full upper lip.

"I'm going to have to put this blindfold on you, Gary. I hope you understand." As I approach, he bristles.

"No way. No way are you putting that thing on me." He squares his shoulders and clenches his jaw.

I step closer to the ready-to-pounce Pye and coo softly, "This guy doesn't want you to get your breakfast. What do you think about that?"

The magnificent Pyewacket arches his back, raises his hackles, and replies, "RE-OW!"

Pretending to shudder, I say, "Oh, that does not sound good Gary." I ponder my next move when—

A stern voice crackles over the intercom. "I saw a strange van parked outside, Mitzy. I'm comin' up."

I've never been so happy to hear my father's voice. Well, maybe *never* is too strong a word since we haven't known each other that long, but I'm extremely pleased at his over-protective instincts right now.

The secret wall/door slides open and the menacing frame of my six-foot-and-change ex-con father, topped with a shock of white-blonde hair like my own, fills the large gap. "You know this guy?" snarls Jacob.

I shrug. "He was just leaving. Pye and I were having a little fun." I dangle the blindfold.

My dad, quick to read a room, doesn't miss a beat. "You get dressed. I'll take out the trash."

He grabs Gary by the scruff of the neck and steers him out of the apartment.

"HISS." Pyewacket wishes Gary a hasty retreat.

"Eyes front," growls my dad.

Gary whimpers.

Rapid footfalls descend the iron spiral staircase to the first floor and the heavy metal door leading into the alley slams shut with finality.

A smug grin spreads from ear to ear as I turn to search for my jeans.

"Not so fast, hussy."

Uh oh. Ghost-ma is on the rampage.

"And give me one good reason I shouldn't be angry with you, Mizithra Achelois Moon."

"We agreed that you wouldn't read my thoughts, Grams." It's a feeble comeback.

"Well, let's also agree that all bets are off when you bring men of questionable motives into our sanctuary!"

I open my mouth to protest, but she has a solid point.

"You have hundreds of rare books in that store, priceless family heirlooms in this apartment, and, most importantly—your precious heart." A ghostly tear trickles down her timeless face.

"You couldn't be more right. I wasn't thinking straight. I was feeling sorry for myself because there's nothing to do and I went to that stupid bar next to the train depot . . . I drank too much rum."

"I know a way to stop that." Grams crosses her arms and arches a perfectly drawn brow.

"Just because you were in AA, Grams, doesn't mean everyone is an alcoholic."

"We're not talking about everyone, Mitzy. We're talking about you." Grams freeze-frames for a moment and vanishes.

"Grams? Grams, don't leave like that."

Jacob re-enters in time to hear my last words. "You and Mom fighting?" he asks.

"She's upset that I brought that guy back here and thinks I should go to AA."

He sighs and shakes his head. "She's not wrong."

"What? You think I'm an alcoholic, too?"

He walks toward me and opens his arms. "I'm in no position to judge you, sweetie, but that guy was hiding something. No decent guy drives around in a van with a bed in the back and 'Waterbeds Unlimited' emblazoned on the side."

Unsavory images of last night's drunken escapades dance through my mind. I shiver and slip into my dad's waiting hug. But before I can make any apologies or promises, Grams materializes beside the bed and says a single word that turns my blood to ice.

"Gun."

My whole body stiffens.

Jacob leans back. "What's wrong?"

I keep forgetting I'm the only one who can see

and hear my dearly departed matriarch. "Grams is over there." I gesture to the left side of the bed, between the heavily draped six-by-six windows and the tiger-maple nightstand. "She said 'gun.'"

Jacob's arms fall to his sides and he walks toward the ghost he can't see. "Ask her where."

Grams points to the left finial. "It's under the bed. Between this post and the wall."

"Behind the left leg," I relay.

My dad drops to the floor, shimmies under the bed, and stands up holding a black pistol. He drops it on the bed and uses the edge of a sheet to wipe it clean.

"Dad?"

"Sorry," he whispers. "Force of habit."

I walk to the bed and glance down at the firearm. "That's not mine."

"Probably safe to assume it's Gary's."

"He was definitely looking for something this morning, and it wasn't seconds." I'm a heartbeat too late in realizing that this is not the audience for that joke. But as I recall the way Gary's hand dove under his pillow—

Ghost-ma gasps.

Another thoughtless intrusion into my private musings.

Dad is stoic.

"He works down at the docks. It's probably for protection," I offer lamely.

"It's definitely for protection, Mitzy. But what does he need protection from in Pin Cherry Harbor?" Jacob shakes his head and adds, "The only gang around here is Ethel and her bingo gals down at the Elks' Lodge."

Grams chuckles in spite of the tension.

I glance at the gun and suspicions flood my hungover brain.

Grams clears her throat.

I put up a hand and shake my head. "Dad, I need to get dressed—"

"Ree-ow." A gentle reminder.

"And feed Pye. Why don't I meet you at the diner in twenty minutes and we can discuss Gary and that gun." I gesture to the pistol.

Jacob steps away from the weapon and nods slowly. "When you hand that off to the sheriff, don't mention my name."

"Of course."

He hurries out without a backward glance. Shoulders hunched. Jaw clenched.

"See you in a few," I call as the bookcase door slides shut.

I rub my forehead and stumble to the bathroom. Placing two hands on the marble vanity, I stare into the antique mirror. Things may be strange, but they could be worse. When I did a runner on my previous life and took "Dante's" bus from Arizona to a place north of north, I wasn't exactly leaving a success story in my wake.

"Ree-OW!" A warning punctuated by a threat.

Time to feed the beast, or risk losing a finger.

A firm push of the small decorative plaster panel above the intercom opens the secret door from my apartment to reveal the second floor of my bookshop. I walk out onto the Rare Books mezzanine and Pye whips past, knocking me sideways in his haste to get downstairs.

Sliding my hand down the wrought-iron railing to keep myself upright, I circle down the spiral staircase to the thick carpet on the main floor.

Pye wraps himself between my feet in figure eights as soon as I reach the back room. "It's happening. Simmer down." I grab a bowl and dump a large portion of Fruity Puffs into the vessel.

Pye lifts up on his hind legs and nearly tips the bowl from my hands with his thick skull.

"Here. Here." I set the bowl down and step away. I made the mistake of attempting a friendly scratch on the back during his breakfast—once.

I push "brew" on the coffeemaker and plunk myself into a straight-backed wooden chair.

"Any plans today, dear?"

I gasp and exhale loudly. "Myrtle Isadora Johnson Linder Duncan Willamet Rogers!"

Grams giggles.

Her ghost is tethered to my bookshop, the Bell, Book & Candle, and she makes a habit of scaring the bejeezus out of me with unannounced pop-ins.

"I'll do the sparkly fade-in thing next time. I promise." She clutches at her strings of pearls and curtsies elegantly in her gown.

"You're too much." I pour my java, bravely add some past-the-expiration-date cream, and return to my slumped posture in the chair.

Pye sits back and begins his morning ritual of paw, face, and whisker cleaning, which reminds me it's been a few days since my last shower.

"Ghosts can't smell, sweetie."

I roll my eyes in exasperation. "Grams, my lips have to be moving, all right?"

"Of course. It's so easy to get confused, you know. Everything comes through on the same wavelength and it seems as though it is out loud, so—"

I point a firm finger toward my lips.

"Yes, dear, I'll watch for moving lips." She swirls toward Pyewacket and runs her ghost fingers along his back.

His tufted ears twist like cat satellite dishes, but he's growing accustomed to these energetic exchanges and he purrs softly.

"Time to get dressed and head down to the diner. Dad won't wait too long for breakfast." No sooner do I rise from the chair than Pye prowls over to the metal door leading to the alleyway and rakes his claws down the well-scratched paint.

"He wants to go out." Grams smiles at the creature that used to belong to her and nods like a proud parent.

When I open the door, he drops his rump firmly on my foot and does not budge.

"In or out, Pye?" A crisp autumn wind whistles through the cracked opening.

He is still as a stone statue.

"Come on, Pye. I need to go get human breakfast." I shiver uncontrollably.

He appears to have grown roots into the floor.

I let the door slam shut. "Suit yourself."

Leaving him to his stubbornness, I walk back to the elegant circular staircase.

Tan fur flies past me, and Pye takes up a defensive stance on the fourth stair.

"Uh, Grams? What the heck is going on?"

"Well, I used to take him for walks along the lakeshore. He probably wants you to go outside with him."

"A cat who needs a walker?" I put a foot on the bottom step.

Pye growls softly.

"Pye if I take you for a short walk, will you let me go and get breakfast?"

He shakes his hackles down and prances up the stairs.

I wag my head and approach the wall-mounted candle that must be tipped down to activate the mechanism which slides open the bookcase revealing my plush apartment.

Grams vanishes into the wall and I catch up to her in the glorious *Sex and the City* meets *Shopaholics* closet, which is larger than my entire previous crappy apartment.

"There's a whole section of lovely yoga pants, leggings, and tank tops over there." Grams points to a series of built-in drawers.

I open a drawer to reveal more fashionable workout gear than I could wear in a year—if I actually worked out. I pull out random pieces and admire them. "Grams, you were sixty-five when you died, and you said that you'd been ill for over a year, right?"

"That's right, dear. It was hard on Odell, but he was by my side until the end."

My question has nothing to do with her laundry list of ex-husbands. "What I'm getting at is the hip-factor in this closet. I get the vintage couture—you had money and you bought whatever you liked, but this drawer full of too-hot-for-Bikrams workout gear doesn't seem like your style."

A ghostly giggle flutters through the hallowed fabrics.

I look up and give my Ghost-ma a suspicious glare.

"Truth time?" she asks.

"We say, 'keepin' it a 100.' But whatever you want to call it, this closet just became your confessional." Hands on hips, I wait.

"When I told my lawyer that I wanted to change my will and leave everything to you, he encouraged me to buy you all the gifts I'd wanted to give you during those years your father forbade the family from contacting you—when he thought you were better off not knowing about him."

My arms slip to my sides. "You mean grumpy old Silas Willoughby told you to buy indulgent presents for a granddaughter you'd never meet?" I could not picture that hound-dog-cheeked man encouraging such extravagance.

She shrugs and floats to the far corner near the floor-to-ceiling shoe racks.

"Grams?"

"Well, after he'd been reading in one of the books about a way to keep a soul from crossing over . . ." She nods and grins sheepishly.

"So you're well and truly stuck here? It's not one of those unfinished-business kind of things?"

"I'm pretty sure I can stay forever, dear. Are you upset with me?"

"Upset? Are you kidding? I spent the last ten years thinking I was an orphan, and now I have a grandmother—and a dad."

"REE-ow!" The sound of imminent retribution.

"Oh, dear! You best take Pyewacket on that walk before he does something drastic."

I quickly don a pair of seriously punk-rock pocket leggings, a side-cinch tank, and a thick hooded cardigan. I fire off a quick text to my dad and force my phone into the tight little pocket on the thigh.

Grams swirls toward a pair of lightweight hiking shoes . . . and before Pye can cause me any harm, I'm ready.

This time when I open the side door into the alley, a blur of tawny fur and black tufts shoots past me without hesitation.

A brisk wind blows across the lake and howls between the buildings as I hurry toward the low wall that dead ends the backstreet.

Pye leaps five or six feet in the air, heaves his powerful back legs against the dumpster, and sails over the wall with ease.

I kick, push, and struggle to lift myself up and over the four-foot barrier.

Once I brush off the debris and straighten my sweater I catch the flash of sunlight, dancing across the waves. I have to remind myself that I'm looking at a massive freshwater lake and not an ocean, but the way the surf is crashing on the shore, that's a tough sell.

Pye is deftly leaping from one boulder to the next and heading toward a raised rocky outcrop.

I zip up against the stiff breeze and add a plucky little pep to my step with a jog toward the promontory. The terrain dips down before it rises back up to the berm that separates the sand and rocks from the dune grass. As I crest the hill, the muscular Pyewacket is crouched low, inching over the boulders in extreme stealth mode.

By the power of Grayskull! I do not want to see a rabbit or seabird murdered before my breakfast. I run toward the fiend making as much noise as possible. "Run little bunny or whatever you are! Flee before death becomes you!" I flap my arms and create a general nuisance of myself.

Pye freezes and only the tip of his oddly short tail twitches.

I rush up behind him, screech to a halt, and throw up a little bit in my mouth.

CHAPTER 2

Spinning away from the horrible sight, I wiggle my hands in the "oh that is ookey" dance while gulping in fresh air. My insides turn cold, I can't lift my arms, and my stomach is performing a pre-heave churn.

As I struggle and fail to extract my phone from the overly snug pocket on the leggings, movement on the road catches my eye. Hooray! A patrol car cruising along First Avenue.

It takes all of my strength to force my arms into the air. I wave my hands helplessly and jump up and down.

Tires screech.

Lights flash.

A car door slams.

My eyes widen and my tummy tingles—in the

yummy way. If this were one of my student films, I'd tell the camera operator to push-in and get every detail of this arrival.

Sheriff Erick Harper walks toward me in the finest pair of well-worn blue jeans I've ever inspected. And I am inspecting the crap out of these.

He waves.

I close my gaping jaw and try not to stare at the T-shirt that is straining to contain his well-defined pecs under a brown leather bomber jacket.

He smooths back his loose blonde bangs and nods. "What's going on, Moon? Why'd you wave me down?"

Oh, right. The thing . . .

Pye chooses that moment to growl fiercely.

"Hey, I told your grandmother and I'll tell you the same, you can't have that wild critter running loose. You have to put him on a leash."

Unable to contain my scoff, I reply, "Pyewacket? On a leash? You can't be even a little bit serious, Erick?"

"I've asked you to call me Sheriff Harper, Miss Moon." He smiles a little, but tilts his head as though he's scolding a small child.

Which instantly triggers my intense dislike of condescension. "How's that workin' out for ya?"

He shakes his head and walks toward me. "Now, what's this all about?"

I cover my mouth with one hand and gesture to the rocks with the other.

He looks back and forth. "These rocks? I know they look a bit strange, but the locals call this Boilerplate Beach because of the way the water shaped—"

"Not the rocks! That!" I interrupt his geology lesson and make an "up and over" motion to indicate something on the other side of the rocks.

He climbs higher and looks down.

His hand goes for his radio. But he's in civilian clothes—such lovely, perfect civilian clothes—and there is no radio.

"Maybe call it in from the car?" I suggest.

He turns and eyes me in a way that is both insulting and also arousing.

"You're not going to accuse me of murder again are you?" I stick my hands on my hips.

He shakes his head. "You do seem to be some kind of magnet for corpses."

"Rude!"

He chuckles. "Why don't you tell me how you managed to find this one?"

His smile kinda melts my insides.

"I'll grab my notebook from the car. Don't go anywhere, all right?"

"Yes, Sheriff. I promise not to leave town." I roll my eyes for emphasis, in case he misses the sarcasm.

He takes off in a quick jog, and a grin slinks

across my face as I forget all about feeling insulted. When he returns, I tell my tale. But we'll skip ahead since you were there.

". . . So I walked up to see what Pye was stalking and—" I cover my mouth and shiver. "It's soggy, and swollen, and maybe a little scorched?" There is definitely something roiling violently in my gut.

"That'll do, Moon. Definitely looks like a drowning, but I can't account for the burning you ment—" He closes his note pad and leans toward me. "You all right?"

His concern is swoon-worthy. Or maybe I'm—

Strong arms catch me and guide me down the hill, away from the "finding."

Pyewacket growls once before he leaps from the mound and races back toward the bookshop.

"Coward," I mumble.

Erick pats my shoulder mechanically. "You're no coward, Miss Moon. I did two tours in Afghanistan and I've been in law enforcement for almost six years—still unsettles me."

The deep emotion in his voice, combined with his physical nearness, threatens to topple me a second time. "I'm fine. I just haven't eaten any breakfast."

"I'd drop you at Myrtle's Diner, but I have to wait for the medical examiner. Is there someone you can call?"

After ten years spent believing I was an orphan, my knee-jerk thought is "no." But I'm not an orphan. I have a dad. A living, breathing father. "I can call my dad," I say with a foolish grin.

Erick nods.

The industrial-strength fabric of the stretchy yoga pants refuses to cooperate and no matter how hard I battle, I can't seem to extract my phone.

A low chuckle fills the early-morning quiet. "I'll call him."

Before I can respond, Erick phones Jacob and tattles on me.

I wave my hand frantically. "Give me the phone."

His eyes twinkle as he passes it over with a warning, "Make it short. This is an active crime scene."

My eyelids squeeze to slits and I glare. "Yes, Sheriff." I snatch the phone. "Dad? Yeah, totally fine. I just found the thing wedged in the . . . I don't want to talk about it . . . No, I can walk . . . Sure. Ten minutes sounds great . . . All right. Bye" I pass the mobile back to Erick.

With the cell in one hand, he helps me to my feet with the other. "Are you sure you can make it to the diner?"

The wooziness is gone. Irritation is quickly replacing it. "I felt a little light-headed, I'm not a basket case."

He raises his hands in surrender and backs away. "I'm sure you understand the importance of keeping a lid on this ongoing investigation, right?"

I tilt my head and purse my lips. "You know this town better than me, Erick. Tally will probably tell me about this before I can place my order."

Pumping up the stern official-ness of his gaze, he adds, "I'd appreciate it if you don't pour fuel on the fire."

A sudden thought strikes. "You grew up around here, right? I mean, you pretty much know everyone. Did you recognize—it? Wasn't there a tattoo on the arm?" My brain is calling up the image my tummy does not want to review.

He grins. "You better get to breakfast, Miss Moon. And I recommend you leave this to the professionals. Understood?"

I nod in a completely noncommittal way and hurry off toward the diner. I can be very professional. He'll see.

The sight of Myrtle's Diner warms my heart and shifts my restless stomach to a more acceptable rumble of hunger. As I push open the door, Jacob slides out of the booth and meets me in two large strides.

Strong arms encircle me, and my father's reassuring voice whispers, "It's a little odd to hear your voice on Erick's phone—first thing in the morning. If I hadn't just ushered Gary out of your place, I might think there's something you're not telling me about your relationship with Sheriff Harper." He chuckles.

Basking in the moment of parental concern, I allow myself to entertain the idea. The truth? I wish there was something I wasn't telling him. Sadly my unrequited longing for Sheriff Too Hot To Handle is still the best-kept secret in Pin Cherry Harbor. And trust me, keeping a secret in this podunk town is a real feat!

I hardly have a chance to slide my eighty-eight percent polyester covered bottom into the booth before Tally sets a mug of steaming-hot coffee on the table.

"Morning, Mitzy." She smiles and nods.

"Good morning, Tally. How's your daughter?" I slip my hands around the ample mug.

Tally bobs her head a few times but her flame-red bun remains firmly perched on top of her head. "Well, she's right as rain and twice as welcome. I don't know how I'd make it through the weekend rushes without her."

"Good to hear. We'll have two specials." I smile as the older woman scurries off to the kitchen, and I glance back toward the cook.

Odell Johnson, my grandmother's first husband, gives me a friendly salute with his spatula through the orders-up window.

Dad slides the sugar toward me and I push it straight back. "Cream only."

He smiles and chuckles. "I'll add that to 'doesn't share fries.' I'm learning all your secrets." He returns the sugar to the wire holder at the end of the table and fixes me with a fatherly stare. "So, what happened out at Boilerplate this morning?"

I shake my head sternly. "Not only was I warned to keep my mouth shut by our bossy local sheriff—and there's nothing going on there, by the way—but I also do not want to talk about that on an empty stomach." My tummy twirls in warning.

Jacob leans back against the red vinyl-covered bench seat. "Maybe you should move out to the estate with me. You seem to attract trouble, and I'd like to be able to take better care of you." He breaks eye contact. "Make up for lost time, you know?"

Both of us wish we could get back the years he spent in prison and all the years before that, when he didn't know I existed. But all we have is now. My mom had a one-night stand, she ended up pregnant and never told the guy—cut to Grams' Last Will and Testament and me escaping my old life to unexpectedly find a family in Pin Cherry.

The phone on the wall rings and disrupts my reverie.

Jacob stiffens and lays both hands flat against the silver-flecked white table. He exhales slowly through his nose.

My super senses spark, and I feel Jacob's fear as strongly as if it were my own. "What's wrong, Dad?"

"Bells. Alarms." He leans back and sighs. "It's a prison thing."

I nod and sense the emotion fade. But the lull is short lived.

Tally answers and mumbles, "Right away." She looks at me as she hangs the receiver in the cradle.

My chest constricts.

She disappears into the back and reappears followed by the sheriff. Tally shakes her head and rushes out of the kitchen, looking pale and worried.

I can't tear my eyes from the silent movie playing out through the orders-up window.

Erick approaches Odell at the griddle and puts a hand on his shoulder.

Odell turns toward the visitor and his lined face transforms from crusty, old diner-owner to broken-hearted man in the space of thirty seconds. He steps away from the cooktop, nods to the sheriff, and takes a moment to collect himself as Erick slips out the back exit.

I'm frozen in mid-sip of coffee when Odell turns and locks eyes with me.

Pain grips his face and his eyes glisten with unshed tears. He swallows and walks out of the kitchen in a straight line toward our table.

I set my cup down. He knows the victim. I recognize that anguish on his face, or do I feel it in my bones? It's the same ache that gripped me for years after the news of my mother's fatal accident was delivered by my babysitter. "Can I get you—?"

Tally hands him the glass of water I gladly would've retrieved.

He waves it away and places both hands on the edge of our worn table. "I'm going to need your help, Mitzy."

"Of course. I'll do whatever I can, but what do you need?"

"That body you found—" His voice breaks and he lifts a hand to keep us quiet while he struggles for composure. "That was my little brother."

CHAPTER 3

My father and I exchange pained glances and fall silent as Odell explains how the medical examiner used to book private guided fishing tours on one of Walt's boats every summer. "He knew it was Walt as soon as he saw the tattoo."

"The mermaid?"

Odell stiffens and mumbles, "You saw it?"

"Only for a second. Then I flagged down the police car." I reach out and place my hand tentatively on top of Odell's fist, hardened by decades of work. "I'm so sorry. I'm so very sorry." I glance up at my father.

Jacob shakes his head. "Walter was a good man, Odell. He'll be missed."

I pat the gnarled knuckles and add, "I wish I could've known him. What can I do, Odell?"

He swallows once and coughs to clear his throat. “Walt had some struggles these last few years. Sheriff says they’re treating this as suspicious circumstances but they haven’t ruled out suicide.” He gestures toward my father. “You found evidence the cops missed on his case, so I figure I’d get you to poke around and see who done Walt in—”

“I’m no—”

Odell again lifts his hand to shush me. “Walt was a lot of things, but he ain’t the type to kill himself. Somebody is gonna pay for this, and I’m bettin’ you’re my best shot at getting to the truth.”

I look at my dad, back to Odell and shrug. “So, you’re hiring me?”

A hint of a smile tugs at the corner of Odell’s downturned mouth. “I already got you on the ‘free burgers for life’ plan. I was hoping you’d consider that a down payment.”

I squeeze his hand. “Of course. I’d do it for free. I’m just making sure I have my story straight for Erick. I mean, Sheriff Harper.”

Odell and Jacob exchange a glance I don’t appreciate.

“What?” I force my face into a mask of innocence. “He told me to leave it to the professionals, so—”

“Professionals,” my dad says with a scoff. “Lotta good that did me.”

Tally nudges Odell out of the way and lays two plates on the table. Mine contains scrambled eggs with chorizo and jalapeños, a heap of home fries, and one strip of bacon. Jacob's "special" consists of two massive blueberry pancakes and four sausages.

Odell inspects the order and nods his approval.

I still don't understand how he knows exactly what folks want for breakfast, but I suppose after running a diner for nearly half a century, some things are second nature.

"I'll let you dig in, but come round later and I'll fill you in about Walt." He raps his knuckles on the table and returns to the kitchen.

Jacob and I eat in silence. With grub this good in front of me, I tend to stay focused.

I finally set my fork down and lean back.

My dad wipes a little syrup from the corner of his mouth and grins. "I don't want you getting yourself into any hot water with the sheriff."

An image of Erick and me lounging in a hot tub flashes through my mind. I imagine what his chiseled chest must look like under that tight tee he wore this morning.

"A father might be concerned about a smirk like that."

I wipe all expression from my face. Somehow I had allowed the lascivious grin to slip from my mind to my mouth. Oops. "I'm always in trouble with the law around here. Seems they don't like outsiders or newcomers."

My dad raises one eyebrow. "Trust me, they're not real fond of convicts-come-home either."

My dad robbed a big box store and did some hard time. There, we've got that out of the way. He's reformed and we're figuring out how to build some kind of relationship after twenty-one years of my life spent thinking he either hated me or might be dead.

He pushes his plate back. "I have a meeting with Cal's attorney. I guess she's actually my attorney now . . ."

A quiet sadness settles over him and he sips the last of his coffee.

"I'm sorry you didn't get a chance to talk things over with your father before he was—before he passed away." I stumble over the polite way to discuss my grandfather's murder and sigh in frustration.

A hopeful light brightens Jacob's grey eyes. "Maybe he'll become a ghost like Isadora?"

"According to Grams, that's not how it works. But what do I know? I have exactly one case study to draw from."

He nods. "I'll catch up with you later. You'll be at the bookshop?" He slides out of the booth.

"Yeah, Twiggy wants to go over inventory, then

I'm back here to meet with Odell, but we could grab supper somewhere."

"Why don't you come out to the estate and we'll take the boat over to Chez Osprey before they close the island for the season."

"Sounds fancy."

"Is that a bad thing?" Jacob tilts his head.

I shrug. "I'm not used to fancy. Back in Sedona I reused my coffee grounds until the filter ripped or the brew looked like weak tea. I took a mostly cold shower three times a week and washed my clothes by hand in the bathroom sink."

He chuckles. "Preaching to the choir, Mitzy. I might've been raised with money, but after Cal cut me off and I ended up in prison . . . Well, coming back into all this is kinda throwing me off balance. But I don't want to take you out there because it's fancy. I want to show you the Osprey because it was your grandmother's favorite place. Not just the restaurant—the island was special to her."

I reach into my pocket to pay the bill, but my dad beats me to the punch and lays a fifty dollar bill on the table. I open my mouth to protest.

"I have a lot of father-daughter moments to make up for, honey. Let's agree that you'll never pay for a meal in my presence. Give your old man that much, all right."

"All right." I stretch out the hem of my tank top

and feign a curtsy. "What time should I be at the manse?"

"Manse?" Jacob screws up his face in confusion.

"Short for mansion."

No response.

"I was just trying it out."

He laughs. "Come out as early as you can. That way we can take our time out on the lake."

"I'll try, but Grams will want me to get all dolled up. You know she filled a closet with clothes for me before she even knew me?"

A pained expression washes over my dad's face. "It was selfish of me to forbid the family from contacting you. I thought your life would be better without a convict dad, but Isadora and Cal would've done right by you." He sighs. "I can't go back in time, but I'll do my best to make it up to you."

"All we have is today, right?"

"Right." He puts a strong arm around my shoulders and gives me a squeeze. "See you later—at the manse." His strong shoulders shake with laughter as he exits the diner.

CHAPTER 4

Walking back down Main Street, toward the bookshop, I soak in the view of the sun-drenched great lake. How much longer can this gorgeous autumn weather hold? The locals always talk about the storm of 19-something-or-other and the blizzard of 20-something and I'm worried a former Arizona girl might not survive in sub-zero temps.

I'm also not looking forward to this inventory thing, but Twiggy was Grams' best friend and she works for the entertainment—not the money—so she isn't someone I want to annoy.

She orders supplies, gets the "drawer money" for the register from the bank each day, and seeks out rare tomes from all over the world to add to our collection.

Since I know absolutely nothing about running

my own bookstore and can barely navigate around the place, if Twiggy calls a meeting, I attend.

The large, intricately carved wooden door is unlocked when I arrive. Twiggy must've let herself in the side door. As far as I know, I possess the only key to the one-of-a-kind front door, but she and my dad have keys to the side entrance. I pull the chain out from under my shirt and smile as the sunlight bounces off my special key's well-worn brass surface. A weighty triangle barrel with teeth on all sides.

For a moment, I step back and study the door. A centaur chasing a maiden through delicate woodland. A faun playing a flute for a family of rabbits dancing around his cloven feet. The shadow of a winged horse passing in front of the moon. A wildcat stalking a small boy.

I kneel to get a better look at the cat. It has tufted ears and a short tail like Pyewacket. Pressing my face closer, I swear the feline has the same scratches above its left eye, but that would be too—

The heavy door swings open and knocks me to my ample behind. "Geez Louise!" I press a hand to my throbbing forehead.

Twiggy's cackle fills the street.

This would be the "entertainment" I mentioned earlier. My clumsiness provides her endless amusement.

"Just wearing the clothes ain't gonna make you more coordinated." Twiggy gestures to my yoga attire.

"I was looking at the door. That cat— Oh, never mind." I stand, brush the dust off my rear, and march inside.

"You gonna wear that getup for inventory?" Twiggy hooks a thumb through the belt loop of her dungarees, shakes her helmet of grey hair, and chuckles.

The breeze is all but gone, and I feel sweat in places I'd rather not mention, but I won't let her win. "Yep. I'm wearing it all day."

"Suit yourself, doll." She stomps past me with her usual bull-in-china-shop grace and retrieves a clipboard.

I reach for it.

She swishes it back. "No siree. You climb. I write."

"Fine. Where do we start?"

She sizes me up and shakes her head. "Well, I don't want to send you up a ladder right outta the gate." She walks toward an area beneath the Rare Books Loft.

I follow.

"We'll start you off in children's literature." She points to a long, low bookcase behind a row of rainbow-colored benches festooned with stuffed animals.

Refusing to acknowledge the insult to my dexterity, I plop down on the floor and slide out the first book on the shelf. "What do you need to know?"

"How much room is left?"

Bewilderment scrunches my face. "What? Don't you need the title or the author or a code?"

"Nah. The computer tracks all of that when I scan 'em in and out. I need to know how much room is left on that shelf, so when I go to the estate sale on Thursday, I can buy accordingly."

With extreme precision, I push the book back onto the shelf. I stand, straighten my tank top, and take a deep breath. "I'm sure you find this 'hazing the new kid' shtick amusing, but I have a murder to solve. So, if you're done pulling my leg, I'll be going."

Her face pales and her skin prickles as Grams races through Twiggy and floats directly in front of my face.

"What happened? Who died?"

Before I can answer, Twiggy whispers, "Is she here?"

"Yes," I reply and gesture to Grams' general location. "As for the murder, I'll tell you both together. This morning when I took Pye for a walk, he discovered a body on the lakeshore."

Twiggy and the ghost ask in unison, "Who?"

"Erick slipped in the back of the diner and broke the news to Odell while Dad and I were eating breakfast. It was Walter Johnson, and they think it's probably suicide."

"Not in a million years," cries Grams.

"Odell asked me to look into it."

Twiggy remains uncharacteristically silent.

Grams covers her mouth with a ring-ensconced hand. "Oh, Twiggy, I'm so sorry."

I look back and forth from the ghost to her former best friend.

"Tell her, Mitzy. She can't hear me." Grams urges me to pass along the condolences.

"Grams says she's sorry to hear about Walt." A moment of clarity hits me. "Did you know Walt?"

Twiggy remains still as a statue.

Grams swirls closer to her old friend, but looks back at me. "Rumor was that they were engaged back when I was off partying with my second husband, Max Linder. Walt had a run in with the law and he headed up to Canada—"

"He didn't come back?" I ask.

Twiggy's eyes attempt to focus on me.

Grams shakes her ghostly head. "Nope. Poor Twiggy. You know, after Max was killed in the accident, I came back injured and alone. She was my only friend. She's the one who convinced me to attend AA meetings—saved my life." Grams' eyes sparkle wistfully. "Prolonged it, at the very least."

I wave my hands to get her attention and ask the question another way. "What about Walt?"

"He got a girl pregnant up in Canada. He did the right thing by her, but he and Twiggy never spoke again."

As I stare at Twiggy's no-nonsense exterior, there's a split second where the wounded woman underneath the armor is exposed.

"Give her a hug or something, Mitzy." Grams swirls around Twiggy and manages to do nothing more than give the traumatized woman a severe case of the chills.

I step closer and give Twiggy's back a clumsy pat.

She flinches and looks at the floor. "I'll handle inventory. You get over to the diner and talk to Odell." She chokes out a ragged exhale and stomps off to the back room.

I look to Grams. "Are you sure she'll be all right? Maybe I should stay?"

Grams waves me off. "Twiggy's a tough old broad. She's been making her own way for decades. The best thing is to let her be. No sense digging up hurts that she's buried so carefully."

I shrug. So much for sharing the burden.

Grams raises a finger to respond.

I point to my lips and shake my head, but add, "I get it. Let sleeping dogs lie."

At the word "dogs" a low menacing growl emanates from Pye. He peeks down from his perch atop the half-wall separating the children's section from the rest of the bookshop. One golden eye shames me for uttering such blasphemy.

"You better get over to the diner, honey."

"Copy that." I walk toward the front door but pause when I recall my supper plans with my dad. "And you better get started on an outfit for tonight." I smile as Grams eagerly floats my way.

"What's the occasion?" She's terrible at concealing her glee.

"Dad said he wants to take me to Chez Osprey before they close for the season."

The anticipation slips from her face and is quickly replaced with longing. "I thought I squeezed every last drop from life, but I'd give up all my designer gowns for one more trip out to that island."

Desperate to lighten the mood, I chime in with, "Ahem, those are my gowns now, Missy. And I'll thank you to keep them safely in their closet heaven!"

She snaps out of her mood and chuckles. "Oh Mitzy, you're such a card!"

CHAPTER 5

The weather has taken a sudden turn for the worse, and I break into a jog as a foreboding wind knifes across the lake and into my skin.

I fight the whistling fury of the gusts to pry open the door.

All eyes turn as I blow into the diner.

I rake my fingers through my wild, white-blonde locks and rush to a booth.

Odell catches my eye through the orders-up window and the hot oil sizzles as he drops down a basket of fries.

The booth behind me empties and I glance around. A couple of tourons (my clever compound word for tourist-morons) taking selfies or foodies or whatever in the corner, and three locals bellied up to the counter are all that remain.

Odell brings out a plate of golden crisp beauties and slides onto the bench seat opposite. "You want some?"

I stare longingly at the plate of perfectly cooked french fries. "I'm still digesting that delicious breakfast."

Half of a grin tugs at the corner of his mouth. "I can eat and talk."

Despite my verbal protest my hand seems to have a mind of its own as it reaches for a golden beauty.

He doesn't touch the fries, but instead straightens the little white tubs of fruit preserves in their plastic display case as he talks. "My dad died in a hunting accident when we were kids. My mom did the best she could, but Walt was always a handful. When the cancer took her fifteen years ago . . . Well, Walt took it real hard."

Why did that number sound so familiar? Fifteen? I look at the tattered, unused cigarette poking out of Odell's shirt pocket behind his apron strap. Oh right, he quit smoking fifteen years ago. Coincidence? I think not.

"I did my best to keep tabs on him, but he's a grown man. What could I do?"

It feels like a rhetorical question, so I refrain from answering and steal another fry.

Odell takes all the packets of jam out of the

little holder and sorts them by flavor. "He ran a pretty decent bed and breakfast out on Osprey Island and then he expanded into boat tours—the chartered fishing trips I mentioned. I thought he was doin' all right."

I nod to indicate I'm following the timeline.

All the strawberry packets go in one stack. "Then we had that dry summer. The fishing was poor and the tourist traffic dwindled, and of course, winter came early and stayed late. About six or seven months ago, a big fire destroyed his lodge out on Osprey . . ." Odell's voice fades out and he looks out the front window.

I swallow as quietly as possible and softly ask, "Did he have insurance?"

His fist comes down hard on the table, sending the tower of orange marmalades skittering.

I slide the jellies back toward his side of the table, nod encouragingly, and slip a fry into my mouth despite the stares from other patrons.

"No insurance. What's worse is that he used the inn as collateral for the whole boating business. What a mess." Odell takes a precision trimmed thumbnail to an imaginary stain on the squeaky-clean table for a moment before he resumes stacking the packets.

"Did he have to sell the boats?"

He fixes me with his intelligent coffee-brown

eyes and shakes his head. "That right there—" he gestures to me "—that's the kind of thinking that would've saved Walt's life."

I take that to mean Walt did not sell the boats and I wait for further information.

"He came to me for money." Odell swings his arm wide to include the whole diner. "It might look fancy, but most months this place is farther in the red than I'd like."

I make a mental note to ask Grams how I can use my newfound wealth to help Odell without insulting him.

"Once I turned him down he worked his way down the food chain." He rubs a hand across his lined face and exhales. "I can only imagine the kind of 'help' he uncovered." Odell presses both palms against the worn edge of the table and leans back.

I wipe my mouth with a thin paper napkin and wait an extra beat. This is the point in the movie when there's always one last sliver of crucial information. No such tidbit drops, so I ask the obvious question. "You think he took money from a loan shark?" I have no idea if that's a real-world term, but I've heard it uttered by many an actor.

"Some kind of predatory lending, no doubt." He shakes his head and looks down, no longer interested in fruited-jam segregation.

"But why would they kill him? Seems like it'd

be harder to collect the vig." I don't even have time to pat myself on the back for my stellar *Get Shorty* reference before Odell knocks me down a peg.

"Who are you? Don Corleone?" He slides out of the booth. "Look, I don't want you puttin' yourself in any danger. Just see if Silas can get a copy of the medical examiner's report and I'll take it from there."

"You bet. If the ME says murder, then I'll have a little chat with Erick." I smile too eagerly.

In spite of his ill humor, Odell's mouth turns up on one side. "I'm sure you meant to say, Sheriff Harper. And I'll be the one having that chat, Mitzy."

"Of course," I lie. It's only a little white lie though. What's a tiny fib between friends?

Odell shakes his head and returns to the heat of the kitchen.

I bus my own table and slide my plate into the dish bin behind the counter. "See ya tomorrow," I call as I exit Myrtle's Diner. I best take this opportunity to walk over to the Piggly Wiggly and get a box of Fruity Puffs and a pack of toilet paper before Grams entangles me in the lengthy process of "dressing for dinner." Except they call it supper around here—supper and pop. I grin as I walk.

Straight down Main Street to 4th. The ancient blue-and-yellow sign bears a mere hint of its original vivid coloring. I enter to the now familiar "bing-bong" and the solitary cashier turns and gives me the "locals" nod. My first few visits were met with a rapid and shockingly perky "Welcome to the Pin Cherry Piggly Wiggly. What can I help you find?" Now that she's established my resident status, I receive the far less off-putting nod. We're both relieved.

I grab a four-pack of toilet tissue and make my way to the cereal aisle. Unfortunately my simple journey is interrupted when I reach the endcap and come face-to-dangerously-straight-part with an unwelcome greeting.

"Figures you'd be the one to find his body," snipes the short and stout Deputy Paulsen.

I chew the inside of my cheek while I search for an appropriate response.

Her pudgy little hand caresses the grip of her firearm with an unnerving sense of anticipation.

I can't seem to find a reason to stifle the response that is creeping toward the tip of my tongue.

She juts her chin up at me like a schoolyard bully.

And out it tumbles. "Maybe if I keep doing your job, Erick will make me an honorary deputy." I smile tightly to conceal my utter glee.

Rage seethes in her dark eyes and her knuckles whiten as she clenches her pistol grip. She sputters and spits before she manages to snarl out her response. "Sheriff Harper knows what you're up to, punk."

Every "p" and "t" in her retort spritzes me with a mist of spittle. I pointedly wipe the spray from my face. "Enjoy your shopping, Pauly." I slip past her and allow myself a silent giggle as I strut toward the breakfast foods.

She sputters something incoherent in my wake.

As soon as I turn the corner and get out of her line of sight, I break into a run and snag a box of Fruity Puffs as I race past. Olympic relay teams would be hard pressed to master such a smooth transaction. My only goal is to make it to the register and exit the store before Deputy Paulsen can think of an actual comeback.

I am one stride from the end of the aisle and I shift my weight to take the corner at maximum speed.

How could I have known there would be an "Early Thanksgiving" display of canned pumpkin—?

I hit the tower of canned goods at top speed.

Tumbling horribly as cans sail across the grocery store like confetti from a cannon.

I manage to control my slide and protect my face. As I push up to all fours, a familiar voice delivers the *coup de grâce.*

"Ya dropped something, *deputy.*" Paulsen's derisive laughter echoes off the metal ceiling and bounces up from the worn linoleum.

A pack of toilet paper and a box of Fruity Puffs hit the floor near my head.

I do not look up.

The laughter continues until the scrape of a door silences the mockery.

I collect my shopping and limp to the register.

"Clean up at the pumpkin castle," crackles over the loud speaker. The clerk looks at me as though I set out to intentionally storm her vegetable ramparts. She clacks the handset back on the hook and chomps her gum.

I set my two items on the belt.

She stares at me and chomps several more times.

I slide the items closer.

She doesn't move a finger. "That'll be thirty bucks."

I open my mouth to protest, but honestly that "fine" seems fair. I fish the money from my pocket and set it on the belt.

She does not offer a bag.

I take my shopping, dispense the customary nod, and hobble out.

CHAPTER 6

My return journey down Main Street is less a victory lap and more a walk of shame. My knee throbs from the embarrassing incident at the Piggly Wiggly and the frigid air bites into my skin, adding insult to injury.

To distract myself from the discomfort, I run through what little I know about the body I unluckily discovered.

Walt Johnson's death is most likely related to his money troubles. But in a town like Pin Cherry Harbor, I can't picture a loan shark capable of murder. I'm going to have to extend my search radius.

If Walt were as desperate as Odell says, then he would've cast his net far and wide to get himself out of a tight spot. I could see if my Ghost-ma knows anything about a possible seedy side of Pin Cherry or the surrounding communities.

But for now, I'll focus all my energy on icing and elevating my swelling knee, and eventually getting ready for dinner with my dad.

That's something I never dreamed I'd hear myself say. Dinner with my dad!

After my mom died, I used to create all kinds of fantasies that would involve me tracking down my dad or my dad finding me . . . but the common thread was always the happily-ever-after for a super unhappy child.

My actual meeting with him turned out very different from any fantasy scenario, but I couldn't be happier to have him in my life.

The cold wind sends me into a spasm of uncontrollable shivers. I shuffle-limp as fast as I can and pull open the massive carved door leading into my bookshop. Grams is waiting for me.

Despite my physical pain, I at least have my wits about me enough to look around for customers before I start babbling to my resident ghost. "I had a little accident at the grocery store."

"Oh, dear, did someone attack you?"

"No, nothing that exciting. I was trying to avoid Deputy Paulsen and instead took out a massive display of canned pumpkin!"

Ghostly laughter fills the bookshop.

"It's not funny."

"Let's see what we can do about that knee. Grab some ice from the back room and toss it in a plastic bag. You should elevate it for at least twenty minutes, but then we'll have to start evaluating your fashion options for supper!"

After collecting the ice as instructed and shelving the Fruity Puffs, I stumble toward the circular staircase and slowly pull myself up to the Rare Books Loft. I squeeze my four-pack of toilet paper under one arm and place the bag of ice in that hand, while I pull the secret candle handle with the other. The bookcase slides open with satisfying mystery and I limp into my apartment.

Grams is already in the apartment, "Sit down. Sit down. Put your leg up. I'll keep working on options." Her aura seems to glow as she swirls around and vanishes through the wall, into the closet.

I fluff the pillows on the four-poster bed and place two behind my head and two under my leg. After I manage to balance the bag of ice on my throbbing knee, I sink back into the cloud of comfort. A heaviness settles onto my eyelids and I am all too aware of last night's lack of sleep.

The happy sound of Grams arguing with herself over colors and fabrics transports me to dreamland. My vivid naptime fantasies include a world where Sheriff Harper returns my affections and

Walt is miraculously resuscitated so he and Odell can repair their relationship before it's too late—

"...too late! Mitzy, you have to wake up. You're sleeping too late!" The keyed-up voice of my Ghost-ma penetrates the fog of my glorious siesta.

"I'm up! I'm up!" I'm not actually up, but I shout my irritated-to-be-awakened response and rub the sleep from my eyes. The bag of ice on my knee has turned to tepid water and has a slow leak in one corner. I hoist my leg up and push the pillows out of the way so I can stumble to the bathroom and pour the rest of the "bag water" down the drain.

"Finally," she mumbles as she drifts back into the walk-in.

After I lower myself on the padded mahogany bench in the center of the closet and get my leg situated comfortably, I gesture for Grams to hit me with the details.

"Well, dear, I tried to pick something practical since you'll have to walk down the wooden dock, climb into a boat, ride across the windy lake, and climb out on the other side."

The dress she selected is lovely, curvy, and snug. I'm happy to note that there won't be any wind blowing up my skirt. She also selected a sensible yet stylish kitten-heel that flares out at the base. And if I know my grams, that flare is exactly too wide to slip between the planks on the dock. "You thought of everything."

"Like I said, dear, Chez Osprey is one of my favorite places. I made countless trips during my healthy years in Pin Cherry. I hope you and Jacob have a memorable evening."

"Thanks Grams." My stomach growls rudely. "I think I'm going to text Dad and see if we can do an early dinner, or supper. All this knee cracking nonsense made me miss lunch." I fire off a quick text and Jacob replies that he is more than happy to meet up sooner. He even offers to come to me to give me, but he puts "Grams" in brackets, time to get ready. I chuckle as I set down my phone and return my focus to my primary mission. "Anything I should know about the island?"

"Well, I haven't been for some time. That is, before I died. Obviously, I haven't been since."

"Obviously." I nod for her to continue.

"But in its heyday, Osprey Island was a magnificent oasis. A beautiful inn, five-star restaurant, and gorgeous hiking trails through pine-and-birch-covered hills." Grams shakes her head. "Near the end, I heard rumors that things had shifted a bit. There were a couple of new establishments on the island and some of them were run by less than reputable owners."

"Did you ever go to Walt's place?"

Grams takes a minute before she answers. Her gaze is serious. "Odell warned me to stay away from Walt's place. He was worried his brother would try to shake me down for cash."

"Did he?"

"What do you mean, dear?" The innocence in her ethereal eyes makes her look twenty-five. Which is about ten years younger than her chosen "ghost age" of thirty-five.

"I don't know everything about you, Grams, but I've learned enough to know that you seldom do as you're told. So, when you went to Walt's place, did he ask for money?"

Grams clutches one of her many strands of pearls and giggles. "Oh Mitzy, you know me better than you think. Walt's place was no Chez Osprey, but it was a nice place for families and hunters. His Canadian wife had left him to raise his daughter on his own and the sight of the little girl's poorly fitting clothes broke my heart. I told him I couldn't give him a loan, but I offered to pay for clothes for little Diane, and the gas to get her across the lake to school on a regular basis."

"Did you ever check and see if he actually used the money for the daughter?"

Guilt flickers across her face. "I was busy with the bookshop."

We wordlessly agree to shelve that conversation

and I get ready for my outing with Jacob in relative silence.

However, when the intercom buzzes, I feel completely unprepared despite the fact that I picked the earlier time. I mean, I'm technically ready, but I feel like a girl getting ready for her first father-daughter dance. I press the mother-of-pearl inlaid button and say, "Come on up." Anxiety pushes my voice an octave higher, but I force myself to plunk down on the overstuffed settee and wait patiently.

The hidden bookcase door slowly slides open and Jacob Duncan makes his entrance.

Grams gasps. "Oh, my handsome boy."

"Dad, you look amazing. Where did you get a suit?"

"My wardrobe does consist of more than prison coveralls, Mitzy."

At first I feel terrible for my thoughtless comment, but then I catch the sparkle of mischief in my dad's eyes. "You got me," I concede.

He chuckles. "Good thing we saved you a drive out to the estate. I remember how long it used to take my mother to get ready—"

Jacob's skin prickles as Grams swirls around him in protest.

"I don't think she appreciated that remark." I point to his goosebumps.

"Why don't you get them?" he asks.

"I'm no paranormal expert, but I've always been able to see her and communicate with her . . . Maybe it's different for me."

His eyes search the air and come up empty. "Well, wherever you are Mom, thanks for bringin' Mitzy into my life."

Ghostly tears spring to her eyes and she gushes, "Oh my! Tell him how much I love him, Mitzy."

I relay the message and smile warmly at my dad.

He takes an awkward breath and blinks back his emotion. "What are we waiting for? Let's get down to the docks and head out on the lake."

I wink at my Ghost-ma. "Bye, Grams."

"Have fun, dear." Her eyes hold equal parts joy and sadness.

When we reach the slip where Dad parked the Duncan yacht, the docks and Final Destination are bustling with workers and patrons, but I'm happy to report no sign of Gary. The wind picks up and the waves on the lake turn rough and choppy. Before I have a chance to shiver, my father slips off his suit coat and drapes it over my shoulders. "Thanks, Dad."

"Happy to do it sweetheart."

The warmth created as my heart swells with love is more powerful than any insulating effect of the woolen suit coat. He helps me board the yacht and we weigh anchor for Osprey Island.

The lake is frightening and powerful this close-up, not quite the "fun" I had anticipated. The waves are massive and my stomach churns.

"I suppose I should've told you to take some motion-sickness pills," says Jacob.

"You'd think it would've been something that over-prepared Grams might have mentioned."

"Try to focus your eyes straight ahead and imagine you're riding a horse." My dad looks at me and shrugs. "Whenever Cal took me out on the lake, he used that analogy to help calm my stomach."

"So you're telling me motion sickness is hereditary?"

"Sorry." He grins sheepishly.

I attempt to implement my father's suggestion. However, I haven't ridden a horse since fourth-grade summer camp. The violent chopping of the waves and the wholly unsteady feeling under my feet is nothing like my faint memories of equine adventures.

By the time we reach the docks at the foot of the impressive Chez Osprey, my stomach is in full protest.

"You are definitely a shade of green," he says.

I nod and clamp my lips together. I refuse to

throw up in front of all the patrons of a fancy restaurant, or worse, stain my grandmother's cobalt-blue vintage couture.

Jacob disembarks first and offers me a hand. He steadies me as we walk down the long wooden dock and offers me a seat on an ornate carved bench tucked under a massive pine tree. "Let's just sit here a minute on *terra firma* and let your stomach settle. What do you say?"

"That sounds fantastic." I gaze over the frightful grey waters where several smaller boats in a tight group race across the angry waves. "They don't seem to be suffering any setbacks from the weather."

"I don't imagine weather or anything else gets in the way of guys like that."

I pull my gaze from the lake and stare at my father's clenched jaw. "What do you mean?"

He shakes his head.

"Seriously, Dad. What are you saying?"

A hardness sets into the planes of his face and he speaks without emotion. "That larger boat in the center is carrying contraband. The two boats on either side carry gunners and cell-jamming equipment. Redundancy is key. The boat in the rear watches the radar. They have to remain in a tight formation to appear as a single vessel. If anything comes within their safety ring, they go silent and shoot to kill." He exhales and looks at the crushed granite beneath the bench.

My chest tightens and I'm desperate to diffuse the horrible prison memories that must be rolling through my dad's head. I choose one of my classics: gallows humor. "So you think the Canadian syrup lords are bringing in some hot maple?"

He turns and his angry scowl melts into shock and finally amusement. "Somethin' like that." He chuckles again and pats my knee. "We better get in there before they give our table away."

I glance around at the "no one" queuing up and gingerly rise to a shaky, but standing, position. "Let's do this."

Jacob offers me his elbow and we walk up the steps toward an impressive split-rock entrance punctuated by thick pine double doors.

Before he can reach the handle, the door opens and a young man dressed like Daniel Boone, complete with raccoon-tail cap, waves us inside. "Welcome to Chez Osprey. The finest vittles in the north."

"Thank you," I say.

"The Maiden of the Lake will seat you."

The Native American headdress with a single—I'm assuming, osprey—feather and the buckskin shift must be the most politically incorrect restaurant uniform in the history of ever, but at least the girl looks to be of native descent. I'm actually not sure if that makes it better or worse.

"Welcome to Chez Osprey and Fish-Hawk, the sacred island of the Anishinaabe. I hope you will enjoy the food of my people." She picks up two menus and walks toward the dining room. Her warm-brown moccasins make a light swish across the polished wooden floor.

Jacob and I follow. The click-clack of my heels seems disrespectful. A few early-bird diners look up, but most ignore my entrance.

"Water from the island's spring will be served. Can I get you a birch beer or the wine list?"

I shrug and nod toward my father.

"Bring us two birch beers and some bannock."

She smiles and slips away.

A strange silence hangs in the air and I catch Jacob staring out the window with a pained expression tightening his jaw.

"So you used to come out here with Cal and Isadora, I mean, Grams?"

His eyes are slow to focus on my face and his mouth hangs open for a moment before he responds. "The last time was when they celebrated my high school graduation." He takes his napkin and lays it in his lap.

A server dressed in black trousers and a long-sleeved black button-down fills our water glasses and departs.

Jacob looks at my eyes, but I don't feel as though he sees me.

"I felt invincible that day. Cal made a grand gesture and promised to buy me any car I wanted if I kept my GPA at 3.5 or above for my entire freshmen year at college. Isadora shed a few tears and gave a water-glass toast that got the attention of the entire restaurant. The owner came out and offered Cal an expensive bottle of champagne from his private reserve."

"But Grams is an—"

"Oh, I know the drill, Mitzy. Isadora went to meetings every week and Cal would tag along at least once a month. Reminders were given, sobriety chips were displayed . . . The owner begged our pardon."

"Did it embarrass you that Grams was an alcoholic?"

"Who knows what motivates a spoiled rich kid, eh? As soon as the big showy supper ended, my buddy Darrin picked me up and we drank a case of Hamm's down at the cove and nearly drown taking a drunk skinny dip."

I wasn't sure which part of this rattlesnake to grab. "Are you an alcoholic?"

"Me?" Jacob's eye's narrowed and he shook his

head slowly. "Nope. I got zero excuses for my behavior."

I felt bad for Grams and I snapped, "Alcoholism isn't an excuse. It's a disease."

He finally surfaced from his dive into memory pond and nodded his agreement. "I get that now, but as a kid it was harder to be objective."

The birch beers and bannock arrive. The distraction sends me down a self-reflective spiral.

That tunnel vision of childhood was all too familiar. As a young orphan, I had convinced myself that Jacob had abandoned my mom and me. While in reality, she could've called him anytime but chose not to drag her one-night-stand into unplanned fatherhood. Dreams of a father desperately searching for me had kept an eleven-year-old girl from giving up on life. Truth is a double-edged sword. Now that I know the rest of the story, it's up to me to build a relationship with my dad.

I work a dense yet flavorful bite of bannock around and wash it down with a tentative sip of clear birch beer. The crisp earthy flavor with its whisper of mint is a pleasant surprise. I set my glass on the table and catch my dad watching me wistfully. "Did you know Walt Johnson?" I ask.

Jacob grins. "You're a big fan of left field, aren't you?"

"I wanted to change the subject and that body

just loomed up in my mind. I've been told that I don't have a social filter."

"What's that supposed to mean?"

"Back in Sedona my friends frequently referred to me as Loose Lips, or sometimes just Cake Hole, because I also enjoy dessert. Not relevant, but I was always the one in the group that would ask the outrageous questions or proposition guys way out of my—"

Jacob holds up a hand for me to stop. "I'm not sure I want to hear this unsavory story about my baby girl." He chuckles, shakes his head, and takes a long drink of his water.

I mentally slap myself on the forehead. What a stupid thing to say to my dad. My cheeks are flushed and I gulp some water in hopes of cooling my skin.

He graciously changes the subject. "I don't remember much about Walt. I knew he was Odell's brother and I probably heard Isadora mention him once or twice, but we never went to the lodge, or even to that side of the island. I don't think Cal liked her to have anything to do with the Johnson men."

"Makes sense." However, I had learned a slightly different version of history. "Would it surprise you to learn that Grams did visit Walt's place and even gave him money for his daughter's clothes and education?"

Jacob raises one eyebrow. "It shouldn't. That woman never listened to anyone." He smiles appreciatively. "You're very much like her."

I furrow my brow. "Thanks. I think."

CHAPTER 7

The remainder of dinner is all business—the eating business. The Maiden of the Lake and her cohorts do not disappoint. Locally harvested onion and mushroom soup, wild rice, venison loin stuffed with blueberry and watercress, and a sumptuous dessert of acorn flour crepes with braised crab apples in maple syrup.

Despite my slightly distended abdomen, I'm not quite satisfied. "Dad?"

Jacob takes a sip of his roasted chicory "coffee" and grins. "I'm beginning to recognize that tone, and it sounds like I'm about to be wrapped around your little finger." He sighs and leans back in his plush leather chair.

"Do we have time to visit Walt's place on the island?"

He nods, wipes his mouth, and places his napkin on the table. "Let me see if the Duncan name can get me a quad or a couple horses. Not that you're dressed for either, but if you want to see the charred ruins of a dead man's dream—who am I to say no?"

"Thanks, Dad." I smile gratefully, but the idea of bouncing along on a four-wheel bucket of bolts or a four-legged bag of bones does not delight.

Jacob returns with a spring in his step. "Turns out Cal and Nimkii were lifelong hunting buddies. He was looking for a way to pay his respects, so supper is on the house and he'll have two mustangs saddled and waiting out front in about fifteen minutes." He places a small pottery mug in front of me. "He also gave me this snakeroot tea for you, to help prevent motion sickness on the trip back. If you drink it now, he said it should kick in by the time we get back on the boat."

"Snakeroot?" Wrinkling up my nose, I take a tentative sip. The peppery-ginger flavor is pleasing, so I down the whole cup, before standing and tugging my fitted dress down. "Maybe this was a bad idea . . ."

"You can ride side saddle," offers Jacob. "Nimkii said it's a short, easy ride. We'll be back before dark."

Dark. I hadn't even considered the perils of

being in the wild northern woods in kitten heels after sunset! The Arizona desert has scorpions, rattlesnakes, tarantulas, and javelina, but the thought of coming across a moose or a bear causes an involuntary shiver.

"Are you cold?" Jacob leans toward me with concern.

I shake my head, look down at the floor, and mumble, "Bears?"

He laughs a little too long and puts a reassuring hand on my shoulder. "Too far south for the polar variety and I don't know many black bears that can swim this far out."

I huff my annoyance and walk toward the entrance.

"Daniel Boone" appears from a side hall and scurries to open the front door.

I nod and display a half-smile.

Jacob stops and gives the guy a big handshake. "My daughter and I are going for a quick ride over to the old Walleye Lodge and Tavern. If we're not back by sunset, you get your rifle and come find us." He slips a wad of bills into the young man's hand and pats him on the shoulder.

The boy looks down at the veritable fortune in his fist and enthuses, "Yes, sir. I don't have a rifle, sir, but I'll bring Mr. Nimkii. He's a deadeye shot."

"Thanks." Jacob nods and follows me out the door.

I lean in and whisper toward his ear, "Should I be worried?"

"Not at all. I never had to work as a kid. Cal and Isadora spoiled me. I was just looking for an excuse to pass along my good fortune since I inherited my father's estate."

I smile with pride. "That was really nice, Dad."

"I'm full of philanthropic generosity. I have Cal's, I should say, my lawyer working on a legal defense fund for wrongly accused prisoners and a job placement resource, too. I know I joke about how tough things were after I got out—but it's no joke. Not many businesses wanna hire a felon."

I nod, but can't begin to understand the true price of my father's wayward choices.

The clickety-clacking of horseshoes on the wide flagstone path heralds the arrival of a youthful stable hand and our two mounts. A large red horse with a flowing mane and a spirited gate, and a smaller, tan, more subdued equine with short dark spikes of hair down its neck follow the kid.

"I'll take the tan one," I call.

My father chuckles. "When discussing horse-flesh that color is called roan, and the large mare is chestnut."

I scowl. "Fine. I'll ride the *roan* mare."

"Starlight is a male, a gelding," the boy announces. "He's real gentle."

I fume silently. So I'm not a horse expert, but I'm not an idiot. I'd like to see one of these two make a half-caff, skinny, caramel macchiato without any help.

Jacob walks over and pats the chestnut mare on the head. "What's her name?"

"That's Cranberry," the helpful lad answers.

My dad boosts me up and I take a shaky perch on Starlight while he whips his leg up and over Cranberry's back like Wyatt Earp.

The stable hand gives our horses a little swat on the rear ends and Jacob and I begin our adventure. It only takes me a couple of minutes to realize that riding sidesaddle is my only option in this tight-fitting ensemble. I hike up my dress and hook my knee over the saddle horn. From what little I recall, this is acceptable horsemanship. Most of my bare, left thigh is exposed, but at this point I don't really care about decorum, I just want to keep from falling on my backside in the middle of the woods.

"How you doing back there, Mitzy?"

I take a moment before I answer. "I'm hanging in there."

Jacob chuckles. "You want to pick up the pace?"

"That's a hard pass." I exhale loudly to indicate my utter lack of amusement.

The sun filtering through the dense pine-and-birch forest is mesmerizing. I lose track of time and slip into a daze. I completely understand why Grams loves this place. There is only the wind fluttering through the leaves and the soft thud of horses' hooves on the well-worn trail.

"Did you hear anything from Silas regarding the medical examiner's report?" asks Jacob.

I nearly lose my tenuous hold and slide right off my saddle from the shock of the voice piercing my trance. Once I regain my balance and let my heart beat return to a normal rate, I reply, "Nothing yet. But don't you think it's strange there wasn't any gossip in town about an explosion or some kind of fire?"

"I do."

The tone in my father's voice indicates so much more than agreement. "So you think Odell is right? You think someone killed Walt?"

"Not sure. It's not like Walt and I were close. And as you know, I only recently got back to town myself."

I didn't want to intrude on the beauty of this island forest with a heart-to-heart discussion about my dad's time in prison. I return the discussion to Walt. "Maybe we'll find something in the ruins that will help us figure out what happened to him."

Jacob responds by pulling back on his reins and uttering a commanding "whoa." He dismounts with grace and skill.

I attempt to follow suit, but experience less success with Starlight. He tosses his head frantically and sidesteps. I slip back and forth on the saddle and have to drop the reins to grab hold with both hands and prevent a fall.

Jacob grasps my horse's bridle and whispers a few calming words. He wraps both sets of reins around a low tree branch and helps me dismount.

As we give the horses a wide berth, the remains of the Walleye Lodge and Tavern spread out before us. I am surprised to see a small travel trailer parked beside the charred carcass.

Jacob puts a hand on my arm and we both hesitate.

"Hello? Hello? Anybody home?" says Jacob.

No response.

We approach the trailer and Jacob knocks firmly, but not threateningly, on the small door.

It does not open.

Before I can mention that I might have heard a clicking sound, my father shoves me firmly away from the door and puts his body between the trailer and me.

"Hey, it's Jacob Duncan. Not a looky-loo. Not the sheriff. We were friends of Walt's. My mom, Isadora Duncan, used to be married to Odell. We don't want any trouble."

He backs farther and farther away from the trailer, pushing me behind him as he speaks.

The door to the trailer swings open and the menacing double barrel of a shotgun appears followed by the determined face of the young woman whose finger covers the trigger.

Her coal-black eyes scan Jacob up and down. She leans left to get a glimpse of me in my hiked up dress and kitten heels, and chuckles. "So you finally got out of the big house, eh Jacob?"

My dad nods solemnly. "That's right. And this is my daughter, Mitzy." He steps to the side and I peek around his large shoulder.

"I'm Diane. Walt's kid." She lowers the gun, but she doesn't set it down. "If you're looking for my dad, he left on a fishing trip a few days ago, and I don't expect him back until day after tomorrow, eh."

I squeeze my hand around my dad's arm and suck in my breath. She doesn't know. We are going to have to figure out how—

"Diane, I hate to be the one to tell you, but he won't be coming home." Jacob's voice cracks a little when he says "home."

Her hand tightens around the barrel of the gun

and it shakes a little. "What'd you mean?" She smooths her sleek black hair back from her high cheekbones and the nostrils of her proud nose flare slightly.

"The sheriff found a body washed up on Boilerplate Beach this morning. I'm sorry to say the tattoos identified him as Walt Johnson. I'm sorry for your loss, Diane."

"What are you talking about? No one called me. I think if—my dad was dead, someone would call me, you know." She breathes rapidly and her eyes glisten.

"Does anyone know you're living out here?" He shrugs and adds, "I'll admit, I just got back into town, but I had no idea anyone was living out here."

Diane leans the gun up against the trailer and sinks onto the creaking metal step below the door. The whole trailer shifts toward her weight. She doesn't cry, she shakes her head and mumbles.

"Is there anything we can do for you, or get for you?" I ask, helplessly.

She doesn't look up but continues to shake her head. "I told him not to mess with those guys. Geez, I warned him."

Jacob takes two careful steps in her direction and stops when she looks up. "Which guys?"

She buries her face in her hands. "Never mind. It's done and dusted."

Her sleeves fall back and reveal a delicate vine of ivy leaves encircling her right arm. Where have I seen that? Before I can stop it, the image of the body on Boilerplate Beach looms in my mind. The mermaid tattooed on Walt's right shoulder had a vine of ivy wrapped around its own right arm. Both father and daughter shared this image of remembrance for a woman who had abandoned them. I wonder if Ivy knows how much Walt and Diane miss her?

Emotions are swirling too close to the surface for me. "We're sorry to have bothered you, Diane. We should get back to the mainland." I tug Jacob's sleeve. "Let us know if there's anything we can do," I call out as we walk toward the horses.

Diane doesn't look up. Her hair covers her stoic face and the tendrils of ivy are lost under a curtain of black. She doesn't wave or make any attempt to stand.

Part of me wants to try to use my gift to pick up on her feelings, but I'm all too familiar with the feeling of helplessness that follows hearing this kind of news. I wish I could tell her I've been there and it gets better with time, but that would be a lie. Every day I was in foster care, every new placement, was just a painful reminder of the fact that I had no mother. No family in the whole world to take me in and care for me when I needed it most. I'm immensely grateful my grandmother left me her bookshop and her fortune, but I would've been so much more thankful if she had scooped me up and pieced me together when I was a shattered, homeless eleven-year-old.

Jacob gives a final wave to Diane's bowed head, and Cranberry leads the way back to Chez Osprey.

CHAPTER 8

The return trip across the lake to Pin Cherry is quiet. Quiet in that there is no conversation. Nature however, puts on quite a show. The waves surge, the wind rips across the massive lake, and the boat's twin engines strain to fight their way to shore as the sun slips into the indigo horizon. I'm grateful for Nimkii's effective tea taking on the monumental task of keeping down my supper.

Jacob flanks the dock with the practiced ease of a seasoned northshoreman. He leaps onto the thick weathered planks, rope in hand, and secures the boat.

I grin and imagine what it would've been like to grow up in Pin Cherry, enjoying fishing, swimming, and boating with my father.

"Mitzy?"

"Um, yeah?"

"Where did you go? I called your name three times." He smiles, but looks concerned.

I swallow the truth. "Just distracted with all the Diane stuff."

Jacob takes my hand and helps me transfer from tilting watercraft to wooden pier. Before he releases my hand, he mumbles, "I'm sorry about your mom. I'm sorry I wasn't there for you."

"Mmhmm. I know." I pull my hand free and cross my arms over my stomach. The mood ring on my left hand shimmers a purplish-grey—which is new. Maybe that's the color for the mood of resentment. I look down at the evenly spaced boards and focus all my attention on placing my feet to carefully avoid jamming a heel between two planks. It's not an actual possibility, but the false task prevents a deeper dive into dead-mom talk. A topic I prefer to avoid at all cost.

Jacob drives his pickup truck with determined caution and drops me under the street light in front of the Bell, Book & Candle.

I decline his offer to walk me up to the apartment.

Grams is hovering behind the thick wooden door of the bookshop—swirling anxiously.

As soon as I see her ghostly presence, I burst into tears.

She circles around me. "These darn useless ghost arms! I need to give you a proper hug."

I nod, swipe at the saltwater on my cheeks, and run up to the apartment.

Grams materializes next to me as the bookcase door slides closed. "What happened?"

I kick off the shoes and shake my head. "I need a shower. Alone." I catch the hurt in her eyes as I give her the brush off, but I keep walking toward the bathroom.

I turn the water on full blast and drop my dress in a heap on the floor.

The hot water pummels the tension in my neck and shoulders. My tears mix with the spray as I shove my face directly into the pulsing streams.

Steam fills the room. Time melts away.

This luxury of a hot and uninterrupted shower is something I've come to appreciate more than I ever dreamed possible. There is no privacy in foster care and no time for self-indulgence. I lived with good families and bad. Foster mom #3 and foster mom #9 were kind and generous women. Number three gave me a sense of place and the courage to embrace my intelligence. Number nine gave me enough love to allow me to accept my wider than average hips and my unusual bone-white hair. It was the first ounce of self-acceptance I learned. But no one ever let me talk about my mother. No one ever let me weep, rage, or sit silently and remember. My belongings got packed in trash bags and my feelings got buried—deep.

But today something cracked open. I know how Diane feels and I'm not going to let Walt's death be swept under the rug of small-town propriety.

I turn off the water, smooth back my hair, and let the rivulets trickle down my back. I reach through the steam for a towel to wrap around my torso, like every A-list actress in the movies, and walk out of the bathroom to announce my intentions.

I make it exactly one half a footstep out the door before Grams swoops down in concern.

"Mitzy, what's happened? It's so much better to talk about it. Ask for help if you need it. Don't be afraid to admit that you're powerless and that you need something, someone outside yourself, to help you work things out."

The psychobabble tainted with Alcoholics Anonymous aphorisms grated on my nerves when I first came to Pin Cherry, but now I understand that it's the way she expresses her love. She struggled through something monumental and she found a program that worked for her. I take a deep breath and accept the lifeline. "Did you know Diane was living in a tiny travel trailer on the site of the burned-out lodge?"

Her ghostly features pinch with regret. "No, I'm sorry to say. Once I got sick, I lost contact with Walt. Odell and I became quite close in my final years and I didn't want to do anything more to hurt him."

I nod. "Well, she is. She's living in a crap little trailer next to a pile of charred wood, all by herself. She didn't even know Walt was dead."

Grams drifts toward the large six-by-six windows and gazes at the brooding blue-black sky and the moonless waters for several minutes before she answers. "I'm sure she wasn't living there alone, Mitzy. I would guess that Walter was living there with her until the accident."

"It was no accident. And I intend to prove it."

Grams spins slowly and floats toward me, never breaking eye contact.

"What do you mean?"

"I saw that body. Something wasn't right. I can't put my finger on it, but I sensed something."

"Sensed? Are you embracing your gift?" Grams pushes in for a close face-to-ghost-face. "Are you saying you were reading the energy? Was it the energy of the place or of Walt's body?"

I shrug. "How would I know? This is all so new to me." I hold up my hand and spin the mood ring. "I saw plenty of energy workers in Sedona. Some were frauds but a few actually seemed authentic. I never believed in that stuff. I never gave it a second thought." I move into the closet and rummage through the drawers in search of my favorite T-shirt.

Grams floats a respectable distance outside the doorway and continues to interrogate me.

"Tell me more about what you felt. And try to remember if there was anything else. Visions. Sounds."

"There was nothing else; at least nothing I noticed. But after the initial shock and nausea, I did feel a dark energy. Is dark the right word?"

"Dark is fine, darling. You should call Silas."

Unable to find the T-shirt, I slip on a soft pair of shorty pajamas. "Yeah, he should have a copy of that medical examiner's report by now."

"I wasn't talking about any report. I meant that Silas might be able to help you understand what you're feeling."

"I am not exactly sure what I could tell him. He won't understand."

"What do you mean?" Grams places her bejeweled hands on her hips. "Silas, of all people, will be supportive of your gifts. He was a huge help to me when I was learning to hone my ability. I only ever had visions, though. Clairvoyant is what it's called. As far as we know you're clairsentient, which means you feel things. Maybe you felt something from the body's spirit or aura."

I chew the inside of my cheek and try to wrap my head around this idea. This concept that all the airy-fairy woo-woo nonsense I was exposed to while working in various coffee shops in and around Sedona, Arizona might actually be real. I mean, the last few years brought me in contact with a steady diet of vortexes, aura cleansing, chakra alignment, palm reading, you name it. But I never for one minute believed that any of it was true. And now I'm standing here talking to my Ghost-ma about energy I sensed coming from a corpse! I'm going to need to sleep on this.

"I agree. A good night's sleep—"

I stare daggers at Grams and point meaningfully to my lips.

"I'm sorry, dear. You're right. Your lips didn't move and it's none of my business. You get some sleep. We'll talk about it more tomorrow."

I'm in no mood to touch the gun we found under the bed. The gun that is now resting on the right side of my bed like a dangerous lover. I choose to ignore it and hope it will return the favor.

Tucked between 800-thread-count Egyptian cotton sheets, I find no peace. Images of the body on the rocks, twisting vines of ivy, and Diane's heartbreaking trailer spin unceasingly in my mind. I stretch my arm to the right and feel for the coarse but reassuring fur on Pyewacket's front paw. He yawns and his whiskers tickle my arm as he moves closer. I scratch his wide skull between his lovely tufted ears and deep-throated purring shakes the bed.

CHAPTER 9

The next thing I know, the crisp light of morning in almost-Canada is blasting through my windows and jolting me upright. Note to self: maybe invest in some blackout blinds.

"It's rather late, dear. You should get down to the diner and let Odell know what's going on."

I hastily change from my flimsy PJs into my standard jeans and T-shirt. This tee features a jumble of Scrabble tiles with the tagline, "I just bought this book at IKEA."

Hurrying across the loft and down the spiral staircase, I carefully step over the "No Admittance" sign chained across the bottom.

"I thought I heard you thundering down the stairs." Twiggy appears from the back room, cup of black coffee in hand.

"I've got to head down to the diner and talk to Odell. You need anything from Rex's?"

An amused smile parts Twiggy's lips. "Look at you running around town like a local. Nah, I don't need nothin'."

A quick nod and I leave through the side door. Once in the alley, I slip my grandmother's mood ring out of my pocket and push it carefully onto the ring finger of my left hand. The small oval stone stares up at me like a dead piece of coal. Today it refuses to change colors or share its shimmering secrets. The more I stare, the less it cares. I shove the ring back in my pocket and make my way through the brisk morning breeze to the best cup of coffee in town.

I push open the door to Myrtle's Diner and Odell's normally welcoming eyes are filled with questions. I slide into a booth and Tally sets down a steaming mug of coffee and a small melamine bowl of individual creamers. I nod my thanks.

"He's crankier than usual today. Looks like he hasn't slept."

The top of the creamer peels back easily and I watch the white liquid cloud the oily black surface of my java. I swirl the spoon slowly and savor my first sip.

There are three other patrons. Two regulars at the counter and someone tucked behind a newspaper at the table in the far corner. His well-shined shoes look expensive. Not from around here. I roll my eyes and chuckle. Wow! I'm turning into a bona fide local.

A crash in the kitchen pulls my attention to the orders-up window. Tally races out with a broom and Odell returns to the grill. His mouth pinched in a hard line, his movements tinged with anger.

The door scrapes open and I instinctively turn my head. Silas Willoughby nods and slides into the red-vinyl bench seat opposite mine. He lays a small folder on the table and pushes it across.

"Bright morning to you, Mitzy. I believe this missive contains much-anticipated information."

I spin the folder around and scan the contents. The ME's report does not disappoint. They're ruling Walt's death a homicide. A few unexpected tears try to escape, but I blink them back as I close the folder. Of course, this means Erick will be looking into the murder and I'll have to play nice with Deputy Paulsen, but at least there's a chance Diane will get some justice.

Odell delivers a new plate with a fresh breakfast to my table and nods toward the folder. "That it?"

"They ruled it a homicide," I say with a slight crack in my voice.

"You on the case?"

"I already was."

Silas interrupts our terse exchange with his order. "I'd like to partake of the special, if it's not too much trouble."

Odell nods and walks back toward the kitchen.

I call out quietly, "I met Diane yesterday."

His footsteps hesitate, but he seems to change his mind about something. Odell does not return to the table.

Silas harrumphs once and chews the corner of his mustache.

"What?" I ask.

"They are not close. Odell never trusted Diane's mother, Ivy. In fact, I seem to remember him inventing a clever moniker—something akin to 'Evil Ivy.' Drove a wedge between him and his brother, and therefore between him and his niece. Regardless, Ivy caused a great deal of trouble for Walter back in the day. She was a woman of ill repute."

I stare at Silas and shrug. "Is that supposed to mean something to me?"

"In your jargon, I believe she would be referred to as a lady of the night, or perhaps a gentleman's hostess?"

I nearly spit take my coffee. "In my jargon, she'd be a prostitute."

Silas is obviously offended by my base language.

"It is my understanding that she danced for payment. I am not aware of any escort services."

"So, a stripper." I take another sip of my wake-up juice.

He shakes his head and frowns. "As you will. However, she took a sizable portion of Walter's money and saddled him with a daughter, whom she clearly never desired. The poor man did his best with Diane, but if your grandmother hadn't intervened on behalf of the girl's education . . . I fear things might have been far worse."

"Diane is living in a thimble-sized trailer beside a pile of rubble. Things got worse."

"And why would this be any of your concern, Mitzy?"

"I know what it's like to lose the most important person in your life and be left with nothing." I stare into the old man's milky-blue eyes for a second before my gaze drops to my untouched breakfast.

"I acknowledge your frustration. But your situations are far from similar. Diane is a full-grown woman with a nearly achieved bachelors degree and the ability to make a new life for herself."

"Walt left her nothing but a mess. He had no insurance on anything and his boats are most likely going to be repossessed. The trailer she's living in probably isn't even paid for!"

"I fail to see the connection between Diane's

problems and your tone. However, if you feel some philanthropic urge, I am certain we can allocate funds to assist Walter's offspring in her time of supposed need."

I lean back and gaze at Silas, taking in his smooth shiny head, unperturbed expression, and rumpled tweed coat. He's right. I can afford to help Diane. I've never been in a position to help anyone before. The thought never occurred to me. I pick up my fork and dive into my lovely scrambled eggs and perfectly browned home fries.

"So where's this Ivy chick now?" I mumble through a mouthful of food.

"Manners, Mitzy." Silas carefully places a paper napkin on his lap and pulls a second one from the dispenser at the end of the table to tuck into his collar and protect his faded bowtie. "It is my understanding that Ivy returned to Canada once she had bilked young Walter of his funds."

"Nice girl." I roll my eyes. "Any chance you have a connection at Immigration? I mean, INS?"

The vinyl creaks as Silas leans back and strokes his thumb and finger down across his bushy mustache. He almost grins. "A fascinating idea. Is there something you're not telling me?"

My fork halts midway between my nearly empty plate and my full mouth. My eyes tentatively look up toward Silas. There is a strange, commanding power in his eyes, not the aged tired man who stared across the table earlier. I lower my utensil, pick up my napkin, and swipe it across my mouth. "What are you talking about?"

"I am certain you know exactly what I'm talking about, Mizithra."

He uses my proper name. My throat tightens. He senses something. Is it my posture? Can he see my aura? I have zero experience interacting with alchemists, so I'm not sure if this question is genuine or if he's testing my honesty. Grams thinks he can help me understand my gifts, but . . . I suddenly have to wonder why the immigration idea *did* pop into my head? Did I think it up or did that idea come from somewhere beyond me? Maybe I do need help. I swallow hard and lower my shaking hands to my lap.

He leans forward and his eyes seem to bore into my soul. "Go ahead. I'm listening."

"Grams, er um Isadora, wanted me to tell you. But I don't know—I'm not sure—it seems crazy."

"If your grandmother feels it is pertinent, I propose that it behooves you to share your news."

A calm sensation floods over me and I breathe a huge sigh of relief. Did Silas do something? I guess it's now or never. "She thinks I might be clairsentient. Maybe she's projecting, or it's wishful thinking. But that's what she wanted me to tell you."

Silas inhales and steeples his fingers beneath his jowls. "I suspected as much. Has she given you the ring?"

My hand involuntarily touches the lump in my left pocket.

He nods. "She has."

"That's creepy. How did you know?"

"I observed your hand move, dear. No magic involved."

"Do you think I have an actual gift, or whatever?"

"Tell me exactly how events unfolded when you placed the ring on your finger."

"Do you mean today or the first time?"

"Both. Begin with the first time."

My fingers trace the outline of the ring in my pocket as I speak. "I was messing around in her jewelry box, and for some reason I slipped that particular ring on my finger. At first the stone was totally black, so I asked what kind of ring it was. Then Grams spent all this time explaining what mentoring is and went on and on, and to be honest I kind of zoned out. But when I looked back at the ring, it wasn't changing to any of the colors she mentioned. It looked like it was moving, like there was a storm inside the stone. If that makes any sense?"

Silas takes a slow, measured sip of his coffee and

dabs his mustache with a napkin before he answers. "Go on."

"For a minute I felt something and it almost seemed like I saw something in the swirling mist inside the stone. I'm not sure. It all happened so fast. It was probably just my imagination playing tricks on me because of everything Isadora was saying."

"And today?"

I squeeze the ring nestled in the fabric of my skinny jeans. "Today there was nothing. I slipped it on, looked down at the stone, and it stayed black."

He drags his prayer-hands down the flesh of his chin, bounces his head lightly on the tips of his fingers, and his lips quiver with the promise of words—but no sound escapes.

"What did you say?" I ask.

"What did I feel?" he replies.

His tactic of answering my question with a question is not only irritating, but also unsatisfying. I open my mouth to toss a little snark in his direction, when a phrase pops into my head. I repeat it aloud without hesitation. "You feel curious." I jerk my head back and the hairs on my arms stand on end. A chill runs through my whole body and my mouth waters in the icky way it always does right before I throw up. I want to get up and run to the bathroom but I can't move.

"And that's your first lesson." Silas briefly smiles with a satisfaction I have never seen on his face before, and then he calmly takes another sip of coffee.

Sliding out of the booth, I stare at my lawyer. My mouth opens and shuts like a fish gasping for air, before I find my voice. "I gotta go."

He nods calmly. "Good day, Mitzy."

CHAPTER 10

BACK AT THE APARTMENT, I can't stop pacing or biting my fingernails. Which is a new bad habit, because I used to pride myself on never having such a vice. The stress of the morning, combined with the strain of not understanding my gift and the pressure to find Walt's killer—it's all too much. I gnaw viciously on another innocent fingernail.

Grams flickers in and out, desperate to help me but unable to break through my anxiety attack. "Honestly, if you just sit down and take some deep breaths, I promise it will help. I've been where you are. In truth, I've been much lower, sweetheart, but I've definitely been where you are. When I started reading those old books out there and discovered how to manage my gift, everything just made more sense to me. In the beginning, the visions are what drove me to drink, but in the end, learning how to interpret them and even use them gave me some power over my life. I may be an alcoholic in recovery, but studying the psychic arts is what saved me. I would never discount the value of the program. The program worked because I worked it. But learning to be a 'wise woman' and to embrace my visions, that's what truly transformed me."

It's possible that I've been pacing for hours or days. Maybe Grams has a point?

I lower myself onto the overstuffed settee and take three deep breaths. I don't feel better, but I do feel different.

"That's it. Now take three more."

I reluctantly follow her instructions and have to admit that my heart rate is beginning to return to normal. But before I can find any real sense of calm—

Twiggy's voice blasts through the intercom and shatters my fragile peace. "Hey, Silas is down here. He says it's important."

I exhale in frustration and press the mother-of-pearl button next to the speaker to reply. "Can you send him up, please?"

A staticky click is the only response.

The bookcase door slides open and Silas shuffles in. The meek, unassuming lawyer who stands before me bears little resemblance to the wise and powerful alchemist who sat across from me in the booth at Myrtle's Diner.

"I received some information from my INS contact." He looks at me with something like pride in his eyes. "Ivy did return to Canada after Diane was born, but she didn't stay. Or at least she didn't stay put. I've come to understand that the DEA has built quite a case file on Ivy Johnson, a.k.a. Ivy Lapointe."

"Drug enforcement?" So many things are swirling through my brain I can't grab hold of anything. Ideas. Words. Images. Some of it feels like a memory and some of it feels like a dream.

Grams rushes to my side. "Ask him if Walt was involved?"

"Grams wants to know if there's any mention of Walt?"

"There was." Silas takes a seat and waits.

"Well, what did it say?" I ask. But before he can answer, I fire off several more questions. "Was Walt implicated in some kind of drug scheme? What would they even be doing? She's in Canada, right? Is there some kind of illegal maple syrup trade?"

"To address your last question first, yes there is. However, Ivy and her cohorts were into a far more lucrative operation. They were trafficking counterfeit opioids."

Grams gasps and clutches one of the many strands of pearls around her spectral neck.

"Counterfeit opioids? And I thought meth was bad," I mumble, as I recall a foster brother who peddled that nasty crap at school . . . They didn't catch him until a high school sophomore overdosed. I probably should've turned him in, but at the time I was pretty busy fighting for my own survival.

Grams rudely ignores my reverie and blurts, "What's your next move, Mitzy?"

Her question interrupts my unhappy trip down memory lane and I stare through the grandmotherly apparition while I search for something resembling a plan. "I need to get back out to the island."

Silas stands and his mouth tightens with concern. "What are you considering?"

"I need to get back out to that island and find out what these 'other' operations are that popped up on the far side of the island."

"That sounds like neither a well-thought-out nor safe plan." He clears his throat but does not continue.

"What other choice do I have?"

"Perhaps you could convince Deputy Paulsen to do your dirty work for you." Silas tilts his head.

Talk about your impossible odds! An unsavory image of me lying on the floor of the Piggly Wiggly surrounded by the detritus of a toppled canned-pumpkin tower flashes in my mind. "I'm not sure if you've noticed, but Deputy Paulsen pretty much hates me."

Grams giggles like a schoolgirl. "And when have you ever let that stop you?"

I gasp in mock horror. "Well I never!"

Silas stares at me with concern. "I assume Isadora made some comment which you failed to share?"

I nod. "You seem to be the one with all the diplomatic gifts. What would you suggest I use as incentive for Deputy Paulsen to do my work?"

"It's my understanding that high-profile cases go a long way toward boosting one's political ambitions."

I scrunch up my face as I replay the cryptic advice from Silas. Grams moves in closer to blurt out her interpretation, but I put up a finger and motion for her to give me a moment.

Silas slips a pair of tarnished wire-rim glasses from his interior coat pocket, rubs the rose-tinged lenses, and hooks the stems over his large ears. He glances about until his gaze lands firmly on Grams. "My, my, Isadora. You are as breathtaking in spirit as you were in life. Perhaps one day, I will unearth an incantation that will bestow me with the blessed ability to hear your charming voice once again." He sighs wistfully. "But until then, I am grateful for these spectacles and their gift of sight beyond."

I turn away to hide the misty emotions clouding my vision. The bond between Silas and my grandmother, as I understand it, is completely platonic. Yet there is some deeper connection that I can't comprehend. Perhaps it's the magic? Perhaps the bond between mentor and protégé? A bond that can transcend death must be deeper than any one-dimensional love.

Grams whispers, "It is, dear. It is."

My throat feels like a tiny frog is fighting against my instinct to swallow. I cough a little before I announce my plans. "I'll head down to the police station. It's time to light a fire under this investigation into Walt's murder."

Silas nods appreciatively.

Grams gives me a slow clap and a chuckle.

I roll my eyes. And to avoid involving Silas in our teasing banter, I simply think my response. *Really, Grams? The slow clap?*

She giggles until ghostly tears touch her shimmering cheeks. I shake my head and open the bookcase door. Pyewacket bounds through the door knocking me onto the settee, which in turn jostles its current occupant, Silas.

The inconvenienced man stands and straightens his rumpled coat. "You have spoiled every ounce of decorum out of that feline, Isadora." He harrumphs into his mustache and exits.

"Pye, what are you up to?"

The dog-sized caracal sprawled across my bed, next to that pesky handgun, holds something down with one paw while tugging on a piece of it with his dangerous incisors.

I approach to take a closer look and he gives a low guttural warning growl.

"Look here mister, I'm the one that pours the Fruity Puffs in this house. So if you would like to continue to receive your pampering, then you better show me what's under that paw."

To my utter shock, the spoiled beast pulls back his paw to reveal a small silver key dangling from a neon-yellow foam disc.

I reach for the object and receive no further threats. "What kind of keychain is this?"

Grams whizzes over. "Boat key. The foam disc floats! Isn't that clever? That way if you drop your key overboard you have time to recover it. Isn't it ingenious? I don't know who invented it but—"

"Grams, I don't need the whole history of floating key chains. I grew up in the desert and don't know a whole bunch about boats, but I get it. Keychain floats. Probably means this is the key to a boat. The second time I say the word "boat," I *feel* beyond a shadow of a doubt that this is the key to Walt Johnson's boat.

"Mitzy! What does it mean?"

There's no time to scold her for eavesdropping on my thoughts. "I have no idea, Grams. I'll give it some thought on my walk down to the station."

"What about the key?"

A smile slides across my face. "I'll give it to Deputy Paulsen as a show of good faith."

"My precious little cuddle muffin knew exactly what you needed." She drags her ghostly fingers across Pyewacket's back and he arches towards her as though he can actually feel her touch.

I spin the keychain around my finger and head down to the station.

Despite my many trips to the police station since my arrival in Pin Cherry Harbor, the uniformed officer manning the front desk is a new face. "Hello there, would you happen to know if Deputy Paulsen is in this afternoon?"

Without so much as a glance in my direction he mumbles, "Take a seat. I'll let her know you're here."

"Would you like to give her a name?" I ask.

He picks up a telephone, dials a three-digit extension, and announces, "There's some lady here to see you." And he drops the receiver back into the cradle with a thunk.

Moments later, the short, squat form of Deputy Paulsen rounds the corner and catches sight of me. She halts and slides her hand down to her pistol grip. "Here to cause more trouble, Moon?"

"Not on your life, ma'am. I was actually wondering if I might have a private word?"

Her eyes narrow, and she chomps on either a cud of gum or plug of tobacco. Who could be sure?

"I'll talk to you in interrogation room one. You've got five minutes."

I obediently lead the way to interrogation room one, as my familiarity with the station extends to said interrogation rooms. She follows me in, unnecessarily kicks the door shut, and continues to fondle her weapon.

I take a seat and assume a docile and cooperative posture. "I'm sure you know that Erick—"

"Sheriff Harper."

"Of course, I'm sorry. Sheriff Harper asked me to stay out of the Walt Johnson homicide, but I have an important piece of information. The kind of information that could literally make a career in a small town like Pin Cherry. I didn't want to bother him with it, seeing as how he told me to stay out of things. But I had to tell someone, and I feel like you're the second-in-command around here." The acid roiling in my stomach will certainly give me away. I'm not sure if I can last the full five minutes with this level of suck-up-itude.

"You better not be yanking my chain, Moon. What's this information?"

"Were you aware that Walt's daughter, Diane, is living out on the island?" I'm fairly certain she knows this, but giving her the opportunity to display her superior knowledge should put me right where I hope to be.

"Between the two of us, you're the new kid in town. If that's all you got, I have a job to do."

"Of course. Of course you would know that. But, maybe you didn't know that her mother is the focus of an international DEA investigation?"

You couldn't smack the shock off her face with a baseball bat.

I swallow the smug grin struggling to display itself on my face. "Her maiden name was Lapointe. It sounds like she's part of a huge opioid smuggling ring. I mean, a bust like that—that's the stuff of legend." I clench my fists under the table and swallow everything else I want to say. The look on the deputy's face is everything.

"If the DEA is running some kind of sting in our territory, then I'm sure they filed proper paperwork. Go ahead and pat yourself on the back for being a good citizen. I'll take it from here."

I smile as innocently as I'm able. "Thank you,

Deputy. I knew I came to the right person." I drop my gaze to the floor hoping to appear humble, but genuinely wanting to hide the victory dancing in my eyes.

She grabs the door handle and motions for me to get out of the interrogation room.

"Oh, I almost forgot." I hold up the almost-glowing foam disc and dangle the silver key. "My cat brought this in. He was with me when we found — Anyway, I'm sure this belonged to Walt Johnson.

Paulsen snatches the keychain from my hand and shakes her head. "You just have a knack for destroying evidence, don't you?" She whips a plastic bag from her back pocket and drops the key inside. "Probably not a single usable print . . ." She continues to grumble under her breath.

Before I say something I'll enjoy more than I'll regret, I get myself out of the station.

Not a resounding success, but I'll take it.

CHAPTER 11

The sun is high overhead and the welcome warmth encourages a lazy pace down the cracked sidewalk. I'm not sure what it is about the town of Pin Cherry Harbor, but it genuinely feels like home. For the first time in a long time, I feel happy, and lucky—and loved.

Unfortunately, my half-celebration is cut short as Sheriff Erick parks next to the curb on Main Street and gets out of his cruiser. I toy with the idea of walking past without giving him so much as a glance, but when he calls out my name, I have no choice but to stop.

He steps onto the sidewalk and walks toward me with one hand extended.

I naturally walk forward to see what he has for

me. However, it isn't exactly natural. Turns out the uneven sidewalk has it in for me and two steps into my "meet cute" I catch my toe on an angled edge of concrete and crash into the deliciously firm chest of the local constable. To be fair, he doesn't exactly handle things with stunning grace himself.

"Oh shoot!" He fumbles to set me upright and brushes against my bikini-top area. "Sorry. I'm so sorry, Miss Moon." Erick steps back and rubs his hand against his pant leg as though he has touched a toad rather than my fully clothed left boob.

I choose to draw attention away from my tumble by directing a spotlight on his. "I like a guy to at least take me to dinner before he tries to get to second base."

Erick's face turns as red as a pin cherry.

"I may have to change your nickname from Sheriff Too Hot to Handle to Sheriff Too Handsy." The joke falls flat and I shrug.

He's still rubbing his hand against his pant leg and I'm beginning to feel more than a little offended.

"Did you have something for me?" I prompt.

"I think you dropped this at the crime scene." His voice is tense and his manner uncomfortable. He places a business card in my hand.

I don't have the heart to tell him that I've never

taken a business card from anyone in my entire life. So, I glance down at the card and see the name of a rare-books dealer embossed on the thick paper. Curious. Who knows where this could lead? I choose to feign responsibility. "Oh, yeah, I've been looking for that. Thanks." I move left to continue on my route back to the bookstore and he slides the same direction. I zig to the other side and he zigs the same way. I stop, smile, and glue myself to the sidewalk until he moves around me. "Good day, Erick," I call as he strides toward the station.

He mumbles a response and disappears into headquarters.

I skedaddle back to the bookshop with two new pieces of information.

Once I'm safely ensconced in my apartment, I whip out my phone and search for "Lars Gershon," purveyor of rare books and antiquities.

Grams is strangely absent from the apartment and the lack of an audience is disheartening. I offer my wonderful news to Pyewacket. "You'll be happy to know that I successfully conned Deputy Paulsen into investigating Ivy Lapointe. And that's not all I accomplished."

Pyewacket rolls onto his back, stretches lazily, and yawns.

"What else did I uncover you ask? Well, I'll tell

you. The business card of one Lars Gershon was found at the crime scene. Perhaps a coincidence. Perhaps not." I can almost hear the "dun, dun, dun" of the movie soundtrack—in my mind.

A shower of white light bleeds through the wall and interrupts my report.

"Did I hear you say something about Lars? Lars Gershon?" Grams' face is whiter than usual.

"Yeah, Erick gave me this." I fan the business card. "I looked him up and he seems to have a legit business. Or at least he seems to have a legit website."

"Oh, dear. Oh, dear, dear, dear." If Grams had corporeal legs, I would say she's pacing. But in her case, it's more like swirling or spinning.

"It sounds like you might know Lars, Grams. Is that true?"

She shimmers to a halt and fixes me with a guilty stare. "I may have had some dealings with Lars. If you know what I mean."

Just a quick reminder, my Grams is a bit of a skank.

"Now now, Mitzy, I told you there's a very wide line between a skank and a woman of means who knows what she wants."

"The line's not that wide, Grams."

She shakes her head and swirls toward the plump settee. I'm sure she thinks she's sitting on it, but from where I stand the view is a strangely unsettling, see-through, hovering sensation.

"Lars was fascinating. He was well-traveled, spoke seven languages, including Latin. And he used to bring me trinkets from all over the world."

"And how do you suppose his business card showed up next to Walt's corpse?"

"Well, I have no idea. I don't think Lars even knew Walt."

"You don't think, or you don't know?"

"That doesn't make any sense, Mitzy. What I meant to say was I never introduced Lars to Walt, and Walt never mentioned meeting him to me. But I hardly know everything that goes on in this town." Grams straightens the lovely burgundy tulle of her gown and fiddles with one of the rings on her left hand.

I step closer. "Is that a gift from Lars?"

She becomes so still I fear her spirit has somehow disconnected from the apparition.

"Grams? Grams?"

She flickers for a second before rocketing toward the coffered ceiling.

"What exactly happened between you and Lars?" I ask.

"Why don't you see if you can schedule a meeting with him."

I gaze up at my floating Ghost-ma and chew the

inside of my cheek. "That sounds a lot like you're not going to answer me. Is this misdirection or transference?"

"Don't waste your time psychoanalyzing a ghost, Mitzy. Just call the number on that business card and see if you can set up a meeting with Lars."

I tap the digits into my phone and a friendly-voiced woman with a hint of a southern accent answers on the second ring.

"Gershon Antiquities, how may I help you?"

"I was hoping to speak to Lars if he's available."

There's no response, but I know I didn't drop the call because I can hear short quick breaths on the other end of the phone.

"Hello? Do we have a bad connection?"

"Oh no, it's fine. I'm sorry. I just got the news an hour ago, and I haven't had time to figure out what to tell people. I'm sorry. It's just—"

"What news?"

"Did you know Mr. Gershon?" she asks.

I decide to fabricate what I don't know. "He was a close friend of my grandmother, Isadora Duncan."

A sharp inhalation on the other end of the line precedes the response. "Oh, my condolences."

"Sorry?"

"I'm sure she'll want to come to the funeral."

I feel like I've slipped into an Abbott and Costello routine. I can't imagine why my dearly departed grandmother would want to come to her own funeral and I'm tempted to say as much to this flighty southern belle. But I choose the "more flies with honey" option. "I'm afraid I'm a bit confused. My lovely grandmother passed away a few months ago. I was simply reaching out to Lars in hopes of gaining a better understanding of her book business. You see, I've inherited the bookshop and—"

Intense sobbing on the other end of the line interrupts my unrehearsed lie.

"Miss, are you all right?"

After two ragged gasps and one unladylike nose blowing, she responds, "Mr. Gershon is deceased. I only just received the call . . . I don't have any details. I'm so sorry."

The line goes dead. I pocket my phone and look up at Isadora. "Bad news, Grams."

She floats down with a slow and deliberate flourish. "He's gone, isn't he?"

I nod.

"When I saw that business card, I had one of my little visions. Like I used to get when I was alive. I saw his face, but it was a ghost. I haven't had any visions since I died, and I wasn't sure what to do." She floats to the window and shakes her head.

"It's all right Grams. We both have a lot of things to figure out. But one thing is for sure, there's a connection between Walt and Lars. I'm sure of it."

CHAPTER 12

THEY SAY that the early bird gets the worm. *They* can have their worms. I prefer to roll out of bed at the crack of 10 AM.

As soon as my feet hit the floor, Grams rushes out of the closet. “Oh good, you’re finally up.”

Rude.

She narrows her gaze and continues, “You should see if Jacob will take you back out to the island. Maybe Diane knows something about Lars.”

“And if you would’ve given me a moment to wake up, that was exactly what I was about to say.”

She smiles with pride. “Great minds!”

I can’t handle this much perkiness before my first cup of coffee. I zombie-walk into the closet, struggle into yesterday’s skinny jeans, and grab a clean T-shirt. This one sports a cuddly kitten and the tagline "You look MEOW-velous!" I slide my feet into a pair of flip-flops and stop in mid turn as my hand brushes against the ring still shoved in my left pocket.

Grams hovers just outside the closet, her face a mix of anticipation and concern.

I pull the band out of my pocket and slip it onto the ring finger of my left hand.

We both hold our breath. Although, in her case it hardly seems as noteworthy a feat as it does in mine.

"Anything?" she asks.

"No. Wait—" The black cabochon shifts in hue to a yellowish-amber. "Something's happening."

Grams floats into the closet and hovers over my right shoulder.

We watch together as the curved stone seems to simultaneously grow in diameter and depth. The scene shifts to a swirling royal blue and I swear I can almost see an island taking shape amongst the waves. "Did you see it?"

"No, dear. I saw the color change a bit, but that was all. How about you?"

"It was probably my imagination." I let my hand drop to my side. The ring feels like a ten-pound weight.

"Nonsense. You have a gift. You have to believe that. What did you feel?"

I shrug. "I didn't feel anything this time. I thought I saw water and maybe an island."

Grams inhales sharply and clutches her pearls. "You *saw* something? Have you ever had visions before?"

My mind is inundated with images from my past. I basically survived foster care by creating alternate realities within my mind. What a loaded question. I'm not exactly sure how to answer her. A hand pats my back, and I nearly jump out of my skin. "Who's there? What was that?"

"What is it, dear? What happened?"

"Someone—or something—touched my back!"

Grams moves closer to me and her ethereal fingers reach toward my arm. "Did it feel like this?"

As her ghostly energy comes into contact with my skin, a surge of unfamiliar sensations race across my skin. My eyes widen to saucers. "Yes."

"Oh, hallelujah! We've made a connection, Mitzy. I can actually touch you." Otherworldly tears spring from her eyes, and for the hundredth time I wish she'd been buried with a handkerchief.

I sink to the floor of the closet and let my head fall into my hands. What is happening to me? Visions inside rings. Physical interactions with ghosts. It's all too much for me.

Grams whispers, "I know your lips didn't move, dear. But I have to say something. You're a witch."

I shake my head and put up my hands to stop her.

"You can call it a wise woman, a psychic or an empath, if that makes you feel better. I told you before and I know you didn't believe me. But you can't continue to deny your nature. I never had your gift, or maybe gifts. I had a few wonky visions, an occasional premonition, nothing extraordinary. Most of what I learned I read in books or heard about from Silas. I practiced and practiced, but it always seemed like the more energy I tried to control the sicker I got."

I look up. "Are you saying that you died from an overdose of magic?"

"I'm sure modern medicine would have chalked it up to the predictable liver failure of an alcoholic. But I stopped drinking a long time ago. Even if you count the relapses, it was fifteen years, eight months, and three days since I had my last drink. That's counting back from the day I died of course."

"Of course." Math may not be my favorite subject, but even I can solve that equation. "The day dad went to prison?"

"Indeed. I believe the hardest thing in the world would be for a mother to lose a child. But the second hardest thing is to feel so awfully responsible for letting that same child down, and knowing that he'll waste fifteen years of his life paying for a crime he never should've committed."

"You're not responsible for his actions, Grams."

"I know. I know. Grant me the wisdom to know the difference. You'd be surprised how many times you can say that in fifteen years." She shakes her head as though the memories can be erased and returns to an earlier topic. "Anyway, Silas was quite confident that my illness was a result of overloading my system with more power than I knew how to manage. I kept studying and trying new meditations and spells, hoping one of them would help me find a way to go back in time and make different choices."

"What?"

"It was foolish. If I had spent half that time and energy on acceptance, I'd still be alive today."

I get to my feet and run my hands through my haystack of white hair. "And then I'd still be an orphan."

A beautiful light fills her eyes and her smile nearly breaks my heart. "You're right! If my death is the thing that brought this family together, I'd do it again without hesitation." She swooshes toward me, wraps her glimmering arms around me, and I feel like I've slipped into a bubble of love and protection.

I swipe at the tears adorning my cheeks and chuckle. "Time for the humans to have breakfast."

"Certainly. I'll be here when you get back."

"Speaking of breakfast, where's Pyewacket?" Grams disappears, and I make my way to the Rare Books Loft. She reappears a few moments later, giddy and bursting to tell me what she's discovered.

"Out with it." I circle my hand in the "continue" gesture.

"He's stretched across the desk in the back room and Twiggy is hand feeding him Fruity Puffs!" she whispers.

A strong urge to race to the back room and taunt Twiggy swells inside. I fight the urge.

Grams nods her approval of my decision.

"I'm off to the diner. Okay? I'll get a hold of Jacob when I get back and see if he can take me out to the island today."

"I hope he has time to stop by before you leave. I'd love to see him."

"I'll see what I can do." As soon as I step out of the bookshop, I regret my decision to leave without a jacket. But in the fight between shivering and starving, my stomach almost always wins. I break into a jog and cover the short distance to Myrtle's Diner in no time. When I open the door, I am pleased to discover my father already occupying a booth.

He waves me over and I slide in across from him. The mouth-watering smell of Odell's cooking engulfs me.

Tally is en route with my coffee and Odell salutes me through the orders-up window with his metal spatula.

Smiling at my dad, I say, "I was gonna call you after breakfast."

Jacob thoughtfully chews his mouthful of pancakes and washes it down with a swig of coffee before he replies. "What can I do for my favorite daughter today?"

"Don't you mean your only daughter? If I have a half-sibling out there somewhere, I'd like to know right now. I don't think I can handle anymore family surprises."

Jacob chuckles good-naturedly. "Nope. No siblings. Your mom was the only one who let one slip through the five-hole."

I scrunch my face in horror. "Five hole? Is that appropriate to say to me?"

He struggles to swallow his coffee and stifle his laughter simultaneously. Lucky for me, swallowing wins the battle and he avoids spewing hot coffee across the table. "It's nothing like that, Mitzy. It's a hockey term. It's the zone at the bottom of the net between the goalie's skates."

A sigh of relief escapes. "I guess I didn't learn a

lot of hockey terminology in Arizona. But I could probably tell you more than you would ever want to know about dry heat or javelina."

He nods comically. "I'm sure you could. As of right now, I have no questions on those topics."

Tally slides my breakfast onto the table and I dig in. Not as well mannered as my father, I talk with my mouth full. "Can you take me out to the island today?"

He tilts his head and eyes me suspiciously. "What do you need on the island?"

"Couple of things."

"Like what?"

I don't particularly like the set of his jaw. "I have some questions for Diane."

"And . . ."

After a few more bites of my fluffy scrambled eggs and a long sip of my wake-up juice, I answer, "I was hoping we could take a little trip around the perimeter. Maybe just get a feel for the whole island."

He sets down his fork and fixes me with a patented fatherly stare. "You don't want to poke that bear, Mitzy."

"You told me there weren't any bears on the island." I attempt to school my features into a portrait of innocence.

"Don't give me that look. You and I both know

what's happening on the other side of that island, and I'm not about to sail into those unfriendly waters unarmed."

"But I thought— I mean, it's not legal for you—do you even have a gun?"

"Yeah, I'm not about to violate my parole by carrying a gun. But you seem like a girl who doesn't know when to mind her own business—"

"Dad!" I shout my protest, but the truth is, I have no right to be offended. He couldn't be more correct.

He chuckles and adds, "What I was going to say was, I know a guy. He can teach you a thing or two about firearms. I don't want you carrying a gun without knowing how to handle yourself."

"Oh." I nod cooperatively. "But can we at least go back out to Osprey—or is it Fish-Hawk Island—and talk to Diane?"

Jacob exhales and puts his hands up in surrender.

CHAPTER 13

My second ride on the Duncan estate watercraft is less upsetting to my stomach than my first adventure. I also remember to wear a thick hoodie and Jacob gives me something called a "slicker." I pull both tightly around me to keep out the biting wind. Because as luck would have it, the second we left the dock, black rain clouds rolled in.

Jacob shouts over the roaring twin engines, "You okay?"

I don't bother using words. I simply nod my head.

We take the now familiar route to the small pier in front of Chez Osprey. With crappy weather and choppy waves, my dad doesn't waste any time getting us across the lake.

The engine slows and Jacob slides into a slip

with ease. He jumps off the boat, ties us off, and reaches down to help me ashore.

"Nice bit of drivin' there, Dad."

He chuckles. "Didn't want to risk bringing up your fancy breakfast."

"Do you think Nimkii will let us borrow the horses again?"

"Of course." We hurry up the steps and knock on the heavy wooden door of the restaurant.

Jacob thumps his fist several times. "They're only open for supper. Hopefully somebody in the kitchen will hear us knocking."

No one answers.

"Maybe we should just go out to the stables."

Jacob looks at me and grins. "That brain of yours is always cooking isn't it?"

He leads the way around the far side of the building and I run my fingers along the curved log surface. I like the feel of the smooth logs and the pattern of dark brown knots against the pale golden timbers.

As we approach the stables, Nimkii walks out with two saddled horses trailing behind. He stops and stares at me with a strange gleam in his eye. "I see the spider brought me a message of truth."

My father and I exchange a confused glance.

"Pardon me?" I say.

Nimkii hands Starlight's reins to me as he says,

"I was told of your coming. I was told you would need horses." He gives me a slight nod and his smoothly plaited salt-and-pepper braid swishes gently.

I fear my grandmother has found a way to cut her tether from the bookstore and interfere on a broader scale. "What do you mean you were told? Who told you?"

"Today, spider was the messenger. There are many messengers. But we do not always listen."

The way his eyes look beyond my exterior—the way they bore into my soul—makes me uneasy and self-conscious. The words he speaks seem like a message crafted just for me. Does he know about my gifts? Can he sense something just by looking at me?

"Let me give you a boost, Mitzy." Jacob circles around and helps me into the saddle. Then he swings into his like a Wild West cowboy and tells Nimkii we'll be back in an hour.

The Native American proprietor nods solemnly and walks into his establishment.

Starlight's hooves splash into the deep puddles dotting the trail leading to Diane's trailer. Both horses slog along without hesitation and I marvel at the multitude of colors and smells surrounding me in the glittering damp forest. The leaves are changing in earnest now and the golden oranges, burnt siennas, and crimson hues draw my full attention.

As soon as we enter the clearing, I feel it. Something isn't right.

"Trailer's gone." My father's voice is quiet but concerned.

I give my mount a little kick and call to my father, "It's not gone." I manage to get Starlight to stop as I hop down, sliding precariously in the wet meadow grass. I move toward the still smoldering remains. My father's damp footsteps squeak and squish as he approaches. "Someone burned it to the ground," I whisper.

"Get back on your horse, Mitzy. We need to get out of here."

"It's all right, Dad. Whoever did this is long gone."

"What do you mean? How can you possibly know that?" He puts a hand on my arm.

"I just do, okay? Let's look around—and make sure Diane wasn't in the trailer when it happened." Why am I suggesting we look for something I absolutely do not want to find?

My father's hand slips off my arm and we circle in opposite directions around the carnage.

I'm glad I swapped out my flip-flops for tennis shoes when we stopped by the apartment to grab my hoodie. I pick up a fallen branch and poke through the charred debris.

"I don't see any human remains." Jacob's voice carries notes of relief and hope.

"Maybe she was kidnapped," I propose. "Maybe whoever killed Walt thought she knew something."

"We're not even sure what Walt was into. What makes you think Diane would've known anything about his dealings?"

"Call it daughterly intuition. If Walt was the most important person in Diane's life, I find it hard to believe she had no idea what kind of trouble he was dealing."

"Well, if someone kidnapped her, maybe the sheriff can ping her phone or something."

I flick a large piece of melted plastic siding over and stop dead in my tracks. "I don't think that's going to be possible."

My dad hurries to my side. "Is it Diane?"

"No. It's her phone."

"Speaking of phones, we better call this in. The sheriff needs to get a team out here." My dad reaches for his phone. "No reception."

I stoop over and pick up Diane's phone. I press the home key and tap in a six-digit code. The phone unlocks.

"How did you do that? Is that some kind of millennial thing?" Jacob leans toward the phone in my hand.

Turning slowly, I stare at my dad's face. At first I don't see him clearly. It's almost like I'm looking through water and he's on the other side of the swirling liquid. He snaps into focus and I look from his face to the phone and back up. "I have no idea. I think I heard the numbers—somehow." I check the recent calls and the name at the top of the list is "Ivy." "The last call she made was to her mom."

"That doesn't seem suspicious. I'm sure she was letting her know about Walt's death."

"But everyone said Ivy left Diane behind. Walt raised her on his own. How would Diane even know how to get a hold of her unless . . ."

"Unless what?" Jacob stares anxiously. "I'm starting to recognize that look. What are you thinking, Mitzy?"

"I'm thinking either Diane was an accomplice in her father's murder or she's about to be the next victim."

Without another word, Jacob scoops me back onto my horse and sets a fast pace toward Chez Osprey. I find myself bouncing along and hanging on for dear life.

We thunder up behind the restaurant. My dad leaps off his horse in one smooth move and runs in through the back door to the kitchen.

A moment later he returns with Nimkii in tow.

They're arguing about something. My father points to me. Nimkii points to me. My father throws his hands up in exasperation. Nimkii goes back inside and returns with a shotgun and a handgun.

My dad looks at me and shakes his head.

I carefully disentangle myself from the saddle and walk toward the pair. "So, what's going on here?"

My father crosses his strong arms over his broad chest. "He thinks we should race over to the other side of the island and see if we can find Diane before the smugglers take her to Canada."

Nimkii turns to me with his calm retort. "And your father thinks I am a foolish child who acts impulsively and without the blessings of Mother Earth."

I have no interest in getting in the middle of it, so I withhold my opinion.

Nimkii holds the handgun out for me to see as he points and explains. "This is the safety. Hold the gun in your dominant hand, lay a finger alongside the trigger, and rest that hand in the palm of the other hand. Like this." He demonstrates. "You use this sight here, and when you have the target between these two marks, pull the trigger. The clip holds thirteen rounds." He hands me the gun, grip first. "The safety is on."

With an audible swallow, I take the gun. A quick look at my dad does nothing to calm my racing heart. I shove the cold steel against my back and under the waistband of my jeans.

Jacob's ferociously chewing the inside of his cheek and shaking his head almost imperceptibly.

"I have actually shot a gun before, Dad. I grew up in Arizona. Remember? Sure, some of my foster families were new-age, patchouli-wearing hippies, but some were good ol' redneck cowboys. I may not be a deadeye shot, but I can probably provide some cover fire." For a split second there's a glimmer of pride in Jacob's eyes, before it's replaced with fatherly concern.

"No one is taking any risks today. Nimkii called it in. The sheriff is mobilizing a team. We're just going to observe and report. Everybody understand?" He waits until we respond.

My Native American gun handler and I both nod.

Nimkii saddles up a large paint named Biscuit and leads the way across the island.

The colorful trees hold no magic for me on this trip.

The weather takes a turn for the worse as Nimkii guides us through the dense woodland. Any semblance of a trail has long since disappeared. If my father and I had tried to make it across the island on our own, we would have gotten hopelessly lost.

The rain pelts down in sheets and I'm reminded of the monsoon season back in Arizona. Of course, the loamy, dark soil of the island absorbs the water nearly as fast as it falls. No danger of a flash flood here.

The lead horse stops.

"Once we reach the twisted pine tree, we'll have to leave the horses. It's only a short walk to the top of the bluff. But we want to stay out of sight of their lookouts." Nimkii gives Biscuit a little kick and we resume our silent and soggy trek.

Eventually, I feel water seeping through my jeans from the wet saddle beneath. Just when I thought things couldn't get more uncomfortable.

Nimkii signals for us to stop and he and my father hop off their mounts with ease.

I fumble around and catch my hoodie on the saddle horn as I struggle to climb down from Starlight's back. Hooked like an old jacket, I dangle with my feet still inches from the slippery, wet ground.

Jacob hurries over, unhooks me, and sets me on my feet as though I'm a small child.

Nimkii takes my horse and lashes it to a thick birch tree just out of sight.

"No more talking beyond this point. When I give you the signal to stay down"—he pushes his hand toward the earth—"stay as low as you can. All right?"

I nod.

"Whatever you say." My dad looks at me. "You sure you want to keep going?"

"Yeah, I'm sure." I don't feel sure. I feel like I have a large gun stuck in the back of my waistband and I wish it wasn't there. I also feel wet and miserable. But the thought of what might happen to Diane if we don't at least slow the smugglers down . . . I'm willing to press on.

The three of us move forward in solemn single file.

Jacob carefully holds branches out of the way for me, but the tangled mess of raspberry vines twisting across the forest floor on this side of the island is not as thoughtful. The sharp thorns scratch into the flesh beneath my jeans. Geez! And I thought all the needle-covered plants in the desert were dangerous.

Nimkii gives the signal for us to stay low.

A moment later, the silence is replaced with the sound of boats, a woman shouting orders, and gunfire.

Jacob pushes me into the mud and covers me with his body.

Nimkii crawls over to us and whispers, "Not gunfire. Backfire."

Jacob helps me to a low squat and quietly offers an apology.

The cold mud actually soothes my scratched legs, so why complain?

When we finally reach the edge of the bluff, Nimkii leads the way into a well-hidden lookout behind two huge granite boulders.

From our vantage point, we can see a flurry of activity on the rocky beachfront.

Five small speedboats tug against their anchors in a partially hidden cove. A little boat swerves between the others, with its engine coughing, spitting, and backfiring as it struggles against the waves.

Three collapsible yurts, covered with tree branches for camouflage, stand on the shore and could serve as temporary storage or sleeping quarters.

Most of the smugglers must be in one of them. Other than the pilot of the noisy motorized craft, only two men can be seen paddling a canoe out to the nearest boat, and a lone woman stands on shore with a clipboard.

The hairs on the back of my neck tingle. There's something strangely familiar about the woman. We're probably three or four hundred yards away, but something about her hair . . .

I creep closer to Jacob and tug his arm. He slips back from the lookout and gazes at me questioningly.

We're not supposed to talk, so I look around until I find a thick twig. I try to write in the mud, but my scratchings are illegible.

He leans in and pushes back my hood. His voice is a low whisper in my ear. "What?"

I follow suit and lean my lips next to his ear. "That woman is Diane."

His head whips towards me and narrowly misses my cheekbone. I lean back and fall—you guessed it—on my rear end into the mud.

Jacob reaches for Nimkii, taps him furiously, and signals him to pull back. We move as fast as we can in a low crouch and remain silent until we get back to where we tied up the horses.

Nimkii loosens the reins and we hastily mount up and ride into the protective cover of the dense forest.

Once we're a safe distance from the smuggler's cove, Nimkii halts and looks at my dad. "What is it?"

"I think we got played. That woman on the beach is Diane. She doesn't look like a victim to me."

"I'll ride back and warn the sheriff." Without so much as a "by your leave," Nimkii digs his heels into Biscuit's sides and disappears in a pounding of hooves and splattering mud.

I look at Jacob. "Can you get us back?"

He nods. "Probably."

By the time we find our way back to Chez Osprey, Sheriff Erick, Deputy Paulsen, and four uniformed officers I've never met are huddled inside the stable.

At the sound of our horses approaching, Deputy Paulsen pulls her gun.

"Easy Paulsen. That's Jacob and Mitzy." Nimkii shakes his head and quickly sidles up next to me. I attempt to hide my surprise as he slips the gun out of my waistband while he helps me climb down from Starlight's saddle.

"Let me take that horse for you, Mitzy." He leads our mounts to the stable and I'm sure there's a soft thunk of a gun being hidden at the bottom of the feed bucket.

Jacob and I approach the tight knot around the sheriff to share our news about Diane.

Sheriff Harper turns and examines me from head to muddy shoes. "Did you fall off your horse, Moon?" His smile touches his eyes and he chuckles softly.

Jacob steps up and takes control of the discussion. "Look Sheriff, I don't know what Diane and her mom are up to. But both of them seem like solid suspects."

Erick shakes his head. "When I got the call from Nimkii about the burned-up trailer and Diane possibly being kidnapped, I gave Odell a quick call to see if he had any information about Walt's other businesses. Any possible enemies."

I chime in to support my dad. "Well, we just saw Diane. She didn't get kidnapped. Looks like she's running the whole thing down there."

Erick steps away from his other officers and lowers his voice. "That's just it. Odell gave me the only number he had for Diane and told me to let her know about Walt. I called her yesterday to let her know about Walt's death. She headed back to college a week after the Pin Cherry Festival. Apparently, she attends the University of Minnesota down on the Minneapolis campus." Erick shakes his head. "So I don't know who was at that trailer, or who that woman was on the beach—but it sure as heck can't be Diane."

My knees get a little wobbly and I look up at my dad. "Whose phone did we find?"

Erick's head snaps in my direction. "You found a phone?"

I feel around inside my hoodie and pull out the phone I believed belonged to Diane. "We thought it was Diane's phone. The last number called was 'Ivy.'" I hand the phone over. "Maybe it belongs to whoever burned down the trailer?" I can't very well tell Erick that the tingling prickle running through the hairs on the back of my neck confirms my suspicion, but they do.

He takes the phone and presses the home key. "It's locked." He looks at me. "Was it unlocked when you found it?"

I have absolutely no intention of telling Sheriff Harper about my visions, feelings, or voices. "Mmhmm."

My dad arches an eyebrow.

"Paulsen, get this phone back to headquarters and see if they got a way to crack the code."

"10-4 Sheriff." Deputy Paulsen yanks an evidence bag out of her back pocket, bags the phone, seals it, and snarls in my direction. "You probably wiped any useful prints off the evidence, amateur." She brushes past me with a purposeful shoulder shove.

Outwardly I school my features to the portrait of innocence, but inwardly I smirk knowingly. Maybe I did mess up the prints, but it was worth it to get that peek at the recent calls.

Jacob puts a protective arm around me and announces, "Mitzy and I are gonna head back to the mainland. Looks like you guys have this under control."

As we hurry back to the boat, he whispers, "We better have a chat with Odell."

I nod fervently and try to ignore the squish squish of my feet in my soggy tennis shoes.

CHAPTER 14

After a shivery boat ride and a bumpy drive in my dad's F100 pickup, the dried mud on my jeans is itch-tastically unbearable. I beg Jacob to drop me off at the apartment so I can take a quick shower before we go to Myrtle's Diner.

I make it two steps inside the front door of the bookshop before Twiggy's commanding voice bellows from the back room. "Take off the wet shoes."

Don't ask me how she knows, but I have no intention of disobeying a direct order from my mission-critical volunteer employee. I slip off the wet tennis shoes and tiptoe on my mushy socks.

A loud exhale and the endless spinning of the paper towel dispenser echo from the back room.

I hop over the "No Admittance" chain, circle up the wrought-iron staircase, and rush into the apartment to avoid confrontation. However, before the bookcase door can even slide shut behind me, my Ghost-ma is all over me.

"What happened to you? You are in a state! Did you fall off your horse?"

What is it with everyone thinking I don't know how to ride a horse? I'm pretty sure I performed above average, but I don't have time to debate the finer points of my equine skills. "I need to take a shower and meet Dad at the diner."

Grams swooshes in behind me. "Not before you fill me in on the details of your muddy escapades."

I left the wet slicker on the boat for future adventures, so I start by peeling off my slightly damp hoodie. It proves an ineffective signal.

"What did Diane say? Did she cooperate?"

"Grams, I have to shower. Shoo! I'll fill you in after I've decontaminated myself."

Grams vanishes in an angry sparkle.

Turns out, it's far more difficult to remove wet, muddy skinny jeans than you may have imagined. After a great deal of tugging, wiggling, and unladylike exclamations, I am finally free of the filthy denim. I drag myself into the shower and regret that I don't have time to fully enjoy the luscious steamy water. However, I rapidly change my mind as the hot water brutally stings the raspberry-thorn scratches on my legs. I wash my hair in haste and leap out of the shower like a cat who fell into a swimming pool. I yank on clean undergarments and call for Grams to return. As I fluff my hair into a publicly acceptable shape and apply the bare minimum of makeup, I bring her up to speed on the "Diane is not Diane" dilemma.

"Well I never! Who do you think that woman is?"

"That's what we're hoping Odell can figure out."

A jarring thud comes from the bedroom, drawing both Grams and me out of the bathroom.

The ever-helpful Pyewacket has knocked a photo album off the bookshelf.

"Pye! Bad kitty! Bad!" I shake my finger in his general direction.

He grooms his whiskers as though he hasn't a care in the world.

Grams swirls toward him. "It's all right my sweet kitty," she coos as she drags her ghost fingers down his spine.

I crouch to collect the album, and admonish Grams. "Stop spoiling him. I'm the one who has to deal with his moods and his acting out when he doesn't get his way. I can't begin to imagine the indulgent life that cat had before you crossed over."

Grams chuckles. "It's not all that different from your life now, honey."

My hands hang in midair and I stop collecting the photographs that have spilled from the plastic pages and stare at my ghostly grandmother. She's right. I literally had all of this handed to me on a silver platter. Sure, I survived losing my mother and some pretty awful foster homes, but I've hardly put in more than two decades on this planet and now I've inherited a fortune. Maybe I should follow my dad's example and set up some kind of philanthropic foundation. I look up and Grams is nodding furiously.

"Re-ow." Informative, perhaps even an agreement.

"Yes, Pye. I've discovered your exhibit and I understand you're upset that we were ignoring you. Come over here and let me scratch you between the ears. Will that make things better?"

Pyewacket slinks across the floor with the abject superiority only felines can display and rubs his head against my knee—aggressively.

He knocks me off balance, the album falls, and more pictures slide out. "Geez Louise!" I set the album on the floor and begin collecting the scattered images a second time.

"REE-ow!" That one sounds dangerous.

I used to be able to ignore his outbursts, but there is something important in that missive. I stop what I'm doing and stare at the photographs spilled across the floor. I can't quite place the era, but there are several pictures featuring a hand-carved sign for the Walleye Inn and Tavern. "Grams is this Walt?"

She floats over my shoulder. "Yes, honey, that's Walter."

He looks nothing like my discovery on Boilerplate Beach. I pull the photo closer and my mouth goes dry. "Grams. That's her."

"Her, who?"

"The woman who's not Diane. The woman on the beach, running the smuggling operation."

"Oh my stars." Grams anxiously flickers in and out.

"You know her? You actually know this woman." I tap my finger on the face in the picture.

"That's Ivy. That's Walt's ex-wife, Ivy Lapointe," she whispers.

"The woman does not age. She looked exactly like this when we saw her at the trailer. If this was taken before Diane was born . . . She must be nearly fifty now," I whisper. Dropping to my backside, I stare at the picture, and then tilt my head to get a better look at the furry fiend who made this mess. "I'm beginning to suspect this wasn't an accident, Robin Pyewacket Goodfellow."

Grams giggles in spite of my severe tone. "I always loved it when Silas called him that."

I stand and tuck the photo in the back pocket

of my jeans. I grab a tank top from the floor, make sure it's right side out, and slip it on. This one says, "Roses are Dead. Violets are blew." and there's a stick of dynamite in the violet. What can I say? I went through an anti-love phase in my late teens.

Donning my simple flip-flops, I walk to the diner, ignoring the sputter of raindrops intent on testing my tolerance.

Good ol' Johan Olafsson drives his tractor down Main Street without a care in the world. I wave happily. Every time I see that guy, I remember how much he annoys Deputy Paulsen and I regret she can't see him in action right now.

Inside the nearly empty restaurant, I find Odell and my father with their heads close together across the table in the back corner booth. I approach slowly. My dad is the first to look up.

"Hey Mitzy. You're not going to believe what Odell told me."

With both hands resting on the table, I tilt my head and say, "Let me guess. The woman we thought was Diane—the woman we saw running the smuggling operation—it was Ivy Lapointe."

Jacob and Odell stare at me like I have two heads.

"Now, how in the Sam Hill do you know that?" says Odell.

I extract the photo from my back pocket and slap it down in the middle of the table.

Odell takes one look at it and let's out a long low whistle. "I ain't seen this photo for twenty years. You find this at the trailer?"

While part of me is anxious to take full credit, I feel I would be remiss if I didn't let the gentlemen know the intricate part my cat played in discovering the helpful picture. "Actually, the one and only Pyewacket knocked a photo album off the bookshelves and scolded me until I found this in the mess on the floor."

Jacob shakes his head and exhales. "That cat has always given me the creeps. It's like he thinks he's human. He looks at you like he knows things."

"Always? How long has Grams had Pyewacket?" I ask.

My dad looks up and to the left. "Hmmm, I can't remember him not being around. She must've gotten him when I was too little to notice—maybe even before I was born."

I narrow my gaze. "You must be mistaken. Cats don't live forty plus years!"

Jacob shrugs. "They do when they're spoiled beyond all reason."

Odell picks up the photo and rubs his thumb over the face of his brother. "I let you down, Walt. I let you down and I'm real sorry."

Anxious to move away from the heavy emotion, I volunteer my theory. "I think Ivy killed Walt. Maybe she killed Lars too."

"Do we actually know if Lars is dead?" Jacob squints his eyes and leans back.

"Lars Gershon?" Odell looks from me to my dad and back to me again.

"Yeah, Sheriff Erick found his business card near Walt's body. He thought I dropped it, so he returned it to me. I called to follow up on it yesterday and his assistant was pretty upset. She had just gotten a call about an hour before. Lars is definitely dead."

The door of the diner scrapes open and Sheriff Erick hustles into the room. "Should've known I'd find you three scheming."

I throw a hand on my curvy hip and reply, "I've never schemed a day in my life, Erick."

Sadly, I am woefully unprepared for the guffaws that erupt from Jacob and Odell. In fact, the delectable local sheriff adds a chuckle of his own.

"Wow. Just, wow." I stare daggers at the three of them.

Odell slides out of the red vinyl booth and straightens his grease-stained apron. "You just checking up on us, Sheriff? Or you got something to report?"

"I have a possible ID on the woman—"

"Ivy Lapointe," I blurt.

Erick's shoulders deflate and he shakes his head. "How do you do that?" There is a lovely hint of admiration in his eyes.

This time I kick the meddling Pyewacket to the proverbial curb and take full credit. "It's a gift." I get a tingle on my bare ring finger. I didn't realize how much of the truth I was actually telling.

"We're still looking into how Walt's tied up in this whole mess. The actual Diane wasn't able to provide much information. She said she'll come up from college tomorrow and give us whatever she has on her mother, but it doesn't sound like much. They've been estranged almost Diane's whole life."

I can't imagine a mother not wanting her own child. It was hard enough for me to cope with my mother being taken from me by a tragedy. I don't think I would've been able to hold it together if she had straight up abandoned me. I keep my thoughts to myself and slide into the booth next to my dad.

"Hungry?" Odell winks in my direction.

"As ever," I shamelessly reply.

He heads back to the kitchen and the familiar sounds of burgers sizzling on the grill and fries bubbling in hot oil fill me with joyous anticipation. I can't imagine a better smell than freshly fried potatoes! With the possible exception of freshly fried potatoes being fed to me by the crisp, slightly woodsy smelling Sheriff Erick!

"Is there anything else you're forgetting to tell me, Moon?" He takes a step closer.

Startled back to the present, I hope and pray that Erick can't read my mind, and I'm about to say no, when I remember Lars Gershon. "It might interest you to know that Lars Gershon is also dead."

Erick raises an eyebrow, shakes his head, but eventually nods. "We got a call from Lake County first thing this morning." He tilts his head and grins as he adds, "But I appreciate you keeping me in the loop." He hooks a thumb over his Sam Browne belt and I am powerless to prevent my eyes from following the gesture toward his thinly concealed abs.

Jacob hits me square on the floating rib with an elbow jab.

I pop my eyes up like a schoolgirl busted by the principal and blurt, "Thanks for stopping by, Erick."

He hesitates for a minute and I'm not sure if his expression is confusion or hurt. "I better be gettin' back to the station." He nods to the table in general and walks out without a backward glance.

Which is fortunate, because if he had looked back, I would've gotten busted a second time.

CHAPTER 15

BRIGHT AND EARLY the next morning—which is around 9:00 AM for me—and armed with the photo of Ivy Lapointe, I take a little drive south to Gershon Antiquities in my sporty silver Mercedes 300SL coupe with gullwing doors.

The trees at this latitude include a wider variety of species and are starting to melt from bright greens to light yellows. But if the local gossip is to be believed, when autumn hits its stride up here in the great North, the rainbow of colors will be breathtaking. I'm actually looking forward to it after the palette-teaser on the island. There's a lot more vegetation in Sedona than people assume, but most of the trees are some version of pine so the fall-color display is a little less spectacular.

I have to remember to ask Grams about

Pyewacket. I have a hard time believing my dad's version of that story. A forty-year-old cat! I don't think so, Dad. The city limits sign for Grand Falls races into view and I check my phone for the final directions to the antique store.

After parking on the near empty street, I'm stunned to discover Gershon Antiquities is not so much an antique store as a dealer who specializes in high-end private collections.

"Welcome to Gershon Antiquities. How may I help you?"

That's definitely the southern drawl from the telephone. "Hi, I called earlier about Lars. I'm so sorry for your loss. I'm Isadora Duncan's granddaughter." I secretly hope that name carries as much weight as my dad believes it does.

The petite redhead scurries out from behind her immaculate Louis XVI desk and shuffles over as fast as her snug, narrow pencil skirt will allow. "So nice to make your acquaintance. I'm so sorry I hung up on you." She puts a hand to her forehead. "Where were my manners?" The hand drops to her side and rubs the fabric of her skirt. "I was just so flabbergasted by the news about Mr. Gershon. I hadn't had a chance to collect myself. Again, I'm so sorry, Miss—"

"Mitzy Moon. Isadora is my paternal grandmother." Not sure why I felt the need to add that, but I will definitely remove it from my future repertoire. If my extensive background in film and television has taught me anything, I need to walk around this establishment and search for hidden clues, and I need to get her talking. "That is a gorgeous desk." I gesture to her previous perch.

"Oh, isn't it a divine desk? I just adore French antiques. There was a famous firm in Paris, Maison Jansen, which just made the most wonderful items. This exquisite little writing table is custom-made solid walnut, with silver leaf mirrored *verre églomisé*, reverse painting. And it's in perfect condition! They don't make pieces from solid quarter-sawn oak with lovely dove-tailed construction like this anymore."

I bite my tongue. Apparently, it's not that hard to get her talking. I didn't understand a word of that diatribe, other than "desk."

"Are you looking for something in particular, Miss Moon?"

"I feel like I'll know it when I see it. My grandmother's taste was rather eclectic, and I'm looking to continue that theme in the decor." I can almost see the character I'm playing. Maybe a mid-1990s Michelle Pfeiffer? Or perhaps an early-2000s Nicole Kidman? I throw myself into the role. I study each piece as though my life could depend on purchasing it.

"That vase is a lovely addition to any home. It's from a large estate sale we coordinated out on the island. Most of the items were what we like to call 'hunting lodge chic,' but there were a few high-value pieces that we brought into our collection."

An estate sale on the island? I can't imagine smugglers selling off their goods so publicly. Chez Osprey seemed completely intact. She can't possibly mean . . .

"If you're interested in any jewelry, let me know. I have a private room with special lighting and a large mirror."

Keep it general. Don't pounce, I tell myself. "I'd love to see the jewelry."

She leads me into a small room off to the side where a three-tiered glass jewelry case glows with precious gemstones. The pin lighting bounces off the exquisite stones and casts a tantalizing sparkle against the walls and ceiling. It almost makes me want to buy some jewelry.

"Where do you get these wonderful pieces?"

"I'm sure you know there's an aging population this far north of the big city. People move up here to get some peace and quiet in their golden years, and many of them don't have close relatives. Some of the sales come during their lifetime to finance home repairs or bucket-list trips, but a great deal of our stock comes in through our estate sales."

"Like the one out on the island?"

"Oh yes, but that was what we call a 'live one'." She giggles into her hand.

I have to ask. I can't possibly contain my question any longer. "Oh that's devilish. What does that mean?"

She blanches and lets a self-conscious gasp escape her thin lips. "I shouldn't have said that."

"Nonsense. It's just us girls. You can tell me." Now I feel like every mean girl in every high school movie that has ever been made.

"Oh, all right. We call it a 'live one' when someone sells off their estate before they die. This man was in a huge hurry to unload not only his quality items, but he wanted us to get rid of everything."

"Oh that seems beneath you." I shake my head and pretend to understand.

She tiptoes closer and puts a hand on her chest. "I know! Right? We're designed to deal with high-end items. I can assure you I've never before had to find a home for a singing trout on a plaque."

I'm not sure how I prevent myself from blurting that it was probably a walleye—from Walleye Lodge. But she's said enough to convince me that the "estate sale on the island" was held by Walt Johnson. Now I found my connection; all I need is a motive.

"Were there any other dealers helping you sell off his items?"

"It's so funny you should ask. We rarely split commissions, but as I mentioned some of the lower-end items just didn't fit with our clientele. So we partnered with a pawnshop"—she whispers the last two words and shakes her head indignantly before continuing—"over in Round Rock. I'm sure they did great with their part of the inventory."

"Do they pay you a finder's fee or something?"

She looks at me as though I've just grown horns. Her southern accent takes on an edge. "Are you with the police?"

"Hardly! I'm just nosy." I fake chuckle as long as I possibly can and feign interest in a few baubles.

I'm about to leave when a section of military pins and medals catch my interest. "Are these from the estate sale on the island?"

She leans in and whispers, "Honestly, I should've sent them to Round Rock. But Lars, God rest him, insisted."

"I'll take 'em."

"Which ones?" She eyes me suspiciously.

"All of them." I strut out of the pretentious side room and up to the register, waiting for her to catch up.

She scurries after me with her tight-kneed mermaid waddle, carrying the tray of medals. "I'll ring these up for you right away, Miss Moon."

I swallow my glee. "Can you gift wrap the whole tray? I'll pay whatever extra for that." That'll teach her to judge a baby-face chick in skinny jeans. I might not look the part, but I'm loaded. Clearly, I say none of this aloud.

She hands me a lovely golden package tied with a silver ribbon.

I take my purchase back to the car and stew over this new information. I know Walt was in financial trouble, so the estate sale makes perfect sense. But what if there's more to it? Erick said something about Diane coming up from college. I need to make sure Odell introduces us.

I'm tempted to drive to Round Rock and question the pawnbroker, but my stomach is anxious to get back to the diner. For a couple of reasons.

I wave to Odell as I enter the diner and he throws down a burger.

"Hey, Tally, how's business?" I ask.

She glances around the room and her snug flaming-red bun holds firm on top of her head. "Looks like you're it, Mitzy."

I chuckle and take a seat.

"You want pop or coffee?"

I snicker at the northern expression and reply, "I'll have a soda. Thanks."

She nods and hustles behind the counter to retrieve my beverage.

I pull out my phone to look through my notes. Found Walt's body Monday morning. Talked to Diane—I delete Diane and type Ivy. Talked to Ivy on Tuesday. Heard about Lars Gershon's death on Tuesday. I set my phone on the table and lean back. With my eyes closed I replay my first visit to the burned-out site of the former Walleye Lodge.

The woman's long black hair definitely gave her a youthful appearance, but why did we assume she was Diane? I guess Jacob assumed it was Diane and I simply followed his lead. No. She introduced herself as Diane and my dad didn't argue. But he probably hasn't seen Diane in more than fifteen years. It could be pretty easy to mistake the remembered face of a five-year-old girl for the transformed face of the woman living in a trailer next to the destroyed lodge that used to belong to her father. I study the image of the woman's face in my mind. Now I recall the lines around her eyes. Little lines around her mouth. A crease between her eyebrows and the mole on her left cheek. There were subtle signs of age, but for the most part time has been kind to Ivy Lapointe. Fifty might be the new thirty, but not many women her age could pass for a twenty-year-old.

That tattoo! That was no tribute to a missing

mother. That tattoo of ivy on Ivy's arm—talk about on the nose—is probably what inspired the tattoo of "ivy" on Walt's mermaid's arm. It's tattoo *Inception*!

Odell sets my plate on the table and slides in the bench seat across the table from me. "Seems like that little brain a yours might blow a gasket." He chuckles and interlaces his fingers, twirling his thumbs absently. "You find out anything about Walt today?"

The image of Ivy evaporates and I reach down to the package on the seat next to me. I push the present across the table toward Odell.

"What's this? It ain't my birthday."

"Just open it."

He rips into the gold tissue paper and stops as soon as he exposes the Purple Heart. His fingers reach down and tenderly rub the medal. "Where did you get this?" he breathes.

"I paid a visit to Gershon Antiquities today. I discovered Walt had a big estate sale. And I'd have to say that sale must've been before the fire."

Odell looks up at me, his face a swirl of confusion, disbelief, and anger. "Can't believe he sold off my grandpa's medals!" He shakes his head. "I'm not sure how he got his hands on them in the first place."

"How much do you know about the fire that destroyed Walt's lodge?"

Odell runs his fingers across a few more pieces of his grandfather's military legacy before leaning back and letting a heavy sigh escape his chest. "Not much, kid. Like I told you before—I cut Walt off. I told him I wasn't bailing him out anymore and that was pretty much the last I heard from him. 'Course, it's a small town and I heard about the fire, but once I learned Walt was all right, I just let it lie." He leans forward and rests his elbows on the table. "Why do you ask?"

"Something tells me it wasn't an accident."

"Well, he'd a been a bigger fool than I imagined if he burned down that place without having any insurance."

"I'm not entirely sure Walt burned it down. And I've also got a pretty solid feeling that it wasn't an insurance scam."

Odell tilts his head and fixes me with a puzzled stare. "What are you cooking up over there?"

"Don't you find it strange that Walt sold everything he had that was of any value, and apparently some things that weren't even his, before the fire? I mean, doesn't that seem a little too convenient?"

"I see your point. But if there was no money in it, why burn it down?"

I nod, but push my idea. "Maybe it was a warning. Maybe he got in with the wrong people and they were trying to scare him, for some reason." I chew on the inside of my cheek and add, "Walt must've suspected something was up . . . Or maybe he was trying to raise enough money to pay them off?"

"I guess it makes about as much sense as anything else. But Walt's gone. It's not like you can confirm your theory."

This is exactly the conversational opportunity I was hoping for but don't want to jump in too quickly and lose my chance. "I thought you might introduce me to Diane, when she comes up this weekend."

Odell slides out of the booth with a chuckle and raps his knuckles on the table before he walks back to the kitchen. "Whatever you need, kid. Whatever you need." He sighs and the metal spatula scraping across the grill signals the end of our discussion.

I'm not stupid enough to think I outsmarted him, but I am pleased he's going to allow me to play through. Now it's time for me to mosey on over to the police station and see if I can't continue my winning streak and weasel a few more answers from Erick.

Just as soon as I finish my fries . . .

. . .

The uniformed officer obsessed with the Furious Monkeys app has a pint-sized sidekick—a curly-haired child of five or possibly ten. I have no idea why. The police station is fairly quiet, but as I scan the room it becomes clear that there's been an invasion of Mini-Mes. I approach the counter and give the small girl a wave. "Is it 'take your mom to work' day?"

The little girl giggles and looks away.

Her mother does not look up from her phone.

The little girl's eyes widen and she stares at my white-blonde hair. "Why did you cut your hair, Elsa?"

I shake my head. "I don't think we've met. I'm Mitzy Moon."

At that pronouncement, Furious Monkeys puts down her phone. "Here to see the sheriff?"

"I sure am."

The little girl leans toward her mother and whispers, "Why does Elsa want to see the sheriff? Is she in trouble for turning someone into ice?"

The mother looks at me and for the first time actually seems to realize I am a human standing across from her in this reality. She stares at my hair and chuckles. I wish I could say it's the first time I've endured that reaction.

She turns to her daughter and announces,

"That's no Disney princess, sweetheart. In fact, just last month she was accused of murder."

The little girl gasps. "Don't worry, Elsa, your sister will save you."

For some unknown reason, that innocent phrase gets me right in the gut. I swallow hard and blink back unwelcome emotions. I borrow Odell's term of endearment. "Thanks, kid." Shifting my attention back to the mother, I ask, "Is Erick in his office?"

Furious Monkeys has already returned to the world inside her phone and nods without looking up. I sashay through the swinging gate and find my way to my next quarry.

Erick looks up as I enter and quickly closes the folder in front of him. "Do you have something to tell me?"

Don't worry, I got a peek in the folder before he flipped it shut. He was studying a report with a Coast Guard seal at the top for some reason. The neat, orderly printing caught my attention. I refrain from answering his direct question and instead help myself to an uncomfortable seat in his dilapidated office chair. "I feel like I've already given you quite a bit, Erick. It's time you shared a thing or two with me."

His rolly office chair squeaks as he leans back. "Is that so?"

Seems like he's in a fairly decent mood, so I

push on. "Can you tell me about the fire that burned down Walt Johnson's tavern?"

He hesitates and slides the folder in front of him underneath a stack to his left. "What's got you so interested in that fire? It was months ago."

"Were there a lot of personal effects lost in the fire?"

He leans forward. "That's an odd question, Moon. Walt was living in the owner's quarters when the place burned down and his daughter was at school. It stands to reason they had personal effects in those rooms, doesn't it?"

Two can play this game. "Does it?"

His eyes twinkle as he replies, "Has anyone ever told you you're an infuriating woman?"

I lean back and laugh heartily. "If I had a quarter for every time someone said that. Well, I'd be—oh, that's right, I am."

He shakes his head. "The fire happened at the tail end of winter—almost spring. We had a huge, unseasonably late snowfall this year, and the fire marshal wouldn't send anyone out to the island. He said there was no way to get a sufficient water supply with everything still pretty iced over and that dispatching a helicopter would be a waste of funds. He took one look at the color of the smoke and said it looked like an accelerant had been used. He figured the deep snow surrounding the lodge would prevent the fire from spreading and he made the call to let it burn out. We'd already confirmed that Walt had gotten out safely."

I ponder the details carefully and find the timing of the blaze and the deep snowfall a little too convenient. "The fire was in April?"

"Early on, if I remember correctly."

I nod and lean toward his irresistible jawline. "And when did you realize who had set the fire?"

"I don't know who set the fire, Moon. Maybe no one. There was no insurance policy, no insurance claim, and no investigation. What are you getting at?"

I put my hand on the desk and tap my fingers. "That's some real shoddy police work, Erick. I spent some time at Gershon Antiquities today and learned that Walt had a massive estate sale in late March, before the fire. *Right* before the fire. Doesn't that strike you as odd?"

He avoids making eye contact and leans away from my tapping fingers. "There's no telling what that guy was up to. What are you getting at?"

"What I'm getting at is that whoever burned down the lodge was sending Walt a message. Maybe he sold off all his possessions because he needed money. He couldn't sell the lodge because he owed more than it was worth and he was using it as collateral for his boats. He couldn't burn it down for insurance money because he let the insurance lapse. Maybe someone burned it down in an attempt to push him farther into a corner. They wanted to take away his options."

Erick straightens up in his chair and clenches his jaw. "You think Ivy had something to do with this? It sounds like you think she was trying to push him into the smuggling business. That right?"

I smile as I hoist myself out of the chair and walk toward the door. I turn, look over my shoulder, and give Erick a little wink. "Seems like it would be something worth looking into, Sheriff."

He grumbles something about being the one to direct the investigation.

Unable to resist, I add, "Oh, and you should ask Paulsen if that boat key belonged to the deceased."

He stands, fumbles for a comeback, and ends up with, "What key?"

I grin, raise one eyebrow, and exit.

CHAPTER 16

Back at the Bell, Book & Candle everything is silent. Twiggy has gone home for the day and I've checked all the high places for any sign of Pyewacket. He's gotten the jump on me one too many times and I'm growing extra cautious. As I reach the top of the circular staircase, the beautiful tomes displayed on every desk in the Rare Books Loft surprise me. Each volume is opened to a specific page and a set of white gloves rest atop every manuscript. Tomorrow must be the monthly event that Twiggy mentioned. I've been told that my grandmother was generous with her collection—to a point. She would allow scholars and researchers from around the world to make reservations to spend a day with any volume from her rare books collection. It must be quite a sought-after appointment. There was a book on every one of the twenty-five reading desks.

I'll have to remember to put on pants before I stumble out of the apartment tomorrow morning. I reach up and grab the candle handle next to the empty spot where *Saducismus Triumphatus* usually rests and pull the lever down. The hidden bookcase door slides open with a satisfying whoosh. I step through and crash directly into a huge corkboard on wheels. "What the—?"

Grams materializes. "Watch your language, young lady."

"What the heck is this doing in the middle of my apartment?"

"I like to call it *our* apartment." She giggles. "Twiggy brought that up earlier. She announced to the room that you had requested tacks and string, but she didn't want you making any holes in the walls."

I open my mouth to protest, but then I remember that every good detective movie I've ever seen has a murder wall. I mean, sometimes it's a missing-kid wall, or a pyro wall, or a kidnapped-woman wall . . . Well, you get the idea. It's a visual place to organize my suspect list.

I rip open the package of tacks, grasp one between my thumb and forefinger, and press it through the picture of Ivy Lapointe with great satisfaction.

I step back.

Grams chuckles.

I spin around. "It's a start. Rome wasn't built in a day."

"A stitch in time saves nine. There's a hole in the bucket, dear Liza." Grams is laughing uncontrollably now.

"I don't think I like it when you use my tactics against me. Leave the sarcasm to the living."

She floats closer and puts an arm around my shoulders. I feel the tingle of her energy mixing with mine. It's not quite real; there's no weight to her presence. But there's a satisfying comfort nonetheless.

"I tease because I love, Mitzy. You are truly an amazing granddaughter and I know you can solve this case."

I wish I felt as confident as she thinks I should. I pull out the photo album that my helpful rescued caracal knocked down and thumb through all the pictures from the Walleye Lodge and Tavern. There really was a preponderance of taxidermy monstrosities in that place. But even an untrained eye like mine can see the finer pieces tucked amongst the hunting trophies and old fishing poles.

In fact, some of the elegant items look downright out of place. "Grams?"

She zooms in so quickly my heart skips a beat.

"What do you need, dear?"

"Probably a package of Depends would be handy!"

"Oh Mitzy, you're such a hoot."

"Grams, you have a lot more experience with antiques. Do you see anything in these photos that would've had some real value?"

She looks over the items and there is an occasional "Oooo" or an "Awww" and finally an "Oh my goodness!"

"What is it?"

"Well, that Bengt Nordenberg painting over the mantelpiece is worth a small fortune. And it was Cal's. I have no idea how Walt had gotten a hold of it or why it would've been placed on display at the lodge."

I take one of the index cards from the stack provided by Twiggy and write down "stolen antiques" and I pin it up on my corkboard. A few more card-worthy ideas come to mind and I also copy the notes from my phone. No matter how I attempt to arrange the cards, I can't make many solid connections between the random "leads."

"Any luck?"

"Nope. They make it look so easy in the movies. You put stuff on a board, tie some string around a few tacks, and 'bingo,' you've got your man—or woman, as the case may be." I step back and look at my arbitrary array. "Mine just looks like a really sad vision board."

With the wall of clues to my back, I pace down the row of six-by-six windows, stopping abruptly when I notice the handgun still lying on my bed. Oops! Looks like I forgot to call Sheriff Erick about that. As I walk a little closer and stare down at the pistol, another plan takes shape.

Jacob mentioned some friend of his could take me to the shooting range and teach me about guns, or something. Maybe I should just hang on to this pistol and—

"Mitzy Moon! Don't you make me use your proper name! You will do no such thing. In fact, I insist that you pick up your phone and call the sheriff immediately. You have no idea where that gun has been." Grams floats directly above the handgun and stares at me with ghostly fury until I retrieve my phone and dial the sheriff's station.

"May I speak to Sheriff Harper, please?" I stick my tongue out at the bossy apparition who is still giving me the stink eye.

Grams nods victoriously and I'm forced to look away from her pious grin.

"What? Oh, yes. You can tell him it's Mitzy

Moon." Without any further questions, my call is transferred. "Hi, Erick. It's Mitzy . . . Oh, I know. But here's the thing, Erick, I need you to come to my apartment and pick up a most-likely-unregistered gun."

There is a deafening silence on the opposite end of the call.

"Are you still there? I said, I have a gun that doesn't belong to me and I was hoping you would come and pick it up."

He explains how that's not in his job description and asks me why I don't just bring it down to the station.

"For one thing, I don't want to get my fingerprints on it. I've already been accused of murder once in this town. Lord knows what you'd try to pin on me if I pick up that gun. And the second thing —" I look at Grams and shrug.

She points wild finger guns at me and throws her hands up in the air like she's crazy.

Stifling a chuckle, I continue, "And the second thing, I don't know the first thing about guns." I smile at my grandmother and wink.

She nods with approval.

"Thank you, Erick." I end the call and update Grams. "He's on his way."

She takes a lap around the room and gasps. "What about the murder wall?"

"Oh, Humpty Dumpty!" My desperate search around the room for a place to hide a giant rolling corkboard reveals no ready-made stash room. Hopeless. I grab the thing and wheel it toward the closet, but there is no way it will fit through the door. Panic rises in my chest. It's a short walk from the sheriff's station to the bookstore.

"He'll be here any minute," shrieks Grams.

"Not helping!" I retort.

Maybe the bedspread could be thrown over the top, although that seems almost more suspicious. And with my luck the gun would fall on the floor and go off. And with even more of my luck, I'd shoot myself.

I wheel the board back toward the secret door when Grams' face pops right through the cork. I gasp and step back. "Grams! Honestly."

"You'll forgive me once you hear what I have to say." I throw my hands up and roll my eyes.

"You only have about five things tacked on the board, sweetie. Maybe just take them down."

Raising a finger to admonish her for scaring just a little bit of pee out of me—once again—I hesitate and have to admit her suggestion is actually a solid plan.

She smiles.

I hastily pull the tacks out, collect the index cards and the picture of Ivy Lapointe, and shove them in between two photo albums on the bookshelf.

My phone rings. It's him! I have to calm down. Geez! I attempt to slow my breathing before I say, "Hello?"

Erick's sexy voice caresses my eardrum. "I'm here, but the door's locked. Are you planning on letting me in?"

"Be right down." I push the panel, race down the stairs—manage to avoid tripping over the "No Admittance" chain—and unlock the front door. No matter how prepared I thought I was, the sight of Sheriff Erick posted up outside my door, back-lit by the streetlamp, is more thrilling than I care to admit.

"So where's this gun, Moon?"

"Follow me, Erick." I put a little wiggle in my waddle as I lead him upstairs. "I have to ask you to turn around, Erick. I can't reveal all my secrets on our first date."

He opens his mouth as though he might protest. Instead he shakes his head and does as he is told.

After I'm sure he's not watching, I reach up and pull the candle handle. The bookcase slides open and I announce, "You can turn around now."

Erick gives a low whistle. "Always full of surprises."

I lead him into my boudoir and tingles race over my skin. If only he were here for more than an armory related errand. "That's it over there, on the bed."

As Erick walks toward my bed, I can't resist the urge to mentally undress him, mentally put him in the bed, and mentally join him.

"Behave yourself, young lady," whispers Grams.

I shake the vision from my head and attempt to strike a professional pose.

Grams whispers in my other ear, "And what profession would that be?" Fresh snickers echo through my head.

Erick takes a pen from his front pocket, pokes it through the trigger guard, and carefully places the gun in an evidence bag. "I don't suppose you're going to tell me where you got this?"

I shrug. "I just moved in here. The cat dragged it out from under the bed. Who knows where it came from?" I hope my face looks as innocent as my voice sounds.

He shakes his head. "Unless you have any other unregistered firearms, Moon. I'll be on my way."

I had hoped he would stick around and interrogate me a little more, but it seems the presence of my bed has thrown off his law enforcement instincts. I convince myself this can only happen because he's trying to resist his powerful attraction to me. Maybe he needs a little nudge. "Are you sure you don't have time for a drink?" I giggle nervously.

He blushes the appropriate shade of pink. "I need to get back to the station. I appreciate you calling this in." He gives a gentlemanly tip of his head and walks out of my apartment.

What's that line I'm thinking of? Oh yeah, I hate to see him go, but I love to watch him leave.

A loud ghost groan comes from somewhere behind me.

"Let me know what you find out about that weapon, won't you Erick?"

His chuckle follows him down the stairs.

Eager to catch a last glimpse, I follow at a respectable distance, and lock up after he leaves.

Confident that a good night's sleep will bring clarity to my investigation into Walt Johnson's murder, I pin the photo of Ivy and my notes back on the corkboard before collapsing into bed.

Sadly, dreams of Erick elude me, and when Pyewacket pounces on my chest at the ungodly hour of 8:00 AM, I feel more relief than anger.

"Come on, buddy. Let's get you some Fruity Puffs and me some wake-up juice." I lean heavily against the plaster medallion above the intercom and yawn as the bookcase slides open.

"Great Expectations!" I slam my hand against the button a second time and twist away from the opening to hide from view while the door slides shut.

"RE-ow." The standard Threat Level Yellow version of "Feed me."

"Don't you dare start with me, Pye. The entire loft is filled with hoity-toity academics! I can't go prancing out there in my shorty jammies."

"Reow." Quiet insistence.

"Well, I vote no." Turning my back on the indignant feline, I stumble into the closet to find some socially acceptable duds.

"You always look nice in blue," enthuses Grams.

My heart thuds against my ribs. "Holy Hera, woman! I am not awake. I have not had coffee. And I've already been ogled by at least twenty book nerds!"

Grams sighs and disappears through the wall.

I grab a navy-blue T-shirt that reads, "A large group of people is called a 'no thank you,'" and a pair of black leggings. Blue and black don't really go together, you say? Tell that to Eddie Izzard.

Now armed with pants, I confidently reopen the door and stride onto the loft like I own the place. Which, of course, I do.

Stares and whispers oscillate across the loft like a brisk summer wind over a wheat field.

Teetering between offended and delighted, I pause.

An oddly familiar pair of shiny men's shoes

tickles a memory, but I'm preempted from further investigation by a low growl from Pyewacket. Before I can react, he charges down the circular staircase, darts between two rows of bookcases, and the bookshop is filled with a blood-curdling yowl.

Hurrying after him, I skitter to a halt just behind his arched back and bared fangs.

What is this guy doing in my bookshop? "Gary? You read?" That came out much more condescendingly than it sounded in my head. Dockworkers can read, he just didn't— Never mind, I'll only dig myself a deeper hole. I try another tack. "What are you doing here?"

If guilt had a signature expression, it would be the look on Gary's face. "Hey, you. I was wondering if you wanted to hook up again sometime?"

Is this guy for real? He still doesn't remember my name and he's hitting on me? I'm honestly tempted to encourage Pyewacket to maul him.

Gary swallows audibly. "Can you call off your cougar, or whatever?"

Now you get what I was saying about him not striking me as the literary type, right? I don't have time for this jerk. "Pye, wait for me in the back room or no Fruity Puffs for you."

Pyewacket drops one more insolent hiss before complying with my request.

"Seriously, what are you doing here, Gary?"

"Can't a guy buy a book?"

A quick glance at the self-help book in Gary's hands that promises to guide you to financial freedom through knitting, and I literally laugh out loud. "Don't get your yarn in a twist." My sense of humor sails over Gary's head, but let me be clear—the play on words was totally intended.

He shoves the volume in his hand back on a random shelf and takes a step toward me. "Okay, you got me. I just wanted to see you again. I don't really read."

Bingo! Before I can offer a snarky response, I hear the whispered word, "Danger." I step back and look around. There's no one else in the stacks, and no Grams hovering above us. Now I'm hearing voices? My life just keeps getting weirder. "Gary, I got a lot on my plate right now. I'm not looking for a relationship or even a two-night stand. You're nice, it was great, let's keep in touch. Buh-bye." Without waiting for his reply, I hustle into the back room and dump Fruity Puffs into Pye's bowl. Thankfully Twiggy has already brewed coffee and I eagerly pour myself a steaming mug of liquid alert.

"You're up early, doll." Twiggy clomps over to the computer, slides the mouse, and types something into an open document.

"So the book nerds upstairs, they're all researchers?"

She doesn't look up or stop typing. "They make reservations, they follow the rules. I don't ask a lot of questions."

"But—" I don't have the energy to play this game today. "Do you need help?"

She turns around slowly and cocks one eyebrow. "From you?"

I shake my head. "You're right. It was a stupid question. I'm off to find some breakfast, and see if I can't get a little more information from the sheriff before I meet Diane."

Twiggy swallows hard and crosses her arms. "You think her mom did it?"

I shrug. "I'm sure Ivy is involved. Whether she's the one who killed Walt or if she just put him in harm's way, I don't know yet." I stand up, rinse out my mug, and set it in the dish drainer. "I'll keep you in the loop. We're gonna figure out who did this."

I make it all the way past the bistro table and have one foot out the door of the back room before Twiggy says, "Thanks."

I nod and keep walking.

CHAPTER 17

THE FLAT GREY morning light promises nothing. After an uneventful breakfast and a "goose egg" on the boat key at the sheriff's station, I shift gears. Seems like the perfect day to go check out the pawnshop. I drive to Round Rock in no real hurry, warily watching the rough waves on the lake and the dark clouds gathering on the horizon.

Hoping to catch the pawnbroker in a chatty mood, I park my gullwing Mercedes a couple of blocks away. Wouldn't you know? Mother Nature chooses that moment to bless us with an intermittent autumn shower. By the time I push open the door beneath the three white globes, I look more like a drowned rat than an heiress.

Perfect. Actually perfect, not sarcastically.

I swipe a thumb under each eye and pull my

clingy wet T-shirt off my chest. I want the guy to talk, not gawk.

Poking around the shop, on an intense search for nothing, I finally draw the owner's attention.

"Are you looking for anything special, Miss?"

I run my fingers through my hair and wipe a little more water off my face. "I'm looking for a present for my grandmother's birthday. Do you have anything that might appeal to an older generation?" I replace the lid on the yellow, smiley-face cookie jar and grin helplessly at the shopkeeper.

He walks out from behind the counter and returns my smile. "Well, aren't you a thoughtful granddaughter. Let me see what I can find."

"She has pretty eclectic décor. A lot of antlers, and for some reason one of those singing fish on a plaque. Have you seen those things?"

He turns and shares a chuckle. "You're not gonna believe this, but a few months back, I got a whole load of stuff from a guy's place out on the island. And I'll be darned if there wasn't one of those plaques in the mix. We've sold a lot of things from that batch, but I'll show you what we have left."

Fantastic. I follow him around like an eager puppy and he shows me all manner of taxidermy and hunting-lodge décor.

"Do you have any paintings?"

The shopkeeper slaps his thigh as though I'm

the most hilarious person he's ever met. "Well, gosh darn it, you must be psychic."

He has no idea. "Oh, you're too much," I reply.

"There was one that we held against a pawn ticket. The fella needed cash and wanted to unload everything, except one painting he said he'd buy back when he could. That ticket expired a couple weeks ago and he didn't show up, so I put her out on the floor." He walks down an aisle crowded tightly with souvenir X-Men glasses, nondescript pottery, and rusty washbasins. We turn the corner, go up two steps, and pass into a space I'll refer to as "pawnshop chic."

"If I remember correctly, those three over there all came from the island—including the one from the expired ticket. But as you can see, there's quite a selection here." He raises his hands and gestures to the many horrible paintings of dogs and other animals playing poker adorning the walls. "I'll leave you here for a few minutes so you can look around."

It only takes me a moment to locate the Nordenberg. Seems like Walt purposely kept it from Lars Gershon's greedy eyes and had every intention of recovering it. I carefully lift it off the wall hook and check the price tag dangling from a crooked piece of scotch tape on the back. $75. If my grandmother is to be believed, this painting is literally worth tens of thousands, and here it is in a pawnshop for $75. I can't believe my luck.

Stifling my glee, I meander the narrow pathways and climb up and down some additional stairs, before returning to the front counter.

"Looks like you found something."

I smile broadly. "I sure did. This will go perfectly in her sitting room. Thanks so much for taking the time to show me around." I carefully lay the painting on the counter.

"Oh, I'm so glad this one is finding a new home. The man who pawned it used to stop by with his pawn ticket and make sure I was still holding it for him. Each time, after he came by, I'd be tempted to make him some kind of deal. He always looked so desperate to buy it back. Then one day he stopped coming. Poor man."

I don't have the heart to tell this kind man that Walt will never visit the pawnshop again.

He picks up the painting, pulls the price tag from the back, and retrieves a small order pad to write down the five-digit code from the tag. When he reaches the price, he hesitates and looks up. "I tell you what, let's call it sixty."

The gesture catches me off guard and I almost yell out my status as a wealthy heiress. Fortunately, I realize his offer isn't intended to be offensive. He genuinely thinks I can't afford the painting and wants me to be able to give my grandmother a lovely present on her birthday. I am touched, and I simultaneously feel a little bit rotten.

"Thank you. I appreciate it."

He rings up the sale and I fish some cash out of my pocket. Luckily I have a lot of fives and ones, which reinforces the poor, young-girl angle of my con.

He takes the money and I lift the painting off the counter.

He reaches out a hand and grabs the frame.

For a moment, I worry that he's on to me and I'm tempted to yank the painting from his hand and run.

"It's still raining out, dear. Hold on a minute. I'll get a big trash bag and wrap it up real nice for you."

This guy is killing me. I'm going to have Silas anonymously send him money just as soon as I set up that philanthropic organization. Note to self: set up philanthropic fund thingy.

The owner returns with a black trash bag, slides the painting inside, rolls down the top, and tapes it shut tightly.

I thank him profusely, grab the painting, and escape before he can kill me with any additional kindness.

As soon as I get back to the car, I rip off the

trash bag. Why? I'll tell you why. Everyone knows that important stuff is frequently stashed behind family photos and—

Aha! One corner of the kraft paper backing is loose. Walt's visits to this painting were no sentimental journey.

I slip my hand carefully beneath the brown backing, feel around slowly, and—Yahtzee!

As I extract the single sheet of paper, I imagine all sorts of fantastical findings, including a possible treasure map. Instead, there are columns of numbers that have no relevance to my life.

Dates? No.

Phone numbers? No.

Addresses? I don't think so.

Safe deposit box numbers? How would I know?

Who cares? I bought a most likely stolen painting and discovered a hidden something or other. I'm going to go ahead and celebrate the crap out of that.

Let it be known that some, or all, of the posted speed limits may have been broken as I rush back to Pin Cherry Harbor. I burst into the apartment and am immediately underwhelmed by the lack of fanfare. "Grams? Grams? Where are you?"

No reply. I lean the painting up against the end of the four-poster bed and walk back into the bookstore. The Rare Books Loft is emptied of its studious bibliophiles, but two or three customers are still milling around on the first floor, so I can't go calling out for my Ghost-ma in the middle of the shop. Instead, I walk downstairs and find Twiggy in the back room. "Have you seen Grams?"

She turns slowly in her chair and gives me a look that can only be described as insufferable. "Now, how exactly would that happen, doll?"

"Right. Sorry, I keep forgetting I'm the only one who can see her. Well, except for Silas, but that's because of the glasses— Never mind. I'll keep looking."

As I walk out of the back room, Twiggy tosses a nugget of knowledge in my direction, "She always loved the top floor of the printing museum. Have you been up there?"

I shake my head. "Thanks. I'll check it out." I slip between the stacks and push open the metal door marked Employees Only.

The smell of ink, machinery, and history fills my nose. I run my hand over the gears and levers of the Gutenberg press. Someday, perhaps she'll tell me the story behind this collection, but today I have more urgent matters to discuss. I hurry up the staircase, trying to push away other memories clamoring to be acknowledged. "Grams? Grams? Are you in here?" I'm not sure why I'm whispering, but somehow being in the museum feels more like being in a library than being in the bookstore.

A sparkling ball of light floats toward me, and Grams materializes.

"That's the one you like, right?"

"Yes. That is the least alarming entrance." I smile warmly at the apparition. "What were you doing in here?"

Her face radiates with a light that actually makes me feel happier. "Come over here and see what I've been working on."

I follow her to a sturdy wooden workbench backed by hundreds of varied-sized cubbies. Beneath the bench are seven or eight thin drawers. One of them stands open, for display I assume.

Grams spins around and smiles at me. "Not for display. I opened it. I've been working on it for almost two weeks! And I finally got it open this far." She spins like a whirling dervish.

"You opened the drawer? I thought you couldn't move physical things. How did you—?"

"Who cares about that?" Grams' ghostly fingers point to a piece of parchment on the table. I lean over and see a quill pen resting on the blotter next to a sheet of parchment, bearing the phrase "I love you Mitzy" in a wriggly, scratchy hand that could be attributed to a child.

Tears spring to my eyes and salty drops make

blotches in the ink. "Shoot, sorry Grams. So sorry, I've ruined your note."

She hugs one arm around my shoulders and whispers, "You couldn't possibly ruin anything if you tried. I do love you, Mitzy."

"And I love you, Grams."

After basking in the familial love that's been missing from my life for a decade, I remember why I came looking for her in the first place. "I have to show you something, too. Come back to the apartment."

She chuckles, and her ghostly eyes twinkle. "I'll race ya." She disapparates and I rush down the stairs, charge through the bookshop, and thunder up the circular staircase. Foolishly thinking I can beat a ghost. As my hand reaches up to pull the candle handle, Grams' face pops through the sliding bookcase door. "I win."

CHAPTER 18

After an early supper at Myrtle's Diner, I saunter into the police station with every intention of telling Erick about the painting. Instead, I am bombarded with such a distracting flurry of activity I fear I'm in the wrong town. Even Furious Monkeys has managed to set down her phone.

Leaning over the counter, I nearly have to shout, "Sheriff Erick here?"

She jerks a thumb over her shoulder toward his office and I take that as permission.

Pushing past the swinging gate, I weave my way through the throng of unfamiliar faces and into Erick's office. Imagine my surprise when there's a gorgeous brunette in uniform sitting on the edge of his desk, joking with him in a much too familiar way.

"Ahem." I clear my throat loudly.

She turns and smiles warmly. Her crisp light-blue shirt is adorned with a colorful display of ribbons above her left breast pocket. "Good morning, ma'am. I'm Captain Truby of the US Coast Guard District 9." She extends her hand.

My hand shoots out reflexively and we exchange an awkward handshake. "Mitzy Moon, owner of the Bell, Book & Candle." I'm not sure why I added that, but it seems like titles are an important part of this trade.

She turns toward Erick and says, "I'll tell Junior you asked after him. He's a sergeant first class now. Anyway, I'll see if I can get the major crimes unit to cooperate. Read my report." She gestures to a document, printed in a remarkably neat hand, lying on his desk.

The same one Erick slipped into a folder on my previous visit.

She gives him a playful slug to the shoulder. "They argue about districts and control all day long. But the bottom line is if it happened out there on that lake, that's my jurisdiction. They can rattle their sabers all they want, but when it comes to the water, it's mine." She punches one fist into the other palm and marches out of Erick's office, giving me my first glimpse of my favorite law enforcement officer.

"Hey, Mitzy." He sighs and shakes his head.

Did he just use my first name? Holey moley! It's happening. My knees are wobbly and my stomach is flip-flopping. He just used my first name. I should talk now. I should say something nice to him now. He looks exhausted, and stressed, and like he could use a shoulder massage. Don't say that. Dear Lord baby Jesus, don't say that. I go with, "What's all the ruckus out front?"

"It'll be all over the papers, so I might as well fill you in." He leans back in his chair and stretches his arms behind his head.

I am filled with anticipation, hoping that his shirt might come just a little untucked. No such luck. "What's going to be in the papers?" I ask.

"We traced that key—" He pauses and fixes me with an exasperated but warm stare. "A concerned citizen turned in a boat key which we traced back to Walter Johnson. The Coast Guard mounted a search for his boat. But it was the FBI divers who located the wreckage of Walt's boat first, and further investigation uncovered signs that a bomb had been placed aboard the vessel. They found evidence of a meth lab too, so it looks like Walt was cooking for Ivy. Whoever planted the device used the chemicals and a detonator to trigger the explosion. So it's definitely homicide, and possibly a lot of other things." He exhales and his hands fall firmly into his lap.

"What kinds of other things?"

He looks out the window of his office and scans across the frenzy of activity. "We've got members of something like six different law enforcement agencies out there trying to work as a joint task force while they fight over who gets credit. DEA. Tribal police. Coast Guard. Major Crimes. Homeland Security. FBI. And I'm sure I'm forgetting somebody."

"What about the *Men in Black*?"

He looks up at me and his blue-grey eyes fill with genuine concern. "The who?"

"You're not going to sit there and pretend like you never saw the movie *Men in Black*, are you?"

The creases vanish from his forehead and the worry in his eyes evaporates as a huge belly laugh grips him. Once he recovers, he looks up at me and smiles. "Thanks, Moon. I needed that."

I'm enraptured by the smile, but I mourn the loss of that momentary first-name-basis thing. Once again, I am Moon. "Anything else I can do?"

"Yeah, you can keep your nose out of this. Way out of this. Take one look out there and you'll see that I've got my hands full. I don't have time to babysit an amateur sleuth, poking around in dangerous business where she doesn't belong."

"I'm not sure if I should be insulted or flattered, Erick." I smile in what I hope is a seductive yet friendly manner.

"Take it however you want, Moon. Just back away from this, all right?" He stands and I get the distinct feeling that our banter is over.

I nod in the most noncommittal way possible and take the long way out of the station. If my meandering exit provides me with a nugget or two of information, what harm could that do?

My super snooping at the sheriff's station garners me some juicy tidbits. I mentally pat myself on the back as I hurry down the unseasonably sweltering sidewalk to the promise of air-conditioning at Myrtle's for my meeting with Diane.

As soon as I enter, there is something off about the energy in the diner. Yes, I know I just referred to the energy in the diner as though it's a real thing. I twist the ring on my left hand around and around my finger, afraid to look down and possibly experience another vision. Instead, I march to a booth and slide in, desperately struggling to ignore the tickling hairs on my forearms.

Odell gives me the customary wave through the orders-up window and Tally delivers my soda. "Are you enjoying the Indian summer, Mitzy?"

"Are we still allowed to say that?"

Tally looks at me as though a horn has sprouted between my eyes. "What else would we call it, dear?" She toddles over to offer refills to the patrons at the table in the front corner. While I sneak a peek at my ring.

It shifts from black to deepest blue and then to cold blue-grey. I don't want to admit how much it looks like the vast swath of water between here and the island. Something shimmers deeper within the image and I lean forward to get a better—

"Hi, are you Mitzy?"

I look up and know in an instant that this is Diane. She has her mother's cheekbones and the same shiny, straight black hair. "Yes. And you must be Diane. Have a seat. I'm so sorry about your dad." I blurt it all out too quickly. My heart is racing and my head pounds with anxiety. Part of me is embarrassed that she caught me staring into my ring, while most of me is just incredibly uncomfortable discussing the death of a parent.

She tosses her bulging backpack onto the seat and slips in beside it. "Thanks. It's been tough. My dad was all I had, you know?"

Boy did I. "Yeah, I get it."

Tally sidles up to the table and tilts her head at Diane in that "you poor thing, how sad for you" kind of way. It was a look I grew to hate in the years following my mother's death. No matter how sincere it was intended, it always felt false and patronizing.

"What can I get ya, Diane?"

Diane smiles with more kindness than I could ever have mustered less than a week after my own mother's death. "Thanks, Tally, I'd love a piece of pin cherry pie, with a big scoop of ice cream and extra whip."

"Coming right up."

Diane seems like a solid person. Maybe we have more in common than I assumed. But I can't shake the heavy feeling of dread. So I try to drive it away with relentless banter. "So, Odell says you're going to college down in some place called the Twin Cities. Do you like it?"

She nods. "Yeah, my campus is in Minneapolis. But the cities are so close together, I guess that's how they got their name." She shrugs. "I like it all right."

"What's your major?" I can't believe I just ask that stupid question. I feel like a giant movie cliché.

"I'm studying forestry."

And silence.

Boy, this girl is not giving me anything to work with. "Oh, interesting." I grab a jam packet and tap it back and forth between my fingers, completely out of conversation topics.

"Are you going to the community college?" she asks.

It almost seems like that question is meant to put me down. I raise my guard a little before I respond. "No, I'm Isadora Duncan's granddaughter. I own the bookshop and the museum." There, let little miss college student deal with the fact that I'm a business owner in this community.

Diane leans back and a strange glint flashes in her eye for a moment and quickly disappears. "Oh right, I forgot about your connection to the Duncans."

I have no idea what she means by that snarky comment, but I am liking Diane less and less. I decide to ask the question that is the Achilles' heel of every college student. "So what do you plan to do after you graduate?" I lean back and cross my arms smugly.

She doesn't miss a beat. "Oh, I plan to put my forestry degree to use developing Osprey Island. Of course, it will be an ecologically sound development plan." She presses her lips together in a fine line.

Tally arrives with Diane's pie and a plate of fries for me. I take a break from the *stimulating* conversation and happily munch on my fried pieces of perfection.

"Wow, you really like french fries," she muses.

"Yeah. I figure I might as well eat what I want while my metabolism is still racing."

She shrugs and daintily picks at her slice of pie. After two more bites, she sets down her fork and pushes it away.

Having firsthand knowledge of the deliciousness of the pie at Myrtle's Diner and the exquisite creaminess of the ice cream, I find her gesture personally offensive. I slide my empty plate to the end of the table and ask, "You gonna finish that?" Pointing to her pie.

She gives me a look similar to Tally's "horn in the middle of your forehead" expression, but shakes her head.

With a huge smile, I reach across and slide her pie within striking distance. The platter is clean in moments. However, despite my physical satisfaction, my energetic antennae are still tickling. "Are you close with your mom?"

The query has the desired effect and Diane is thrown off balance.

For a split second I feel something beyond dread; something cold and frightening. Darn it. I wish I had a better understanding of these powers.

She smiles. "Since you're new around here, you might not know the story. It's a little hard to talk about. My mom left right after I was born, and I haven't seen her since."

"Oh gosh, I'm sorry. I didn't know. I just thought since she was on the island on Tuesday, you might have run into her."

Diane's eyes darken and her jaw muscles flex as

she grinds her teeth together. "What makes you think my mother was on the island on Tuesday?"

A wiser person would've avoided answering the question. But that isn't my style. "Well, I ran into her at Walt's trailer, out there next to the charred remains of Walleye Lodge. I thought maybe she let you know she was coming to town. Maybe she's here for the funeral?" I offer this option with zero knowledge of any funeral plans.

"I have no idea." Diane unzips her backpack with far too much care and fishes around inside for a second.

I catch a glimpse of the contents, but look away before she notices.

When her hand reappears it contains a couple of crumpled bills that she sets on the table. "I've actually got to go to the mortuary right now. Like I said, if it was my mother that you saw, I had no idea she was in town." She launches out of the booth dragging her pack behind, and looks out the front door.

"So, it was nice meeting you, Diane."

"Sure. You too." She slings the bag over one shoulder and leaves without so much as a wave to her uncle Odell.

He looks through the window and shakes his head.

I add a few bills to the wadded up cash Diane

left on the table and I knock a coin loose while attempting to flatten the bills into one pile. I pick up the coin, which is about the size of a quarter, but it's definitely not a quarter. Imagine my surprise when I read the word "Canada" embossed on the face of the coin next to the image of a deer-thing, possibly an elk. It has large antlers and it kind of looks like the elk I've seen back in Arizona. I slip the coin in my pocket, wave to Odell, like a decent person, and walk back to the bookstore.

The scene that awaits me in the apartment could best be described as a silent movie. Silas has on his special glasses that allow him to see the ghost of grandmothers past, and Grams is doing her best Marcel Marceau pantomime in an attempt to communicate with the aged barrister—who can only see, but not hear her.

She sees me and sighs with relief. "Oh thank heavens! I was absolutely running out of ideas. Now you can translate, Mitzy."

"Hello, Silas."

"Good afternoon, Miss Moon."

"Oh please, Sheriff Erick is bad enough. I don't need two people in this town calling me Miss Moon."

Silas chuckles and his magicked glasses make his eyes appear twice as large as normal.

"Mitzy, you need to stop spinning that ring

around your finger and tell Silas what's going on," chides Grams.

When she's right she's right. I take a seat in the scalloped-back chair and interlace my fingers to keep them from shaking. "Silas?"

"Yes, Mitzy."

"Grams wants me to tell you something."

He nods and his jowls wiggle waggle.

"She thinks I need to learn more about my gift."

"The gift may be hereditary." He looks up at Grams and they both nod in agreement. "What kinds of things have you been feeling?"

"It mainly seems to happen when I wear the ring." I show him the circa 1970s mood ring. "I felt some emotions that came from Grams and I felt some other strange things. The weirdest was today at the diner. I felt this odd sense of dread. And then I met Diane, and—"

Silas puts up his hand, gesturing me for me to stop. "Did you feel the dread before you met Diane or *as* you met Diane?"

Closing my eyes to shut out any distractions, I replay the events at the diner. "I definitely felt the dread before she came in. But I also felt something uncomfortable after she arrived. She's not that nice a person." I look over at Grams. "I'm actually kind of surprised you paid for her college. Something isn't quite right about her. And she said she was going to use her forestry degree to develop Osprey Island. She gave me some nonsense about how it was an ecological development plan, but I kind of wonder how the Tribal Council is going to feel about that."

Silas strokes his thumb and forefinger over his bushy mustache and Grams swirls around the room like a maniacal ghost merry-go-round.

"Oh, and there was this." I reach into my pocket with my left hand and fish out the Canadian coin, but as soon as it touches the band of my ring, images flood through my head. Diane on a plane. Diane's passport. Duffle bags. Plastic wrapping. Diane driving a car. Duffle bags, but no clothes.

I drop the coin on the floor, stand, and step away from it as though it's a rattlesnake.

"Tell me exactly what happened, Mitzy." The calm voice of Silas utters a single command.

I describe events as best I can with my limited vocabulary of these strange occurrences and I explain the images that I saw.

Silas stands and stares through his glasses at my grandmother's ghost. "Isadora, she may possess more than one gift."

My grandmother rushes toward me and wraps her phantom arms around me.

Awkwardly, I attempt to return the embrace. I can feel the tingling of her energy against my body and I feel safe and loved. But I have no idea what is going on. "What is he talking about, Grams?"

"Well, as I told you, dear. I only ever got visions. Some people call them premonitions. But if Silas is right, and you can feel things and see things, then you may have more than one gift." She smiles like a proud mama.

A chill races across my skin and I place a hand over my mouth to stifle a gasp. "What does it mean if I heard something?"

Silas takes off his magic spectacles and walks toward me, emanating a strange and commanding power. "Elaborate."

"Earlier today, downstairs in the stacks. Pyewacket was terrorizing this guy, who I'm pretty sure is named Gary. And when Gary walked toward me, I heard the word 'danger'."

Silas cleans the glasses meticulously and slips the curved metal arms over his ears. "Do you know what this means?"

I shake my head nervously.

"I believe you are a true psychic, Mitzy. You receive messages audibly, visually, through sensations, and even sometimes through a sense of knowing that cannot be explained. These are valuable gifts. But you must learn to decipher the messages, or you will waste countless hours running in circles pursuing phantom wisps of ideas that you can never comprehend. The true gift of a psychic is not in receiving the information, it's in properly translating the tidings."

Despite every effort to nod my head, no part of my body will move. Somehow this sad little orphan is suddenly special beyond measure. First a family, and now I have some incomprehensible gift or maybe gifts? It's all way too much.

Grams is shamelessly listening to my thoughts and sobbing uncontrollably. I'm sure they're happy tears. But all I can think is how much I wish my powers could give her a ghostly handkerchief. I look up at her and we share a tearful chuckle.

"Let's begin with the images from the coin."

Good ol' Silas. Always the voice of reason.

CHAPTER 19

After my crash course in Psychic Powers 101, I decide to give myself a pop quiz. I drive down to the train depot office and the docks. It seems like a good time to get a little more information from Gary about where he got his gun, and why.

The truth of the matter is I have no real context for the strange message, "Danger," that I heard when I bumped into Gary in the bookshop, but I also don't believe his visit was as innocent as he proclaimed. I park my car in the train depot parking lot. A car stops in the road to let me cross as I walk the block and a half to Final Destination, the dive bar where I first met Gary. I'm feeling so small-town that I almost wave, but I can't actually see the driver through the tinted windows. I pick up my pace and ignore the uneasy feeling in my chest.

As I enter this cubic zirconia in the rough, the scent of decades-old cigarette smoke, beer-stained carpet, and cheap cologne assaults my senses. And I mean just the regular five, not my supernatural ones. Gary is bent over the pool table in the back and I'm not proud to say that I instantly recognize him by his best feature.

I approach the table and lay a quarter on the bumper.

"I got this table all night," he says without looking up. His pool stick slides along the bridge he creates with his finger and smacks into the cue ball, which sends one of the solids rocketing into the corner pocket.

"Nice shot. You come here often?"

He stands with a quick jerk, smiles, and lays down his pool cue. "Well, what have we here?"

It's painfully obvious that he has not yet had the pleasure of recalling my name. "Moon, Mitzy Moon." I give him a wink.

His face pales in the dim light of the Pabst blue ribbon fixture slung low over the peeling green felt.

Not the best or worst reaction I've received since arriving in Pin Cherry Harbor. "Did you ever find your *phone*?" I emphasize "phone" in a way that I hope helps him understand that I in no way mean phone.

He leans back, tilts his head, and narrows his gaze. "Did you find something in your apartment?"

"Maybe." I prefer to keep it noncommittal until he admits what he actually lost. "What kind of phone did you lose?"

His fists ball up at his sides and he grumbles in a low and threatening tone, "The dangerous kind."

I raise my eyebrows and nod. "I did find something dangerous. However, since I'm so new in town, I thought it would be best to let the sheriff handle it."

Gary's expression flips from shocked to furious in the blink of an eye. He grips the bumper of the pool table and his knuckles shift to white as he growls, "That better be a joke."

I shake my head. "What do you need such a dangerous phone for in a safe little town like Pin Cherry?"

"You better mind your own business. And hope that nothing comes back on you."

I narrow my gaze. "Don't threaten me, Gary."

Gary's hand dives into his pocket. He pulls up his phone and taps at the screen. "Don't go anywhere. I gotta make a quick call." He steps outside.

Taking the liberty of collecting all the pool balls, I rack them and start a new game with a fresh break. I happen to knock in a solid and a striped, so I'm sizing up my best shot when the door opens behind me. I choose to play it coy and pretend to be too involved in my game to acknowledge Gary's return.

Footsteps approach.

As I feel a surge of anger that does not belong to me rising in my chest, I hesitate a moment too long.

Some kind of damp, musty smelling cloth bag is pulled over my head and a strong arm encircles my neck. I kick, scratch, and attempt to yell for help. But despite my lungs screaming for oxygen, I can't breathe.

My eyes open and after several minutes, I can make out thin cracks of light above me. I'd like to move my hands, but they're securely tied in front of me. I lean slowly to the left and feel cold metal beneath me. That is when I notice the movement. No matter how still I remain, I still feel bobbing and swaying.

I'm on a boat. And not the fun party-song kind with T-Pain.

I'm in the bottom of a gasoline-smelling boat on the lake.

With no idea how long I was unconscious, I could be a mere one hundred yards from the bar, or I could be out in the middle of one of the five largest freshwater lakes in the world.

Panic grips my heart. My breathing races and I can hear my heart beating like a drum in my ear.

No one knows where I am.

I didn't tell anyone where I was going.

I didn't leave a note.

I could suffocate.

Calm yourself, Mitzy. You can see daylight, and that means you can breathe. Stay calm and use what you've got.

What I've got is nothing. I'm stashed in some boat, on some lake, with no food or water.

Explore the whole space. You might be surprised by what you find.

I don't know where this calm voice is coming from, but it's driving me insane. Apparently, there is a perfectly serene half of my brain that isn't at all rattled by my sudden kidnapping.

I twist to get my feet under me and that's when I discover there's also a rope securely knotted around my ankles.

I scoot along the floor like a seal out of water and see what I can find. There's something that feels like a lifejacket. Then a small metal case. I try the latch and it pops open. Inside I feel around and can identify Band-Aids, packets of what must be antibacterial ointment—basic first-aid stuff.

Basic first-aid stuff might include scissors!

I meticulously search every inch of the metal case.

Aha! Scissors.

I grab those and slip them into the front pocket of my jeans for later use.

Continuing my search, I find something that feels like a boat cushion, some empty plastic bags, several large canvas duffle bags filled with tightly wrapped bundles covered in thick plastic, secured with tape.

Finally, pushed up against the metal hull, two cases of plastic bottles. I stretch the wrap secured around the bottles, with my teeth and tied hands, until it tears and wiggle one loose. I twist off the cap and sniff at the contents. Smells like nothing more than bottled water.

What if it's laced with something?

Unless it's laced with strychnine, how much worse could your situation get?

I have to agree with Tranquil Mitzy. I decide to take a small sip and wait an arbitrary amount of time to see what happens.

I take my sip and secure the lid.

I scoot back to my original location, set the bottle next to me, extract the scissors, and begin the process of snipping my way to freedom with the equivalent of child's safety scissors.

Having no way to calculate the passing of time,

I judge halfway through one loop of the rope encircling my wrists to be enough time to deem the liquid in the bottle safe.

I take two more sips and replace the cap.

After I make it all the way through one loop of rope, the boat rocks suddenly and loud voices on deck drift through the cracks.

There's no time to cut through the remaining rope. I twist and pull my wrists and yank my hands free as fast as I can, but my race against time is for nothing. Whoever boarded has no interest in the cargo. They go straight to the main cabin and fire up the engines.

This new purposeful movement could be bringing me closer to home or taking me irretrievably farther from rescue.

The worse news is that the aroma of fuel intensifies. A wave of nausea turns my skin cold and clammy.

My hands are now free and I untie my ankles as well, but to what end. I lean back against the curved hull, close my eyes, and for some reason think of Pyewacket.

Crazy, brilliant, irritating feline. He serves no purpose but to annoy me on a daily basis. However, the thought of never seeing him again breaks my heart.

Robin Pyewacket Goodfellow, if I should never see you again, I would like to say, I think I love you. It's an unfamiliar emotion. It might be considered transference or objectification. But you've done more for me during our short acquaintance than any humans I can think of in my twenty-one years on this planet.

If I'd had the chance to grow old with you, Pye, I would've considered myself lucky. However, it seems my impulsive snooping is what finally did me in. I sit here in the hull of some mysterious vessel, motoring across some enormous body of water, to some unknown destination. Whatever happens, I'm glad I had the chance to be your friend.

P.S. Don't blame Gary. It's not his fault. I actually never saw who put the bag over my head.

I'm not sure why I am so anxious to clear Gary's name at this point. Something about the smell of the man who grabbed me didn't register as Gary. What am I actually doing right now? Am I "clairodorant?" If I were examining the evidence, I'd say he was the most likely suspect.

For all I know, that call he received might've instructed him to nab me.

I should've been paying attention, counting the minutes, or listening for sounds. There will be no way for me to re-create the trajectory that my kidnappers took and lead the police to the stash.

Of course, since there's no chance of being rescued, details hardly seem important.

The engine cuts off and the voices on deck resume. As I strain my senses, I may even hear voices coming from farther away, possibly the shore or the dock.

Metal grates against the rough surface and clunks over my head. There's a splash followed by the whizzing sound of a rope sliding over the side of the boat. I don't know a ton about maritime happenings, but I'd say we just dropped anchor.

There's a steady rhythmic splashing and a soft thunk as something bumps the side of the boat.

My first instinct is *Jaws*; my second is a small craft.

Something metal slaps against the side of the boat and one, wait no, two people climb down what must be a chain ladder and hop into the smaller craft. They shove off and the rhythmic paddling grows faint.

I wait several minutes, unsure of my next move.

If there's no one else on the boat, this is as close as you're going to get to shore. Whatever shore it is. Now's your chance.

My chance to what?

Swim for it.

What? I can't believe what I'm hearing. Or

what I'm telling myself. Everything is jumbled in my head.

Get off this boat.

All right. All right. Geez! Other Mitzy is getting pushy. I take a deep breath, twist the ring on my finger and try to feel for other people who might still be on board.

Still unclear as to how my gifts work, or how to interpret the messages, the best I can do is get myself out of this hold and hope no one is standing guard.

I take a piece of the rope, tie a knot around the water bottle, and tie the other around my waist. I have no idea where I'm going, but I grew up in the desert. Water is life.

I creep toward the dimming slivers of light and push against the hatch. It does not budge.

I'm locked in. Of course I would be locked in. When you have valuable cargo, you don't just leave it sitting out in the open.

Valuable cargo? Assuming that's not me, what else is down here?

I feel my way back past the lifejackets and the first-aid kit to the tightly wrapped plastic bundles. Attempting to rip through the plastic with my fingers is unsuccessful, so I retrieve the scissors and slice one open. The resulting spillage sounds like the tiny beads in a Native American rain stick.

I tip the package to staunch the flow and reach in with my fingers. Small round bits with smooth edges—pills! Oh, *Mighty Aphrodite,* they're pills.

Drugs!

Somehow, I know in my gut that I'm on the smuggler's boat. But before I can plan my next move, my eyes are drawn to the mood ring . . .

And clear as day I see an image of Diane's backpack. When she unzipped it in the diner to dig out her cash, there was something in the bag. Something plastic. I only saw a corner of whatever was bundled into her bag, but if I can get one of these to shore and—

Now is your only chance.

The calm voice in my head makes perfect sense. It's now or never.

I grab a life jacket, tie the webbing strap around one of the un-opened plastic-wrapped bundles, and slide back toward the hatch.

This time I take a methodical approach and feel around the edges for hinges or hopefully . . . Bingo! A handle.

I give the handle a cautious twist, but the metal on metal screech is loud enough to wake the dead.

My throat tightens and I freeze in horror.

I don't know how long to wait. Two minutes? An hour?

No footsteps. No voices.

I push upward and the hatch squeaks open.

I shove the lifejacket and bundle of pills through first. Then I wait.

No gunshots. No running footsteps.

Risking a peek, I push my head through the opening. The sun has slipped out of sight and the whistling of a crisp twilight wind is gaining strength.

I slither out of the hold and crawl across the deck toward the edge. I peep over the side and see nothing but blue-black water as far as the eye can see. It's only a matter of time before the boat swivels on the anchor and this side faces the shore.

Arizona may not have ten thousand lakes, but I did take a couple of trips up to Lake Powell. And I happen to know that when you jump off the deck of a boat into the water, it makes a large, loud splash.

I need that ladder.

Crawling across the deck to the other side of the boat, the top of the chain ladder hooks through two metal loops before it disappears over the side. I glimpse over and see the shore, but the wind is pushing the boat away from land in a wide arc. I might have a minute at the most to climb down the ladder unseen.

Waiting until the breeze swings this side of the boat out of sight of shore, I crouch below the rail.

It's now or never. "Never" brings fresh spikes of fear to my skin.

I slip my arm through the lifejacket and throw my legs over the side. My foot slips on the metal step and my left leg pushes through the ladder, catching me in a most uncomfortable position. I stifle a scream, untangle my water bottle and rope from the ladder, readjust my limbs, and start down a second time.

The wind has picked up. My side of the boat whirls back toward danger. The water is just below me. If I jump there'll be a small splash. If I wait . . .

I jump. The splash is not enormous, but it's also not unnoticeable. I hope whoever has watch—wasn't. I hold the lifejacket in front of me and kick my feet under the water as hard as I can.

No more splashing. No more sounds. I'm slipping through the water like a—

Oh, dear Lord baby Jesus, what is in this lake? Are there such things as freshwater sharks? Do beavers eat people?

I kick my legs faster and my quads burn. Daylight is gone and the dim afterglow is slipping away.

I'm still fifty yards from shore. The muscles in my legs are going to explode before I ever make it to land.

Something bumps into me and a squeak escapes my mouth.

I duck my head under water to hide my conspicuous white hair. When I pop up, shouts from the beach shatter the hushed air.

Kicking as though my life depends on it, and let's be honest it does, I race toward shore. Something else bumps me, but this time the hard impact on my hipbone confirms it's a rock.

Land! I get my feet under me and stumble my way to dry land. I unhook the lifejacket and drag it up into the trees, out of sight.

I'd love to stay here until morning so that I have more light to find my way, but by morning I'm sure to be discovered.

With the plastic-wrapped bundle of contraband under my right arm, I move through the trees slowly but steadily. I can feel the ground stretching upward before me.

By the time I risk a backward glance, the smuggler's fire on the beach looks far below. I must be near the bluff where Nimkii, my dad, and I first spied Ivy Lapointe.

Pushing past the row of large granite boulders, I soon feel the familiar stinging of the thorns on the raspberry vines as they tear at my skin. I've honestly never been so pleased to be in so much pain.

I continue forward, following a sense of direction that is not my own. Exhaustion tugs at my muscles, and despite my desire for the safety of human contact, I'm forced to crawl into the deep underbrush before I collapse.

Multicolored sunlight filtering through the trees coaxes me awake.

For a split second, I smile and stretch my arms. But then the intense pain in my legs and the abject fear in my heart heighten all my senses.

There are voices. Multiple voices in the forest.

Part of me wants to call out and be found; the other part realizes the inherent danger in mistaking enemy for friend.

Creeping farther into the thick ferns, I wait in silence.

I could swear they're calling my name. However, that's little consolation. It wouldn't be that hard for the kidnappers to obtain my name. I did introduce myself to Gary right before I got nabbed. I continue to wait.

Rhythmic vibration trembles the ground beneath me. Those aren't footsteps. That's a horse!

The smugglers do not have horses. That must be Nimkii. It has to be.

Struggling with my decision, I hesitate, unable to make a choice. Luckily the loud and somewhat worried voice of my father makes the decision for me. "Mitzy? Mitzy, it's all right. It's Dad."

I crawl out onto the trail. My throat is too clogged with emotion to call for help.

Thundering hooves clamor to a halt nearby. The solid thud of my father's feet hitting the dirt and his strong arms scooping me up is one of the top five moments of my life. Guaranteed.

"I've got her!" he calls. Other voices and shouts blur as the safety envelops me and I struggle to hang on to consciousness.

Truly believing nothing could improve on this moment, I've never been so happy to be wrong.

An angelic light seems to surround Erick as he jogs down the trail toward my dad and me. The look of concern and relief on his face threatens to break my heart.

"We need to get her to the hospital, Jacob." Erick grabs his radio and directs the police boat to stand by at the dock below Chez Osprey. Then his strong hand reaches for my leg with unexpected tenderness. He carefully slides up my pant leg and mumbles, "There's quite a bit of blood."

At first, I can't imagine where the blood came from, but unwelcome memories of the thorny raspberry vines worm their way to the surface. However, that pain is instantly pushed away by a more urgent memory. "Pills," I whisper, and weakly gesture toward the underbrush beside the trail.

Erick removes his hand from my leg, nods, and

prowls into the scrub. After several minutes he surfaces with the tightly wrapped plastic package, which I stole from the cargo hold. He looks at me and tilts his head in the most endearing way. "This looks like a standard bundle of counterfeit opioids. Probably has a street value of about $3,000, give or take. The smugglers trade this stuff for meth. No money to launder . . ." He shakes his head and sighs. "I'm not even going to ask, Moon. I'll take your statement once the doctor patches you up."

Jacob walks toward his horse.

"Wait," I manage to whisper.

My dad stops. "Sheriff, she's got more to say."

Erick hurries over. "I can handle the rest, Moon. I am the sheriff, in case you've forgotten."

His words are gruff, but his gentle blue eyes are brimming with tenderness. My information is crucial, so I force my exhausted brain to focus. "Diane —" I cough and my arm is too sore to make any effort to cover my mouth. "Diane had a bundle like that one. Pills. In her backpack."

"All right, Moon. We'll check it out. She's staying at the hotel by the Coast Guard station." He pats my dad on the shoulder and adds, "Get her to the hospital, Jacob. I'm sure Deputy Paulsen would love to pick up Diane. I'd ask Truby, but she's sweeping the far side of the island to see if they can intercept the smugglers."

With that, my dad jogs toward his horse, carrying me like I'm nothing more than a sack of groceries. He gingerly places me on Cranberry's back and swings up onto the horse's haunches, behind the saddle, as he kicks us into motion.

The ride back to Chez Osprey is longer than I remember and far more uncomfortable. Every aching muscle, bruise, and scratch throbs with pain. I don't have a clear memory of being transported from horse to boat, but at some point I wake up in the hospital. Woozy from whatever medication is dripping through my IV, I scan the room almost expecting to see Grams floating next to my dad.

No such luck.

However, I'm pleased to see the room contains my three favorite guys. My dad, my lawyer, and my secret crush.

Jacob leans forward and squeezes my hand. "I've got quite a lot to tell you, sweetheart. But the sheriff needs to get your statement. My news can wait."

Erick approaches the foot of the bed and smiles, in what I prefer to believe is more than a professional way. "Miss Moon, are you strong enough to give me your statement?"

Consenting with a careful tilt of my head, I hold up a hand. "I need a sip of water first."

My father grabs the dusty-rose-colored plastic

container from my bedside table and turns the straw toward me. As I take a long sip, he offers up some commentary. "That was smart of you to tie that water bottle to your waist." His voice cracks a little and his eyes are misty. Another thing I seem to have in common with my father, offering practical advice or compliments rather than expressing deep emotion.

Sheriff Erick retrieves his notepad and clicks his pen. "I'm ready when you are, Moon."

"Did you get Diane?"

Erick's hands drop to his sides in surrender. "If it will move this interview along . . . Paulsen brought Diane in yesterday. The girl still had the pills on her, but swore that she was trying to return them. She wouldn't say if they came from Ivy, but the packaging was identical to the bundle you found on the smuggler's boat." He exchanges a defeated look with Silas. "That was all we got out of her before she asked for a lawyer."

I roll my head to the left. "You?"

Silas harrumphs into his bushy mustache. "Isadora would've wanted it."

I can't help but wonder if his use of the past tense is for Erick's sake. I know how persuasive Grams can be, even with only the power of pantomime. I raise an eyebrow.

"We are discussing options with the district attorney." Silas smooths his whiskers and looks away.

Erick raises his pen and pad a second time. "How 'bout that statement, Moon?"

I relay the story of being grabbed from the Final Destination, but I leave out anything remotely related to the terror that I felt. I explain how I escaped from the boat, swam ashore, and came to be discovered on the trail by my father.

"Is there anything else you remember, Miss Moon?"

As I open my mouth to say no, a snippet of conversation pops into my head. The voices on deck had been shouting about something. I close my eyes and force my unwilling brain to replay those terrifying hours trapped in the dark, damp hold.

"Did she fall asleep?" asks Erick.

Silas clears his throat and replies, "I believe she is attempting to access the memory."

Leave it to Silas to make it sound so complicated. As I drift deeper into the recollection, I hear the phrase, ". . . the drop on Saturday. We get rid of the girl on the way. Ivy said tie her up and throw her overboard, and let the lake do the rest." I shiver involuntarily as the words reveal how close I came to death. My eyes pop open and I blink several times to push the emotion back down.

"Did you remember something?" Erick's pen is poised above his pad.

"They said something about a drop this Saturday." I choose to leave out the bit about how they planned to dump my body. My dad looks like he's holding it together by a thread as it is.

"Did they say where the drop was?" Erick raises a hopeful eyebrow.

I shake my head.

"That's okay. If you think of anything else, you give me a call. All right?"

"All right."

Erick walks out of my room and stops to give instructions to the deputy guarding my door. Poor Deputy Paulsen. Of all the things she would like to be doing, protecting me has to be at the absolute bottom of her list.

Silas walks over and nudges the door closed.

My father leans in and squeezes my hand with renewed force. "Don't ever pull a stunt like that again. You hear me?"

I'm certain I didn't pull this stunt on purpose. I'd like to defend myself, but twenty-twenty hindsight has clearly shown me that venturing into a seedy dive bar without so much as leaving a note wasn't my best-laid plan.

"I suggest you share your news, Jacob," prompts Silas.

My father nods. "Right. I've decided to hang onto the railroad business. Cal left it to me in the will and I could sell it for a pretty penny, but I don't need the cash. Keeping it in the family seems like the right way to honor his memory and thank him for having enough faith in me to change his will. But the real news is that when I was going over the books, I found some things that didn't add up. I wouldn't have thought much of it, but those discrepancies along with what happened to you . . . I'm not sure how much to share with the sheriff."

There's definitely something Jacob is leaving out of his story, but at the moment the biggest question on my mind is how did everyone know where to look for me? "How did you find me?"

Silas chuckles and Jacob shrugs before he replies. "I guess we have to give Pyewacket most of the credit." He looks at Silas, and the lawyer shakes his jowls affirmatively.

"Pyewacket? That cat can't even find his own Fruity Puffs. I can't imagine how he helped in a missing-persons case." I want to chuckle but my tender throat rebels and delivers a fit of coughing instead.

My dad offers me water as he launches into the story. "When you didn't turn up for breakfast at the diner, I went to the apartment. As soon as I opened the bookcase door, Pyewacket started running circles around the room like he was possessed."

I attempt to lift my hands in a "who cares" gesture but the muscles in my arms are too exhausted from my lengthy swim to respond. So I mumble, "He is possessed."

Jacob's eyes widen as he adds, "No argument here." He eagerly continues, "He pulled a pair of chewed up shoes out of the trash can, spilled a glass of water from the bedside table, and knocked a photo album off the bookcase. All in the space of about sixty seconds. I had no idea what he was trying to tell me, so I rang Silas."

Silas bobs his head several times before picking up the story. "Pyewacket has always shown a curious affection for the unseen. I took the various clues he provided and made a list of their potential meanings. Eventually I came to understand that the boat shoes, the water, and the photo album containing pictures of Chez Osprey, Walleye Lodge and Tavern, and, of course, Ivy Lapointe, could only mean one thing."

My father jumps in with the solution. "We suspected you were in a boat on the water, somehow connected to Ivy. When the general manager down at the depot reported your car in the parking lot, I made the connection to the bar." He looks at Silas, back to me and shrugs. "I'm not proud to say I roughed up Gary pretty bad."

"Is he the one who grabbed me?"

"Sounds like he was a middleman. Ivy had something on him and delivering you was going to make 'em square."

"That slime ball didn't even know my name. If I hadn't introduced myself, none of this would've happened."

"I wouldn't be so sure. According to the story I . . . dragged out of him, Ivy texted him a picture of you after we met her on the island. It was just small-town bad luck that he'd already . . ." My father blushes and clearly doesn't know how to refer to my one-night-stand with Gary.

I jump in and rescue him. "We'd already met." I nod for him to continue.

"Yes. So he was just following orders." Jacob's jaw clenches and his gaze hardens.

A fresh set of horrifying chills slithers down my spine. "Wait, that was before I even knew Ivy was involved."

Jacob looks down at the floor. "When I introduced you as my daughter, she saw an heiress and an opportunity. She was planning on asking for a two-million-dollar ransom."

Too shocked to respond, I can't help but wonder if I'm worth two million.

As though he reads my mind, Jacob mumbles, "I would've paid whatever they asked to keep you safe, Mitzy."

My throat tightens with emotion. "Let's hope you never have to."

My father tries to turn my frown upside down. "I guess it's a good thing that gun fell under the bed before he had a chance to use it."

I would have to agree. And I would also have to nominate Pyewacket as feline most likely to have knocked it under the bed. It seems that cat not only has his own set of multiple lives, but he's appointed himself my personal guardian caracal.

"So if there's going to be a drop on Saturday . . . What day is it?" I ask.

"Today is Saturday." Silas strokes his bushy grey mustache.

I fight through the pain and force myself into a sitting position. "I need to get out of here. If I can get my hands on that packet of pills, I might be able to figure out more information about the drop."

My father rises to his full six feet and change and places a firm hand on my shoulder. "You've done more than enough for our local law enforcement. They'll take it from here."

My mind is racing. I look down at my left hand and see the ring is gone. "My ring!"

"I've kept it safe for you, Mitzy." Silas fishes

around in the breast pocket of his brown tweed suit coat, retrieves the ring, takes an unhurried stance, and places it in my hand.

I slip it on my finger and wait. I recall the image of the pills tumbling through my fingers in the hull of the boat. There were also large duffle bags of some kind. At least ten? It was so dark I can't be sure. I focus on the image of the tumbling pills and stare into the ring.

Nothing.

Silas puts a hand on my arm and whispers, "Clear your mind. Don't force information into the vision, simply let it unfold."

I breathe in and out, trying to push the images of boats, pills, icy water—all of it—out of my mind. I look back at the ring and see greenish-gold swirls. For a moment those stupid boat shoes appear and I nearly lose my focus. I exhale and push that image away. It is quickly replaced by a photo of my late grandpa Cal Duncan holding up a moose's head by the antlers. I remember this photo from his office at the train depot, and the man next to him . . . Nimkii!

My eyes pop open. My throat goes dry.

Jacob leans toward me. "What? What is it?"

"A photo from the wall in grandpa Cal's office at the train depot. The hunting photo, with the moose and Nimkii."

Jacob looks at Silas. "Do you think he's involved with Ivy?"

Silas smooths his mustache twice before answering. "We'll have time to unbraid that wreath at a later date. But I am certain the vision of the train depot is no coincidence."

My father's face lights up and he nods enthusiastically. "The discrepancies in the cargo manifests. This could be the connection. I'll let the sheriff know." He steps into the hall to pass his information on to Deputy Paulsen.

Silas squeezes my hand. "You're getting better, Mitzy. Each time you practice using your gifts, they will improve."

"Can you get me out of here?"

"I will not be party to you taking any further risks." Silas harrumphs and crosses his arms.

"I'm just anxious to see Grams."

The barrister's stern expression softens and he nods. "I'll see what I can do."

Hiding behind a pleasant smile, I silently plot—and once I'm out of here, I'll see what I can do.

CHAPTER 20

BEFORE I CAN PUT a second foot onto the floor inside the bookshop, Grams is all over me.

"Don't you ever scare me like that again, young lady. Do you hear me?"

Making a conscious effort to peer around the stacks, I make sure it's all clear before answering. "Yes, Grams. I've already received sufficient lectures from Jacob, Silas, and Erick."

"Well I don't give a rat's behind! You can hear another one from me. The very idea! Wandering into that shady establishment, without so much as a word to me." She crosses her bejeweled limbs over her vintage gown and scowls.

At times like these, I have to admit I'm grateful she's not a vengeful spirit.

"You are going to experience some vengeance if you pull a stunt like that again."

I point to my lips and shake my head. She knows the rules about reading my thoughts.

She stares at me, and I worry there might be flames flickering in her ghostly eyes. Before I can negotiate a truce—

Pyewacket leaps off the stairs and literally bowls me over. His rough tongue must be removing a layer of skin from my face, yet I can't bring myself to push him off. He's the reason they knew where to look. I scratch him roughly between the tufted ears and eventually roll out from underneath his affectionate assault.

I rush up the circular staircase into the apartment. The painting lies untouched on my coffee table. I slide my fingers under the paper backing and extract the piece of paper for the second time.

"What is this? It has to be important. No one hides a piece of paper in the back of a painting just for grins and giggles."

Grams is still sulking and refuses to respond.

Holding the sheet, I pace the length of the apartment as I stare at the random columns of numbers. Not dates, or phone numbers, or addresses, or—

"Geocaching!" I shout to the four walls.

Despite her anger, Grams materializes. "What are you going on about?"

"I finally figured out what these columns of numbers mean. It's a list of latitudes and longitudes that directs you to a physical location where something has been hidden. It's called geocaching. It's all the rage with my generation. Don't get me started. But this might be how Walt was planning to cut Ivy out of the exchanges. He knew he could make a lot more money without a middleman. He could've been carefully building up his supply of meth while he ferreted out Ivy's Canadian contact."

"That does make sense. Especially if he found out about what Ivy was doing to Diane."

"What do you mean? How do you know what Ivy was doing to Diane?"

"I know you only met the girl the one time, but I've known the child her whole life. She's a good girl who loves her father, and never wanted anything to do with her mother."

This information doesn't fit with my impression of Diane in the diner, but Silas did tell me that interpreting the messages is the most important part. The feeling of dread could have been related to Diane's regret, or fear of someone discovering she was in possession of the pills. Maybe? It's all so confusing. "If Diane was meeting with Ivy on Walt's behalf, why?"

"I don't know the whole story, dear, but Silas came by and asked if I'd have a problem with him representing the girl. She told him she had enough information to make a deal."

"What information?" I pace toward the four-poster bed.

"She wouldn't tell Silas until they gave her a mutiny."

Turning slowly, I squint at the apparition. "A mutiny?" Laughter grips me and my aching muscles protest each guffaw. "I'm pretty sure you mean immunity, Grams."

"Oh yes, that makes much more sense. I was so flustered about you disappearing, I wasn't thinking straight."

"Ree-ow." Proud with a hint of humility.

Stooping to scratch his insufferable belly, I reply, "Yes, Pye, it is fortunate that you were thinking straight."

Grams descends to coddle the daylights out of the large fur baby while I make another lap around the apartment and stare at the list of numbers.

If I'm correct about these numbers indicating geocaches of methamphetamine, there must be fifteen secret stashes. No matter how fast Walt was cooking, I doubt he could stash this much and keep up with Ivy's orders. Maybe she didn't burn down the Walleye Inn. Maybe Walt burned it down himself!

I spin around and look at Grams. "Maybe Walt burned down the Walleye to throw Ivy off his trail. Maybe he convinced her that his lab blew up. That's a thing, right? Meth labs blow up all the time. Don't they?"

Grams nods encouragingly. "I've no idea, sweetheart. That's more of a 'your generation' thing, but I'm sure they do. That seems to be the only option that makes sense, because you said he sold off all his valuables in an estate sale before the fire."

"Exactly. So he knew there was going to be a fire, but I don't think Ivy knew about the estate sale."

Grams asks, "What about the business card?"

"The business card for Gershon Antiquities that Erick found near Boilerplate Beach wasn't wet or burned, so it couldn't have washed ashore with Walt. Someone saw that body before Pyewacket and I discovered it. If that someone was working for Ivy—" A shudder chills my skin as I wonder what may have happened to Mr. Gershon. "What if Ivy figured out the plan? What if she suspected Walt of double-crossing her and sent someone to shake Lars down for information?"

"Do you think that's how Lars ended up dead?"

"No idea. But Walt was keeping this painting at

the pawnshop for a reason. If Lars had known about this list"—I wave the sheet of coordinates—"I'm sure he would've handed it over without a fight."

"That poor man." Grams sniffles. "He died for nothing."

I grab my phone and type in the first set of numbers from the secret list. It appears to be in the middle of the lake. "How am I going to check this out? I definitely can't involve Dad." As I stare at the blinking dot on my phone, a lovely plan unfolds. "It's just a boat ride. No one will even know where I've gone."

"Mizithra Achelois Moon! You will not go hunting down these dangerous drug caches on your own!"

I lay the piece of paper down, take a picture, upload it to the cloud, and slip the paper under the lining on the back of the framed painting.

All the way down the circular staircase and to the heavy metal side door, she's lecturing me about the folly of youth.

Grams stops right below the red "Exit" sign.

I step outside and close the door quietly behind me. Part of me feels terrible that she's trapped in the building and can't continue to scold me all the way down the alley, but the other part of me is happy to escape the voice of reason.

With my dad's new duties at the railroad and

his hunch about drugs getting stashed in the train cars, I'm sure he's in his office at the train depot comparing manifests with scale receipts to see if the weights check out. I should be able to drive out to the mansion, commandeer the Duncan family watercraft, and check out the first geocache location before anyone misses me.

The large granite stone bearing the Duncan family crest with a large "D" in the center marks my turn. The blur of black-and-white birch trees lining the curving drive is still a little mesmerizing.

I find myself wondering if Ivy was searching Walt's trailer for this list.

The sheer size of the "manse" never ceases to impress. It sits majestically on the shore of the enormous "great lake" that graces the entire region and manages to rival its beauty.

Another random thought interrupts my architectural admiration: Was Walt really cooking meth on a boat?

Two soaring gables sit astride a magnificent entrance, and light spills through massive windows. The entire home is faced in split rock, and at least three chimneys poke through the steeply sloped roof. A terraced patio hugs the side of the home and works its way toward the surging waves.

I park on the flagstones and hurry up the manicured walkway.

Even though the maid is working today, she has no reason to question my presence at the mansion. I decide to show a hint of personal growth and leave a note for my father on the marble countertop.

Hey Dad,

Just borrowed the boat for
a quick errand on the lake.
I'll be back before dinner.
Mitzy

Determined to learn from past mistakes, I copy the latitude and longitude of the first stash under my name, just as a precaution. I grab a bottle of water from the fridge, remove a doughnut from the box on the counter, and traipse down to the boathouse.

The keys are in the ignition. I take a deep breath, start the engine, and reverse out of the slip. So far so good. I pull the throttle back and shift into what I hope is "forward."

Using the GPS app on my phone, I set the latitude and longitude of my destination and tap for directions. I push the throttle lever to increase my speed and struggle against the large waves.

The first drop is less than half a mile away, and

the sun shines brightly from a nearly cloudless sky. At least I don't have to worry about getting caught in a rainstorm. Easy peasy, lemon squeezy.

Approaching the dot on my phone, I expect to see some kind of buoy or flotation device marking the location. But even though the map tells me I'm literally on top of the cache, I see nothing.

Come on, Moon, think like a smuggler. A flotation device visible on the surface of the water would be seen by anyone passing by. Granted, it's an enormous lake and it would be a heck of a coincidence for someone to happen upon the stash, but it could happen.

So I would need a marker—that's below the surface!

Gazing down at my mood ring, the image of something shimmering beneath the surface flashes across the cabochon. I search around the boat and find a long handled net, I assume for grabbing fish.

Steering the craft in a circle, I keep my eyes focused on anything beneath the surface. As I widen my arc, a quick flash of silver on the right-hand side catches my eye. I slow the boat to a mere sputter and make another circle.

There it is! I tighten the perimeter.

It takes me a while to figure out how to drop anchor, but eventually I get that sorted out and return my focus to the slippery task of scooping up the shiny float.

Approximately twenty tries later, I finally manage to snag whatever is beneath the shimmering float and hoist it up toward the boat.

A large aluminum hook held aloft by a thick Mylar float. Walt may have been stupid, but he was also a genius. Looks like he even put some kind of beacon on there to assist in locating the caches in inclement weather. Nice touch.

I begin the tedious process of pulling the rope up hand over hand and eventually reach the yellow Pelican case. I'm all too familiar with Pelican cases from my days in film school. All valuable equipment gets stored in Pelican cases. They're nearly indestructible and always watertight.

I set the case on the deck, pop the latches, and gasp at the sheer quantity of what has to be methamphetamine.

Panic grips me. I close the case and scan the horizon in a 360. Okay, looks like the racing heart was all my own doing. There is no imminent threat.

Time to head back. I raise the anchor and am busily cursing the lazy speed of the winch, when approaching sirens echo across the water.

The flashing lights are soon followed by the familiar voice of Captain Truby, blaring across the waves. "This is the United States Coast Guard. Cut your engines and put your hands in the air."

Well, this is awkward.

Captain Truby's Coast Guard cutter approaches mine in a bouncy yet direct route and the two officers on deck manage to keep their extremely large and terrifying guns trained on me.

Their vessel knocks into mine and one of the armed men secures the two boats, while the other keeps his weapon pointed directly at my heart. I believe that's called a "kill shot."

She boards my boat and crosses her arms. Black bloused trousers, a black shirt and cap, and an orange reflective vest have replaced the spiffy uniform she wore to Erick's office. Her mirrored sunglasses bounce back my worried expression, and I imagine that right behind those lenses she's staring straight through me. "Don't I know you?" she asks.

I keep my hands up in the air and reply, "Yes, ma'am. We met in Sheriff Harper's office. I'm Mitzy Moon."

"And why exactly are you pulling up a smuggler's cache of drugs, Miss Moon?"

Wait a second. How does she know what I was pulling up? Maybe that "beacon" is some kind of— Images flash through my mind: half burned papers from the ruined trailer; the carefully written list of latitudes and longitudes; the meticulous printing on the report on Erick's desk.

"Walt didn't make the list! You wrote it. You made the list of geocaching sites and Walt planted the meth. He turned on Ivy. He was a snitch." In my mind, the hero's theme music swells.

"That's enough, Moon." Without turning toward her men, she commands, "Take her into custody."

The two armed officers board my vessel. One places me in the all-too-familiar handcuffs and hustles me back onto the Coast Guard vessel. The other officer takes possession of my dad's boat. Boy, am I going to have some explaining to do.

Our caravan of two makes a hasty return to the marina outside the Coast Guard office in Pin Cherry Harbor.

CHAPTER 21

The spartan Coast Guard office is almost as no nonsense as its leader Captain Truby. She ushers me to an uncomfortable-looking metal chair and pushes me into it without any of the niceties I've come to expect at the local sheriff's station.

"Please state your full, legal name for the record."

This is going to hurt her more than it hurts me. "Mizithra Achelois Moon."

She hesitates a moment and taps her pen on the table. "Spell it."

"You can call me Mitzy," I offer, before I painstakingly enunciate each letter of my mouthful of a name.

"When did you become involved in the drug trade in Pin Cherry Harbor, Mitzy?"

I have half a mind to tell this woman how incredibly rude I find that insinuation, but somehow I manage to hold my tongue. "I'm not involved in the drug trade. I was following up on a lead."

Captain Truby's humorless laugh echoes off the cold linoleum. "That's the first time a drug trafficker has used that particular line." She rolls her eyes at the armed officer standing in front of the door.

At this point, it seems painfully obvious that she knows nothing of my family standing in the community, or my recent inheritance. She actually believes I'm some kind of drug dealer. I feel it's in my best interest to dispossess her of this notion as quickly as possible. "First of all, Captain Truby, I am the heir to the Duncan fortune. It seems unlikely that I would deal drugs as a side hustle. And second of all, I was investigating Walt Johnson's murder. I stumbled across a clue that was clearly overlooked by the local constabulary." I attempt to lean back smugly, but my handcuffed wrists pinch against the hard metal bar of the chair. I'm forced to hunch forward meekly.

"I'm not sure if calling out your relation to local ex-con Jacob Duncan is your best defense, Miss." She leans back. "He's the only Duncan left, isn't he?"

The snipe at my deceased grandmother and my murdered grandfather hits below the belt, but I'm not about to let it show. It looks like convincing her is going to require a bit of muscle. "Can someone remove my phone from my back pocket?"

She nods to the other officer and he steps forward. "Do you have anything sharp in your pocket? Is there anything in there that's going to hurt me?" His tone is firm, no-nonsense.

"Just my phone." I recall my banter with Gary just before I was kidnapped and add, "It's not a dangerous phone."

He pushes me forward with one hand and extracts my cell phone, laying it on the table in front of his commanding officer.

"Look at the most recent images," I say.

She taps the home button. "It's locked."

"1234," I blurt.

Captain Truby shakes her head and taps in the code.

She doesn't say anything, but even her tightly controlled facial expressions can't hide what she's feeling. My extra sensory perception picks up on a bit of shock, and possibly a hint of guilt. "As you can see, Captain, that's your writing on that piece of paper. I discovered it hidden in the back of a painting, which came from the Walleye Inn. Once I realized those were GPS coordinates, I went on a little geocaching hunt. You just happened to find me—as I found it."

"That's an interesting story, Moon. Do you think it will hold up in court?"

The waves of threatening energy rolling off Captain Truby knock my confidence sideways. Something is completely off. She and I both know that it's her writing on that piece of paper.

A terrifying question knifes into my consciousness. If Walt wasn't working with her to set up a sting, what's the other option?

"Throw her in the hold. I'll notify Ivy one of the drops has been compromised. We'll deal with this intruder later."

Oh. That's the other option. Walt *was* the middleman. Captain Truby isn't setting up a sting, Captain Truby's on the take. I'm starting to wish I'd listened more carefully to my dad's lecture.

Rough hands yank me out of the chair and toss me into a claustrophobically small, all-white cell with only a metal bench. Handcuffs and all. Oh, and I voluntarily gave up my phone and my password. Pure genius.

I haven't even had a chance to settle into my pity party before the cell door opens and a familiar shape is shoved through. "Silas?"

CLANG! The metal door slams shut, leaving us to stew in our own juices.

His brown suit looks no more rumpled than usual, and the subtle aroma of pipe tobacco follows him into the cell. "Good afternoon, Miss Moon. The maid found your missive out at the Duncan estate and notified your father. He in turn, telephoned me, and I was in the process of securing a watercraft when I received a call from Sheriff Harper. He had issued a BOLO for you and the vessel. Fortunately, a local fisherman heard the announcement and recognized the *Tax Sea-vasion* as the missing Duncan boat. He was kind enough to inform the sheriff that the Coast Guard had taken it in. I assumed you'd gotten yourself into trouble, as usual." Silas tilts his head and strokes his grey mustache with thumb and forefinger. "I came to offer my assistance." His stooped shoulders and well-worn tweed coat beg to differ.

"Well, as you can see, I have everything under control."

This statement brings a much louder chuckle from my lawyer than anticipated.

I ignore the implication. "Looks like we have some time to kill. What's the deal with Diane? It's just us. You can tell me what's going on, right?"

His jowls brush across his stooped shoulder as he checks to make sure the cell door is closed. "Diane hunted down Ivy several years ago and inadvertently got Walter involved in drug smuggling. She desired a relationship with her mother, but Ivy simply required access to more boats and Walter's permits. He had the freedom to operate his fishing vessels in Canadian waters without the least inconvenience from authorities."

"But why did she have pills?"

"Ay, there's the rub! Diane came to suspect Ivy of blackmailing Captain Truby because of some compromising photos she caught a glimpse of during her travels in Canada. She put two and two together and imagined that if Ivy could obtain the protection of the Coast Guard, she would no longer require Walter's services. Diane offered to sell the pills at school if Ivy promised to protect Walter."

"That didn't pan out." I exhale the weight of my sadness and ask, "Is that why she was returning the pills?"

"That is her story. However, Diane claims Ivy wouldn't accept the return and swears she's innocent of Walter's demise."

A cold sweat beads at my temples, and I wonder if it was blackmail that drove Truby to defile her duty to country, or was she always a rotten apple? "So, if Ivy didn't kill Walt—was it Truby?"

"I fear it was Truby. Perhaps we are nearer to danger than we realize." Silas strokes his mustache thoughtfully.

An involuntary shudder takes me. "This pretty much seems like maximum danger."

"Agreed." Silas nods. "I'm quite sure the authorities aren't looking for a link between Truby and the explosive device recovered from Walter's boat—"

"The list!" The shout draws a scowl and a shushing from Silas.

"I beg your pardon? There's a list?"

"The list of latitudes and longitudes that I found in the painting."

"I fear I'm missing a vital piece of information. To which painting do you refer?"

"It's from the estate-sale stuff, but it went to the pawnshop, not Gershon's. If the site where Walt's boat wreckage was found matches up with one of the locations on the list—we got her!"

"If you say so . . ." Silas harrumphs and paces the two small strides to the door. He peers out the porthole and returns. "Stand up and let me see those handcuffs."

I do as I'm told and lift my wrists as best I can, behind my back, toward Silas.

He places his hands over the metal cuffs, mumbles a short phrase, and the handcuffs drop to the floor.

"Neat trick. Can you please teach me that one?" I'm not too proud to beg.

Silas slowly bends and retrieves the manacles from the floor. "With your propensity for finding yourself in these types of altercations, I do see the benefit. And as we seem to have nothing but the luxury of time on our hands, I believe now is the perfect moment for a lesson."

There's barely room for both of us to sit side by side on the metal bench, but we wedge ourselves in and Silas locks one side of the handcuffs around my right wrist.

"The basis of all alchemical solutions is transmutation. In this situation, the position of the lock must simply be reformed."

I scrunch up my face. "That doesn't make sense."

Silas leans back and grooms his mustache. "Let me think of another example." His eyes slowly slide from side to side as I imagine him searching for relatable parables. "Ah! Imagine you are holding an ice cube in your hand."

"Okay."

"Eventually the heat from your hand melts the ice, correct?"

I exhale. "Yeah, that's heat versus cold. It's not the same thing as locked versus unlocked."

"That is where you're wrong, Mitzy. It is precisely the same. Place your hand over the lock and visualize ice melting."

I do as I'm told, and, as you might expect, nothing happens.

"Your lack of belief directly affects your efficacy." He places my hand over the lock and his milky-blue eyes stare deeply into my disbelieving grey ones. "You can feel the lock. You can feel metal binding against metal. Now begin to soften that metal, feel the metal give way. Feel the lock slipping, feel it release."

The shock of the handcuff dropping into my lap jolts me out of the trance. I was completely under Silas's spell. I could see and feel everything he described, and then the handcuffs came off. It can't be that easy.

"Would you like to try it on your own?"

"Do the Duke Boys like to drive fast?"

His face shows no sign of recognition.

I search my brain for a snappy comeback without a pop-culture reference. Nada. So, I go with, "Yes."

Silas picks up the handcuff and once again locks one side around my wrist. He sits back and gestures for me to proceed.

I place my hand over the cuff, take a deep breath, and close my eyes. I go through the list just as Silas had described. I feel the metal, I feel it binding, I feel it softening, I feel it release. The handcuffs drop!

"I did it!" My whoop of joy is not appreciated.

Silas places a finger to his lips and mustache.

"I did it," I whisper.

"Excellent. Stand up," instructs Silas.

I do as I'm told.

Silas pulls both my arms behind my back and secures the handcuffs over both wrists.

"What are you doing?"

"Some secrets are best kept, Mitzy."

The door to the holding cell opens and Silas hunches over and becomes feebler before my eyes. His hands shake and his voice falters as he asks, "What's going on? I have no idea what's going on."

Captain Truby fills the doorway menacingly and replies, "I'm sorry you got pulled into this, old man, but your client was poking her nose where it didn't belong." She steps out of the way, and her officer enters and grabs both Silas and me by the arms. He drags us out and waits for his next command.

"Take them down to the Duncan boat. We'll toss them overboard out by Leif Erickson's Abyss."

I stifle a gasp as one officer roughly directs us out of the office and down the ramp to the dock while the other keeps his weapon at the ready, in case we get any ideas.

Silas gives me a little wink before he trips and falls on the wooden dock.

The officer drops his hand from my arm to retrieve Silas and, for the second time in as many days, I dive into the icy waters of the greatest of lakes. As soon as the cold knifes into my skin and sucks the breath from my lungs, I regret my genius plan. With freezing water soaking my clothes and pulling me deeper and deeper, I'm having a lot of trouble re-creating the sense of calm that allowed me to release my handcuffs in the tiny cell.

Bullets ricochet off the surface, and one pierces through the water near my head.

I kick my feet and manage to get underneath the dock. My lungs are screaming for air, and my brain refuses to cooperate. I'm fighting my every instinct to kick to the surface and gulp in some air—when an unexpected calm settles over me.

And this is how I go out. I guess I must be dying.

As my heavy, wet clothing drags me down, the handcuffs drop off. I stroke desperately at the water, pulling myself toward the surface. Toward the air I so desperately need. As I surface, a loud splash disturbs the water behind me.

Oh great, one of her henchmen is after me, and I saw Ashton Kutcher in *The Guardian*, so I know these Coast Guard guys can swim like sharks. I paddle hard, down the length of the dock, and tuck between two boats. When I surface to grab another breath of air, sirens pierce my eardrums. Normally the sound of sirens would bring me comfort, but after discovering Captain Truby's dodgy connection to the smugglers, I'm not sure whom to trust.

The rhythmic splashing of a swimmer powering through the water approaches.

I'm shivering uncontrollably now, and only adrenaline pushes me to swing around the boat and head for shore.

There are no more gunshots, so I guess the marksman abandoned his target practice for some old-school Marco Polo.

I'm not normally a strong swimmer, but the terror surging through my veins gives me a determination I never thought possible. My knee scrapes across some rocks. Shore! I pop my head above the surface and someone shouts, "Get down!"

With no way of knowing whether the command is meant for me or someone else, I submerge my unwilling body into the icy liquid.

A single shot fires.

Am I hit? I can't be sure if the lack of feeling is shock or just the numbing cold.

Strong hands grab me and drag me to the rocky beach.

This is it. This is what my father warned me about. This is what I get for sticking my nose into other people's business.

"Mitzy? Miss Moon? Can you hear me?"

That voice . . . I recognize that voice.

A hand slips under my neck and tilts my head back, while a stubbly cheek brushes against my lips.

If this is some attempt to finish me off, I don't understand.

Strong fingers pinch my nose, and as I open my eyes, I'm greeted by the parted lips of Sheriff Erick descending toward mine.

I blink rapidly, cough, and wave my hands.

Less than an inch from contact, the sheriff pulls his face away and shouts, "She's all right!"

I make an effort to sit, but Erick's hand pushes my shoulder down. "Wait for the paramedics, Moon. Your days as a mermaid are over."

His laugh covers the distress in his eyes. If I had waited a half a second more, his lips would've been on mine. Damn these near-death experiences and my over eagerness to live. Next time—

A stretcher scrapes across the rocks, and two strong sets of hands lift me in unison. As the paramedics hoist the stretcher and carry me toward the waiting ambulance, my eyes linger on the enticing vision of Sheriff Erick in his clingy, wet uniform, and his chest heaving a sigh of relief.

You will be mine, Erick. Oh yes, you will.

CHAPTER 22

I'M STUCK in the hospital overnight for "observation," but the only thing I observe is my father's need to stare at me with extreme disappointment and drink endless cups of coffee to stave off sleep.

"Dad, you can go home and get some sleep. I'll be fine. I'm sure Erick rounded up Truby and her goons."

"I'm not leaving this room until Ivy Lapointe is locked up. A woman who corrupts a decorated Coast Guard officer is more dangerous than you can imagine."

Seems like my dad might be underestimating my ability to imagine danger right now. "Can you at least go and check on Silas?"

Jacob reluctantly agrees, but before he makes it

past my hospital bed the door to my room swings open.

"You have a visitor, Miss Moon." The nurse steps aside and in walks my attorney. Apparently, none the worse for the wear, save a light bruise on his left cheek.

"I realize greeting the sunrise is not your custom, but I managed to convince Odell that you were in desperate need of proper sustenance. He's agreed to open thirty minutes early. Would you and Jacob care to break your fast with me?"

By the time I convince my father, two nurses, and one doctor that I'm perfectly fine, the half hour has passed, and we arrive at Myrtle's Diner along with the rest of the early risers.

Jacob pauses with his hand on the door. "You guys head in. I'm going to have a word with Sheriff Harper."

"Go easy on him, Dad. He got there as fast as he could. Plus, I think he shot a guy for me." I smile and blush with admiration.

Jacob scowls. "Order me a special. I won't be long."

Silas Willoughby and I instantly become small-town heroes. But you know me, I would never let that go to my head. We simply slip into a booth in the diner and nurse our bumps and bruises with strong cups of coffee and, of course, large slices of pin cherry pie, *à la mode*. The new breakfast of champions.

A strange man approaches our table and lays a business card in front of me.

"We will not be granting any interviews," says Silas.

Without a glance at the card, I know this is no reporter. Expensive haircut. Tailored suit. Manicured hands. And his shoes— Wait! I've seen those shoes. I pick up the card. Rory Bombay, Proprietor, Bombay Antiquities and Artifacts.

"Perhaps you were acquainted with the previous owner, a Mr. Gershon?"

I gaze up from the card. I can't be bothered to close my slack mouth. Those green eyes and that hint of stubble . . . He was in my Rare Books Loft. The thought of him being so close to my apartment —to my bed . . . I'm not sure if I'm turned on or terrified.

"Silas Willoughby. I'm Miss Moon's solicitor." Silas shakes the man's hand. "So nice to make your acquaintance. How can I be of assistance?"

Without taking his eyes off me, Rory replies, "Miss Moon has a book in her collection that I am most anxious to purchase."

A strange feeling slithers across the table. My attention shifts from the dreamy dealer to Silas.

He's putting up defenses. He's anxious. He's—he's effectively shut me out. "What's going on?"

Silas reaches across the table, picks up the card, and slides it into his breast pocket. "I will telephone you on Monday to discuss the particulars. To which book do you refer?"

Mr. Bombay's eyes never leave my face, but something sparks deep within the emerald pools when he utters the title. "*Saducismus Triumphatus*."

Silas rises from the booth and swells with power. "Monday, Mr. Bombay. Good day."

The mysterious gentleman smiles and turns to leave. He places a hand on my shoulder and adds, "I'll look forward to it."

My skin tingles and blood surges to my face. "That man has magic fingers," I whisper.

"Precisely my concern," mumbles Silas.

My eyes widen with shock, but I don't have time for a follow up.

Tally sashays over to the table. "Either of you need a hotter upper?"

I slide my cup of coffee to the end of the table and Tally expertly fills it within a hair's breadth of the top, never spilling a drop.

"Thanks, Tally."

"Any time, superstar." She winks and hustles off

to attend to the other diners in the unusually crowded cafe.

Silas chuckles, wipes a bit of ice cream from his bushy mustache, and changes the subject. "You did quite well with your seaside performance. I was unsure if you would comprehend my meaning, but I was much pleased when you took advantage of my feeble old stumble and dove to freedom." He smiles like a proud father.

I swallow my delicious mouthful of pie before I ask, "What if I hadn't gotten the message? Did you have a backup plan?"

Silas exhales and pats his belly full of pie. "I prefer to focus on the success, rather than the what ifs."

I wonder if he would have taken a bullet for me? Or if he has some power that he planned to use, but didn't have to. Either way, I guess I should listen to his wise words and simply celebrate the victory.

Sitting with my back to the door, I hear it open but it's the grin on my mentor's face that gives away the identity of our guest. I twist in my seat, eager to fill my senses with a slice of sexy sheriff, but I'm crestfallen to note that yesterday's deliciously clingy uniform has been replaced with a completely dry and pressed set. How rude.

"If it isn't our local hero, Mitzy Moon. Jacob said I could find you here."

Several heads in the diner nod their agreement, and two gentlemen raise coffee cups in a toast to my celebrity status.

The sheriff chuckles as he approaches the table. "He's filling out some paperwork. Could be awhile. He said not to wait."

"Eighty-six the special, Odell," I call across the diner.

He tosses me a metal-spatula salute through the orders-up window.

"Do you already have a new case for me?"

"Not today, Moon. I'm here to inform you that even heroes have to make official statements."

Boy, this guy is all business all the time. Maybe I'm wasting my fantasy life on dreams of him letting down his guard and whispering sweet nothings in my ear. Maybe I should spend that energy on a little fantasizing about Rory—

Silas clears his throat loudly.

Once again, I've let my inner delights display themselves on my face. I can almost see the twinkle in my own eyes. "Of course, Erick. Silas and I will come down to the station as soon as we finish our pie."

Erick taps his fingers on the table, nods, and as he leaves, tosses this gem in my direction. "So I'll see you in less than two minutes?" The door closes and mercifully muffles his laughter.

"Your reputation precedes you." Silas gives me an overly formal nod and savors his final bite of pie.

As predicted, my celebratory meal rapidly disappears.

Tally clears our plates, offers more coffee, which we decline, and Silas hands me a napkin.

As evidence of my extreme personal growth, I accept the napkin. Look what a protégé I'm turning out to be.

Odell Johnson makes his way out of the kitchen toward our table.

"Hey, Odell, that was some real fine pie."

He nods his agreement. "I just wanted to thank you for doing right by Walt. You and I both know Diane only got wrapped up in all of this to try to get him squared away. He might not've always made the smartest choices, but he was a good dad." Odell sniffles, wipes his nose with the back of his hand, and says, "Must be allergies."

I smile warmly. "Yeah, I hear they're real bad this fall."

He nods. "Diane's gonna testify against Ivy. She feels terrible about Lars Gershon—Diane does, not Ivy. She let it slip to Ivy about the estate sale before the fire and the DA figures that's when Ivy went lookin' for that fancy painting. She had no idea Walt had stashed it with the pawnshop guy. Poor

Lars. He woulda had no idea what Psycho Ivy was after."

Silas mumbles something under his breath that sounds a little like, "Ah, that was the moniker." But I'm not entirely sure what a moniker is, so I turn my attention back to Odell.

He continues, "Sounds like the DA will drop Diane's charge to a misdemeanor for her cooperation, and he's gonna let her off with some community service. It could've been much worse if you hadn't uncovered that whole conspiracy. I still can't believe Captain Truby let herself be taken in by that good-for-nothin' Ivy. Truby's father must be turning over in his grave. He was a decent man. Made a lot of sacrifices for those kids. At least Junior turned out all right."

Junior must be the younger brother that served in Afghanistan with Erick. I don't bother asking. The details aren't important. What's important is to let Odell thank me profusely in his own quiet, convoluted way.

Silas slides out of the booth and lays a few bills on the table. He places a hand on Odell's shoulder and says, "And you are also a man of fine character, Odell." He walks toward the door and calls back to me, "I'll see you at the station, Mitzy."

Odell chuckles. "If you're not careful, they'll start charging you rent down there." His belly laugh fills the diner and a little tear wets the corner of his eye.

Laughing along, I salute Odell as I leave. He was the first friend I ever made when I came to Pin Cherry Harbor. Maybe I'm not such a bad judge of character after all. Who knows, my luck with men might be about to change.

End of Book 2

~ A NOTE FROM TRIXIE

Another case solved! I'll keep writing them if you keep reading . . .

One of my favorite parts of bringing Mitzy to life has been the wonderful feedback from my early readers. Thank you to my alpha readers Angel, Michael, and Andrew. HUGE thanks to my fantastic beta readers who gave me extremely useful and honest feedback: Veronica McIntyre, Renee Arthur, and Nadine Peterse-Vrijhof. And big hugs to the world's best ARC Team – Trixie's Mystery ARC Detectives!

Three cheers for my brilliant editor Philip Newey! Any errors are my own, as my outdated version of Word insists on showing me only what it likes and when it feels so moved.

I'm a huge fan of Mitzy and Pye on the cover. Thanks, GermanCreative!

Google can give an author all kinds of helpful information, but there is absolutely no substitute for "straight from the horse's mouth." Thanks to my "horses!" Morgan, thank you for getting me squared away on Odell's Army backstory. Kylie, thank you for answering my foolish questions about tattoos and for coining the phrase "tattoo inception!" And finally, thank you to Josh for all the years you begged for a caracal! I was never as brave as Grams, but your passion for them sent me down the "rabbit hole" and once I learned all I could about the little beasts—I knew I had to have one—even if it lives only in my mind.

Now I'm writing book four in the Mitzy Moon Mysteries series, and I think I may just live in Pin Cherry Harbor forever. Mitzy, Grams, and Pyewacket got into plenty of trouble in book one, *Fries and Alibis*. But I'd have to say that book three, *Wings and Broken Things*, is when most readers say the series becomes unputdownable.

I hope you'll continue to hang out with us.

Trixie Silvertale (November 2019)

PARANORMAL COZY MYSTERY

Wings & Broken Things

TRIXIE SILVERTALE

Sittin' On A Goldmine Productions L.L.C.

CHAPTER 1

THICK WHITE FLAKES float lazily toward my outstretched tongue. The inviting aroma of mulled wine and cider drifts through the air and, for a moment, I almost put my arms out and spin. This must be what it feels like to live inside a snow globe.

Except for the chainsaws.

Yes, you heard me correctly. Chainsaws.

At the indefatigable insistence of my volunteer employee, Twiggy, I'm attending my first Northern Lights Yuletide Extravaganza. Most people would probably call it a winter carnival, but the good folks at the Pin Cherry Harbor Chamber of Commerce felt that the event needed more pizzazz.

Did you picture jazz-hands? Me too. However, not mentioned in the invite is the fact that every living soul in town is in attendance, despite the late hour. And "late" in Pin Cherry is anything past 8:00 p.m. I'm sure the rest of our fair city looks like a ghost town.

As I stand next to the chainsaw ice-sculpture carving competition, I have to admit they definitely add the promised flair. Despite the ear-drum-blowing stuttering and revving of the saws, I am mesmerized by the beauty being revealed within eight-foot-by-three-foot columns of ice. The one of an angel almost seems to move its wings.

The magical fluttering of the giant flakes of ice dust makes me feel like I'm part of a Norse fairy-tale. All I need is a blonde-haired, blue-eyed Viking god to walk through the glittering mist—

"Erick?"

"Ah, Miss Moon, perhaps you are not as quick with names as I had hoped."

My disappointment is quickly replaced with a welcome surge of heat as the tall, dark, and green-eyed Rory Bombay scoops up my mittened hand and presses his lips to the thin wool. I can feel the intensity as clearly as if that stubble-kissed chin had touched my skin.

I let him thread my arm through his as I fall into step beside him. I'm not sure what brings him up north from his antiquities business in Grand Falls, but I'm not complaining. "Oh, Mr. Bombay, I remember your name. I was . . . it's not important."

"Please, call me Rory. And may I call you Mizithra?"

I want to blurt, "No you absolutely may not ever call me that," but his emerald eyes twinkle with mischief and I quickly retaliate. "Only if you'd like this to be our last date, Mr. Bombay."

His laughter swirls around me and I feel beautiful and sophisticated. The elation lasts an entire seven seconds before a huge baby stroller smacks into my knee and sends me sprawling on my ample behind in the snowbank beside the shoveled walkway.

The young mother's apology is swallowed by the screams of her drastically unhappy toddler.

A strong hand, clad in soft, black kidskin leather, reaches down. I grasp the lifeline and Rory Bombay pulls me up much too quickly. I crash into the firm planes of his chest and inhale sharply.

"I beg your pardon, Mitzy. Either you're light as a feather, or I don't know my own strength. I'm sure it would be the former." His full lips curve in a suggestive grin.

I should warn him that flattery will get him everywhere, but I'm trying to turn over a new leaf since I ran out on my flat-broke barista existence in Sedona, Arizona, for places so far north they could be mistaken for Canada.

"Is this your first Yuletide in Pin Cherry?" He

gently slips my arm through the crook of his as he inquires.

I like that he's jumping on the chamber's branding train. "Yes, I recently inherited the bookshop on Main Street and First Avenue from my grandmother and this will be my first winter here."

He clucks his tongue. "Oh dear. Are you prepared?" He slides my arm free and spins me out as though I'm his longtime ballroom dance partner. "Let's see. The boots look sufficient for an average winter, but if there's a blizzard like the one in '84 . . . The jeans are flattering, but you'll succumb to hypothermia in minutes when the true storms hit. You should definitely get a lovely pair of silk-lined snow pants."

I smile and play along. "What about the jacket?"

He pulls off his glove and rubs a section of my sleeve between his thumb and long artistic fingers. "Down is good, but this can't be rated for more than ten below. You'll need to upgrade before the solstice."

The word pricks the hairs on the back of my neck. I'm certain that if I slipped off my left mitten and looked at my recently deceased grandmother's magically enhanced mood ring some image would appear. Some kind of warning detected by my budding extra-sensory psychic powers. "Solstice?"

His smile holds a secret that vanishes like quicksilver. "I meant Christmas, of course. It can get down to seventy below zero in the heart of Jack Frost's realm." He scoops me back to his side and continues, "May I tell you a bit about this lovely time of year?"

"Of course."

"First stop, the glögg." He pauses at a booth and says, "Två."

The fresh-faced blonde with thick rabbit-fur earmuffs hands him two steaming mugs. He lays a fifty on the counter, nods, and picks up the two beverages. He does not ask for change.

With my work history as a transient barista, I have a deep appreciation for big tippers. I beam with genuine admiration as he hands me one of the drinks. "Do you speak Swedish?" I ask.

He chuckles. "Ah, you recognize your native tongue?"

I shake my head. "I'm not Swedish."

He looks at me with open appreciation. "Those eyes, grey as a winter storm cloud? That snow-white hair? You are not only Swedish, my darling. You are a Scandinavian goddess."

Despite the cold, my cheeks flush with heat.

"Let me show you to your palace, M'Lady." He leads me toward the lakeshore where a sparkle of lights like an enormous diamond dances through the snowfall.

"It's beautiful," I whisper.

"Come inside and try your glögg."

I follow him into the glowing structure constructed of thick blocks of ice, cut from the great lake that serves as the backdrop to this winter wonderland. The semi-transparent cubes sparkle from within. I take a long pull from my warm mug. "What is this?"

"Glögg means 'to burn or mull.' A brew that is lovingly crafted from old family recipes that include red wine, port, brandy, and spices. It is always served warm and is a favorite on St. Lucia's Day, but is, of course, delicious whenever the temperatures turn chilly."

I eagerly drain my mug in greedy gulps. The liquid trickles down my throat and warms my tummy. "It's delicious."

He clinks his mug to mine, takes a big swig, and continues, "Legends tell of King Gustav I Vasa of Sweden who created a warm drink made from German wine, sugar and spices. His drink was later named 'glödgag vin,' meaning 'glowing-hot wine.' The name eventually transformed to glögg by the late 1800s."

The warmth in my middle is spreading and creating a general softening of all my senses and I can't seem to tear my eyes away from the glögg-wet lips of the enticing Rory Bombay.

The sparkling lights.

The close quarters within the walls of the ice palace.

The deep thrum of his voice.

"Moon?"

That voice? I recognize the sound, but Rory's lips aren't moving.

"Moon, are you actually out socializing?" A friendly hand pats me on the back as though I'm part of some type of sports team.

My mulled brain sloshes a little as I turn. "Erick?"

Behind me, a disappointed sigh escapes my tour guide.

Erick steps rather close and the scent of my mulled wine is quickly replaced by the sharp citrus-woodsy smell of my secret crush. "Who's this?" He gestures to the man at my side.

I wait a beat while the scene plays out in my always-making-a-student-film mind. I sense a tinge of jealousy from Erick, even though he's never bothered to take me up on my blatant flirtatious advances. I have tripped and fallen on him at least three times, and he's saved my life twice, so maybe he thinks we're going steady. In my "mind movie" he slugs Rory in the jaw and tells him to keep his manicured hands off his girl. In reality, I introduce them. "Erick Harper, this is Rory Bombay, the new owner of Gershon Antiquities."

Rory steps forward and extends his hand. "Of course, it's Bombay Antiquities and Artifacts now."

Erick snags the outstretched hand and shakes it firmly several times. "And it's Sheriff Harper."

Even in my deliciously spiced state I pick up on the chill that settles over our trio when Erick adds his honorific to the mix.

"Always a pleasure to meet the local authorities, Sheriff." Rory recovers quickly and pulls his hand back.

The feeling passes and I wonder if Erick will offer to buy me a caramel apple. But before I can see my culinary dreams fulfilled his radio crackles to life. "Sheriff, we have a 962H on Pin Cherry Lane."

Erick depresses the button on the side of his mic. "10-4. En route."

I ask the question that is begging for an answer. "What's a 962H?"

The faint, possibly imagined, whisper of jealousy has vanished and Erick's striking face is tense with duty and a touch of worry. "Leave this to the authorities, Moon." He glances to my left. "Nice to meet you, Mr. Bombay. I'm sorry, but I have to respond to this call immediately."

"It was a pleasure, Sheriff Harper." Rory nods stiffly.

Erick tips his head in a way that insinuates a brim to his non-existent hat. "Enjoy your evening, Miss Moon."

I'm sure he knows there's virtually no chance of that happening now that my wheels are spinning. I can Google things, Erick. Maybe I'll buy myself a police-band radio. I mean, what's an heiress to do if not meddle in the affairs of her community—or at least her community's sexy sheriff.

Rory slips his arm around my waist and leans close to my ear. "Did I ever tell you about the time I survived a two-day blizzard by building an igloo?"

I don't even need my extra senses to pick up on Rory's desperate attempt to erase all memory of Erick from our evening. Maybe it's the mulled wine, or the Yuletide magic, or the mesmerizing twinkle of lights in the snow castle—whatever the reason—I snuggle into Rory's warmth and reply, "Where did you learn to build an igloo?"

CHAPTER 2

The weak light of morning doesn't have a chance of rousing me from the deep sleep afforded by my flannel sheets, electric blanket, and thick down comforter.

However, the rude bomb of tan fur terrorizing my chest gets the job done effortlessly.

"Pyewacket!" I shove my grandmother's rescued caracal off, despite his history of saving my life. A girl's gratitude has limits—

I spin right and breathe a huge sigh of relief when I see my large bed is devoid of company. And, upon further inspection of the luxurious four-poster bed, I deduce that I slept alone. Lucky for me, because if Grams—

"Good morning, Mitzy. Are you wondering how you got here?"

The splash of recovering alcoholic's condescension in my ghost grandmother's voice does not escape my notice. I carefully clear my mind of all snark so that she won't have the usual satisfaction of reading my private thoughts. "Good morning to you, Myrtle Isadora Johnson Linder Duncan Willamet Rogers."

She scoffs and swirls toward the high, coffered ceiling.

You see, my dearly departed grandmother, previous owner of this swanky apartment and the three-story bookstore on the other side of my secret door, was a bit of a skank herself.

"Mizithra Achelois Moon!" Ghost-ma dives toward me in a fury. Clearly she's broken our "no thought-reading" rule.

"Takes one to know one, Grams."

"Well, I never."

"We both know you did. At least five times!" I guffaw loudly as I stumble toward the bathroom.

"How many times do I have to tell you, there's a big difference between a sk—"

"Grams, the only thing that made you a 'woman of means, who knows what she wants' was a few decimal points in your bank account."

"Tom-ay-to, tom-ah-to." She crosses her bejeweled limbs over her burgundy silk-and-tulle Marchesa gown and shakes her head. She may have passed away in her early sixties, but at her chosen ghost-age of thirty-five she looks like an aristocratic older sister.

"Don't I at least get some points for coming home alone?" I gesture magnanimously to my empty four-poster bed.

A mischievous light twinkles in her ethereal eyes as she floats down to my level. "Before you get too comfortable up on that high and mighty horse of yours, you might want to chat with Twiggy."

I swallow audibly. "Oh." You see, Twiggy is Grams' former best friend and my one and only employee, although she works for the entertainment not the cash. I would not be able to run the bookshop without her—and she knows it. I shudder to think what humiliation I will have to endure over my first cup of wake-up juice.

"RE-ow." Which is Pye-speak for "Feed me." I'm slowly but surely learning to decipher the subtle variations in his pointed mewing, and he seems to have no trouble understanding English, so we have a workable system.

"Come on, you bossy fur ball. Let's get your Fruity Puffs before someone loses a finger." I press the plaster circle of ivy vines above the intercom and the secret door from my apartment to the Rare Books Loft glides open.

Contrary to my normal morning stomp-shuffle,

I tiptoe across the thick carpeting of the loft and down the metal leaves of the spiral staircase. But before I can set a hesitant foot on the main floor—

"Mornin', doll. How's that glögg treating you?" Twiggy's cackle echoes off the tin-plated ceiling and bounces back toward my ears like tiny arrows laced with mockery's poison. Her arms are crossed over her flannel button-down and her helmet of grey hair does not move as she shakes with laughter.

"Fine," I mumble. And this is the entertainment of which I spoke.

"I hate to burst your bubble, but I think that slick-talkin' Bombay fella was a whole lot more interested in gettin' inside your bookshop than anything else."

More grating locker-room snickering.

I pour some liquid alert into a possibly clean mug and slump into a stiff wooden chair. As the caffeinated potion seeps into my veins a thought bubbles to the surface. "Wait, what?"

"By the time I bumped into you at the Yuletide Extravaganza, you were three sheets to the wind and he was workin' overtime trying to convince you he was a perfect gentleman and only wanted to 'safely escort you home.' Well, I told him to shove off and managed to get you home in one piece all by my little lonesome." A volley of chuckles.

I gulp down more java and respond, "I remember him being very courteous and I'm sure he would've walked me home like a gentleman if you hadn't interfered." I scowl at her across the rim of my mug. Now that I'm waking up, I recall how interested he was in my Rare Books Loft, and I've come to realize it's freezing in here. "I've got to get some warm clothes on and find a proper breakfast."

A quick trip to the closet later, and I'm stomping through the fresh snowfall on Main Street toward Myrtle's Diner in a thick hoodie that says, "Eat, Drink & Be Meowy." This should get a chuckle or two at breakfast. The more I get to know the owner, Odell Johnson, the happier I am that he and my grandmother reconciled in her final days. It seems like her life would've been quite different if she and Odell had stayed together. However, then I would never have been born or had the good fortune to wind up in Pin Cherry Harbor.

A large black industrial floor mat sits just inside the door, adorned with chunks of muddy snow and ice in various stages of liquefying. A quick glance around the quaint diner proves that last night's festivities were attended by plenty of out-of-towners, or tourons as I prefer to call them. Every red-vinyl booth is filled to bursting, and all of the low four-tops are taken as well. I spot an empty stool at the counter and make a beeline, before I lose my last chance at a hot breakfast.

The grey crew-cut-topped head of Odell pops into the orders-up window and he gives me the standard salute with his metal spatula. I've come to learn that there's no need to place an order. Odell prides himself on knowing exactly what people want. I reach out and my hand encounters an empty space where my cup of coffee usually sits. At this point, I realize the lively flame-red-bun-topped head of the best waitress in Pin Cherry is missing. I shout above the din of the bustling restaurant, "Where's Tally?"

"Not coming in today."

"Is she sick? Should I check on her?"

Odell shakes his head. Something in his expression plucks a nervous chord in my heart.

"Everything okay?" Before he can answer, the man next to me slips off his stool, folds his newspaper in half, and slaps it down on the counter before he walks out.

Odell nods toward the paper. It takes a moment for me to realize that I've never before read a newspaper. But now that I've left the new-age mecca of Sedona, Arizona, and the high-tech life of a barely employed barista, I guess I'll start reading the newspaper like a local. I pick up the copy of the *Pin Cherry Harbor Post* and smooth it out on the counter in front of me. There above the fold is a shocking headline.

LOCAL VET INVOLVED IN HIT AND RUN.

Knowing that Odell served as an Army cook back in the day, I look up, concerned that he's the veteran. He shakes his head and motions for me to keep reading. As my eyes scan over the dancing black letters, I see that our beloved veterinarian, Doc Ledo, was mysteriously struck down on his way home after a late-night emergency surgery on a local service animal. Worry washes over me, but before I can say anything Odell intervenes.

"Tally won't be in today. Went to check on her brother at the hospital. No news yet." His metal spatula scrapes across the grill and the lines in Odell's face seem to deepen with additional years of concern.

He walks out from the kitchen and puts a plate in front of me. Perfectly scrambled eggs and chorizo with a side of deliciously browned home fries. He spins around and fills a mug with coffee, setting it down in front of me and emptying the pot down the row of waiting cups at the counter.

I gobble down my breakfast and chug the coffee. Wiping my mouth on a napkin, I bus my own dishes and make a fresh pot of coffee. The door scrapes open and two more patrons enter.

Snagging a couple menus from the stack, I show the new patrons to the recently vacated stools at the counter. As soon as the fresh pot of coffee is ready I make a round, filling cups and fetching to-go boxes.

When I return the pot to the coffee maker and brew up another round of black gold, I catch Odell smiling as he works. I lean on the ledge of the orders-up window and say, "I was just a poor working stiff before Grams left me a bookstore and a pile of cash."

He chuckles and replies, "Thanks."

It takes a little finagling to figure out the "no-tech" cash register, but before long the dwindling breakfast crowd turns into the lunch rush and the next time I look up it's nearly three o'clock in the afternoon and Odell is serving up a piece of pie topped with creamy vanilla ice cream.

"Hey, you better take your state-mandated break." He sets the pie on the counter and fills a fresh mug with coffee.

"Still the best pin cherry pie in town."

"The tourists should all be back on the road by now. I'd sure appreciate it if you could check on Tally. You know she's awful close to her big brother, Ledo. I can't imagine how upset she must be."

"Hit and run? In this town? Do they have any leads?"

I should be offended by the rumbling laughter coming from Odell, but it's to be expected.

"Seems like you're getting yourself quite a reputation in this town. You planning on running for sheriff?"

"No thank you. I prefer to stick my nose where it *doesn't* belong and actually solve cases."

We share a laugh and I greedily finish my pie. "Maybe I'll stop by the station on my way to the hospital."

"Sounds like Mitzy Moon is on the case." Odell chuckles as he clears my plate and I head out to see what I can uncover about the driver who struck down the man who saved Pyewacket's life.

Outside, the sidewalk resembles a poorly designed checkerboard. Some sections are shoveled clean and sprinkled with salt, which I've learned prevents ice from forming on the concrete when the temperatures inevitably drop below zero as the sun sets. But in front of the abandoned or closed businesses, the snow is piled high. So I play an unwelcome game of hopscotch as I make my way to the sheriff's station. But as luck would have it my incredible coordination betrays me at precisely the most inopportune moment.

I hop up and over an un-shoveled section of sidewalk, but instead of landing on a lovely shoveled square with a generous sprinkling of salty grit, my foot hits a perfectly slick patch of icy terror. One foot goes left, the other goes north, and before I know what's hit me, I'm on my back in the man-made snowdrift left by the plow the night before. Flailing like a turtle on its shell, I desperately seek some purchase in the deep snow. My suffering is put to an end as two strong hands grip my waving arms and pull me to my feet.

"Oh my," I manage to utter by way of a thank you. I don't think I've ever been this close to Erick without having tripped and fallen on top of him! I can actually feel the heat of his body through his thick winter uniform jacket. I have an inexplicable urge to lick the word "SHERIFF" on his badge, but even in Arizona the legends of tongues sticking to things in the frozen north had reached my ears—so I manage to control myself.

"You might want to consider attending a survival course, Miss Moon. I realize this is your first real winter, and we wouldn't want you freezing to death simply because you don't know how to get out of a snowbank." He barely has the decency to finish the sentence before he's gripped by uncontrollable belly laughs.

I choose to press the only advantage I've ever had and step closer to the luscious blonde-haired, blue-eyed Sheriff Erick Harper. "Are you offering me private lessons, Erick?"

He shuffles backward, falters on the same patch of ice that claimed me, but somehow manages to keep his feet underneath him. He clears his throat nervously and offers another round of sound advice. "You be careful out there, Miss Moon. And get yourself some thermal long johns or some snow pants. You'll freeze to death in no time in those jeans."

I'm definitely flattered that he's looking at my jeans, but I have a job to do. "I'm on my way to see Tally. Can I let her know if you have any leads on the driver of the car that struck her brother?"

A pained expression grips Erick's face and he shakes his head solemnly. "It's a real shame about Ledo. He's a great guy and has always been more than fair about taking care of pets, even when families fall on hard times. He saved my little Casserole's leg and wouldn't even let me pay him extra for coming in on a Sunday."

There are so many things to unpack in that statement, I don't know where to begin. But, let's be honest, we both want to know the same thing. "Is Casserole a cat or a dog?"

Erick blushes, looks down at his boot, and kicks at some frozen chunks of dirty snow left behind by the plow. "Casserole was a potbelly pig."

"Was? Was Casserole's name a self-fulfilling prophecy?"

Erick looks up, and his steel-blue eyes soften with memory as a warm smile spreads across his face.

I can feel my heart melting inside my chest like an icicle in the sun.

"Casserole died of natural causes when I was on my second tour in Afghanistan." For a moment there is a flash of pain, but it vanishes quicker than a lightning strike, and the muscles in Erick's cheeks flex as he clenches his jaw and hardens his expression.

"Sounds like a long story. Maybe you'll tell me over a slice of pin cherry pie sometime . . ."

Erick gives a noncommittal shrug.

"Do you have anything on the driver?" I figure it can't hurt to ask again.

"I feel like I'd be wasting my breath if I told you to stay out of this, Moon. But rest assured that I will find out who did this to Doc Ledo, and I'll make sure they pay."

The hard edge in Erick's voice and the menacing energy drifting off him in waves sends a very non-wintry chill down my spine. Beneath that soft "Andy Taylor" folksy exterior lurks a soldier who's had to make hard decisions, and will make them again.

"Good day, Moon."

As the delicious distraction that is Erick stalks down the street toward his cruiser, I become uncomfortably aware of the melting snow trickling down the inside of my boots and possibly even my pants.

In addition to the freezing wetness, my feet are throbbing with fatigue. Looks like my life of leisure in Pin Cherry has softened my edge. After a busy day on my feet at the diner, all I can think of is a long hot bath and my cozy bed.

Seems like my trip to the hospital can wait until tomorrow.

CHAPTER 3

HAVING HAD the unique experience of reading the local paper yesterday, I decide for a repeat with today's breakfast. There are only three of us at Myrtle's Diner this morning, and someone has abandoned his or her paper at one of the four-tops. I pick it up, slide into a booth, and smooth it out on the silver-flecked white Formica table. Top story: MISSING ANGEL BREAKS WIDOW'S HEART

It seems that a three-foot-high memorial statue containing the ashes of Oslo Jorgensen was stolen from the front porch of Olga Jorgensen on Saturday night. The article goes on to explain that the angel was a custom-ordered memorial, which contained the ashes of the woman's dearly departed husband.

The inscription read, "On angel's wings you were borne away, but in my heart you shall always stay."

I lean back and take a long, comforting sip of my hot java. Who would steal a memorial? Did they know the husband's ashes were inside? Is it vandalism or just theft? There's no photo of the stolen statuary, but the image that accompanies the story is far more haunting: just footprints in the snow, leading away from her house. Reminds me of a poem, however this time it would appear the thief carried the angel. There is some sort of marking—

Tally slides my plate onto the table and interrupts my musings.

I inhale deeply. "That smells delicious. I think Odell was seriously off his game without you yesterday. I know he's happy to have you back. How's Ledo doing?"

Tally nods her head rapidly and the tight flame-red bun perched on top bobs with it. "He's doing real good, you know? The doctors say—" Her voice catches in her throat and I put a hand on her arm.

"I didn't mean to upset you, Tally. I'm so sorry about what happened. I know they're doing everything they can for him. And I heard that one of the veterinarians over in Broken Rock is going to come up twice a week until Ledo's back on his feet." I realize my mistake too late.

Tally's eyes fill with tears and she scurries into the back room.

I want to smack my forehead on the table. Back on his feet! Such an idiot! The poor doctor will probably be paralyzed from the waist down because of the thoughtless motorist who left him to die in the street, and I say "back on his feet." I suddenly lose my appetite.

Odell wanders out from the kitchen and quietly slips onto the bench seat across the table from me. "Don't beat yourself up kid, Tally knows you mean well. Ledo's always taken care of her. It's gonna take a while."

I lean forward and whisper, "I feel like such an idiot."

"Don't sweat it. Eat your breakfast and then go figure out who did this to him. That's the best thing you can do for Tally right now." Odell slides out of the booth, raps his knuckles on the table twice, and saunters back into the kitchen.

He's right. That's the best thing I can do for Tally right now. A good portion of my appetite is restored by Odell's encouraging words. I eat half my scrambled eggs and all my home fries. Draining the last of my coffee, I nod my thanks and walk out of the diner.

On my return trip to the bookshop, I notice all the footprints in the packed snow covering the sidewalk. Mostly different deep-treaded winter boots, I guess. But there's the occasional smooth-soled dress shoe and, of course, my tennis shoes with their cheap generic logo in the arch—

That's what it was! The marking left by that shoe in the snow. The photo in the paper wasn't very clear, but maybe if I go down to the *Pin Cherry Harbor Post*'s main office, I can get a look at the original digital file. Maybe even enlarge it. I mean, on TV they can enlarge images a thousand percent without any loss of resolution, so it can't be that hard. If I can see what brand of shoes the thief was wearing, then I can figure out who stole that angel.

Hold on! I don't have time to get involved in statuary theft. I need to stay focused and figure out who could run a man down in the middle of a snowstorm and leave him for dead on the road. That's my primary mission.

After I change my clothes and add a proper winter coat, Grams informs me that I'll have to take the Jeep.

Having one car was news to me, but learning that one does not drive one's 1957 Mercedes 300SL with gullwing doors during the winter months . . . mind blown.

"And where will I find this Jeep?"

"It's two garages down—toward the lake—from the Mercedes. Same access code."

"Do I want to know what's in that middle garage, or do I have to wait for another season?"

Grams laughs and shakes her head. "I honestly don't remember. It might be artwork, or books, or maybe clothes?" She floats lazily toward the window and gazes out over the frozen lake. "I think some of my life is getting fuzzy, Mitzy. Do you think that's how it starts? First I forget a couple harmless details and eventually it's all gone?"

Her tone worries me. "Grams, come on. You said yourself: you're well and truly stuck here. I think the dead only vanish once they're forgotten, and I'm still getting to know you. So what if you forgot the contents of one of your ancillary garages? You're here. I'm here. What is it you always say? One day at a time. Right?"

Tears spring from her eyes as she closes the distance between us. "Oh, Mitzy, I don't deserve you!"

I awkwardly give her a ghost-hug. "Until I can figure out a way to get you an afterlife handkerchief, I'd call us even. Deal?"

She snuffles and wipes at her translucent cheeks. "Deal."

"I'm off to the hospital. Wish me luck." I casually wonder where the keys are to my "other" car?

"Keys are tucked in the visor."

I almost point to my lips and scold her for

thought-dropping, but I did actually need an answer to that unspoken question.

As much as it pains me to admit it, the best place to start my investigation of the hit and run is by interviewing the sole witness to the crime. Unfortunately, I've always had a strong aversion to illness and hospitals. It's not that I personally have any issue with sick people, but growing up in foster care has left me with a general distrust of institutions. I had been living with foster mom number three and finally finding a tiny bit of comfort after my mother's fatal car accident when I got jumped by a gang of kids on my way home from school. They had only meant to frighten me, but my fight or flight instinct was stuck on "high alert" and I overreacted. I ran like a girl possessed and tripped and fell down an embankment. In addition to the cuts and bruises, I broke my left arm. I never found out who called the ambulance, but when I woke up in the hospital there were two policemen and a woman from Child Protective Services discussing my new placement. Foster family number four was unquestionably one of the worst experiences of my young life. And ever since, I've been less than thrilled with hospitals. However, I'm a big girl now, so I better put on my big-girl pants, get over to the hospital, and see if Ledo can remember anything.

Despite my courageous pep talk on the drive

over, my lack of confidence with winter driving, combined with unpleasant childhood memories, produces a state of agitation by the time I arrive at the Birch County Regional Medical Facility.

As I approach the nurses' station I hesitate and worry they might not let me in, because I'm not family. Before I can make my cowardly exit, the friendly, efficient woman behind the counter notices me.

"Who are you here to see, Miss?"

"Dr. Toledo." My voice lacks any of the confidence necessary to convince her I'm a relative. And at that moment, I also realize I have no idea of the doctor's last name. Just a funny anecdote about how he and his sisters are all named after the towns of their conceptions. A story shared by Twiggy—possibly untrue and definitely inappropriate for this setting.

"And your pet's name?"

My jaw drops, and I gape at the woman for a solid ten seconds. "My what?"

She chuckles. "Ledo has had visits from several pet owners . . . It seems that he's better at remembering the pet's names than their people's. So he's asked us to introduce his guests by the name of their furry friends, or feathered."

I smile and nod. It would appear I'm not the

only person who likes to put things in context. "The name is Pyewacket."

The nurse smiles and nods her approval. "Great name." She walks out from behind the desk and gestures for me to follow.

We make our way down the hall and turn into a room so festooned with flower arrangements that I worry she may have directed me to the hospital gift shop rather than Ledo's room.

"Well, Ledo, it looks like you have another visitor. This one is Pyewacket." The nurse waves her arm magnanimously toward the man in the hospital bed. I mumble my thanks and move hesitantly toward the figure.

"Mitzy Moon! It's so nice of you to visit. I'd get up, but they tell me the legs have gone into early retirement—possibly, permanently."

"I'm sorry." I mumble and avoid his eyes. I don't know what to say. I shouldn't have come.

"Don't be sorry. Look at all the folks who care about me." He carefully gestures to the bouquets.

I glance around the room at the overabundance of flower arrangements and realize how much this man is loved, how little my visit truly matters, and how sweet it is of him to pretend that it does. I thrust a box of Fruity Puffs in his general direction and say, "It's what Pyewacket wanted you to have."

He laughs and then clutches his chest. "Three broken ribs. Don't make me laugh."

"I'm so sorry!"

He gently lifts his arm and takes the box of Fruity Puffs. "No need to apologize, Mitzy. I needed that laugh. And I really need this box of Fruity Puffs. As you can see, I have more flowers than I know what to do with. In fact, could you do me a favor?"

"Absolutely. Can I get you some water or coffee?"

He grips his chest and chuckles quietly. "Now you sound like Tally."

We both laugh a little about that.

"I was actually wondering if you would take these flowers and distribute them at the pet cemetery?"

"We have a pet cemetery?" All I can think of is the horrifying movie, and I have great concern for my personal safety.

Seeming to read my mind, he replies, "It's nothing like the movie. It's just a lovely place where people can remember the unconditional love that their pets provided. The Pin Cherry Harbor Welcoming Committee and the Ladies Luncheon League run a couple of fundraisers every year to pay the property taxes and a part-time groundskeeper. But I have no use for all these flowers and it would certainly brighten the place up. At least for a few hours, before the blooms freeze. But, maybe you could get the paper to take some photos and then the joy will last forever."

I'm speechless. I look at this man who may never regain the use of his legs and I can't comprehend how, even in what seems like his darkest hour, his first thought is for others. A wave of guilt washes over me. My self-absorbed, misspent youth can't be relived, but I am absolutely going to distribute these beautiful flowers and set up a photo shoot with the local paper. And then I'm going to drive to my lawyer's office and set up a philanthropic organization, finally. Mitzy Moon is going to make some attempt to leave the world a better place than she found it.

"Mitzy? Everything okay?"

I surface from my existential dive and reply, "I'm supposed to be here to cheer you up." I force a smile to my face and give my personality an injection of artificial sunshine.

Ledo tilts his head and stares at me wistfully. "You don't have to use kid gloves around me, dear. I know the extent of my injuries and I know the odds are not in my favor. But I didn't suffer any brain damage and I have full use of my hands and fingers. There will be an adjustment period as I get used to life in a wheelchair, but I can still practice medicine. I can still help all my patients, and that's what's truly important to me."

I nod my head, but still can't find my voice.

"I'm not going to pretend it will be easy. I know there are dark days ahead. But I'm not giving up. Giving up is a one-way ticket to somewhere I don't want to go."

"Ledo, I will absolutely take these flowers anywhere you want them to be. And if it's all right with you, I'd also like to find the person who did this to you."

"Well now." He chuckles carefully. "I've heard some mighty fine stories about amateur sleuth Mitzy Moon. Seems like you've done more than your share of legwork for the sheriff since you came into town. When Tally was here yesterday, she couldn't stop talking about how you'd helped Odell get to the bottom of Walt's murder and even got some leniency for little Diane. I'm not interested in retribution or vengeance, but I wouldn't mind making sure someone has to face the music."

"Exactly what I was thinking." I slide a chair closer to the bed, sit down, and pull out my phone in case I need to take notes. "Tell me everything you remember, even if it doesn't seem important."

As Ledo relives the painful memories of the night he was struck down, I keep a careful watch on my grandmother's mood ring on my left hand. Unfortunately, nothing in his tale offers any clue to what might've happened, and he seems to have no memory of the shape, size, or color of the vehicle that hit him. The Doc had been looking down at his phone, searching for the right "walking home" playlist when he stepped into the street without looking and was hit almost instantly.

"Did the vehicle try to stop? Did you hear brakes screech?"

"I honestly don't remember. But even if they had tried to stop . . . with the snow falling . . . the slippery roads . . . I'm sure they did everything they could."

This must be what it's like to talk to the Dalai Lama. The man seems genuinely at peace with what happened. "Can you remember anything else?"

"The doctor here said I might be missing a few memories. I did hit my head and there was a mild concussion, but nothing serious. There's a chance a memory or two may have been dashed away by the pavement, but if I think of anything else I'll for sure let you know."

"All right. I'll start poking around, and get these flowers transported over to the pet cemetery while I organize the photo shoot." I turn to survey the vast array of bouquets and mentally power through a series of options for getting them moved. Behind me, I hear the sound of cardboard tearing, plastic ripping, and a loud crunch followed by a satisfied murmur. I turn around just in time to see Ledo reaching in for a second handful of Fruity Puffs.

"I can see why Pyewacket loves these things. You'll give him my best, won't you?"

"I absolutely will." Gesturing to the arrangements, I ask, "Do you want all of them moved or just certain ones?"

"I'll keep this Winter Wonderland arrangement from Tally and Tilly." He points to a beautiful selection of holly leaves, red berries, pinecones, and silver bells arranged around a snow globe. "But all the rest of them are fair game, you know?"

I nod and begin making a rough calculation of how much space will be needed.

"And when you're talking to the paper, maybe you can ask them to run an article requesting donations to the pet cemetery in lieu of flowers, so we can prevent a second floral apocalypse." He laughs at his own joke and clutches his fractured ribs once more.

"You're not doing yourself any favors, Doc." I chuckle. "I'm on the case."

Having slowly come to terms with the benefits of my inheritance, I call the local florist and offer to hire them to relocate all of the bouquets to the pet cemetery. They happily quote me a price and agree to handle it the very next day. My second phone call is to the local paper, informing them of a wonderful winter photo opportunity and purchasing a half-page, full-color ad offering a reward for anyone who has information about the hit and run to call in with tips—with a note at the bottom asking for donations to the pet cemetery in lieu of flowers. That completes my transaction with our local news outlet.

Now it's time for me to finally sit down with my attorney, Silas Willoughby—who happens to be an alchemist—and set up an organization designed to give back to this community, which I've decided to call home. And of course, I'll see what he can do about getting a copy of the police report so that I can peruse the details of Ledo's accident.

Despite Ledo's calm and friendly nature, the smells and sounds of the hospital are giving me a mild case of the heebie-jeebies. "I better get started on these errands. You let me know if you need any more Fruity Puffs, all right?"

"You betcha!" Ledo stifles a snicker and squeezes his ribs.

CHAPTER 4

After stopping by the bank to withdraw cash and update Tilly, the oldest of the three, on her brother's floral directives, I drive to the newspaper. Apparently, the only place in town that accepts electronic payments is the florist. Everywhere else deals in cash, as though I'm trapped in an old pre-tech-revolution alternate dimension. I mean, I have a passbook in which they type my deposits and withdrawals—with a typewriter! Sometimes I wonder if I'm even in color.

I'm hoping that the heartwarming human-interest story on Doc Ledo, combined with the big ad purchase, will grease the wheels at the *Pin Cherry Harbor Post.*

As soon as I enter the old brick building, which houses the local paper, I can smell the ink. It reminds me of my bookshop, but in a raw, straight-to-the-source kind of way. I approach the birch-clad reception area and ring the bell, which squats below a sign instructing me to do just that.

A kid that looks roughly high-school age wanders out of a back room and nods.

I feel old as I assume that's what passes for a greeting with his generation. "Hi, I'm Mitzy. I purchased—"

"Oh, right. The ad. Sit tight."

Rude. I shudder to think how many coffee-shop patrons I've offended over the years. So, if you're wondering, I'm the pot, not the kettle.

I fish my formerly crisp twenties out of my pocket and continue to "sit tight."

Mr. Manners pauses his rustling of papers and yells, "Dad! Dad, the lady is here about the giant ad." He rolls his eyes and exhales, before turning and walking into the back without so much as a "by your leave."

The next human to burst from the bowels of this journalistic house of integrity is both smaller and more bespectacled than I could ever have dreamed. The man is possibly five feet tall in boots, and his eyewear looks as though it was stolen from a prop comic's trunk.

An ink-stained hand thrusts itself in my general direction. "Miss Moon, sorry about Quince. He's great behind the camera, but not all that comfortable with people."

"Your son is the photographer?"

He nods furiously.

Just my luck. I can't wait to try and pry information out of that "Chatty Cathy."

"I'm sorry I didn't have time to tell you on the phone, but we don't have 'full-color' ads. We're a one-color press operation. Not that we wouldn't love to run color, but our old Heidelberg just keeps whirring away, so it looks like we won't be upgrading to a 2- or 4-color press anytime soon. Not that we could afford it with subscriptions waning and the bloggers scooping all our stories. But, you know, we've been in the newspaper business since my great-great-grandmother moved here and married into the Knudsen family in 1869 . . ."

In case you were wondering, he's still shaking my hand. I twist my hand away as politely as possible and make a desperate attempt to staunch the flow of words spilling from his face. "Wow! What a story. Listen, the one-color ad is fine. I'll go ahead and purchase a two-page spread to draw more attention to the information. What do I owe you?"

His enlarged eyes blink behind his enormous lenses like a confused frog.

I start peeling twenties off the roll in my hand. "Is a hundred dollars enough?"

Blink. Blink. Blink.

"Two hundred?"

"Two hundred is good." Look who suddenly returned!

Quince for the win. I have a sneaking suspicion that two hundred is far too much, but at this point I just want to end this transaction.

"Here you go." I lay the bills on the ink-smudged counter and turn to leave. Luckily a tingle on my ring finger reminds me that I had a second reason for my blatant bribery of the fourth estate. Rounding on Quince, I ask, "Did you take that pic of the footprint in the snow?"

His hands scoop up the cash guiltily before he answers. "Yah."

"You still got the original?"

"Yah."

At least I know this kid's currency. "How much?"

His eyes narrow in confusion.

"How much for the pic? I'll buy it off you right now. You text it to me and I'll pay you."

Something in my short speech has awakened the transfixed patriarch. "Quince doesn't shoot digi-tal. He has an SLR and develops—"

I put my hands up in surrender, because I don't need a history lesson on the invention of the *camera obscura* by Leonardo da Vinci. I'm a film-school dropout, remember? "Awesome. Can I buy the negative and an enlarged print?"

Blink. Blink. Blink.

"Yah. Follow me, dude."

I guess I'm the "dude" in this scenario. I follow the verbose young Quince to a black cylinder, which he spins to reveal a revolving door.

He steps in and I move to follow. He flinches at my nearness and mumbles, "One at a time."

I chuckle as the cylinder rotates and reopens to reveal an empty tube. It's like a magician's trick. I'm fascinated. I step into the tube and rotate the door around me. A sliver of red light expands to fill the barrel as the powerful odor of acids and ammonia hits me.

"Sweet." Again I feel the weight of my age. This guy is probably no more than five years younger than me. Why do I feel as out of place as Arnold Schwarzenegger in *Kindergarten Cop*?

He pulls strips of hanging film out and peers at the negative images.

"Who taught you to do all this?"

"YouTube."

If he and his dad put all their words in a giant lottery spinner and took turns pulling them out . . . "Do you have that footprint pic?"

"You want 'em all?"

"All?"

"I took a bunch of exposures."

"Sure. I'll take all the negatives, but I need you to print out the best one at like 8″ x 10." I have no idea what sizes are standard, but I remember that one from school picture packets. Packets which were never purchased after my mom died because, let's face it, not a lot of foster families want to blow money on orphan pictures for no one.

"They're DCs."

"The photos?"

"The shoes." He unclips the strip of negatives, rolls it up, slips it into a little plastic canister, and hands it to me. "You're the PI, right?"

I spin the film canister in my hand and smile. "I just own the bookshop."

He nods. "I feel ya."

I grin. "DCs, huh?"

"Yah."

"What do I owe you?"

"Depends."

"Depends? On what?"

"You want me to tell Sheriff Harper I sold those"—he gestures toward the negatives—"or did I just lose 'em."

I think I'm getting hustled, and this kid is as good as Emma Stone in *Easy A*. "You look pretty absentminded."

"A hundred."

I count out five twenties, pause, and add two more. "Maybe we never met."

He takes the money a little too eagerly for a truly seasoned gangster.

I nod and slip out through the second-most awesome door in Pin Cherry Harbor. Slick as it is, this darkroom door cannot compete with my secret bookcase door.

I smile at the elder Knudsen as I walk out.

"Quince find that photo for you?"

I expertly palm the canister and shake my head. "He couldn't find the negatives."

"Kids these days . . ."

Whatever else he mumbles is lost to the closing front door.

CHAPTER 5

The weather has truly turned frightful. I saw a sprinkling or two of snow in Sedona, but the temperatures never dropped below zero. As I rush to my car, I can actually feel my eyelashes freezing together.

The heavy door on my four-wheel-drive Jeep sticks a little in the cold, and I whimper as my aching fingers struggle to get a grasp on the frosty handle.

Once the door clicks shut I expect to feel better, but my car has been chilling in the elements for nearly twenty minutes.

I start the engine and fumble my stiff fingers over the dials in a feeble attempt to get hot air pumping through the vents. Lesson number one of my first winter in almost-Canada: just because you turn the spinny knob to heat doesn't mean you will feel actual warmth.

Snow is falling in earnest now and I can no longer see the centerline on Main Street. I suddenly understand why Grams insisted I have a "winter" car and leave the sporty Mercedes 300SL in a nice dry garage until spring.

By the time I pull up in front of the bookshop, a tepid breeze is blowing across my frostbitten knuckles. I shove the shifter into park and run stiffly toward the intricately carved wooden door. My cold fingers cannot grasp the key and, after dropping it in the snow twice, I bang on the door and shout for my Ghost-ma.

Images from the terrifying *To Build a Fire* flash through my mind and panic grips my chest. I'll surely freeze to death right here on my own front stoop—

The slow scrape of metal tumblers interrupts my nightmare.

"Grams? Grams is that you?"

The door pushes open and knocks me on my backside, scrambling to retrieve the key.

The familiar cackle of Twiggy welcomes me home. "You thought a ghost was opening the door? Maybe you are suffering a little Arctic hallucination, doll." She stoops and picks up the key, but offers me no further assistance.

I struggle to my feet in a most unladylike fashion and dive into the relative warmth of the store. "Wh-what are-are you st-still doing here?" I force the words out between my chattering teeth.

Twiggy hands me the key and walks into the back room. She slips into her coat, hat, mittens, and scarf, before turning off the lights. "I was just leaving."

I watch her leave through the side door and scoff, as it slams shut. "She was waiting for me to get back and she likes me and worries about me, whether she wants to admit it or not."

"I agree, dear."

And there goes my bladder, folks.

Grams snickers into her bejeweled hand. "Sorry, honey. Pye and I were worried about you, so I came as soon as I heard you talking to Twiggy. I thought you sensed me."

"I can't even sense my own fingers right now!" I shake with a fresh wave of shivers.

"You take a nice hot shower and you'll feel warmer than a tea cozy."

I open my mouth to protest, but the mere thought of that miraculous shower and its consistently hot water is already making me feel better.

After an undisclosed amount of time thawing my frozen body in the luxurious steam-shower, I slip into my reindeer onesie and wrap a thick towel around my hair. I make a beeline for the inviting four-poster bed and bury myself under the double-thick down comforter.

Pye seems to sense my need for warmth and curls up on top of the covers, adding his significant weight as another blanket.

My fingers and toes appear intact, and my involuntary muscular convulsions have finally ceased. I'd be lying if I said I was looking forward to ever getting out of this bed, but at least nothing was actually lost to frostbite.

"Frostbite isn't nearly—"

I put up a hand for Grams to cease and desist, while I point meaningfully to my lips with the other hand.

"Of course, dear. I'm just glad you made it home safe, you know?"

"Do you know anything about shoes, Grams?"

"Jimmy Choo, Alexander McQueen, Christian Louboutin, Manolo Blahnik—"

My gasping laughter interrupts my fashion-horse grandmother's list of favorite things. "Um, no. I'm actually more interested in skateboard shoes."

"Oh, Mitzy, you're such a card! What would I

know about skateboard shoes? I took a walk or two on the wild side, but I never rode a scooter there."

"A couple of my foster brothers had some skills, but they never included me."

Grams brow furrows with concern. "What's the sudden interest in skateboarding in the winter, dear?"

I shake my head. "I'm sure it's nothing. But every time I think about that photo in the newspaper of the footprint in the snow, I get a feeling—"

She swirls over the bed and Pyewacket bristles as she drifts through him. "Is it your gifts? Are you getting a message?"

"No idea." I relay the story of visiting Ledo, arranging to have the flowers relocated, and then my strange interaction with the teen "blackmailer" who works as a photographer for the newspaper.

"Well, I think the boy sounds very industrious."

"That's one word for it."

"Did he know anyone with shoes like that? Those BCs, or whatever."

"They were DCs, Grams. I'm sure every kid at his—" I leap out of bed so fast I upend Pyewacket.

His retribution rips a tiny hole in the leg of my pajamas.

"Sorry, Pye. You'll absolutely forgive me when you hear my brilliant idea."

He turns away and does a yoga pose named for

his least favorite animal, so I'll simply mention it's a downward "D-word" to avoid losing a chunk of flesh. I take the insulting display of his rear end, pointed in my general direction, in stride.

"What idea? What are you talking about? Is this about the case?" Grams is swirling around me like a Ghost-ma merry-go-round.

"It's about an article I read in the paper."

"You read the paper? I thought your generation was all about the blogging and what not."

I strike an indignant pose, but before I can utter my witty retort Grams belly laughs uncontrollably.

"What's so funny?"

"I know I'm not supposed to read your mind or listen to your thoughts, or whatever this is, but when you . . . those pajamas . . . it just tickled me."

I have to admit I probably don't look super intimidating with a furry belly and little brown antlers hanging off each side of the hood. "Can we get back to my brilliant idea?"

"Of course." She continues to snicker and wipes laughter tears from the corners of her eyes.

"I was about to say that probably every kid at his high school has those shoes. So, what better way to track down the owner of this particular pair of DCs than to go to the high school?"

Grams grows unusually quiet and her eyes dart left and right.

"What's going on? Was the principal of the high school one of your 'special friends?' Did you burn a bridge?"

She floats toward me with a look of morose pity flickering across her face. "You know I love you, Mitzy, and you know I think you are just the most beautiful girl in the whole world, but you can't pass for a high-school girl, sweetie." Her ethereal hand reaches out and I feel the comfort of her energy on my shoulder.

"I'm not going to pass myself off as a student, Grams. Well, not a high-school student." I wink meaningfully.

Her aura lights up like a Christmas tree. "The Birch County Community College!"

I nod and smile as I flash my eyebrows mischievously. "I'm thinking some kind of psychology student who needs to complete a certain number of observation hours or something."

"You swipe it up on your phone and get your backstory straight while I select your character's wardrobe."

"My character's wardrobe? My backstory? Who are you right now?"

"You know I used to write screenplays, dear. Just because I never sold one to a big Hollywood producer doesn't mean I don't know how to dress a set." She giggles like a schoolgirl as she zooms into the closet.

I'll leave her to work her magic in a closet that can only be described as right out of *Sex and the City* meets *Confessions of a Shopaholic.* While I work on my "backstory."

CHAPTER 6

As you may or may not know, I am not a morning person. I do not like bright sun in my face. I do not like rushing all over the place. I do not like it with a ghost. I do not like it with cold toast.

But, today is my first day of undercover work at the school and despite my aversion to the ungodly hour of 7:00 a.m., I'm managing to pull together a "look" that Grams assures me will win the day.

"Do you have your notebook?"

"Kids just record their lessons these days, Grams. I've got my phone. That should cover everything."

"What's your name?"

I spin on my chunky-heeled boots and grin. "Darcy Brown."

She squeals and claps her hands. "Good luck, Darcy!"

I chuckle as I slip out of the apartment and speak the school's address into my phone.

The fifteen-minute drive is a breeze on the newly plowed streets. I turn into the high-school parking lot and take a moment to survey my surroundings while I pluck up my courage.

Busses are pulling into the half-circle drive in front of the school. The students are unloading in a chaotic stream of pushing, shouting, and occasionally, snowball throwing. I think I'll wait right here until the bell rings. I have no interest in this *Lord of the Flies* nonsense.

BRRRRRRRING!

The earsplitting bell drives the children inside. I wait until the aides who monitor the drop-off zone sweep up all the stragglers, and I carefully make my way to the office.

There's a vivacious blonde waif at the counter in a heated exchange with a woman bearing the nametag, "Donna Jo – Secretary."

"But Donna Jo, you know my mom can't drive good in the snow. It's like, not my fault I'm late."

"Can't drive well, Brynley. I'm sure you'd know that if you weren't late to English every single day. I'll write you a pass and I will add your name to the detention roster."

"That sucks!"

"Language, Brynley."

"Principal Puig took my phone and, like, I can't even call my mom. She's gonna be super pissed—"

Donna Jo's face transforms from mildly irritated school secretary to avenging angel in a split second. "I think maybe we need to have a chat with Principal Puig right now, young lady."

I chew the inside of my cheek to keep from snickering. The sheer number of times I've been referred to as "young lady" in a school office . . . No need to dredge up the past. I'm no longer wayward foster child, Mitzy Moon. I'm—

"May I help you, dear?"

A kind, elderly lady labeled "Mrs. Boulton – School Nurse" has replaced the over-reaching Donna Jo. I thank the spirits for my good fortune and step up to the counter.

"I'm Darcy Brown. I'm a psych student from BCCC and I'm supposed to be observing in counseling today."

"Of course, dear. Do you have your authorization form?"

I exhale dramatically and let my shoulders sag hopelessly. "I wish. I went to the department office early this morning, but my professor was snowed in and couldn't meet me on campus. She called in the approval, but the secretary wouldn't give me the form. She's kind of a stickler, you know?" I let my eyes wander toward the principal's office and Donna Jo.

The sweet nurse smiles knowingly and nods. "Well, I'm sure everything is in order, and I know you have to get these things finished before the semester ends." She opens a three-ring binder and makes a few notes. "Write your name on this badge."

She slides an "Authorized Visitor" badge toward me and I'm in such a hurry to complete the transaction I start to write "M" instead of "D." Do you have any idea how hard it is to make that look like a ridiculous and on-purpose flourish? I peel off the sticker and press it onto my Donna Karan suit jacket.

She smiles and reaches for a clipboard.

Movement in the principal's office catches my eye. Donna Jo and Brynley are wrapping things up. I've got to giddyup!

"Sign here, dear."

I sign so fast that I'm honestly not sure which name I write. "Can you point me to the counselor's office?"

"If you wait a jiffy, I'm sure Brynley can escort you on her way to English."

Panic grips my chest. I feel more than certain that Donna Jo will not buy my cockamamie story. If

I don't high tail it out of here, my cover will be blown before the end of first period. "Oh, I'm so late already. I feel just awful. Can you just tell me where to turn?"

She shuffles around the counter as Donna Jo turns to leave the back office. I pivot my gaze and smile broadly at Mrs. Boulton.

The lovely woman slips an arm around my shoulders. "Don't fret, dear. Ms. Olson is very understanding. She'll give your professor a good report. Come along, I'll show you the way."

Donna Jo reaches the counter just as we pass through the doorway into the hall.

I refuse to look back. Never look back. Movie heist 101: once you've successfully passed the checkpoint, never look back. My pulse is racing and I feel sweat evaporating from my hairline. I take a deep breath.

Mrs. Boulton gives my shoulders a little squeeze before dropping her arm. "That's it. Just a few deep breaths and you'll be all set." She pauses and gestures to a closed door. "It looks like Ms. Olson forgot about your appointment, or maybe she got snowed in. She lives down a long dirt road out by Clear Lake. Well, I guess we better head back to the front office and see if Donna Jo can reschedule your visit."

My stomach is flipping like a gymnast in a floor

routine. "Maybe I could just shadow you today? I have to turn in this paper by Friday and my professor never gives extensions."

Her face wants to say "no," but my wonderful little gift of clairsentience *feels* that her heart wants to say "yes." I simply need to give her a reason. Done. "It's absolutely my fault that I waited until so late in the semester to schedule this. I was just so overwhelmed with caring for my grandmother . . . Now I'm going to flunk and I'll probably lose my scholarship." Is that a tear? Did my performance bring a tear to this woman's eye? Oh boy, now I feel sick to my stomach for a whole different reason. It's official: I'm a terrible person.

"Why, aren't you the sweetest thing? Of course you can shadow me. It's actually perfect timing since I have to give my health talk to all the junior and senior classes today."

I grasp her hand in both of mine and gush, "Oh, thank you. Thank you so much. You're a life saver."

After a brief stop in the teachers' lounge to get our coffee, Mrs. Boulton leads the way to her small, sterile office. Her desk is a half-size folding table with a chipped lamp, a notepad, and two pens. In the corner are two spartan, uncomfortable-looking cots covered with white sheets and equally white paper. A thin suggestion of a curtain hangs between the gurneys. Despite the fact that I hated school and have nothing but painful, lonely memories of my pre-matriculation days, I feel terrible about the obvious lack of funding at this institution.

"What can I do to help you prepare for the talks?"

"You don't actually have to do anything, dear. The Birch County Community College students usually just observe."

"Well, I'd like to start a new trend." I smile broadly. "Put me to work, Nurse Boulton."

"Well, alrighty. Boy, I love your attitude, Darcy."

"Oh, it's M—my pleasure." I barely caught myself before I blew my own cover. I have to get it through my thick skull: today I am Darcy. Darcy. Darcy. Darcy. I won't even think the other name. All Darcy. All day.

"Here's the key. You open that grey cabinet over there and get out ten condoms, the sample packet of birth control pills, and a big stack of the abstinence pamphlets."

My feet fail to move and my face is certainly near fire-engine red. I mean, what are the odds that I show up for my undercover routine on the very day of *THAT* health talk? I guess I'll have quite a story for Grams tonight.

"Don't worry, dear. I'll do all the talking."

I gulp audibly and collect our supplies.

The first two presentations are uneventful. A cheerleader named Traice asks an innocent question laden with double entendres, which incites uncontrollable snickering, and a young man named Khlab—pronounced cay-lebb; don't worry, I couldn't figure it out either—wants to know if minors are allowed to buy condoms. His question draws a few hoots from the jocks in the back row.

By the time we get to the junior class presentation right before lunch, I feel like an old pro. In fact, I recognize my office buddy, Brynley, sitting in the center of a group of orbiters. I remember this group of girls too well. Whatever the "sun" said, the "planets" would follow. Maybe my deep dislike of morning has something to do with my overt distaste of "suns."

She's tapping and scrolling on her phone as though her life depends on it, and the surrounding girls are glued to the screen.

Apparently, she got her phone back from the principal this morning. Her family is either wealthy or politically influential. In my experience, those kids can get away with anything.

Nurse Boulton calls the class to order and begins her presentation.

Since it's my third time through, I let my eyes wander up and down the rows of desks. Before my fashion training with Grams, I never would've noticed that Brynley's Marc Jacobs bag is a knockoff, or that one of the orbiters has colored in the scuff marks on her platforms with a Sharpie. A tickle at the edge of my consciousness picks up on a deviation from the speech.

"Oh, is that so, Stellen?" Brynley crosses her arms and smirks.

"It's a valid question." I assume the boy responding is Stellen.

"Not for a creepy little woodchuck stuffer like you!" Her eyes flash, and the "planets" all giggle maniacally.

The boy picks up his backpack and runs out of the room with his head down.

Mrs. Boulton calls, "Stellen. Stellen, you do not have a hall pass."

I put a hand on her arm. "I'll go after him. You finish your talk."

A murmur washes over the classroom. I nearly forgot what a hot piece of . . . property I am in almost-Canada. I put a little *extra* in my "shake" as I leave.

"Stellen?" I walk around the corner, based completely on the inexplicable feeling in my gut. Whimpering and sniffling confirm my hunch. "Stellen, do you want to talk about it."

The young boy shakes his head of dark-brown curls and wipes the tears from his green eyes.

This guy is probably going to mature into a dangerously handsome twenty-something, but the crushing humiliation of high school is completely robbing him of embracing his potential.

"I'm fine. I'll just go to the principal's office and say I was wandering without a hall pass."

"You don't have to do that. We stepped out of class to discuss a private matter. You haven't broken any rules."

The genuine gratitude that pours out of his upturned face nearly breaks my heart.

"For real?"

"For real. Brynley and her pack of hyenas can take a hike."

He chuckles and hiccups a little. "A stuffed hyena. Now that would be something to see."

I narrow my gaze and wonder how the word stuffed can appear in conversation twice in the space of two minutes. I worry that little Stellen might be some kind of psycho serial killer with plans to turn his enemies into trophies. "Stuffed hyena?"

"Oh, yeah. My dad's a taxidermist. That's why they all tease me about my freezer full of dead animals and call me a woodchuck stuffer."

I breathe a sigh of relief. "They used to call me *Powder*."

His whole face lights up. "Like the movie? I

love that film. I mean, my dad loves to skin animals and all that taxidermy stuff, but I want animals to live. I love that movie."

"Too bad we didn't go to high school together, Stellen. I think we would've been friends. You know?"

"Totally." He stares off into the distance. "I don't really have friends."

"Well, you have one now." I put out my hand.

He shakes it as he says, "Thanks, Miss Brown."

Oh crap. So much for giving this kid a little faith in humanity. Probably best to tell him the truth immediately. Rip the Band-Aid off. Right?

"There she is! That's her!"

The skin on the back of my neck prickles before I turn. Donna Jo is frantically waving her appendages at me, and the one and only—

"Miss Moon, I should've known."

As I watch Stellen's eyes fill with hurt and confusion, my usual elated tummy tingles are replaced with sudden nausea. "Hi, Erick."

"It's still Sheriff Harper, Moon." He pulls the cuffs from his belt. "You know the drill."

"Miss Brown, what's—"

I turn away from the betrayed teen and put my hands behind my back.

"Mitzy Moon, you are under arrest for possible child endangerment, false . . ."

The rest of Erick's speech is lost to me. I can't believe things ended up like this. I had no business coming to this school. What was I thinking? I've finally sunk as low as—

BRRRRRRRING!

Spoke too soon.

Doors burst open and the hallway fills with a swarm of loud, rushing students. It reminds me of a slot canyon during a flash flood back in Arizona. It's like white noise, but it can't drown out my shame.

Some students slow and stare at the sheriff and me in the handcuffs, a few pull out their phones and record the event, but most hurry past to their next class.

I search the swirling crowd for Stellen, but he's vanished into the sea of humanity like a pebble in a dry riverbed. However, my humiliation is far from over.

"Darcy, what on earth happened, dear?" Mrs. Boulton's friendly concern stabs into my heart like a knife.

"Long story. I'm really sorry." I can't make eye contact.

"Come on, Moon." Erick puts one hand on my shoulder and one on my cuffed wrists as he steers me, not unkindly, toward the exit.

Donna Jo follows, sputtering all the way. "This never would've happened if I'd been on the front desk. I can assure you that Principal Puig is going to hear about this. I've been saying that Boulton woman . . ."

The rest of her tirade is muffled as Erick places that movie-classic hand on my head as he puts me in the back of the patrol car and slams the door.

He slides into the driver's side, calls in to dispatch, and drives away from the scene with a half-wave, half-salute to Donna Jo.

"That was all for show, right? I mean, you're just going to drive me back to the bookshop and forget this ever happened."

Silence.

"I can explain, Erick."

Rather than a direct answer he depresses the button on his radio and says, "Dispatch, this is Sheriff Harper. Can you let Silas Willoughby know that we're bringing Miss Moon in on possible child endangerment charges?"

"10-4, Sheriff."

The emphasis he places on "Sheriff Harper" let's me know beyond a shadow of a doubt that I've crossed a line, perhaps *the* line, and this is one dust bunny I can't sweep under the rug.

CHAPTER 7

As Sheriff Harper marches me through the station, I feel worse than during any previous walks of shame in memory. The chipped paint on the metal desks and the warped paneling on the back wall fail to amuse.

The cold metal chair in Interrogation Room One feels harsher than I remember, and it's worth mentioning that Erick does not unlock my cuffs before he plants me in it.

"I'll be back once Willoughby shows."

He does not ask if I want coffee. He does not ask if I need a restroom. He does not smile. I really stepped in it this time.

I'm left to stew in my own juices for some time. I suspect Silas is also taking his sweet time in responding in an effort to teach me some additional lesson.

Lesson learned, all right? I know it was a bad idea—now. At the time, it seemed like a completely legitimate way to find the kid who owned the DC shoes. I can't put my finger on why I thought that was so important, but I did. I still do.

Despite the trouble I'm clearly in, I feel—and yes, I mean feel in the weird woo-woo way—in my gut that the shoe print is somehow connected to Ledo's accident. But I'm of no use to Doc Ledo if I'm sitting in the slammer, so I better spend this time coming up with the world's greatest reason for sneaking around a high school under a fake name.

By the time my underwhelming lawyer pushes open the door and joins me in the claustrophobic space, I'm wedged somewhere between relief and frustration. However, I think I might have the perfect cover story.

"Hey, Silas. Do you want to see me get out of these handcuffs?" The reference to one of my previous alchemy lessons fails to garner the desired response.

He does not reply. He scrapes back the chair on the opposite side of the table and heaves his tattered briefcase onto the flat surface as he drops toward the seat with a tortured exhale.

The unwelcome aroma of pipe smoke and denture cream wafts toward me, and Silas smooths his bushy grey mustache with disappointment and frustration.

"I have the perfect story."

He does not smile. He does not wink. He adjusts his brown bow tie and straightens his tweed coat. "These are very serious charges, Mizithra."

Uh oh. It's formal name time. Now I'm actually worried. "How serious?"

"False impersonation, conspiracy to commit criminal impersonation and second-degree conspiracy to commit harassment, disturbing school, possible child endangerment, and giving a false statement. Sheriff Harper informed me that the school district is threatening to push for felony false impersonation, due to the trauma caused to minors. You are facing up to three years in prison."

I don't handle bad news like most people. Ever since my mother was killed in a fatal car accident when I was eleven, I've had an intense aversion to accepting negative information. "Wanna see me get out of these cuffs?" I whisper.

"I would prefer if you would enlighten me as to the impetus of your visit to our local educational institution."

"It has something to do with Doc Ledo's accident."

A faint smile touches his mouth and his hound-dog cheeks quiver. "Would this pertain to 'something' you sensed?" A hint of the patient mentor within emerges.

I nod.

He smiles in earnest. "Go on."

"Ever since I read the article in the newspaper and saw the picture of the footprints in the snow, I haven't been able to get the image out of my mind. I know—deep in my gut—I know it has something to do with the hit and run."

"I see." He leans back and strokes his mustache. "Did you discover any additional information at the school?" Keen interest lights his milky-blue eyes.

I shrug as best I can while in the handcuffs. "About the only thing I discovered is that high school hasn't changed one bit since I went, and the mean girls still rule the world." I think back to the pathetic furnishings in the nurse's office. "Oh, and that the school is severely underfunded."

A large smile lifts his jowls, and Silas scrunches up his bulbous nose as he leans forward. "I can work with that."

"Huh?"

The handle on the door twists.

Silas whispers, "As difficult as it may be, let me advocate on your behalf."

I offer a begrudging, "All right."

Sheriff Erick enters and stands next to the table.

I look up into his blue-grey eyes and smile in spite of my predicament.

"I hope your lawyer has conveyed the seriousness of the charges, Miss Moon."

"Well, here's the thing, Erick. It seems—"

Silas clears his throat loudly and bangs his briefcase from the table to the floor.

I snap my mouth shut and try to apologize to him with my eyes.

"What my client is attempting to explain, Sheriff, is the reason for her entrepreneurial fact-finding mission."

I lean back and my wrist pinches against the back of my chair. Even though I'm in a little pain, I think I'm going to enjoy this.

"This better be good, Willoughby." Erick crosses his arms over his broad chest and I can't take my eyes off his slightly bulging biceps.

"I assure you, Sheriff Harper, my client had the best intentions. You see, the Duncan-Moon Foundation is eager to support positive development and community renovation in our fair city of Pin Cherry Harbor. Having been a product of the foster-care system, Miss Moon had the opportunity to visit many schools in her young life. One of the causes she wishes to champion is proper funding for arts and sciences in our schools. Her undercover visit to the school today was at the behest of the Foundation and was for the sole purpose of identifying the programs most in need of the Foundation's generosity." Silas punctuates his soliloquy with a meaningful head nod and a tamping of his mustache.

I'm so amazed by the yarn my lawyer has spun that I'm leaning forward, hanging on every word. However, Erick didn't fall off the turnip truck yesterday. He stares stolidly at my attorney, but addresses me.

"And what did you find, Miss Moon."

Thankfully, I too have been off the vegetable transport for some time. "I'd have to say that one of the programs most in need is student services. The nurse's office is sadly under supplied and the total lack of patient privacy has to be a violation."

Silas fixes me with a "quit while you're ahead" glare.

Erick's arms slowly uncross and he places both hands on the table as he leans deliciously close to me. "Moon, I don't know if you're this good or this bad, but I hope you have the cash to back up this ridiculous fairytale."

I'm so mesmerized by the proximity of Erick's full, pouty mouth that words have vanished from my brain. Luckily, Silas is unflappable.

"As soon as we complete our evaluation the Foundation will be cutting a check to the Birch County School District, earmarked for Pin Cherry Harbor High School, of course.

Erick stands and shakes his head. "Of course."

"Now, can you remove the restraints from our generous local philanthropist?" Silas smiles pleasantly.

The sheriff scoffs. "Stand up, Moon. Once again it would appear that this is your lucky day."

I silently follow orders and can't help but think that Silas has used his alchemy voodoo to glue my mouth shut, because however hard I try, I can't seem to release my inner snark.

The cuffs come off and I rub the red indentations on my wrists.

"Come along, Mitzy." Silas gathers up his briefcase and leads the way out of the interrogation room.

I take a step toward the door that Erick is holding open, but my right foot catches on the table leg—which is screwed to the floor—and I sail headlong into Erick's rock-hard chest.

He fumbles with the door, manages to catch me with one arm, but has to release the door to keep from losing his own balance. His left hand comes around to lift me back to standing and grazes my boob area, finally releasing my trapped tongue.

"That's the second time you've gone to second base with me, Erick, and still no dinner."

He turns as red as a pin cherry, and I let myself out of the room that seems to have shrunken to the size of a broom closet in the last few seconds.

CHAPTER 8

Silas drops me at the bookshop in his 1908 Model T, which I'm sure isn't winter-worthy, and informs me that someone will retrieve my Jeep after school hours and will contact the school board to see how sizable a donation will be required to erase my transgression.

I walk into the bookshop filled with visceral relief followed by a fit of giggles as I mumble, "We do more before 9:00 a.m. than most people do all day."

"Who does, honey?"

And we're back to Bladder Control 101! "Grams, we agreed on the slow sparkle re-entry. Remember?"

She chuckles. "Right! Sorry, dear."

I slip a belated hand over my mouth and glance around the bookstore. "Are we alone?"

"Not even close, doll," calls Twiggy from somewhere in the stacks. "But if you're asking if there's anyone here who doesn't already know that you talk to ghosts, that answer is 'no.'"

"Touché."

Twiggy and Grams both have a long chuckle at my expense.

"Oh well, I guess no one wants to hear about how I got arrested at high school and Silas had to invent a philanthropic organization to keep me from serving three years in prison."

I dust my hands together as though I'm finished with both of them and head toward the circular staircase.

Grams attempts to intercept me, but I walk through her phantasm—and straight into the immovable object: Twiggy.

"All right, Your Highness. Let's have the story." Twiggy walks to the back room as she calls, "I'll make tea."

I relent and regale the girls with my tale. Twiggy laughs at my misfortune until tears squirt from her eyes, while Grams swirls around the bookshop with a severe case of afterlife anxiety.

"Are you out on bail? Will there be a trial?" She spins upward.

I shrug and reply, "I believe the correct term is 'bribe.' I mean, Silas is going to make the school board an offer and just keep adding zeros until they say, 'Thank you for your donation' instead of 'Lock her up!'"

"After all of that and you still don't know whose shoes?" Twiggy snickers. "You're something else."

I exhale in a loud and offended way. "At least I was trying to follow up on my psychic clue."

Twiggy rolls her eyes. "So you say. Could you see the logo in the snow?"

"Yeah. It was from a pair of DC skateboard shoes. Like I said at the beginning of the story, that was why I went to the school."

"Oh, I got that part, doll. I was just thinkin' that if you could see the logo, then it wasn't covered by snow. I guess the statue musta been stolen right before the storm ended."

Grams freeze-frames and my jaw drops.

Twiggy winks at me. "I'll leave you to chew on that, and you can pour your own refills on tea. I gotta get home and feed the dogs."

"Reeeee-ow." A warning.

"Oh, take it easy, Pye." Twiggy bends and scratches his arched back. "See you three stooges tomorrow." And with one last piercing cackle, she's gone.

I whip out my phone and call Silas. "Hey, I— You're right, a proper greeting would be more civilized." I put on my poshest British accent. "Good evening, Mr. Willoughby. Would you be so kind as to inform me if you've obtained a copy of the police report?"

Grams shakes her head. "You shouldn't make fun, dear."

I point to the phone and nod. "I wasn't making fun."

Ghost-ma "tsks" several times and disapparates.

"Which police report?" I feel his mildly insulting insinuation is directed at me. "No, not mine. I actually meant the accident report from Doc Ledo's hit and run."

Grams reappears right in front of me and I gasp and jump back, nearly falling over Pyewacket.

"I'm fine, just dealing with a little interference on my end. Would you mind bringing the report over? I have an idea."

Pyewacket threads himself around my ankles in a suspiciously supportive manner.

"Yes, I am embracing my gifts . . . All right, we'll see you soon. Thanks."

By the time Silas arrives, I've polished off some leftover "hot dish" (a.k.a., casserole) from the fridge and let Pye out for his nightly prowl.

My alchemist-lawyer enters and, while I lock the front door behind him, he slips on his magicked wire-rimmed spectacles and searches the air. "Ah, Isadora. You look lovely, as always."

She waves and curtsies.

"So, how are you coming on figuring out a way to hear her?"

"My research continues." His face grows pensive.

I hastily change the subject. "Were you able to get the report?"

He hands me a folder and I flip it open. My eyes search through the messy handwriting of the officer on the scene. The ever-annoying Deputy Pauly Paulsen. To say that the woman despises me would be a severe understatement. Ever since I arrived in this town and wound up temporarily accused of murder, that woman has been out to make my life miserable. Hopefully, I can find what I need in this report and avoid having to get additional information directly from her pudgy little face.

"Ah ha!" I stab my finger onto the paper as though I've solved the Millennium Prize.

"What is it?" ask Silas and Grams in unison.

"The time of the accident."

Grams swirls her hands in the universal sign for "continue."

"It says that the snowplow operator found Ledo at 8:45 p.m. and his coat was covered by a fine layer of snow. There were no witnesses. Everyone was at the Extravaganza. It sure was lucky the plow went through that neighborhood when it did."

Silas harrumphs and strokes his grey mustache with his thumb and forefinger. "The plow always goes through The Pines first."

"What do you mean 'The Pines?'"

"What was the location of the accident? Precisely?"

I run my finger across the report. "Says here, the body was found on Pin Cherry Lane between Spruce Street and Fir Street."

"The Pines," repeats Silas in a tone that indicates he's answered my question.

Fortunately Grams floats in with much needed details. "The Pines is the upper-class end of Pin Cherry, dear. The wealthy retired folks, the doctors, judges, and moneyed widows all live in The Pines. The snowplow hits their neighborhood first, because if she doesn't the complaints will be the top story in the *Post*."

"She?"

"Artie. She's been running the plow since my fourth husband and I got back from our honeymoon."

I wave my hands to interrupt any further honeymoon-related information. "That's plenty for now. Let's get back to the accident report." I re-find the bit of data I was about to share before the "Artie" tangent. "Here it is. The actual time of the accident was calculated based on snow accumulation on the body and the known time that the snowfall ended."

"Which is?" prompts Grams

"They say Ledo was struck at 8:25 p.m." I close the folder and look at Silas. "I need crime scene photos."

"That may prove difficult. May I ask why?"

"I need to compare the snow cover on the body with snow cover on that footprint . . ." Instinctively my eyes are pulled to the mood ring. The swirling black clouds shift to pure white and the footprint appears. My stomach clenches and my mouth goes dry.

"Mitzy?" Silas places a hand on my shoulder. "Are you all right?"

"He saw," I whisper.

"Ledo stated repeatedly that he never saw the vehicle." Silas squeezes my shoulder.

"No." The hollow gulp in my throat seems to echo off the tin-plated ceiling. "The thief. He saw the accident." And now I can't breathe.

CHAPTER 9

After a lengthy pep talk from my attorney followed by endless ghost-pats on my back from Grams, I manage to get some sleep, but the pale grey light of morning does not relieve the tightness in my chest.

All night long I struggled to make a decision. Part of me wants to run down to the sheriff's station and share my great lead, but the other part of me wonders how bonkers I'll sound when I state my source as "a feeling."

I need to talk to Artie and see if I can find something concrete to back up my psychic sensations.

"That really is the best idea you've had, dear."

I'm too exhausted to scold Grams for thought-dropping. "Did my whirring brain keep you up too?"

"I don't actually sleep, honey."

"Right. That does make more sense than what I was picturing." I can't keep the image of little ghost beds all filled with ghosts and each one tucked in with sheets, which may or may not be part of their floaty-ghost robes . . .

"RE-ow." Feed me.

Grams runs her fingers along Pye's arched back. "Sounds like you and Mr. Cuddlekins both need some breakfast."

I glance at the menacing form of Pyewacket slinking across the bed with devilish mischief in his eyes, and I tumble to the floor before he can pounce.

"Come on, Pye. Let's get me some wake-up juice." I press the plaster medallion above the intercom and my secret bookcase door slides open as Pye shoves past and races down the stairs. "Geez! Looks like someone's having a Fruity Puffs emergency."

"Oh, Mitzy, you crack me up." Grams snickers and vanishes into the floor.

I'm definitely up earlier than usual. I deduce this from the lack of coffee in the coffee pot and the absence of Twiggy's cackle when I trip over the—"*Pippi Longstocking*!"

Grams suppresses a chuckle.

"That book was not there when I walked in."

I narrow my gaze and size up potential suspects. Grams has recently acquired some limited abilities in the "affecting solid matter" department, but Pyewacket has a long history of torturing me with found objects.

Pye has finished his breakfast and sits innocently cleaning his whiskers and paying me no mind.

"Robin Pyewacket Goodfellow, did you do this?"

He pauses in his ablutions, and for a moment I feel as though he may speak.

He turns and saunters out in silence.

I exhale and retrieve some much-needed coffee from the barely filling pot.

Grams interrupts my java infusion. "I know you didn't ask out loud, but it wasn't me. I'm pretty sure it was there when you walked in, but you just missed it out of pure luck."

I plop unceremoniously into a stiff-backed wooden chair and rub my wounded toes. After two more glorious sips of go-go juice, I investigate the tome.

"STANDARD LEVEL BIOLOGY." I drop the book on the table and get a café au lait refill.

Grams floats toward the book and sighs.

"Nothing? No quip to explain this book's appearance?"

"I have no idea, dear. What would any of us want with an outdated high-school textbook?"

And there go the hairs on the back of my neck. "How do you know it's a high-school textbook?"

Grams waves her ring-ensconced hand toward the book.

As the coffee works its magic, I see the words stamped on, what I have come to learn is, the fore edge of the pages. "Property of Pin Cherry Harbor High School." I run my thumb across the words and smile. "I told you there was something I needed to know at that high school."

Grams whirs toward my face and places a fist on her hip while she wags a misty finger in my direction. "Don't you dare set foot in that school until Silas gets this mess sorted out. I will not last another one of my loved ones landing in jail."

And here come the tears. "Grams, please don't cry." I make an attempt to comfort her ethereal form.

"You need to go talk to Artie. You stay away from that school, and you interview her instead. Promise?"

"I promise, Grams. Am I allowed to grab breakfast at the diner before I track down this 'Artie' woman?"

"Of course, dear."

I pull out the haunches of my reindeer onesie and curtsy. "Why, thank you, ma'am."

After a quick-change that would make the cast of *Saturday Night Live* jealous, I hurry through the crisp air, snow crunching under my feet, toward the diner.

Let the record show, I never expected snow to crunch. I thought snow was always light and fluffy and silent. But I have a new appreciation for the Foley artists on those frozen-tundra *National Geographic* specials. The sound a polar bear makes as he crosses the Arctic is not a movie myth. That's straight up, authentic snow-crunch.

I pull open the door and nearly drool on my own chin when I smell the wondrous breakfasty yum that is Myrtle's. This glorious little touchstone in my daily routine is one of the many things that makes Pin Cherry feel more like home than anywhere else I've ever lived. I might even start to believe that I deserve to have a home.

Odell salutes me with his metal spatula and I take a seat at the counter so I can chat while I wait.

"I'll have the special."

"Already makin' it."

I nod. And that's what passes for "chat."

"Odell said you're looking into my brother's accident. Do you have any leads?"

I smile at Tally as she sets down my coffee, and

direct my answer to them both. "I'm talking to Artie today. I'll know more after that."

Tally's flame-red topknot bobs with fervor. "Bless that woman's heart. She saved Ledo's life."

I nod and smile. "Does Ledo live in The Pines?"

"Well now, technically I'd have to say 'no' because he lives on the opposite side of Pin Cherry Lane, you know? But he walks home from his clinic through The Pines every night, if you're wondering what he was doing."

Her tone is more defensive than I would've expected. "I'm sorry to bring it up, Tally. I only learned last night that The Pines is the first place to be plowed after a storm. I just thought it was fortunate—that's the wrong word." I take a long sip of my coffee before I say anything else stupidly inappropriate.

Tally scurries away to fill other, more deserving coffee cups.

Odell shakes his head. "Tell Artie I said 'hello' won't ya?" He brings out my plate and leans toward me as he slides it on the counter. "Tally's been on edge since the accident. I don't think she's ready to accept Ledo's prognosis."

He raps his knuckles on the counter and heads back to the kitchen.

I wolf down my food, finish my coffee, and yawn indelicately. "Where can I find Artie?"

"Down at the substation."

I lift my hands and nod encouragingly.

"You know where Final Destination is, dontcha?" He snickers.

I pretend not to receive his meaning. "If you're referring to the tavern located near the docks, I've heard of it."

Odell fails to hide his amusement. "Well, there's a city building across the street. Garage is in the back."

"Thanks."

I hurry back to my own garage and climb inside my frosty Jeep. I crank the nonexistent heat and cautiously reverse down the alley. The vacant building next to me has attracted some interest lately, and a couple of days ago I nearly backed over a realtor.

As the waterfront dive bar Final Destination looms into view, I swallow and shake my head. It started out as a fun place to play pool and ended up the site of a kidnapping. But that's another story, and today I need to stay focused on Artie and whatever information she might have.

I drive around to the back of the city maintenance building, and the huge metal rollup garage door is open. Shoot, I hope she's not out plowing the streets. Guess I didn't really think this through. I park partially wedged in a snowbank and run across the street into the substation. A massive dump truck with a plow on the front fills the space. "Artie? Artie? Odell says 'hello.'" A metal chair scrapes across the floor and something crinkles.

As I come around the front of the monstrous vehicle, a small woman with curly grey-brown hair and a thick plaid coat dusts off her hand on her dungarees as she walks toward me. "Hey there, I'm Artie. Don't mind the sour cream and onion dust. A girl's gotta eat."

I like her already. "Hey, Artie, I'm Mitzy." I extend my hand in the customary greeting and she nearly crushes my bones.

"How ya doin'? You said something about Odell? That old scoundrel! He still owes me fifteen dollars for a bet he lost in 1983."

"That sounds like Odell. He's—I mean he was—good friends with my grandmother. I'm looking into Doc Ledo's accident for Tally. I'm just trying to see if there's anything the authorities might've missed."

Artie slaps her hand on her thigh and reaches out to give me a second even more vigorous handshake.

"Well doesn't that just beat all! You're *that* Mitzy. I'm happy to help Doc Ledo in any way I can. Have a seat." She gestures to a paint-chipped perch that looks as cold as it does uninviting. "Have a seat and ask me anything you like."

I stare at the metal chair, barely thirty feet from the wide-open garage door, and can't hide my frown. I was hoping there would be an actual office somewhere, with a door and a heater.

But Artie takes no notice of my hesitation. She scrapes her chair back, sits down, and slides her bag of chips across the scarred tabletop. "Help yourself."

"Sure, thanks." I definitely don't want to offend her, so "when in Rome." I glance at the imposing truck and prompt, "So tell me about your plow."

Her face lights up like a Christmas tree and she launches into a lengthy explanation about horsepower, tandem axles, and several other attributes of her precious "beastie."

"Well, it's quite a machine." I glance up at the cab nearly ten feet in the air and chew the inside of my cheek. "The police report said Ledo's body was covered with a layer of snow. How did you even see him from up there?"

"When you've been doing this as long as I have, you learn how to tell the difference between a snowbank, a dead deer, and a man." Her tone has an edge, which I desperately need to soften.

"Of course, of course. I grew up in Arizona. I don't know the first thing about snow. I could really use a lesson from somebody with as much experience as you." Grams would be so proud of my "more flies with honey" approach. "When you saw how much snow had accumulated on the body, were you the one to point out to the sheriff how long Ledo had been lying in the street?"

"Boy, oh boy. The stories in the paper didn't exaggerate a thing. You really are a sharp cookie." She bangs her hand on the table for emphasis and retrieves her potato chips. Artie crunches through a handful before she answers my question. "I figure it couldn't have been more than twenty or thirty minutes from the time he was hit to the time I found him. The storm was slowing down, and the rate of accumulation had dropped by at least fifty percent since the peak of the storm—which I place at around 6:00 p.m. Once the worst had passed, I headed out and hit the main roads leading to the park—" She stops and looks at me with a warning in her eyes. "Now, don't go telling any of those hoity-toity Pines residents about my detour. I just wanted to make sure everyone could get to the Yuletide Extravaganza. Anyway, I headed over to The Pines by way of Gunnison and started plowing up and down their streets. Of course, Judge Carlson had to come out and flag me down so he could complain about me leaving windrows at the end of the driveways. I explained to him, for the two-hundredth time, that we don't have enough snowplows or operators to clean out resident's driveways, but after forty-some years on the bench, I guess he's earned the right to complain."

"Did you happen to see Ledo walking home from the clinic?"

"I certainly did not. I figure he'd already passed through The Pines by the time I got there, and I can't help kicking myself for coming in on the far side of the development. If I were to come in off Pin Cherry like I usually do, I might've seen who hit him. At least I would've gotten to him sooner; poor man was near frozen solid by the time the ambulance arrived. I called it in right away, set up flares, covered him with a couple of my space blankets. But I didn't dare move him, you know? I've seen enough TV shows to know not to move a body."

"I agree. Was there any debris around the body?"

"Well, the impact knocked him clean out of his winter boots. They were sittin' by the side of the street, but I didn't see anything else."

I shudder as I think about the amount of force it would take to knock a human being right out of their shoes. Poor Ledo. I absolutely have to figure out who did this to him. "Could you show me on a map or something exactly where you found the body?"

"Sure thing. Hold on." She scoots back her chair and heads to the ladder on the driver's side of the massive snowplow. She scurries up and swings into the cab in record time and returns with what looks like an iPad. She taps and swipes furiously before laying the screen on the table. "See this here, that's Spruce and this up here is Fir. Now, I was coming down Pin Cherry Lane and I saw the body in the road right here." She taps her finger on the screen twice and enlarges the image.

I nod my head. "And is there a driveway right here?"

She returns to her chair and shakes her head. "Not on that side of the street. There's the brick wall between Pin Cherry Lane and the houses in The Pines. All their driveways are inside the residential area. But the folks across the street on the other side of the Lane have driveways. This is probably about where 1872 Pin Cherry sits. But I don't recall any tracks comin' across the street. In fact, I don't remember any tracks on the other side of the body. It's almost like whoever hit him, backed away, turned and went the other direction. Unfortunately, my plow scraped up any tracks left in the street when I approached."

It all seems like a dead end. Her information confirms the time of the accident from the police report and that's about it. No new information. No amazing leads.

"Thanks for your time, Artie. I appreciate the

snowfall lesson and I'm glad to know you're the one running this beastie."

She chuckles with modesty as she gets up and grips my hand in another over-zealous handshake, while she pats me on the shoulder with her other large hand. "Any time. Absolutely any time."

I hurry back to my Jeep and wonder how I still have circulation in my fingers and toes. Maybe I'm growing accustomed to winter in almost-Canada. Or maybe my extremities are so numb I can't tell the difference.

CHAPTER 10

My return to the Bell, Book & Candle is far less triumphant than I had hoped. I tug open the intricately carved front door and bump directly into a man backing toward the entrance.

"Can I help you?" I exhale the phrase with a heapin' helping of snark.

"Ah, Miss Moon. My savior has arrived." Rory Bombay slips an arm around my waist and gently spins me between him and—

"Reeeee-ow." A warning.

I laugh in spite of Rory's desperately tense jaw. "I see you've met our mascot, Pyewacket."

Pye responds with a "Ree-ow." Soft but condescending. Clearly he is not a fan of the term "mascot." I'm sure he would prefer "fearless leader" or perhaps "god king." Spoiled little demon spawn.

"As much as I admire your intelligence, Miss Moon. I will be forced to emphatically disagree. That is a deadly predator, no high-school plushy."

"I'll settle him down." I walk toward Pyewacket as I admonish his poor manners. "Pye, Mr. Bombay is a guest. You will not eat our guests." I reach down to scratch his head between his lovely tufted ears and receive a sharp warning thwack from his right paw. I say "warning" in spite of the pain, because he did not extend the claws and claim a chunk of flesh.

Pye runs up the circular staircase before he can be properly scolded.

"Oh, that fiend!" I search the surrounding air for Grams. Oddly vacant. She normally swoops in to defend the little reprobate.

"Thank you for defending my honor, Miss—"

I spin around and wave my hands in surrender before he can finish that sentence. "Look, I've already got one eligible bachelor in this town stuck in the friend zone with this 'Miss Moon' nonsense. Please call me Mitzy." That sounded a great deal more flirt-forward than I intended. I hope he can't see the flush on my cheeks.

Rory's green eyes twinkle with amusement and his broad shoulders relax. "I'm flattered that you consider me eligible, Mitzy."

He nearly purrs my name, and I feel the heat from my cheeks turn into a tingle in my tummy.

Eager to change the subject, I ask, "Was Twiggy helping you to find something?"

He strokes his stubbled chin and shakes his head. "Not exactly."

"What do you mean?"

"I believe her precise words were, 'Get your grave-robbing hind end out of here.'"

I laugh much louder than is appropriate. "That sounds like her. What did you say to get on her bad side?"

"I was enquiring as to the possibility of gaining access to the Rare Books Loft."

"Did you make an appointment?"

He steps closer and lowers his voice to a husky whisper. "I was hoping for a private tour—today."

A fresh ripple of tingles washes over me, but it's quickly erased by a flash of icy warning from the mood ring on my left hand. I can't risk a peek, but I can sense with all my newbie psychic powers that something is not at all right.

Rory steps back and narrows his gaze. "Is everything all right, Mitzy?"

Something about the way he emphasizes "everything" sends another flash of warning through my aura. I'm just spitballing here, because I don't know what to call the area around my body that is not my fleshy actual body. I remember plenty of Sedona woo-woo folks using the word aura like it was a real thing, so I'm trying it out.

Rory takes another step back and straightens his wool coat. "Perhaps I've caught you on a busy day. Next time I'll make an appointment." He bows slightly and disappears out the door before I can reply.

"I thought he'd never leave!"

Adult diapers. This is my life now. I'm twenty-one years old and I'm going to have to start wearing adult diapers because my grandmother is a terror-ghost.

"I'm sorry, dear. But that man is bad news. You get Silas over here. He'll back me up."

"First, I'm going to change my pants, and then you can tell me all about how the road to Hell is paved with sexy, green-eyed men."

"For goodness' sake! At least give Silas a call before you go and change. Then he'll have a chance to get over here by the time you're ready." Grams swirls around me and puts on her very best sad-puppy-dog ghost-face.

I march to the back room and take a deep breath before I try my luck. "Twiggy, Grams caused me to have another accident. Would you mind calling Silas and asking him to come to the bookshop while I go put on some dry clothes."

Twiggy slowly rotates her captain's chair,

turning away from the computer screen and toward me. As her eyes take in what I'm sure is a hot mess, she replies. "Sure thing, Your Highness. Any additional mandates?"

"Not at this time." I head upstairs and leave Grams to haunt Twiggy into submission.

By the time I clamber back down the wrought-iron staircase in my "Never Trust Atoms, They Make Up Everything" T-shirt, Silas has arrived.

"Greetings, Mitzy. To what do I owe the pleasure of your invitation?"

"I'd like to discuss Ledo's case with you, but Grams has more pressing matters." She swirls over his left shoulder, and I see him shiver with the inevitable ghost chill that everyone but me seems to experience.

"Please continue."

"When I came back from interviewing Artie, Rory Bombay was here at the bookshop."

Silas turns and paces between the stacks. "I told you that man was trouble. He's far too interested in *Saducismus Triumphatus*. We may need to upgrade security at the bookshop. Both the physical and the alchemical."

"What's the big deal? So he's interested in reading some books. Is that a bad thing?"

Silas emerges from the stacks and fixes me with a truly intimidating glare. "Do you recall the story of how your grandmother and I discovered the means to tether her spirit to this bookshop so that she might have the opportunity to make your acquaintance after her death?"

Well, clearly I know the answer to this question. Is he testing me, or does he actually think that I never listen to him when he talks? "I actually do remember. Grams wanted to find some way to hang around and because she knew she was dying, she had time to plan for it. You helped her out by reading the books—"

"Precisely." Silas steeples his fingers and bounces his jowly chin as he waits for me to catch up.

"Oh. I see what you did there."

"I'm sure Twiggy can handle getting a physical security system installed. And I can handle the more—magical alarms." Silas moves to the bottom of the circular staircase and unhooks the chain. The "No Admittance" sign drops and he turns to look at me. "Perhaps you should accompany me. Much of this work is beyond your current skill level, but it never hurts to take advantage of an apprenticeship opportunity when one presents itself."

"Sweet! I'm in." The disappointed look in his eye and the ghostly "tsk" from my grandmother warns me too late that my overeager response is inappropriate.

He rethinks his route and steps off the stairs. "We shall start with the side door." Silas and his crumpled brown suit shuffle to the door that leads to the alley.

I fall into step beside him. "Can we talk about my thing now?"

"Certainly, Mitzy."

"So, I went to see Artie at the substation. She was the one who pointed out that the time of the accident could be calculated based on the amount of snow that had accumulated on Ledo's body as he lay in the road."

"Sounds like an intelligent woman."

"Sure. But it doesn't really help me. That information was already in the police report. I asked her if she saw anyone leaving the area, but she arrived long after the accident had happened."

"Driveways?"

I give myself a secret pat on the back before answering. "I asked that. All the driveways in The Pines apparently empty onto the side streets. And the driveways on the other side of Pin Cherry Lane didn't have any tire tracks that crossed the street. In fact, she said there were no tracks in the snow on the other side of the body. Almost like whoever hit him backed up, turned around and drove back the way they came."

"And where did she find the body?"

"She showed me on a map. It was between Spruce Street and Fir Street, just like the police report said. I asked her if she could be more specific and she said it was probably somewhere around 1872 Pin Cherry Lane."

Silas makes a little sound, which I'm not sure if I should identify as a gasp or a squeal. But in my experience Silas does not squeal.

He turns slowly and the look in his eyes is proud and kind. "Then you have your proof."

"Proof of what? Basically every bit of that information was in the police report. I had a weird feeling that whoever stole the angel statue saw the hit and run. But I didn't find out anything new. I didn't get any piece of information that confirms my weird claircognizant message."

Silas raises one thick grey eyebrow. "Didn't you?"

I rummage through the contents of the interview in my mind. It wasn't that long an interview, so it's not difficult to review the facts. "Well, about the only thing that I didn't know before I talked to Artie was the exact place where the body was found."

A smile grips the corner of his normally sagging mouth as he replies, "Indeed."

I glance down at the mood ring on my left hand and the broiling black storm clouds blow away to reveal that pristine footprint in the snow. "What's the address of the house where the robbery took place?" I ask.

"If memory serves, it was 1874 Pin Cherry Lane." His answer is equal parts smugness and satisfaction.

"I think I need to go see the sheriff."

Silas places a firm hand on my arm. "We must attend to matters here, before all else."

It's definitely not a request. An undeniable sense of compulsion floods through my body. However, I'm going to go ahead and convince myself that I've decided to stay of my own free will. "All right. Show me some magic."

Silas removes a marking pen from his inside coat pocket. "This is an ultraviolet marking pen. The symbols I will draw on the doors and window casings will not be visible to the naked eye. However, their power and influence will create the necessary barrier to any malevolent energy attempting to infiltrate the perimeter."

"Infiltrate? Perimeter? Are you like a wizard soldier now?"

"As we have discussed on more than one occasion, Mitzy, I am an alchemist not a wizard. And my concerns regarding the intentions of Mr. Rory Bombay are more than valid. Did your grandmother share any of his history?"

"His history? The man is barely ten years older than me. I doubt he could have much of a history with my grandmother."

Grams floats in with a hint of regret wrinkling her ethereal brow. "I hate to burst your bubble, dear. But that Rory scamp is older than he looks."

I suddenly don't think I want to hear this story.

"Well, whether you want to hear—"

I point to my lips and shake my head. "Lips did not move, Grams."

"Well, you're going to hear the story. It's for your own good." She preens her burgundy gown and begins, "My fourth husband was affectionately called a 'railroad tycoon.'"

I wave my hands to interrupt. "Wait, I thought your third husband was the railroad owner. I mean, didn't my grandpa Cal Duncan own the whole Midwest railway thingy?"

"Let's just say I have a type, honey. My fourth husband, Joe Willamet, was also in the railroad industry. However, he was Native American. I think it was—"

My attention drifts as I wonder if the end of marriage number three and the start of marriage number four, in such a socially adjacent position, have anything to do with each other."

"I'd like your full attention, Mizithra."

Uh oh, formal name time. I think I was definitely onto something.

Ghost-ma clears her throat loudly. "As I was saying, Silas represented me in my divorce from Cal, and we formed a friendship."

I smile at Silas. "Grams says you formed a friendship during her divorce from Cal."

Silas chimes in, "The friendship seemed to solidify *after* I secured her a more than generous settlement from Mr. Duncan."

"Would you two let me tell this story! Silas and I became friends, and as I started filling this bookshop with items that interested me, I began to build what is now the Rare Books Loft. Silas has always been a curious philosopher and he would spend hours paging through the magnificent tomes I'd collected, while I organized the day to day of the bookshop. Eventually, his knowledge of the arcane was as vast as any mortal could hope. He became adept at transmuting matter and other things. And, of course, you know how the story ends."

I could answer, but I feel like Grams just made the biggest jump-cut in movie history. One minute we're talking about someone reading a few books and the next minute that someone is creating a portal between this world and the afterlife—a portal where my grandmother can exist seemingly forever. "In the movie biz, we would say jump-cut to ghost of grandmother past."

Silas chuckles. "I wish I could hear her version. It sounds to me like she may have omitted the most torturous years of trial and error."

"I think you're right about that." Leave it to Silas to keep it real.

"Let's persevere with these protections. I don't believe it would be prudent to allow another night to pass without having taken every measure into consideration."

"Wait, that story didn't tell me anything about Rory."

Silas shakes his head. "Isadora, she has to know the truth. You can hardly expect her to heed our warnings on faith. Hereafter knows *you* never did." Silas wanders off to continue his emblazoning of symbols and Grams returns to finish the story.

"All right, dear. But I will expect to be given as much leniency as I've given you."

I open my mouth to protest, but memories of mumbling names in my sleep, bringing back questionable choices to the apartment, and my recent interaction with Mr. Bombay . . . I choose to nod my agreement instead.

"As my collection gained notoriety in occult circles, Mr. Bombay paid me a visit. He was extremely interested in several of the titles that I'd purchased and offered me exorbitant sums to take them off my hands. But I was more than comfortable, financially, and beyond that, there was something unsettling in his eyes. When I mentioned him to Silas, he decided to do some investigating."

"Silas? Investigating? So what you're saying is, I'm not the only one who likes to stick my nose where it doesn't belong."

A disembodied voice replies, "As a barrister, I have a duty to protect my client's best interests."

"Different words. Same meaning." I snicker.

Grams' ghostly chuckle fills me with a warm feeling of family happiness that I've missed more than I can say for the last ten years. "Please continue with your history lesson, Grams."

"Thank you, dear." She floats in front of the large six-by-six windows and continues her tale. "Silas suspected that Mr. Bombay was not his real name. Perhaps he had established an antiquities dealership under the pseudonym and traveled around the world collecting rare occult tomes and artifacts. Rumors of his collection ranged from fanciful to dangerous. Silas endeavored to test Mr. Bombay's intentions."

"That sounds like a risky plan." I tilt my head and narrow my gaze.

Grams emphatically nods her agreement. "We practiced the, for lack of a better word, 'spell' that would induce truth and then we invited Mr. Bombay to dinner. I set up an elaborate private dinner in the Rare Books Loft. Of course, it was before I had purchased all the lovely desks paired with those wonderful green-glass shaded lamps… Anyway, I had the loft decorated with beautiful lights to create a magical setting."

"No pun intended, I'm sure."

"Oh, Mitzy, you're too much." Grams pushes a shimmering hand in my direction. "As expected, he accepted our invitation and arrived fashionably late with a bottle of 1805 Terrantez Madeira. During the course of dinner, Silas excused himself to open the wine and used alchemical symbols to transmute the liquid into the truth serum, like we had practiced. It was my job to keep Rory sufficiently distracted and entertained—"

I can't contain my overzealous chuckle. "Distracted and entertained? Is that what we're calling it now?"

"Now, don't you start with me, young lady. I'm a respectable woman of means, and I simply needed information. I used the tools that were at my disposal."

I gaze at the elegant apparition of my grandmother at her chosen ghost age of thirty-five and smile. "You definitely were a hot number, Grams. I'm guessing Mr. Bombay couldn't keep his hands off you."

Once again a voice from offstage replies, "You

would indeed be correct, Mitzy." Followed by a deep, guttural chuckle from Silas.

"All right, you two, it feels like you're ganging up on me." Grams pitches a ghost snit.

"Grams thinks we're ganging up on her, Silas. I guess we best behave or I'll never get to hear the rest of story."

"Understood." Followed by a low chuckle.

"Please continue, Grams. I promise no further interruptions."

"Silas returned with the wine and my sparkling cider, and handed us each a glass. Somehow, Mr. Bombay saw through our ruse and switched his glass without us even noticing. Silas ended up drinking the truth-spelled wine and told him everything."

My eyes widen and I shake my head. "To quote Velma, 'Jinkies!'"

"I don't know who that is, dear."

"Not important. Continue."

"As you might've guessed, Mr. Bombay was furious with us and promised he would return with an offer we couldn't refuse. His tone was not friendly."

The ominous threat does not escape my attention. The Mr. Bombay that I met seems flirtatious, but ultimately harmless. And there's still the matter of his youthful appearance. "Okay, Grams, I get that you and Silas had dealings with someone named Mr. Bombay. But how can this possibly be the same guy? Are you sure this isn't a son, or possibly even a grandson of the guy you met?"

Silas shuffles in from wherever he had been marking his symbols and harrumphs loudly. "The information contained in these valuable resources"—he gestures to the books in my shop —"can be used for positive or negative results. Perhaps even a fountain of youth, as well as knowledge. And, to be fair, actions are subjectively interpreted. What some view as positive, others may view in a negative light. Take your grandmother, for instance. Trapping her spirit here in the bookshop so that she could partake of the opportunity to meet a long-lost granddaughter seems wholly positive. However, there are those who would say we have no business tampering with things beyond the veil. And perhaps they are correct."

Grams swirls down in a ghostly fury. "Don't you dare impugn my decision, Silas Willoughby. You are as much, if not more, to blame. Look at all the good we've done for Mitzy. Why, if we hadn't been here when she discovered her abilities... Who knows what might've happened."

Silence.

"Mitzy, tell him what I said. Tell him!"

I do as I'm told.

"My dear Isadora, I wholeheartedly endorse our

decision. I was simply demonstrating the effect of perspective for your dear granddaughter."

I step between my attorney and my Ghost-ma. "No fighting. I don't want to stand here playing the spirit version of 'Telephone!' Let's say I take your side and agree that Rory is trouble. How do I combat his obvious powers and knowledge? I have some gifts that I don't really understand, a dodgy ring, and a giant store full of books I've never opened! That hardly reads like the résumé of someone who saves the day."

Silas adjusts his faded bowtie and smiles. "Fortunately, you will most likely not be called upon to save the day. The protections I've put in place will discourage Mr. Bombay from returning and should also transmute his intentions should he cross any of these thresholds and enter your space. Your grandmother and I shall worry about Mr. Bombay, while you attend to tracking down this angel thief."

I'd actually completely forgotten about Dr. Ledo and the proof that confirms the clairvoyant, or clairsentient, message I received. "Right. Let me head over to call on Erick and see if I can stir up information, rather than trouble."

Grams chuckles openly while Silas has the decency to at least put a hand over his mouth.

"I'll see you two later."

CHAPTER 11

The sheriff's station is nearly deserted and the sullen officer minding the front desk is glued to her phone as usual. Maybe it's time to try a new approach. "So, what level are you?"

She hesitates, but she does actually flip her gaze from the screen of her phone and look at me.

Will wonders never cease? "I was asking what level you're at on Furious Monkeys?"

"Oh, I'm Level 83. This Furious Monkeys is just the best game ever! I so love this game. I don't know how I could make it through a shift in this boring, nothing-ever-happens station without this game. It's a lifesaver. No joke."

The flash of social energy shocks me into silence. I nod and smile.

"Are you here to see Sheriff Harper?"

I manage a brief reply. "Mmhmm."

Her eyes drift back to her screen and she gestures toward the sheriff's office.

I push my way through the swinging wooden gate and walk past the lonely metal desks in their crooked rows, with their messy stacks of paper and random coffee stains. In the student film I'm now making in my mind, this is a dolly shot and there's plenty of doughnut crumbs on the desks as well.

"Hey, Moon, can I help you?"

Oops, got lost in my mind movies again. But I'm pretty sure he didn't call me "Miss." Progress. "Hey, Erick, any leads on Doc Ledo's case?"

Erick's full lips smirk and he shakes his head, already defeated. "You know the speech. And I already gave your lawyer a copy of the police report."

I nod with more understanding than I've ever possessed. "Right. So, I'm sure you already made the connection."

The look on his face gives me all the answers I need. That's the wonderful thing about being an honest, upstanding, and unnecessarily sexy sheriff. Your face always tells the true story. "You should never play poker, Erick."

He chuckles and gestures for me to come into his office.

I let my face display an innocent gratitude, but my strut says "winner winner chicken dinner."

"So what's the connection, Moon?"

"The witness, of course." I really want to drag this meeting out as long as possible. And I only have one tiny piece of information, so I'm going to make it last.

"Witness? There were no witnesses. That's why the investigation has stalled out."

"Then my visit is definitely going to be the best thing that's happened to you all day." I'm not quite brave enough to wink, but I hope my smile conveys the message, "I'm the best thing that's going to happen to you, ever." I wait impatiently for him to beg.

"Is that so?" He leans back in his chair and laces his fingers behind his head.

Like one of Pavlov's dogs, I can't help but glance down toward his belt to see if possibly the corner of his shirt untucks and I can finally get a peek at what I know are absolutely washboard abs.

He clears his throat in a way that makes me feel like I'm not the only one with extrasensory perceptions.

"Right. Based on my investigation, there actually was one eyewitness to the hit and run."

He leans forward on his desk, and as his hands brush past his head a few strands of his gorgeous blonde hair knock loose and hang enticingly over his blue-grey eyes. Boy, this man knows how to derail an interrogation.

"How long are you gonna string me out? What did your investigation uncover?" He smiles in what I'm sure he meant to be innocence, but it's all kinds of enticing to me.

I don't particularly like the tone he used as he said "investigation." I think it's worth mentioning that my investigation has already uncovered far more than his. But I'm not here to play a comparison game. I'm here to get information. "Have you solved the case of the stolen statue?"

He chuckles. "This is starting to sound a little Agatha Christie."

I smile. "So you read detective novels? Does that improve your investigation skills?" I hope he picks up on my ironic tone.

He exhales and leans back.

Shoot. I pushed too hard, like always, and I lost my advantage.

"All right, Miss Moon. I do have an entire town to protect, so unless you have some additional information, I'll need to get on with my day."

When will I learn? "I thought it would be worth mentioning that whoever stole the statue saw the accident."

A little sparkle returns to his eyes and he leans toward me. "I'm listening."

"If you look at where Doc Ledo's body was found, the estimated time of the accident, and the footprints left at the scene by the angel thief, I think you'll see what I'm getting at."

His eyes darken. "Everyone was at the Yuletide Extravaganza. No one saw the robbery either. I can't imagine we'll have any more luck tracking down the angel thief than we did the hit-and-run driver."

Let the record show that I'm very pleased he's using my term "angel thief," and I guess I have to give him just a little bit more. "Well, I'm sure you noticed the footprint at the robbery was left by a DC skateboard shoe."

A smile, not of amusement, but of something more diabolical, spreads across Erick's face. "And now it would seem I've solved a different mystery."

I attempt to hold my features in their portrait of false innocence. "I'm not sure what you mean."

He stands and I struggle to keep my focus. "I think I just figured out what you were doing at the high school. And I'm pretty sure it didn't have anything to do with philanthropic evaluations." He walks around his desk and offers me his hand. I instantly take it without considering the implication. He pulls me firmly to my feet and leans down. "The school board dropped the charges, but I'm sure I could track down a parent or two who would be happy to pick up the ball and run with it. I suggest you get yourself out of my office before I have time to pick up that phone."

I yank my hand from his and scoot past him toward the door. I would like to point out that this takes every ounce of personal willpower I possess, because I would much prefer to have tripped and fallen all over him. "I hope you'll let me know if you turn up the suspect in the robbery, Erick. It was great chatting with you." I hurry out of the station so quickly, I forget to put a little extra wiggle in my waddle.

CHAPTER 12

As I PULL my hood up against the frost-laden air blowing across the now-frozen great lake, I catch sight of the sign above Myrtle's Diner. For the first time in recent memory, I actually can't remember the last time I ate. It certainly was today, wasn't it? I better go in and have some french fries just to be on the safe side. I push open the door and hurry into the welcome heat and delicious smells that await.

Red-vinyl bench seats all stand empty and only one man sits at the counter. Of course, if we all take a moment to remember my incredible luck with men, I'm sure you can guess exactly who's sitting at the counter. Let's say it together: Rory Bombay.

"Miss Moon." He rises from his stool and smiles that glorious, flirtatious, irresistible grin. He strides toward me and extends his right hand.

For some reason, I choose to play nice and extend my hand in return.

He grasps my fingers gently and brings the back of my hand to his lips. The subtle caress of his soft lips juxtaposing the roughness of his stubbled chin is exactly as delicious as I imagined that night at the Yuletide Extravaganza.

"Mitzy, I do hope you will forgive my ill manners at the bookshop. I've always been just a little frightened of cats. You see, my great-grandmother lost a child to a large black cat that was busily lapping dried milk from the child's face and inadvertently sucked away the infant's breath."

Now, I may not have lived through the depression, but I know an old wives' tale when I hear one. And this little anecdote couldn't be less true. In fact, I'm so sure that it is a falsehood that I don't even need to look at my mood ring for verification. However, as soon as the thought enters my mind, I can't resist a quick peek. Just as my eyes dart left, Rory drops my right hand and scoops up the ring-ensconced extremity.

"That is quite a fetching ring. May I ask where you got it?"

"I'd rather you didn't." The little hairs on the back of my neck pick up on a distinct shift in Rory's energy.

He covers as best he can. "Of course. All women must have their secrets."

I notice he doesn't release my fingers. I have no intention of causing further social tension by yanking my hand away, but I really don't want him staring at my ring. Thank heaven for small favors.

"This ain't a Sadie Hawkins dance. Did you come to eat or not, Mitzy?"

"I'll have the usual, Odell."

Rory regretfully drops my hand and invites me to join him at the counter. I feel powerless to refuse. And as I take a seat on the stool next to him, I suddenly wonder if the powerlessness is imagined or if it's caused by something Rory did. I have to shove all of this nonsense out of my head. Mr. Bombay has always been nothing but a gentleman to me, and Grams and Silas filled my head with a load of codswallop that I can't seem to shake.

Rory flourishes his hand near my right ear and produces a shiny copper penny. "A penny for your thoughts, Miss Moon."

Game on. "How old are you?"

He does not lean away. His green eyes sparkle with what I hope is only mischief as he replies, "I do admire your direct approach to life."

"That wasn't exactly an answer."

He lays the penny on the counter, leans back, and takes a deep breath. "I am older than I look.

Perhaps too old to be flirting with a lovely young woman such as yourself. But I've never felt that age should be a barrier or condition to truly exploring the possibilities of getting to know someone."

Now, how am I supposed to argue with that sentiment? If I insist on an answer, I'm going to appear shallow and unadventurous. Either he is sincere, or he is devilishly good at manipulating women. For now, I'm going to put all my eggs in the sincerity basket. "All right, I withdraw my question. But you only get one 'pass' and you've used it up. So you're going to have to answer this next question."

"Fair play to you, Miss Moon."

"Mitzy will be fine. And what I'd like to know is: What is your interest in me and my bookshop?"

"I believe that is actually two questions. Which one would you like me to answer today?"

Oh boy, he is good. "For today, I'd like to understand your interest in me."

"Very well. I find you fascinating. It's a small town and I've heard the rumors. And yet I see you walk through this city with your head held high. You seem to be adjusting well to your new life and your new standing in the community. In fact, I recently heard a rumor that you made a very large donation to the local high school."

As I open my mouth to protest, I see the corner

of his lip twitch as he struggles to keep his strong jaw from quivering with laughter.

I shake my head. I know when I've been beat. "Boy, there are no secrets in Pin Cherry Harbor."

Odell slides my plate in front of me with one hand and refills Rory's coffee cup with the other. "About the only secret that I can think of is what your dad is doing with his fine-looking lawyer down in Chicago."

Despite the wonderfully enticing man sitting next to me, my attention snaps to the curmudgeon serving my burger and fries. "What on earth are you talking about, Odell?"

He shrugs. "Jacob and Amaryllis came in here for breakfast three or four mornings ago and told me they were headed down to Chicago for a big train conference. Sounds like your dad planned to pursue a couple of new contracts and needed some legal advice."

I size up Odell for a moment while I formulate my follow-up question. "So what's the secret?"

"It's not my place to say, but I don't often get business associates sittin' on the same side of the booth when there's only two of 'em." He raps his knuckles on the silver-flecked white Formica counter and saunters back into the kitchen.

So many questions whirring through my head. But the biggest one is, obviously, why didn't my dad tell me he had a girlfriend? I mean, before my mom passed away, I used to fantasize constantly that he would return and they would get together and we would have a family. But I've learned a lot of things about my past that I didn't know before I came to Pin Cherry Harbor, and now the only thing I want is for my dad to be happy.

"If you'll pardon the interruption, I may have some information pertinent to your current dilemma."

"You know something about my dad's business trip?"

"I do not. However, I do know Amaryllis, and she is a lovely intelligent woman who, I would venture to say, has your father's best interests at heart."

Geez, this guy knows how to win a girl over. Whatever reservations I had when I walked through the front door of the diner and saw him sitting at the counter have all but evaporated. He's handsome. He's single. And he finds me fascinating. Silas and Grams are going to have to do a lot better if they want to discourage me from getting to know Rory. A lot better.

Rory drinks his coffee and finishes up the last of his pin cherry pie while I power through my burger and fried pieces of potato perfection. As I lick the salt from my fingers, Rory chuckles.

"I believe my instincts were correct. I thought it

best not to interrupt you while you were eating." He smiles and gives me a very yummy wink.

"It's been nice getting to know you a little better, Rory." I wipe my mouth with a thin paper napkin. "I have some leads I need to follow up, but I hope we bump into each other again."

"I would be delighted, Mitzy." He raises his coffee cup in a toast as I leave the diner, with a wave to Odell and a nod to Rory.

I decide to drive the few blocks over to Pin Cherry Lane, rather than risk potential frostbite walking in these icy, windblown conditions. As I pull into the driveway at 1874 Pin Cherry Lane, I realize I have no plan. But I seem to do my best work on the fly, so here goes. I make my way down the freshly shoveled and salted sidewalk and knock firmly but not threateningly on the front door.

The door opens almost instantly and a frail, white-haired woman standing somewhere between four and five feet tall smiles up at me as her cataract-laden eyes struggle to focus. "Good afternoon, dear. If you're looking for Brynley, dear, she left about an hour ago. Would you like me to get her cellular telephone number for you?"

Oooh, all my psychic senses are buzzing. Footprints in the snow. DC skateboard shoes. Kids in high school have them. This woman has a granddaughter in high school. Brynley—queen of the mean girls. I'm starting to feel rather confident that this theft had very little to do with the actual owner of the statue. "Oh that's okay, I have her number."

"All right then, dear. Who shall I tell her was calling?"

All the psychic powers I have, and I can't get my claircognizance to deliver a name! Come on, regular brain, it's in there somewhere! "Oh, tell her Sadie stopped by." I turn and jog back down the sidewalk before she can ask any additional mind-boggling questions. I hop in my Jeep and back out of the driveway, hoping against hope that Sadie is at least clique-adjacent.

I race back to the bookshop, taking unnecessary risks on the slippery streets and putting my limited winter driving experience to the test. Thankfully, when I get back to Bell, Book & Candle, Silas is tucked into a corner of the Rare Books Loft reading a thick leather-bound book trimmed by gilt edges.

"Ah, Mitzy. Any luck bamboozling the sheriff?"

Grams surges through the hidden bookcase door and floats eagerly beside Silas.

"I'll have you know that I handled myself very professionally and I already have an additional lead."

"What did I tell you about using the tools at your disposal?" Grams giggles like a schoolgirl.

"For your information, I actually went to the

house where the robbery occurred. In other words, I did my own legwork."

Silas carefully closes his book, slides back his chair, and shuffles over to the vacancy on the bookshelf where he replaces his reading material.

I'm extremely disappointed that no one is begging for additional information, so I launch into a voluntary account of my discussion with Brynley's grandmother and my confirmation that the angel thief was positively a high-school student.

"I'm glad to hear your instincts were on track."

"That's it? Are you not amazed?" I look from Ghost-ma to Silas and back.

"Oh, that's wonderful, dear."

"Well, if anyone has any great ideas . . . I need to get back into that high school. I know for a fact that the angel thief is there and I need to find the only eyewitness to the hit and run. I'm taking all suggestions. No idea will be ignored."

Grams slowly swirls up toward the ceiling and offers no brilliant strategies.

Silas strokes his bushy grey mustache with his thumb and forefinger, and unless my ears deceive me he seems to be humming under his breath. I pace toward the circular staircase and am nearly bowled over by a tan fur ball rocketing up the stairs. I jump to the side, and Pyewacket drops something before he races off down the left arm of the U-shaped mezzanine, his back end running catty-wampus to the front. I stoop to pick up his leavings.

"It looks like Pyewacket has figured out how to spend my money." I chuckle and walk toward the nearest trash bin.

"Perhaps you can delay for a moment, Mitzy." Silas gestures to the slip of paper in my hand.

I fan it back and forth. "It's a blank check. With claw marks in it. Apparently, he tore it out of the business checkbook. I'm gonna throw it away."

Silas puts a hand on his slightly round belly and laughs loudly. "Robin Pyewacket Goodfellow, you are a gentleman and a scholar."

I scrunch up my face and stare at my attorney. Is this what dementia looks like, I wonder? "Are you planning on letting me in on the joke?"

"You were looking for a way back into the school. I believe there's no better avenue than to present the principal with your donation in person. In fact, allow me to procure one of those oversized checks that sweepstakes companies are so eager to disperse, and I will see if the principal can organize an assembly for the presentation."

I stare at the blank check in my hand as a wave of goosebumps flutter across my skin from head to toe. That cat is far too human for my comfort.

CHAPTER 13

As it turns out, it's not that difficult to give money to high schools. Silas was able to organize a school-wide assembly in less than forty-eight hours. However, the rush-printing of the giant check proved to be a more monumental task. It cost a small fortune and had to be delivered by courier from Broken Rock. With all the pieces in place and the perfect subdued pantsuit with silk blouse selected by Grams, Silas and I load the giant check in the back of my Jeep and drive to the school.

Despite the secret being out that I am no longer Birch County Community College student Darcy Brown, but, rather, wealthy philanthropist Mitzy Moon, I enter the Pin Cherry Harbor High School gymnasium with more than my fair share of dread.

The bleachers are packed with students, teachers, and—something Silas forgot to tell me—parents. Wow! If I had any prior misgivings about public speaking, I suppose there's nothing like a trial by fire to cleanse them from my system.

Principal Puig stands atop a portable dais, behind a well-worn wooden podium, and speaks into a crackling microphone with the exact amount of feedback that you're expecting. If I were directing this student film, I would definitely instruct the camera operator to slow-pan the crowd and whip-pan to the principal.

"I'm sure you were all more than happy to hear that your second period classes would be canceled in favor of an impromptu assembly." Cheers and hoots emanate from the mass of hormones gathered on the wooden bleachers. "I am pleased to announce that our science program will be receiving a donation designated for new lab equipment, new textbooks, as well as a scholarship available for students pursuing bachelors of sciences after graduation." A smattering of applause from parents and a standing ovation from whom I'm assuming is the science teacher. "In addition, the English department will be receiving a sizable donation earmarked for the purchase of tablets to be used in the classroom, as well as a fund specifically for the library to purchase e-books which can be borrowed and read on the tablets."

This news receives larger applause than I would've thought. But I secretly worry that it's mostly for the tablets and very little for the e-books.

"And finally, a portion of this sizable donation has been set aside to fund a scholarship for a student pursuing an education in the veterinary sciences or veterinary medicine."

I smile and nod to the two people clapping.

"Students, faculty, and parents of Pin Cherry Harbor High School, please help me welcome our generous benefactor, Ms. Mizithra Moon."

Thunderous applause and feet stamping the bleachers assaults my senses. But beneath the din, I can still identify the subtle chuckling of Silas Willoughby. I'm sure he's quite pleased with himself. "Mizithra" is absolutely his doing. I do my best to strut across the shiny, highly polished gymnasium floor without slipping and making the wrong kind of spectacle of myself. As I approach the platform, the principal turns and offers me a hand. I'd like to ignore it and step up on my own like the empowered woman of means that I am, but the very real fear of my innate clumsiness choosing this moment to surface causes me to grab his hand in a near panic.

I manage to get myself on stage without any undue embarrassment and turn to retrieve the giant check from Silas.

Principal Puig returns to the microphone to announce, "Let's give another round of applause to Ms. Moon and the Duncan-Moon Philanthropic Foundation."

Another round of deafening applause answers the call as my eyes search the bleachers for Stellen. The cover story might be that I came to present a check, but in my heart, I'm willing to endure all the pomp and ceremony just to get a chance to apologize to that poor kid. Once again my attention wanders, and that seems like possibly the second or third time Puig had to repeat my name.

"Ms. Moon, did you want to say something?"

"Of course." I have no idea what I'm going to say, and playing dosey-doe with the principal while I'm holding a giant check and trying to get to the microphone proves difficult. Finally, he moves left when I move right, and I make my way to the mic, giant check in tow. "Good morning, everyone."

A general mumbling of something sounding a little bit like "good morning" follows.

Inspiration strikes in the nick of time. "I was here a few days ago on a research assignment from the Foundation and I had the pleasure of meeting several of you. My apologies for the secrecy surrounding my visit, but the Foundation felt it was important to get a realistic and unrehearsed picture of the programs at the high school. And I'm happy to say we found some great ways to help out."

Teachers and parents clap briefly.

I wonder if I'm allowed to do this, but I figure I'm the one holding the big check, so I can pretty much say whatever I want. "One thing Principal Puig forgot to mention, the Foundation has also designated a portion of the funds to remodel the nurse's office. We plan to build private exam rooms, a reception desk, and permanent storage cabinets." When I see the lone figure of Nurse Boulton stand to clap I struggle to blink back tears. I don't know what makes that woman want to think the best of someone she barely knows, but I truly appreciate the vote of confidence. "Well, let's get on with this presentation. And if anyone has any questions for me, I'll be over there under that net hoop." I gesture toward the basketball hoop. Uproarious laughter and a few catcalls from the jocks echo through the gymnasium, but I know that a little self-deprecation goes a long way with this crowd. I step to the left and Principal Puig walks up to stand beside me. I maneuver the massive piece of laminated foamcore into position for the photo op and smile at Quince as he snaps away with his camera for the local paper. Heck, he probably takes pictures for the school paper too. We continue smiling for an uncomfortable amount of time and throw in several obligatory handshakes. As the applause dies down, Principal Puig takes the check and steps to the microphone. "All right. Everyone back to class. You will return to your second hour classrooms and your teachers will take roll. Do not attempt to skip out on the last ten minutes of your second hour. Detention will be given to anyone who does not report for this attendance." Principal Puig turns away from the microphone to address me privately. "Ms. Moon, I wanted to personally thank you for your generosity to our school. Educational funding is always a struggle and we certainly appreciate local benefactors putting the school at the top of their list. If there's ever anything I or Pin Cherry Harbor High School can do for you, please don't hesitate to ask." Another hearty handshake follows.

"Thank you, Principal. One thing you can do: please call me Mitzy."

"Of course. Of course." More handshakes.

"And if it's not too much trouble, could I possibly have a moment to speak with Stellen before he heads back to his second-period class?"

"Stellen? Stellen Jablonski?"

I'd really like to ask him how many Stellens go to this high school, but maybe it's a very popular name in almost-Canada. And I can nearly hear Grams whispering over my shoulder, "more flies with honey." "If that's the Stellen whose father is a taxidermist, then yes."

Principal Puig turns around and grabs the microphone. "Stellen Jablonski, please come to the platform before you return to class."

My eyes search the thinning sea of humanity and I locate the lone fish now swimming upstream. For some reason, tears well up in my eyes and I have to get a hold of myself. I twist my mood ring on my left hand and look up at the ceiling, while I blink back the emotion.

As the boy approaches, Principal Puig points to him and excuses himself to return to school business. I step off the platform and walk toward Stellen.

He stops, looks down at his feet, and stammers, "Hi, Miss Brown, I mean, Miss Moon."

"Hi, Stellen. I was hoping you would give me another chance?"

He pulls his eyes up from the floor and stares at me. "What do you mean?"

"The other day, when we were talking in the hallway, I meant what I said. I am your friend."

He looks up at me, shakes his head and shrugs. "It's okay. I know you were just doing the research for the donation or whatever. I've got friends."

I scan the empty gymnasium for a single straggler and see none. I'm all too familiar with putting on a brave face. In the foster system, I attended a new school almost every year . . . Sometimes two different schools in the same year. There was never anyone waiting for me either. "Yeah, I get it. I was just thinking that you mentioned you like animals. And I thought you might want to stop by my bookstore sometime and see my pet caracal." It's impossible to describe the instant transformation that takes place before my eyes. Stellen's spine gains strength, his shoulders square, and his face seems to glow from within.

"For real? You have a caracal? For real?"

I chuckle and nod. "He's quite a handful and he's addicted to Fruity Puffs, but I think he'd like you."

"That's lit! I have to get some stuff at Rex's after school tomorrow. Can I stop by then?"

"Sure. As long as you have your parents' permission." I don't really know if that's a thing, but I sort of feel like I shouldn't be inviting kids to my bookshop without their parents' buy in.

"Oh. I kind of don't want to tell my dad."

"Maybe you can ask your mom?"

"Um, well, the thing is . . ."

I'd recognize that hesitation anywhere. "Hey, it's cool. My mom died when I was eleven, so, you know?"

Stellen looks up as relief spreads across his face.

"Yeah, thanks."

"You don't think your dad will let you come to the bookshop?"

"Yeah, he'll let me. I just don't want him to know you have a caracal. I mean, like, he'd just want to stuff it. You know?"

I laugh in spite of the seriousness of the accusation that his taxidermist father would target my cat. "Well, Pyewacket seems to have far more than nine lives, so I'm afraid it will be a while before he's available for stuffing."

Stellen snickers and breathes a sigh of relief. "See ya tomorrow." He turns and runs out of the gym.

I feel pretty good about myself right now.

"That was a very kind thing you did, Mitzy."

And now a little squeak escapes my throat. I had completely forgotten Silas was waiting for me. "Boy, you and Grams just never get tired of scaring the bejeezus out of me."

Silas chuckles. "Come along, Mizithra. Let's get you back to the bookstore before you make any more expensive mistakes at this high school."

I follow Silas out of the gym and do my best to ignore the subtle shaking of his shoulders as he continues to be amused at my expense. All in all, this was the best day I've ever had in high school—hands down.

CHAPTER 14

As Silas and I head back to the bookshop, I attempt to reset my expectations to their normally low level. After losing my mother at such a young age and struggling through the foster system for more than six years, I tend to have a general suspicion of positive emotions. It's not that I don't enjoy being happy. Who wouldn't? It's just that in my experience the higher you let yourself climb the farther you end up falling. However, in spite of my internal red flags, I'm actually feeling pretty good about myself. I'm feeling confident in my choices.

I park the Jeep in the garage, and Silas and I walk down the alley. That is, until the heavy metal door of the building next to mine pops open, missing my face by a hair's breadth.

"My apologies, Miss Moon!" Rory Bombay

skillfully grasps my hand and prevents me from stumbling backward and almost certainly landing on my rear end in the muddy slush.

"Thank you. I'm pretty sure I would've been in a lot of trouble if I'd damaged this designer suit."

Rory glances at Silas and back to me. "Isn't it your suit? Do you have an overbearing valet?" He chuckles.

Silas steps forward and disengages my hand from Mr. Bombay's before he replies. "I'm sure you're familiar with Tanya. She's not a dry cleaner to be trifled with." He loops my arm through his elbow and gives me a meaningful tug. "Come on, Mitzy, we have business."

Rory calls down the alley, "Miss Moon, I was hoping I could take you to dinner in Grand Falls this evening."

I glance over my shoulder as Silas hustles me between the brick buildings and call, "I had to skip breakfast, so let's start with lunch and see what happens."

"Perfect. There's a lovely patisserie on 3rd Avenue. Why don't you change into something less restrictive and I'll meet you in front of the bookshop in half an hour?"

Just before Silas steers me around the corner, I shout, "It's a date."

"Mitzy, I thought your grandmother and I were quite clear about Mr. Bombay and his intentions."

I untangle my arm and stop on the sidewalk.

Silas takes two more steps before he realizes I'm not going to budge.

In my best grown-up voice, I announce, "I will take your recommendations under advisement. But I'm old enough to make my own decisions. And let's not forget I have more than the average sense of right and wrong."

Silas turns and walks toward me on the sidewalk. "Those extra senses are exactly what your grandmother and I are endeavoring to protect."

Now that sounded unduly ominous. But I refuse to give him the satisfaction of knowing that he got to me. "It's just lunch, Silas. We'll walk there, eat lunch, and walk back. I'm not getting in a car with him. I'm not spending the day with him. I'm not going away with him for the weekend. It's just lunch." Now that I think about it, the thought of going away with him for the weekend doesn't sound terrible.

"I hope you know what you're doing. However, I fear you do not." Silas walks me to the front door of the bookshop and bids me farewell.

I hurry inside, up the circular staircase, pull the candle handle next to *Saducismus Triumphatus,* and slip into my apartment as soon as the secret bookcase door slides open. I kick off my chunky heels and drop the suit on the floor as I rush into the closet to put on something more in line with my standard fare. Skinny jeans, UGGs, and, despite the cold, one of my favorite T-shirts. The slogan reads "Coffee is Magic" and it has a picture of a witch riding a stir stick over a mug of bubbling java. As I'm touching up my makeup, a sphere of light sparkles toward me and I gaze into the mirror, spellbound, as Grams materializes next to me. "Now that's more my speed." I sigh with relief.

"Well, you've been such a pill about my pop-ins, what choice do I have?" She chuckles and places her hand on my shoulder.

I still can't get used to the idea of actually being able to sense her touch. It's such a strange feeling. It's almost like a hand on my shoulder, but it's weightless and comforting at the same time.

"How did everything go at the school, dear?"

I finish applying my lip-gloss before I answer. "It went pretty well. I didn't trip and fall and I think my little speech was all right."

"What did you say?"

"Is it weird if I say I don't remember?" As I think back over the morning, I literally can't remember one word of my speech.

"That's perfectly normal. I gave a multitude of

public speeches in my day, and I can't remember a single one."

"Well, I'm not sixty-something and I'm still alive, so it seems like I should be able to remember what words come out of my mouth."

Grams seems to experience a flare in brightness. "Young lady, I didn't choose my ghost-age of thirty-five so that you could remind me how old I was when I died! Let's all just stick to the script, shall we?"

I turn and survey my circa-thirty-five-year-old grandmother and shake my head. "Yes, of course, Myrtle Isadora Johnson Linder Duncan Willamet Rogers. Let's make absolutely sure we're sticking to your script!"

I walk through her apparition and Grams swirls after me.

"Are you off to the diner for lunch?"

There's a hint of regret in her voice, and I can only imagine how much she misses Odell. They grew so close at the end of her life.

"Well, you know Odell—"

I point to my lips and shake my head.

"Sorry, dear. It's all so jumbled up. I'll do better, I promise."

"I'm actually having lunch at the patisserie on 3rd Avenue."

As hard as I try, I can't keep thoughts of the enticing, green-eyed Rory Bombay out of my mind. I push the plaster medallion and, just as the bookcase is about to slide open, Ghost-ma summons the strength to push the medallion a second time, slamming the bookcase closed. I spin around. "Grams! How rude."

"Silas and I warned you about him. What on earth are you thinking?"

"I'll tell you the same thing I told Silas. I'm a grown woman, and I can make my own decisions. It's just lunch." I push the medallion and this time, as soon as the door begins to slide open, I shove my foot in. It might seem reckless, but I don't think my angry Ghost-ma would actually risk injuring me.

The angry whoosh of an exhale followed by the swishing, swirling disappearance of Grams confirms my suspicion. I slip out of the apartment and down the stairs as my heart fills with blossoming anticipation. While I'm negotiating climbing over the "No Admittance" chain my lunch date is once again delayed.

"Hey, doll, you headed up to the diner?"

What is it with everyone assuming I can only eat at the diner? "I'm going to lunch, if that's what you're asking."

"Whooee, testy. Is Sheriff Erick still ignoring your many advances?" Twiggy stamps a biker-boot-clad foot and cackles with unnecessary abandon.

"Actually, my lunch date is a handsome, wealthy businessman."

"Well, la dee da, Your Highness. If that's the case, you might want to take the time to chew your food before you swallow." Yet another chuckle escapes from my volunteer employee.

"Wow, everyone is out to give me life lessons today. Did you need something, or did you just come out here for your own amusement?"

"You know how much I look forward to our little chats. But if it's not too much trouble, can you stop at Rex's and pick up some cello tape?"

I have no idea what cello tape is, but I'm not about to ask. "Sure. No problem." As I'm walking toward the front door, Twiggy issues a final warning.

"Don't let your guard down around that man. I know he seems charming, but any guy that handsome and slick-talkin' has got to have an ulterior motive."

I choose not to answer. I've had guys that handsome and even handsomer interested in me before. Hot single girls are few and far between in Sedona. Truth be told, hot single guys are fewer and farther between. Every single guy in Sedona is slathered in patchouli oil and carries a djembe drum! I honestly can't complain about the offerings in Pin Cherry Harbor. Sheriff Erick. Rory Bombay. Mitzy Moon has done all right for herself since she did a runner on her previous life and took up residence near this gorgeous great lake.

Rory is patiently waiting just outside the front door. He's leaned against the lamppost like a movie poster for a hit 1950s picture. His lovely fedora is raked at the perfect angle to emphasize his deep, brooding eyes. The collar of his thick wool overcoat is turned up against the chill and those sexy kidskin gloves hold—a present?

"Is that for me?"

Rory feigns surprise as he looks down at his own hand. "Oh my. What do we have here?" He turns over one hand and places the adorable gold package with its tiny silver bow in his palm. "I suppose you should open it and find out."

Not to harp on the foster-kid thing, but presents . . . They're a big deal! I snatch the present from his hand like a kid on Christmas morning. And by that, I mean the kids I've seen in movies that get presents on Christmas morning, because I wouldn't know from personal experience. "Thank you."

"You might want to wait until you've opened it, Miss Moon."

"What did I tell you?"

Rory smiles that crooked grin that makes my

insides gooey and chuckles. "I'm sure I meant to say Mitzy."

I undo the silver ribbon and open the perfect gold box. Inside is a delicate gold ring that wraps around a cat's-eye emerald. It's breathtaking, and definitely expensive. "Rory! I can't accept this."

"Of course you can. It just came in from a huge estate we're processing and I thought it would look lovely on your hand."

"But it looks really expensive. It just doesn't feel right."

"Nonsense. Consider it a token of our friendship. Now let's get some lunch." He takes the ring out of the box, pulls off my mitten, slips the ring on my right hand, and holds the mitten while I obediently slip my hand back inside. He slides the box and ribbon into his pocket and places my arm through the crook of his elbow.

As we walk across the street, I wonder if it would be rude to ask for the box. It was such a cute box and such a pretty shiny ribbon. Maybe it will come up at lunch. "So there's a bakery in Pin Cherry Harbor?"

"Patisserie, but yes. Where do you think Odell gets those pin cherry pies for the diner?"

"What? I thought he made them himself?"

"Odell? Making pie? Now that man is a genius

behind the grill, but I think that's where his skills end."

I'm a little offended by his low opinion of Odell. "That man" was the first friend I ever made when I came to Pin Cherry and he's been kind and generous to me every day since. I'd like to say as much, but I settle for, "I'm sure Odell could make a pie if he wanted to."

"No offense intended, Mitzy."

I'm starting to think Silas and Grams might've been partially right about Rory. Maybe he's a little too refined and a little too pompous for my taste. As we pass Myrtle's Diner, I purposely avert my gaze. I feel like I'm cheating on Odell by going to this fancy patisserie. Well, I'm pretty sure it's going to be a one-time thing and I'll never go back, and I'll probably never have lunch with Rory again either.

"Are you warm enough?"

"Yeah. My dad got me this coat and it's rated for like seventy below, I think."

"How is Jacob?"

I keep forgetting how small this town is and how much everyone knows about everyone else's business. But it shouldn't surprise me that a man like Rory would have knowledge of one of the largest robberies to happen in the northland in two decades. Sure, my dad's out of prison and he's an upstanding member of the community, now. But I bet there are plenty of people who still think the worst. "He's doing great. He inherited the Duncan estate and he's taken over at the train business—"

"Oh, I heard. Something about a convention in Chicago?" Rory snickers.

I forgot he was present at Odell's "surprise" news. I stop dead in my tracks and put my full weight into my heels.

Rory's elbow jerks against my arm and he comes to a stop, spinning around to stare at me in shock.

"Look, you don't know me that well, so I'm probably giving you more leeway than I should. But let me be perfectly clear, my family is the most important thing in my life and I'm not going to stand here and listen to some outsider make snide remarks and innuendos about my father. He's a decent guy and he paid his debt to society. So if this is going to continue"—I point back and forth between myself and Rory—"then you're going to need to change your tone of voice. Is that clear?" I don't remember exactly when I put my hands on my hips, but that's where they are.

"You're absolutely right, Mitzy. I only know what I've read in the papers or heard through local gossip. I don't know the whole story and I definitely have no business being flip with regard to your personal life. I certainly hope you'll forgive my crass comments and let me make it up to you over a steaming cup of hot chocolate and possibly the best chocolate croissant you'll ever eat."

Hot chocolate and croissants? How am I supposed to maintain my superior air of disinterest when faced with hot chocolate and baked goods? *Julie & Julia*, this guy is good. "I'm happy to give you the opportunity, Rory. Let's hope those croissants are as good as you say." I slip my arm back through his elbow and we make our way to the patisserie with only the sound of the crisp snow beneath our feet.

Despite the promise of hot chocolate and croissants, once we arrive at Bless Choux, Rory insists that I try a slice of their delectable quiche before we jump into dessert. I'm not a big fan of delayed gratification, but the coffee is divine and the flaky, buttery quiche crust could be one of the best things I've eaten in weeks. Odell forgive me. "This is delicious. Thanks for suggesting I switch up my routine."

"I'm so glad you're enjoying your lunch. I hope you will reconsider my offer to take you to dinner."

"Let's see how that hot chocolate pans out before we make any additional plans." I smile and take another sip of my coffee. As someone who's made hundreds, if not thousands, of cups of coffee at an insanely wide variety of coffee shops in the Southwest, I can tell you with a rather large degree of certainty that this is the best coffee I've ever tasted. There's a hint of vanilla and a subtle hazelnut finish. Truly satisfying.

"Perhaps if I give you some details it will help you make your decision. There's a lovely little restaurant in Grand Falls run by a former New York City chef. The hustle and bustle of the big city got to him and he chose to escape all the stress and open a little bistro. The restaurant is set in a converted Finnish pioneer homestead. There's a single seating, Thursday through Sunday nights, and the menu is different each night. The chef chooses his dishes based on local fare and seasonal availability of imported ingredients. The basement is a wine cellar filled with some of the finest bottles you will ever have the pleasure of gazing upon, let alone tasting. He serves hors d'oeuvres in the wine cellar, complete with pairings, about an hour before dinner. Then everyone is called up to the main floor and a five-course dinner is served, followed by a dessert course and digestifs or a pousse-café. I assure you it is an experience not to be missed. Yves Bistro. They have neither a website nor a phone. Reservations can only be made through personal acquaintance with the chef via his private cell phone number."

I am not at all used to the trappings of wealth. Everything that Rory just said sounds like a TV show that I might watch an episode of and then be so disgusted with all the hoity-toity flaunting of money that I would never watch it again. Of course, part of my disdain for money is that I never had any. Thinking back on how my inheritance helped me get out of a great deal of trouble at the high school, and how good it felt to donate money to the much-needed programs at the school, is starting to shift my perspective on wealth. Money can be used for good, and I suppose there's nothing wrong with enjoying a delicious meal with interesting company. I swallow my food before answering. See, I'm learning. "It sounds amazing. I am just not sure if I'm into that sort of thing."

"What sort of thing? Good food? Good company? A truly memorable evening?" Rory leans forward and strokes his finger along the back of my right hand. "I can promise you it will be a very memorable evening."

I hope he can't see the goosebumps on my arms or the way I'm sure my pupils have dilated. I was barely getting comfortable with the idea of having dinner with this man, and now he's making promises about memorable evenings. I'm going to have to get a hold of myself. I finish the last of my coffee and set down the cup. "I'll definitely consider it. It sounds lovely."

He turns my hand over gently and draws a

swirling line down my wrist as he practically purrs, "Are you ready for your hot chocolate?"

"Mmhmm." I feel flushed and words have abandoned me.

Rory walks toward the glass pastry case to place our order, and I promise you I try not to stare. But I can't help myself. His broad shoulders, that gorgeous sweater, and those tailored pants—probably a European cut—that fit in all the right places. Oh no, I'm gawking. I tear my eyes away and glance up and down the enticing display in the pastry case. I have to admit that, for the first time in a long time, I find the food less enticing than the company.

Rory returns with our chocolate croissants and moments later two steaming hot chocolates, with whip cream and chocolate shavings, are delivered to the table. There are only a few other patrons in the bakery, but I know from experience that our drinks must've been pushed to the top of the queue to be delivered so quickly

"Have you always had money?"

He tilts his head. "What an odd question."

"I don't know. You just seem really comfortable being rich. I never had money and this whole inheritance thing is a little unsettling. I mean, making that donation to the school this morning was the strangest feeling I've ever had. I kind of felt like a superhero."

"I think it's wonderful that you made a generous contribution to the high school. And to answer your question, I wasn't born into money. However, I knew from a very young age that I wanted to be financially comfortable and to have the kind of influence that wealth would provide."

It's an interesting and honest answer, but there's an edge in his voice that concerns me. "Did your parents resent the fact that you wanted to do better than them?"

"I'm not sure if 'resent' is the correct word. My father was a butcher and I think he just assumed I would follow in his footsteps."

"Is Bombay your real name?"

A strange crackle of energy storms in his eyes, and when his hand reaches across the table and touches mine, I feel a pull that is not of this world.

"It seems like we're venturing into second-date territory, Mitzy. I hope you'll consider that dinner invitation."

There's a heat on my skin where his fingers touch it. And suddenly there's more than that—a picture flashes into my mind of a building on fire. And then I hear the word "Beware." I lean back in my chair and pull my hand away. I try to be subtle but the muscle that tightens in Rory's angled jaw lets me know that I failed. "I'll definitely consider the invitation, thank you." I slide my chair back and slip into my coat. "I have to pick up a few things at the drugstore for Twiggy. Thank you so much for lunch. It was delicious, and I'm happy to know this place exists."

Rory stands and gives me a little bow with his head. "I also enjoyed our lunch, Mitzy. I hope you will allow me the pleasure of your company again, in the near future." And with that, he scoops up my right hand and kisses it.

I blush profusely under the jealous stares of the other patrons. Quickly slipping on my mittens, I hustle out the door without another word.

As I walk back to Main Street and Rex's, I fret about the psychic messages I received at the patisserie. Normally I would ask Silas or Grams to weigh in, but they've already made their opinions about Rory Bombay quite clear.

CHAPTER 15

THE CRUSHING GUILT of having stepped out on Odell by eating at Bless Choux forced me to eat a midnight microwave pizza last night. Even Pyewacket was uninterested in my leftovers. And the awesome side benefit of eating rubbery, irradiated, Italian food late at night is crazy weird dreams.

In spite of my strong position against rising early, by 5:30 a.m. I can no longer tolerate lying in bed and staring up at the moon-kissed ceiling.

I stumble into the bathroom with high hopes that an invigorating shower will hold me over until the diner opens at six.

The depressing, dull-grey light of the ungodly early morning only serves to reinforce my belief that nothing good comes from "getting the worm."

And I can assure you I'm not referring to the one at the bottom of a tequila bottle.

As I open the side door into the alley a blast of air hits me with such a frozen fury, I stumble backward and gasp for breath as the door slams shut. "*Polar Express!*" I'm not sure if that's what seventy below zero feels like, but I'm not going back for seconds without a whole lot more layers. I shiver my way upstairs and search through the lovely rows of built-in drawers in my mega closet.

"What are you looking for, honey?"

Since I've never been allowed in the closet unsupervised, part of me is expecting this pop-in. "Do you have any thermals? Is that the right word?"

"Of course, dear. You'll find the silk long underwear and sweaters in the fourth drawer down on the left.

Talk about your OCD. It seems like books weren't the only things Grams enjoyed collecting.

"Ahem."

I chuckle as I open the drawer and locate the long underwear. I peel off all my layers and re-dress with the proper base coat of insulation. I put on something called a "turtleneck" under my T-shirt and nearly suffocate before I figure out how to fold down the ridiculously long neck. "From what I know about turtles, Grams, their necks are way more functional than this. I feel like this should be called a spiderweb neck to accurately describe the way it clings to you and threatens to trap you inside its strangling web."

Grams laughs so hard she ghost-snorts, which sends me into a fit of my own early-morning lack-of-sleep giggles.

"Oh dear, I'm super punchy. I better get down to the diner and get some coffee in my system before I crash."

Grams is still recovering, but manages to blurt, "You're such a hoot! What else is on your agenda today?"

"Absolutely nothing. I mean, I think I'll organize the murder wall—which is technically a "hit-and-run wall" this time—and see if I can come up with any more ideas about Doc Ledo's case. But after that, Pyewacket and I will have a long nap."

"All right, dear. You say hello to Odell for me won't you?"

I hesitate and I can feel my Ghost-ma's profound sadness when she realizes her mistake. I turn and smile wistfully.

"He knows how much you cared about him, Grams. I think it would almost break his heart all over to know that your spirit is still here but has no way to communicate with him. He has a lot of fond memories of your last year on this side of the veil. I think it's probably best we leave those untouched."

Little glistening, ethereal tears spring from the corners of her eyes. "You really do have to figure out a way to get me a handkerchief, dear. Gosh, I miss him. There are so many times in my life that I wondered what it would've been like if I'd gotten sober sooner and stayed with him. Can you imagine? Me with only one husband?"

"Everything you did brought you to me, Grams. Remember? No regrets. No do overs. One day at a time. Right?"

She takes a shaky breath and nods. "Of course. We're all just doing the best we can with what we have. The wisdom to know the difference, that's what I learned."

My stomach growls with unnatural ferocity. "Oh, I better get down to the diner."

Grams chuckles and floats over to the zonked-out Pyewacket.

I sigh. "Sure, now he can sleep. All night long he was prowling along the windowsills and growling at the wind. As soon as I get up, he sleeps like a baby."

"You know, Mitzy, babies don't actually sleep that well. Your father was a colicky baby and he kept me up for most of the first year of his life. I'll never forget the first time he slept through the night. I think that's when I started to believe in magic!"

"Seems like you're a bit of a hoot yourself, Grams. Must run in the family." I leave the apartment feeling tired, hungry, and full of the warmth of belonging. But regardless of how prepared I thought I was, when I open the door into the alleyway and catch that icy wind knifing across the lake it still takes my breath away. I fight against the invisible force of what must be a one-hundred-mile-an-hour gust, and manage to get the door closed. The cold propels me to the diner in record time.

As I push open the door and make my blustery entrance, I'm suddenly reminded of my first day in Pin Cherry Harbor. All eyes turn to the door, including Tally and Odell. But instead of silent, unwelcome stares, today's result is far better.

"Good morning, Mitzy," Tally calls as she pours steaming coffee into a fresh mug, which I hope is for me.

Odell salutes me with his metal spatula through the red-Formica-trimmed orders-up window, and I take a seat at the empty counter.

"Special?"

"Done."

Tally sets down my coffee and waits expectantly.

"I'm sorry I don't have more information for you, Tally. But I've at least uncovered the fact that there was an eyewitness to the accident. I shared the information with Erick—Sheriff Harper—and hopefully he'll turn up a lead before me."

Tally blinks back tears and nods hopefully. "I know you're doing your best. I sure do appreciate you looking into things."

"Of course. Anything for Doc Ledo. Me and Pyewacket owe him." I smile and nod encouragingly.

Tally nods briefly before hurrying into the back.

Odell shakes his head. "It's been tough on her. But I know you'll figure this out. You're smarter than the average bear."

I have no information about the intelligence of bears so I'm not sure if that's a compliment, but I give him the old "nod and smile."

"I didn't see you for lunch or supper yesterday? Are you on one of those new fad diets or somethin'?"

I knew this question was coming and I hope my answer passes muster. "After the whole presentation at the school yesterday, I received a lunch invitation, then I ended up crashing for most of the afternoon and had to eat a terrible microwaved disc of probably-not-pepperoni for dinner. Don't worry, I paid the price. Now I'm back at the best restaurant in town, and not likely to make those mistakes again."

Odell chuckles as his spatula scrapes across the grill with the confidence of a seasoned professional.

"I do have one question, if you don't mind?"

"Questions are free; answers could cost you."

"Fair enough. My lunch companion said that you don't make your own pin cherry pie. He said it comes from the bakery on 3rd Avenue. That true?"

Odell locks eyes with me through the orders-up window, slowly sets down his spatula, and walks out of the kitchen with an unhurried but singular purpose. He places both hands on the counter, takes a deep breath, and replies, "My pin cherry pie is made from my great-grandma's recipe. It's won the grand prize at the Pin Cherry Festival every year except 1983, when my mother was too sick to bake and I unsuccessfully tried my hand."

"Understood. Clearly my lunch companion was misinformed."

"Your lunch companion, as you call him, is misinformed about a lot of things. I can't be the first one to tell you to watch yourself around that man."

So much for secrecy. Clearly Odell knows whom I had lunch with and most likely where we had that lunch. "Correct. You are not the first. Silas, Gr— Twiggy, everyone. Everyone seems to think Rory Bombay is bad news. Maybe you're all right and I'm wrong. But all I know is he's been a perfect gentleman and I have no reason to suspect him of anything besides wanting to get to know me." Now, I realize that's not entirely true if we take my psychic warnings into consideration. But that's just between my mood ring and me right now, and I don't intend on sharing those messages with anyone until I get a little more information.

"You're a grown woman, Mitzy. Just keep your head on a swivel, all right?"

"Copy that. You better check on my breakfast. I like my eggs scrambled hard—not burned."

Odell snickers and wanders back to the grill, mumbling under his breath about young ladies trying to tell him how to run his restaurant, or something like that.

Back at the apartment, I have my tacks and my green yarn at the ready, and I'm staring absently at the two items pinned on my hit-and-run investigation wall, which is, of course, not the actual wall because Twiggy doesn't want me making holes with tacks in the lath and plaster. So really it's more of a hit-and-run corkboard, but that doesn't sound very investigate-y. Oh, and I have to use green yarn instead of red, because Grams said red reminds her of blood and makes her uncomfortable.

Anyway, I'm sitting in my scalloped-back chair staring at the article about Ledo's accident pinned on the left and the article about the stolen angel statue tacked on the right. I take out my three-by-five index cards and write "Angel Thief is the witness," and I tack that card dead center. With string leading from one article to the angel thief card to the other article I've established my connection. Now all I need is to figure out who is the angel thief.

I pace down the span of six-by-six windows and marvel at the crazy bright blue sky appearing behind the clouds. Apparently this insane wind is clearing out the cloud cover and revealing a truly magnificent winter scene. I stop and stare out over the frozen, snow-covered lake and blink as the sun sparkles like diamonds off thick white powder and dazzles my vision.

Back to the case. The footprint in the snow was definitely a DC skateboard shoe. The size and brand absolutely—most likely—guarantee the thief was a high-school student. The occupant of the house and owner of the statue is Brynley's grandmother. Brynley is the kind of terrible high-school mean girl who strikes fear into the hearts of her fellow students. The list of people who would like to knock her down a peg promises to be rather long.

I need to find motive. A deeper driving force.

My mood ring seems to turn to ice on my left hand. I risk a glance. The ring is blue-grey and my hand feels heavy. My heart feels heavy. I feel so sad.

I stare into the polished cabochon as the blue-grey swirls away to reveal an angel statue.

Shivers shoot through my body and I have trouble swallowing. I've never seen the statue. This has to be important. This information is—

"Mitzy? Mitzy, are you okay?"

I turn away from the windows and I can't see Grams. My mind's eye is filled with the image of the memorial statuary.

"Grams? I can't make the vision stop. What do I do? I can't see anything else."

"Sit down on the floor, sweetie. Try to sit down. Close your eyes. Take a deep breath and try to focus on this room. You're safe. You're in your apartment. Take another deep breath."

I slide down against the wall and desperately try to focus on the sound of my grandmother's voice. My heart hurts so much. I want that statue. I need that statue. I gasp for air and my eyelids fly open. "Grams! I saw the statue and I thought I was experiencing the widow's feelings, but it was the— I think I felt the— thief!"

CHAPTER 16

I BLINK SLOWLY. My vision is blurry and there is a halo of light hugging the edges of everything. I feel like every patient waking from a coma in every movie I've ever watched.

I wiggle my fingers and toes. Somehow I'm in my bed. Did I faint?

"No, sweetie. You had an episode."

My mouth doesn't want to work, so I'll have to settle for Grams' thought reading.

How did I get in bed?

"I coaxed you to walk over and take off the ring."

I rub the fingers of my left hand together and my ring finger feels naked. *Why?*

"I think you just got too much information at once. Do you remember anything?"

I struggle to blink away the hazy sparkles and think back—

"Keep breathing, Mitzy."

I take a deep breath and force myself to sit up. I slap my cheeks and try to clear my head. "I felt the emotions of the thief, but they're not here. I don't think I've ever gotten a remote feeling. Is that what you'd call it?"

"I have no idea. You'd better call Silas."

I rub my eyes and slide my legs out from under the covers. But they don't quite come out; instead they get tangled in my expensive Egyptian cotton sheets and I fall out of bed onto my head. "Ouch!"

Grams swirls nervously over me.

"Well, my head's clear now." I stand and reach for the ring.

Ghost-ma rushes between my outstretched hand and the mood ring resting on my nightstand. "I wouldn't. Not until you talk to Silas."

"Fair enough." I search the room for my cell.

"I think you left it on the vanity, in the bathroom."

I point to my lips and shake my head. "I'm fully operational now, Grams. Thought-dropping is once again off limits."

"Of course, dear."

Why does it always sound like she's patronizing me rather than complying?

"It's just—" Grams slaps a ring-ensconced hand over her mouth.

"Yeah, now I remember why."

I grab my phone and call my solicitor. Listen to all those grown up words. Phone (that actually has service) and solicitor (like I'm fancy).

"Good afternoon, Mitzy."

I take a moment to remember my manners. "Good afternoon, Silas. I had an episode and Grams said you should come over."

"A feeling?"

"It was like being trapped in a movie in someone else's mind. I—"

"I shall be there posthaste."

SILENCE.

"He hung up on me!" I look at Grams and shake my head. "Mr. Manners hung up on me."

"Oh dear, it must be serious. You should drink some water and have a seat."

I'm too woozy to argue. I walk into the bathroom and slurp some water from the faucet.

A "tsk-tsk" echoes from the main room.

Wiping my mouth with the back of my hand, I venture a peek at my reflection.

The sallow skin and vacant eyes that stare back at me do not look familiar. A memory slams into my consciousness. "Grams, didn't you say that trying to wield too much power is what made you sick?"

"As I explained, honey, the doctors always said it was liver failure, but I knew better."

"How's that?"

"I was never satisfied with clairvoyance alone. I wanted the other gifts too. I wanted what you have and I pushed myself too hard."

"Look at me." I point to my deathly pale complexion. "Is it happening to me?"

"You lie down and we'll see what Silas has to say."

I shake my head and collapse onto the thick down comforter. Seems like Grams is being rather evasive. I'd say it must be as bad as it looks.

The bookcase door slides open and Silas—uncharacteristically—rushes in. "Twiggy was busy tending to a customer, so I made my own way."

From my perch on the four-poster bed, I wave weakly. "Hey, Silas."

He slips his magicked spectacles from an inner pocket and hooks the ends of the wire arms around his ears. "Ah, Isadora. Is it serious?"

Grams nods furiously.

Huh. Seems a little different than the dodgy answer she gave me.

Silas leans over me. Blinks his huge eyes behind the bespelled-glasses, before removing them and placing them in his coat pocket. "Now, let's see what we have." He scans my face and he picks up my left hand. I feel alternating chills and heat on my skin. His eyes dart to the ring on the nightstand. "You were wearing your grandmother's ring when this happened?"

"Yup."

He reaches for my right hand. "And this? Is this yours, Isadora?"

I swallow hard and feel an unbridled compulsion to lie.

Grams shakes her head and then notices that Silas is not wearing his spectacles. "Mitzy, he can't see me. Tell him it's not my ring."

Silas strokes his mustache and looks at me. "What does she say?"

"She doesn't remember," I lie.

"Mizithra Achelois Moon! What on earth are you doing? Where did you get that ring?"

I force myself to think about french fries and how much I love them. But that leads me to thinking about Odell, which leads to a snippet of regret about the patisserie, which sends me right to—

"Mitzy! You tell Silas about that devil Rory Bombay this instant, or I swear I will—"

"All right! All right." I wave Silas away and slide my legs off the side of the bed. I want to walk away from this alchemist before I spill the beans.

"You look unstable. Are you having another episode?"

The concern in his voice breaks my heart.

"As it well should," snaps Grams.

I plop onto the overstuffed ottoman and mumble, "Rory gave it to me."

Silas whips out his glasses, fixes them over his ears, and searches the room. "Isadora, did she say the ring was a gift from Mr. Bombay?"

I scowl at Grams' traitorous nod.

Silas approaches and the stooped, scuffling old man transforms into a commanding force. "Give me the ring."

"Easy, Gollum." I twist desperately at the ring, but my finger is swollen and I can't get it off. "It's stuck."

"I told you that man was dangerous!" Grams anxiously circles.

"It's not like magically stuck, Grams. My finger is swollen from lying around all day and I can't get it off.

"Allow me." Silas takes my hand, without permission, and mumbles something as he marks a symbol on my wrist with his finger.

The gesture fills me with a dreadful déjà vu.

He easily slides the ring from my finger and slips it in his pocket. "There. I'll examine it more thoroughly in my study. I have some specialized tools."

I stare at my slightly thinner finger and whistle, "Boy, if you could bottle that spell you'd have women lining up around the block." I absently rub my bodacious hips.

"It is not a spell, Mitzy. Alchemy is the transmutation of matter."

"Whatever you say." I stare at the bare finger and wonder if there's anything to my episode and Rory's gift.

Grams nods once and crosses her arms over her chest.

Before she can launch into a lecture, the dulcet tones of Twiggy crackle over the intercom. "You got some punk kid down here says you're his friend and asked him to stop by the bookshop."

"*Sweet Home Alabama*!" I jump up and run to the bathroom. Splashing water on my face does absolutely nothing. I still look like warmed-over death.

"What is it? Who's here?" Grams seems more frantic than me.

"It's this kid, Stellen, from the high school. He already thinks I'm a little nuts. I can't let him see me like this."

"But why is he here, honey?"

"Because of me and the undercover thing. I said 'friends' and now I have to . . . Someone stall him!"

Count on Silas to keep cool under pressure. "I'll engage the young man in discourse while you two put Mitzy in order."

"Great. GO!" I push Silas toward the door and dive back into the bathroom.

"Don't panic, dear. We can make a silk purse out of this sow's ear in no time. You get busy with that makeup and I'll see what I can find in the closet."

I shout through the wall after my vanishing grandmother, "Nothing too fancy. Keep it casual. He's a kid."

I dump the makeup bag out on the marble countertop and grab wildly. Concealer, foundation, lip tint, blush . . . Dear lord, I look like a Goth.

Muffled chuckles from the closet do nothing to improve my self-esteem.

Two coats of mascara and a ton of blush later, my face looks almost human. But this hair . . . What am I going to do about this hair?

"How about a nice stocking cap?"

I shake my head at my reflection and walk into the closet. "What the heck is a stocking cap?"

"It's a very fashionable knit hat. There's a variety in the top drawer over there, below the jackets."

I slide open the drawer and grin. Imagine this: cover-up my haystack of white hair with an awesome hat! This is genius. How have I not been wearing hats my whole life? I pull out a red slouchy number and slip it on. Turning toward Grams, I ask, "How do I look?"

Grams chuckles. "Adorable as always. Isn't there some kind of song about a strawberry hat?"

"If you mean 'Raspberry Beret,' then yes. But as far as I know there are no other fruit/hat related songs." It's good to laugh and I feel a little energy surging back into my limbs. "All right. Hat? Check. Makeup? Check. What am I wearing?"

Grams gestures to my black skinny jeans and a striped cashmere boyfriend sweater, which I've come to love. "How about this? Casual, but classy."

"Does it go with the hat?"

"I think there's a matching scarf that will pull it all together."

"Maybe it's just because I'm from Arizona, but do people wear scarves indoors?"

"Oh, it's all the rage once you get up north."

I rummage through the drawer and find the matching scarf. I'm dressed in a flash and scampering down the metal stairs.

"I think I hear her thundering our way now," announces Twiggy.

"Hey, Stellen, sorry I wasn't prepared. I hope Silas kept you entertained."

Stellen nods and takes a couple of steps back. "Hey, Miss Moon."

"Well, now that you've arrived, I shall take my leave. A pleasure to meet you, Mr. Jablonski."

"Okay." Stellen grins nervously.

Silas harrumphs, for what I'm assuming is the loss of civility in today's youth, and shuffles out the front door.

"So, what would you like to see first?"

"Do you really have a caracal?"

"I really do. Although I haven't seen him since this morning. Which is odd, because he usually enjoys barging into my every private moment. Let's have a look around the bookshop and see if we can find him." I start down the first aisle, looking high and low, ready for a sneak attack from either direction. However, no books are pushed on my head and no fiendish fur ball leaps out from between the books. By the time we make it to the back room, I'm actually growing concerned. "Twiggy, have you seen Pye?"

"Yep."

I look at Stellen and shrug. He smiles conspiratorially. "And can you tell me where you saw him?"

"Yep."

Stellen snickers.

"Where did you see him?"

Twiggy slowly rotates her office chair away

from the computer screen and toward my voice. "Now you're asking the right questions. I saw him up in the Rare Books Loft down at the far end of the balcony. He followed me up there when I was shelving books this morning, and I never saw him come down."

"Thank you." I say it sarcastically, but I'm pretty sure you already figured that out. "Come on, Stellen, let's go find us a cat."

We walk over to the circular staircase and I unhook the "No Admittance" chain.

A disembodied voice shouts from the back room, "You hook that right back up behind yourselves."

"Copy that."

I roll my eyes for Stellen's benefit and he chuckles. We hustle up the steps and down to the far end of the balcony. There on the floor beneath the tall ladder crouches the ever-vigilant Pyewacket. He takes one look at Stellen and hisses dramatically.

"Don't worry, it's not you. He's not good with new people."

"Wow. It's true. I've never seen one in real life."

I walk toward Pyewacket and crouch down. "What's up, buddy? Don't you want to meet my new friend?"

"Ree-ow." Soft but condescending.

"What did he say?"

"It's not an exact science. Near as I can tell, he's ambivalent. Maybe sit down on the floor and see if he finds that less threatening."

Stellen quickly sits down and folds his hands quietly.

That's when I see the bottom of his shoes.

"RE-OW!" Game on! Pyewacket launches from his hiding place and thwacks Stellen's shoe furiously, before he rockets across the mezzanine.

Stellen gasps with amazement. "Wow, he's fast. How cool. That cat is lit."

"Hey, are those DCs?" I gesture to his shoes. I really wish I had my mood ring on right now, but even without it I notice the change in Stellen's posture.

"Yeah, everyone has them."

"Yeah, I figured." Something tells me there's more to this story and I think I'm going to hate myself for pushing, but here goes. "Do you want to see something really cool?"

Stellen gets to his feet and shifts his weight uncomfortably. "I guess, but I should probably get going."

"All right. It'll just take a minute."

We walk down the narrow curve of the balcony toward the wider mezzanine and the candle handle to my secret apartment. I reach up and tilt the candle down and the bookcase door slides open.

Stellen gasps. "It's like an episode of Scooby Doo!"

I laugh. "Right?"

He steps forward and peers into the apartment. He looks to the right and surveys the furniture and the built-in bookcases, and then he looks to the left and sees my hit-and-run wall. I'm just about to explain myself when he steps back and looks at me with the strangest combination of guilt and fear in his eyes. "I gotta go." He races down the circular staircase, easily hopping over the chain and running right out the front door.

I think I just got a break in my case. And it's literally the worst thing that's happened to me all week.

CHAPTER 17

AFTER A LONG DEPRESSING chat with Grams, we unanimously agree that I have to pursue the lead, but that I'll do everything I can to minimize the impact on Stellen's young life. The kid just doesn't strike me as a criminal. He must've had a good reason for taking the statue. And even though he's not a member of the "Brynley Fan Club," I refuse to believe that he was motivated solely by spite.

Time to put the wheels in motion with a call to my lawyer. "Silas, I have a situation." I put the call on speaker, so Grams can hear what he has to say.

"Good afternoon to you, too, Mitzy. I sincerely hope it doesn't have anything to do with Mr. Bombay."

Grams rushes in and blurts her concern.

I update him. "Grams wants me to tell you that

it has nothing to do with Rory. I got a lead on the angel statue and I need a home address for the taxidermist. That Jablonski kid's dad."

Silas asks for a moment to make some phone calls and says he'll get back to me as soon as possible.

Grams spirals and I pace as we wait for my phone to ring. When the "ring" finally comes, I nearly jump out of my skin and Grams scatters like smoke in the wind.

"Silas, did you get an address? Okay . . . Okay . . . I have to go alone . . . Well, it's not like she can— All right. I said all right. Yes, I'll call you when I get back." I press end and shake my head. "You'd almost think he doesn't trust me."

"Did he get you the address, dear?"

"Yes, but Silas says he's not pleased with the idea of me going out to the Jablonski property without an escort. He said he agrees only with 'extreme prejudice.'"

"You'd better get going. I'd hate for that child to do anything else he'll regret."

With the sun setting by 4:30 p.m. at this latitude, I bundle up with extra layers for my after-dark mission.

"Silas told me to leave my phone. And for you to call him if I'm not back by 9:00 p.m."

Grams floats slowly down from the ceiling like a

feather on a light breeze. "Call him? How should I call him, honey?"

I place my cell phone on the nightstand and begin Ghost-ma cell-phone lessons. "You see this little indentation here?"

She nods.

"You press that. See how the screen lights up?"

"Yes, I see it."

"All right. I'll open up the contacts and find Silas's number so that you can just press this green button and it will call him. You got that?"

"Of course. I've used a cell phone before, dear."

"I know, but not as a ghost. Do you think you can do it?"

"I opened the bookcase door the other day, remember?"

"Right. But I think you actually closed it, if I remember correctly. Which was a slightly creepy vengeful spirit thing to do."

Grams whirls away in a snit. "Well, you left me no choice."

"I believe it was my wise grandmother who once said, 'You always have a choice.'"

Grams does not respond. I can't honestly blame her. That was a low blow.

The faint sound of ghostly agreement drifting down from above.

"All right. I'm leaving the phone here. I'm

taking the mood ring, and if I'm not back by nine o'clock . . . You know what to do."

"Go easy on him, Mitzy. He's just a boy."

I nod, wrap one more loop of scarf around my neck, and zip up my thick coat.

The moonlit drive out to the Jablonski property only serves to double down on the ominous and eerie nature of my mission. Without the GPS app on my cell phone, I worry that I could become utterly lost. The art of map reading has definitely skipped my generation. But I'm getting a crash course tonight and I'm extremely grateful for the brilliant moonlight.

I make the final turn by the crumbling silo—excellent landmark—and thick trees arch over the road, blocking out the moon. Now I'm faced with being able to see only what my headlights illuminate, and, as the road narrows to a single track through the deep snow, I'm beginning to feel like I might have driven into the middle of a scary movie.

When I break out of the tree cover and my headlights shine on the Jablonski home, it does nothing to calm my nerves.

The dark and dreary cabin looks like every building you've ever seen in a teen horror film. I can almost hear the plodding footsteps of the approaching menace. I shut off the engine and step out of the car. Before I've even taken two steps, a deep voice echoes through the still night and turns my blood to ice.

"What's your business?"

I try to swallow, but my throat is so tight. I pivot slightly and see the shadow of a large man holding something very dead in one hand and something very dangerous in the other. I really hope that's not a gun. I know it is. But by hoping it's not, somehow I can keep myself from fainting. "Mr. Jablonski?"

"You from the school?"

At this point in the storm, I'll climb on any life raft offered. "Yes, yes. From the school." My vocal cords are so constricted by fear that I can barely get the words out. "Stellen?"

"In the house." He gestures with the barrel of his gun. "I just caught this striped skunk. Gonna skin 'em and prep the hide for tomorrow. You wanna watch?"

The blood-curdling scream clawing its way up my throat does not want to be suppressed. But if I have any hope of saving this doomed mission, I have to get over myself. I take a deep breath and remind myself that this is not a movie and this man is just a taxidermist. A taxidermist holding an enormous gun and a dead animal. Deep breath. Deep breath. "Oh, thank you for the generous offer." I can barely force the words past the gagging sensation. "But I think I'll head into the house and chat with Stellen. You, however . . . good luck with that."

"Alrighty then. He's not causing any trouble at school, is he?"

"Absolutely not. He's a very bright boy."

With a low, guttural grumble, Mr. Jablonski stomps off toward an outbuilding and it's all I can do to keep from sprinting to the cabin.

I knock firmly on the door.

The door creaks open and the dim light from a single bulb outlines the boy.

He tries to push the door shut, but I shove my foot in the narrowing opening. "Stellen. I'm not here to get you in any kind of trouble. Is there somewhere we can talk? Please. I promise you I'm not here about the theft."

The door groans open and the light hits the side of Stellen's face. Even in the semi-darkness, I can see his eyes are red and swollen.

"I honestly don't care about the statue. Can we talk?"

"Hold on."

He disappears into the murky interior and returns bundled for the outdoors. So much for my dream of having the conversation inside the slightly-warmer-than-outside cabin.

Stellen pushes past me and marches off into the blue-white moon-glazed snow. The rhythmic crunch-kick, crunch-kick, crunch-kick of his boots in the snow is the only sound penetrating the silence.

Since we're walking away from his father's animal-skinning outbuilding, I follow with slightly less trepidation. Like I said, I don't think this kid is a criminal and if he is I certainly hope I can overpower a sixteen-year-old boy, if it comes to that.

He ducks into a thick stand of small pine trees, almost like a Christmas tree farm, and I swallow loudly before I follow.

On the other side of the trees is a clearing bathed in a pool of almost-silver gloaming from the lunar reflection. There's a small log bench, clearly hewn by hand, and in the middle of the clearing—an angel.

The sight physically stops me in my tracks. The statue is so heartbreakingly beautiful that I honestly expect it to stretch out its wings and bless us both before ascending.

Stellen sits down on the bench and hangs his head in his hands.

I solemnly approach and ask, "Can I sit down?"

He makes a noncommittal sound, so I sit.

"What is this place?"

His voice is thick with emotion. "I call it my memory meadow."

The heavy sadness and the aching need for the

statue wash over me with such intensity that I can't stop myself from crying. "Can you tell me?"

"She was really sick. For a long time."

"Your mom?"

He nods silently.

I know Pin Cherry Harbor is way past where Jesus lost his sandals, but even I don't think they would allow the family to bury Mrs. Jablonski on their property.

As though he knows what I'm thinking, Stellen mumbles, "She's not buried here. Chuckwalla is buried here, but the statue is for both of them."

"Was Chuckwalla a pet?" I hope I got that right. It doesn't sound like a very human name, but these days who can be sure?

Stellen leans back and, for the first time tonight, I see him smile through his tears. "My mom gave him to me as a puppy. He had such a wide body and a cute little round belly . . . He was really the best dog ever. And every time I looked at him, I felt like she was still here, you know?"

"I absolutely do." I can't help thinking about losing my own mother. It would have given me so much comfort to have something she gave me, something alive, to remind me of her.

"It's just— Brynley's always bragging about how much money she has and how much her grandma spoils her because she was her grampa's favorite.

She kept showing pictures of the statue to everyone at school. I wasn't trying to hurt anyone. I just wanted—"

"I get it. I totally get it. Does your dad know?"

Stellen's face turns to a rictus of horror. "You're not going to tell him?"

"Never." I hurriedly change the subject. "Did you bury the dog by yourself?"

"He wanted to take Chuckwalla into that stupid shed and cut him— I couldn't let him. I needed to lay him to rest. Honor him, you know?"

"Yeah, I know." I look around the meadow and I can feel that there is something deeply magical here. But more than one life has been affected by recent events, and somehow I have to try to strike a balance. "Stellen, did you see the accident?"

A fresh set of muffled sobs shakes his hunched shoulders. "Yeah."

Relief floods through my body. "Can you describe the vehicle?"

"Yeah. It was an old 1980 Chevy pickup truck, blue and white, lifted."

The specificity surprises me. "How can you be so sure of the year and everything?"

He doesn't look up. "1980 was the only year of the square-body Chevy trucks that had the egg-crate grill."

Some kids are into video games. I guess this one

is into Chevy trucks. "And you saw it hit the doctor?"

Stellen shakes his head and proceeds to tell me the strangest tale I've ever heard. In the end, the only thing I know for sure is that I have to tell Erick what I've uncovered. And I absolutely have to keep Stellen out of it. "You know I have to tell Sheriff Harper what you saw."

"Do you think I'll go to jail?"

"I don't plan on giving him your name. I'll tell him I have to protect my sources, or something."

Stellen chuckles bitterly. "Too bad you don't work for the paper."

The mood ring on my left hand almost shocks me with the intensity of the electric jolt that shoots up my arm. I'd like to think I cover it up rather well by giving an exaggerated shiver. "You really are a genius. I tell you what, can you return that statue without getting caught?"

He looks at me like I'm crazy. "No way. The only reason it worked the first time was because everyone was at the Yuletide thing."

"Right." I had forgotten about everyone being at the Extravaganza. "New plan. You help me load that thing in my Jeep, tonight, and I'll keep you out of the story completely. Deal?"

He looks out over the meadow and fresh tears fill his eyes. "It's just—"

"You and I will head over to Broken Rock this weekend and we'll get a proper statue for Chuckwalla. Not trying to reward you for your crime, but I'd like to reward you for doing the right thing for Doc Ledo. Make sense?"

He nods. "Can I have a minute? To . . . you know?"

"Of course. I'll wait on the trail on the other side of the trees." I take one last look at this dreamscape and slide through the pine trees—back into the real world.

CHAPTER 18

Back at the bookshop after a slow, silent drive through this otherworldly, glowing snow-covered landscape. I quietly let myself in the side door from the alley and, with a heavy heart, make my way upstairs to the mezzanine. As soon as I pull the candle handle, Grams practically explodes through the wall.

"Oh, thank goodness! I really wasn't sure I was going to be able to work that phone. I was so worried that my sporadic and unreliable ghostly abilities would abandon me when I needed them most." She circles around me, stops, and puts a hand over her mouth. "Dear! You've been crying."

I nod as I walk into the apartment, peeling off my winter layers as I go. "Give me a sec, Grams." I crawl directly into bed, with my clothes on, before I make the call. "Hey, Silas, I'm back at the apartment. I've got you on speakerphone, so let me get you and Grams up to speed, together."

I carefully lay out the details of my visit to what I describe as the filming location for a horror movie, and after setting the stage with the proper level of fear; I proceed to break their hearts in equal measure with the story of Stellen's memory meadow.

Grams clutches one of her many strands of pearls and sighs. "Poor little lamb."

Silas takes another approach. "Speaking as your lawyer, Mitzy, you must dispense of the stolen property before you share your lead with Sheriff Harper."

"He's right, you know? Erick isn't going to stand for you holding out. He'll force you to name the eyewitness." Grams shakes her head in concern.

"Actually, Stellen gave me the perfect idea. First thing tomorrow morning, I'm going to head over to the *Pin Cherry Harbor Post* and sign on as a freelance reporter. Nothing like the fourth estate to insulate my right to protect my sources."

Grams claps her ghostly hands and I can hear Silas chuckling on his end of the phone.

"You are a dastardly force to be reckoned with, Mitzy. I concur that the Shield Law will protect your journalistic sources, but just to be sure I've made myself clear, please drop off the statue to

Mrs. Jorgenson on your way to the newspaper office."

"All right. Fine. The thing is, I don't actually have a cover story for the statue reappearing."

"I recommend you focus on how fortunate it was that you happened upon it and leave before her profuse gratitude is replaced by any questions."

"Will do." I yawn loudly. "You two better let me get some sleep. It sounds like I'm going to have a very busy day tomorrow."

The crisp morning light seeps through my eyelids as Pyewacket head butts me.

"Good morning to you too, my furry fiend." I scratch him between his tufted ears and he purrs loudly. Clearly he's pleased to have once again directed my investigation. "Yes, Pyewacket, you are the smartest kitty. Now, do you happen to know who owns a 1980 blue-and-white Chevy pickup truck?"

He nips gently at my hand and I pull away in mock pain. "Ouch! You little demon! Fine. Thank you for your help. There'll be no further expectations." I walk toward the door and call back, "Come on, let's get your breakfast. I've got a very long to-do list."

As I chug my industrial-strength coffee and

power through a bowl of Fruity Puffs, Pyewacket's vengeful stare tracks every movement of my spoon. I may be taking my life into my hands here, but I can't risk going to the diner and spilling the beans before I have all my ducks in a row. Beans. Ducks. Uffda! (A local term of exasperation, which I've come to love.) It's too early for all this clandestine activity.

Back upstairs I work on making myself presentable, perhaps even a little adorable, since I will have the pleasure of seeing Erick today. Dressed for success, and brutal winter weather, I drive toward Olga Jorgensen's.

As I pull into the driveway at 1874 Pin Cherry Lane I rehearse my speech, especially my exit strategy.

I put the Jeep in "park" and open the rear hatch. The angel statue is a lot heavier than I remember, and the last thing I want to do is drop the ball on the five-yard line. I'm not a sports nut or anything, but I think the analogy holds up. "Put your back into it, Moon." My inner coach gives a little pep talk while I lift with my legs and heave the statue out of the back. I peer around the wings as I awkwardly stumble toward the front door. Setting the angel down on the corner of the porch, I turn it toward the door so the lovely inscription is visible, before ringing the doorbell.

The door swings open and the frail woman smiles up at me. As I'm about to launch into my well-rehearsed speech, she pushes open the storm door and exclaims, "It's back! It's back!" She rushes past me and embraces the angel statue.

I don't think I'm going to get a better out than this. "Is Brynley here?"

The woman turns around with tears in her eyes, "Oh no, dear, Brynley's at school. Shouldn't you be at school, Sadie?"

Uh oh, time to backpedal and make my exit. "Of course. I got stuck in my driveway and I was running totally late. But I'll catch up with her at school. Thanks." I turn and hustle it back to my car.

As I back out of the driveway, I see Olga inspecting every inch of the statue and pressing her hand to her heart. You know what? I'm glad she thinks it's a miracle. To me, that's even better.

There's no one at the front desk of the newspaper. Not that I'm surprised. I ring the little bell several times before Mr. Knudsen wanders out of the back and looks at me with slack-jawed surprise.

"Is anyone helping you?"

I can't stop from looking over my shoulder to see if there was someone I missed, but seeing no one beside myself, I launch into my objective. "Hi, Mr. Knudsen, I was really hoping to do some reporting for the newspaper. Do you use freelancers?"

His eyes blink behind his glasses in what I have come to understand as the mechanism that fuels his thought process.

"We don't really have assignments. You know my grandfather . . ."

That's my cue to interrupt and force the issue. "I tell you what, why don't you assign me a local human-interest story and I'll write it up on spec. If you don't think it fits the style for your paper, we'll call it even. Sound good?" I grabbed a term from the film industry and I hope "spec" means the same thing to journalists. Basically, you write for the health of it and if somebody buys it—hooray.

Blink. Blink. Blink.

"What do you say? Should we give it a try? Just one local human-interest story."

"I guess it wouldn't hurt—"

That sounds like a "yes," people. That's all I need. "Thank you, Mr. Knudsen. You won't be sorry." I'm not sure why I said that last bit, but it sounds like something a cub reporter would say. I exit with a flourish before Mr. Knudsen can change his mind. And now I'm off to the sheriff's station for the *coup de grâce.*

The front desk is empty, so Furious Monkeys is either out sick or on a coffee break. I decide to try my luck with inviting myself directly back to Erick's office.

"Who'd you kill this time?" Deputy Paulsen has one plump hand on her gun and the other holds a toothpick that is picking lord knows what out of her teeth.

"Hilarious. I'm actually doing your job again. Maybe you'd like to accompany me to Erick's office and hear what a real investigation sounds like?"

"One day, Moon. That lip—"

I push past her, but she falls in directly behind me and seems to be taking me up on my offer. I never know when to quit. I was actually hoping for some alone time with Erick. I grin and pick up the pace.

However, I'm stopped short as I come around the corner and see who's sitting in the chair opposite the sheriff. Unfortunately, my quick stop results in Deputy Paulsen smacking into me as though we're a *Three Stooges* outtake.

Erick chuckles. "I'll take it from here, Paulsen." He waves her back to wherever she came from. Bully School, I'm guessing.

"Good morning, Miss Moon. You're up early."

"It happens every once in a while. How's your morning, Erick?"

He shakes his head and shrugs. "Have you met Quince Knudsen, the photographer over at the post?" He gestures to the boy sitting on the other side of his desk.

I shake my head and hope to goodness that my bribe served its purpose. "Don't think I've had the pleasure." I lean forward and reach out my hand. "Hi, Quince, I'm Mitzy."

Quince fumbles the handshake and says something like, "Hey."

I pull my hand back and make eye contact with Erick. I tilt my head meaningfully and ask, "You got a minute?"

"Yeah, we're just finishing up." He hands a business card to Quince. "You give this to Donna Jo and tell her I'm the reason you're late. Got it?"

Quince takes the card, nods, and slips past me out of the office.

I have to admit the kid is good. Apparently he didn't crack under interrogation. Nice to know. I drop into the recently vacated chair and lean back to get a better view of Erick.

"What brings you in this morning?"

"Well, Erick, I have a lead on the vehicle that hit Doc Ledo."

He leans forward and grins. "I can't wait to hear this one. A crime with no eyewitnesses and you suddenly know who was driving the car. Please, Moon, enlighten me."

I don't think I like his tone. "First of all, as I mentioned to you previously, there was a witness.

Whoever stole the angel statue saw the accident. So it stands—"

Erick holds up one finger to halt my word vomit. "About that. I got a very strange call from Olga Jorgensen this morning. She said that God saw fit to give her a miracle and this morning she woke up to find that statue back on her porch. You wouldn't happen to know anything about that, would you?"

I shrug and avoid his penetrating gaze. "The truck that hit Doc was a 1980 blue-and-white Chevy pickup, lifted. But that's not the strange part."

I see a faint hint of recognition in Erick's eyes, which I assume means he already knows who was driving the vehicle. But I continue to spin my tale. "Doc Ledo wasn't actually struck down on Pin Cherry Lane. My source tells me that he saw the truck back up to the spot where the body was found, take Doc Ledo out of the bed of the truck, and position him on the street where Artie found him. My source also says the driver of the vehicle even went so far as to put Doc Ledo's boots in the snow on the edge of the street."

"Well that sounds insane. Who told you this tale?"

"Think about it, Erick. The last thing Ledo remembers was searching for the right 'walking home' music on his phone. Wouldn't he do that as he was leaving the clinic? Not after he'd already walked five or six blocks through The Pines? Clearly whoever ran him down, hit him over on Gunnison Avenue. Then for some reason, known only to them, they loaded him in the back of their truck, drove over to Pin Cherry Lane and staged an accident there. I'm not saying it makes sense, I'm just telling you what my source reported."

Erick leans forward and fixes me with the intimidating stare I'd been working so hard to avoid. "I'll ask you again, Moon, where did you hear the story?"

Here goes nothing. "I'm sorry, Erick, but I can't reveal my sources."

"Nice try, Moon. I'm sure even you realize that protecting a source only applies to journalists." He leans back and rubs his freshly shaven chin. "You can tell me now, or I can charge you with accessory after the fact. Your choice."

"Well that's the thing, Erick. It's all part of a human-interest story I'm doing for the *Post*. So I do have the protection of the fourth estate and I am going to have to protect my sources. You have what you need." I stand and repeat my intel. "1980 blue-and-white Chevy pickup. Silas will be in contact later to see if you've tracked down the driver." I walk toward the door, feeling every one of my heartbeats as though it is a giant kettledrum in an orchestra.

Erick stands, swallows the distance between us in two easy strides, and grasps my arm. "This isn't over."

I've really only got the one tool left in my tool belt, so I step toward him and lean in close as I whisper, "I was hoping you'd say that, Erick."

He immediately drops my arm, mutters something, and stumbles backward.

I leave him sitting on the edge of his desk, flustered, and hopefully wanting more. Let's be clear—more of me, not more information.

I hightail it out of the sheriff's office and straight over to the hospital to update Ledo on my progress.

CHAPTER 19

After a surprisingly upbeat visit with Ledo, I take my overworked hind end to Myrtle's Diner for a well-deserved lunch.

I barely finish stamping the snow off my boots before Tally shouts a happy greeting. "Hey, Mitzy. Coffee or cocoa?"

I take a seat at the counter and ponder my options. "I could use another cup of coffee."

"You betcha." Tally scurries around filling my beverage order.

Odell gives me the ol' spatula salute, and the welcome sizzle of the deep fryer lets me know heaven is on its way.

I grab the abandoned newspaper from the stool next to me and smile when I see the photos of all the flower arrangements at the pet cemetery. Quince did a fantastic job. Even in black and white the arrangements all look beautiful and would surely bring a smile to anyone's face.

"That was a good thing you done." Odell nods toward the paper.

"All I did was make a phone call. It's Doc Ledo that's the real hero around here. In fact, I just came from the hospital."

Tally's hand shakes and she spills a little coffee as she sets down my mug. "Everything okay?"

"He's doing great. When I got there he was just finishing up a meeting with the veterinarian from Broken Rock who's covering for him twice a week, and a traveling veterinarian who's going to cover the office three days a week and handle his house-calls for the livestock clients."

Tally nods and tries to put on a brave face. "Any break in the case?"

"Oh, yes. A big break. I feel like I've told the story so many times that everyone knows. But let me get you up to speed." I give them the extremely shortened version of the eyewitness statement and a description of the vehicle that's been identified.

Odell shakes his head and immediately busies himself with flipping burgers. I have a feeling, much like with Erick, that Odell knows who the driver might be.

"Did the sheriff make an arrest? Are they charging that maniac with attempted murder?" Tally is on the verge of tears.

"Silas is digging into it for me. Hopefully they'll make an arrest this afternoon. Seems like a pretty unique vehicle. But Ledo doesn't want to press charges."

Tally slams the coffee pot on the counter so hard I flinch from the expectation of showering glass. Somehow the amazing pot holds up and I'm spared any injury.

"Why in the H-E-double-hockey-sticks would he not want to press charges?" Tally spins around and marches to the telephone.

I would not want to be Ledo right now. I see her punching the buttons on that wall phone with a vengeance and I can only imagine the ear full of lecture that poor man is about to receive.

Odell sets my plate down and speaks in a low tone. "Come on out back when you're finished."

"You got it." I hope I'm not in trouble, but for now I'm going to enjoy these miraculous fries.

I decide to take an unprecedented approach to my lunch and eat slowly, while I continue reading the paper. I'm definitely impressed with the quality of the photographs. Although the article on page seven, about the Eagles home basketball game, wraps around a fairly blurry picture of the cheerleading squad. Well, I guess they can't all be winners, Quince. Then I notice who's perched at the top of the pyramid—queen of mean, Brynley—and I chuckle. I'd have to say Quince pulled this shot out of focus on purpose rather than accident. I'm liking this kid more and more every day.

I savor the last of my french fries as I read the article about a local philanthropist's generous donation to the Pin Cherry Harbor High School. The obligatory picture of me holding a giant check and shaking the principal's hand nearly makes me spit take my coffee. I look so grown up. Almost like I know what I'm doing. Maybe I should've been an actress? Although, most of what I'm doing seems like I'm making it up as I go along. Maybe improv?

"You about done out there? Somethin' wrong with the food? Never seen ya eat this slow in my life." Odell laughs heartily.

"I was trying on some manners for size. Apparently they don't fit." We share a laugh as I lick the salt off my fingers and wipe my mouth with the thin paper napkin.

I bus my dishes and slip them in the tub behind the counter before I follow Odell out the back door. He takes the ragged cigarette from his shirt pocket, pinches it between his lips, and collects his thoughts.

I stare at that worn nicotine stick and smile. It's just so like Odell to prove to himself every day that he's still strong enough. According to him, he quit smoking fifteen years ago and just keeps the cigarette around like a badge of honor. Anyway, he must've had something to tell me. "So, what's going on?"

"I'm sure Harper will come to the same conclusion as me, but I'm pretty sure that truck you're describing belongs to Johan Olafsson."

Why does that name sound so familiar? Oh right, that's Deputy Paulsen's nemesis. "I've never seen Johan drive anything but a tractor."

Odell nods solemnly. "Yep. Given he's a bit of a drinker, and between the bartender making him weak drinks and the tractor not goin' more than twenty-five miles an hour, it seemed like a pretty good arrangement for everyone involved. But winter isn't the best tractor weather, and it sounds like Johan mighta pulled a fast one on the bartender. Did your witness get a look at the driver?"

"Yeah, but I just reported the information about the vehicle and the staging of the accident." I lower my voice and look around. "Don't mention anything to Tally."

Odell pulls the cigarette from the corner of his mouth and slides it purposefully into the pocket of his faded denim shirt. "What do you mean 'staging' of the accident?"

I proceed to tell him the far-fetched tale of the driver coming down the street, backing up to the precise location across from The Pines, and placing the body on the street.

Odell shakes his head. "I've heard some strange things in my day, but that takes the cake."

"Right? Why would someone who plans to flee the scene of an accident take the time to move the body from Gunnison over to Pin Cherry Lane? And then leave? It makes no sense to me."

"Are you sure the accident happened on Gunnison?"

"I'm only guessing because of what Ledo said about his music. But they clearly moved the body from somewhere."

"Right under that big streetlight on the corner of Spruce and Pin Cherry, right?"

"Yup. That's where Artie pointed on her map of the city streets."

"She always plows The Pines first," mumbles Odell.

Something about that tickles a memory. Think, Mitzy, think. What was it that Artie said? Ah ha! "Except that night she didn't."

"What do you mean?"

"Well, she told me not to say anything, but Artie plowed the streets over by the park first, so everyone could get to the Extravaganza. Then she went around, plowed Gunnison, and came in to The Pines from the far side. Not her usual route."

Odell runs a hand through his grey buzz cut and nods his head slowly. "So if Toledo was hit on Gunnison and the driver knew Artie's route . . . Seems like he moved the doc's body so it would be discovered sooner."

"So you're saying this guy, Johan, has a conscience?"

"Of course. Just because he drinks too much once in a while doesn't mean he hasn't got a heart of gold."

A moment of silence hangs between us and I know we're both thinking about my grandmother and the way her drinking problem tore apart her relationship with Odell—despite the fact that she also has a heart of gold.

"Maybe that's why Ledo doesn't want to press charges?"

"If Sheriff Harper goes for a felony, it won't matter what Doc Ledo wants."

"Then I guess I'd better keep digging. Since my client wouldn't want that to happen."

"You're a good kid, Mitzy. Let's keep this just

between us." Odell pats me on the shoulder and leads the way back inside.

"Mmhmm." Just between me and Odell—and Grams, and Silas.

I'm so amped up I can't possibly wait until I get back to the bookstore. I pull out my phone to call Silas as I'm rushing down the sidewalk.

CRASH!

I fall backward onto the salt-covered sidewalk and my phone flies into a snowbank.

"Mitzy!" Strong arms scoop me up and set me on my feet.

However, I stop the extending hand before it can complete its mission to brush the snow off my behind. "I can handle that part." I brush off the snow and look up into the concerned face of Rory Bombay.

"Are you all right? I was gazing up at the trail that airplane was leaving and the way the sun was illuminating— Anyway, I was distracted and I can't apologize enough for crashing into you. Are you sure you're not hurt?"

I have absolutely no intention of telling Rory how many times I've bounced off my ample backside, but I also don't have time for a pity party. "I'm fine. Honestly, I'm just fine. I really have to get back to the bookshop."

"Let me escort you. Just to make sure there's no further incident."

"Oh, don't worry about it. Excuse me. I need to get my phone. I slide past him and begin digging through the mound of snow left by whoever shoveled the sidewalk. I hope I'm actually searching around the approximate trajectory that my phone took. The snow clings to my mittens, and as it starts to melt the frigid water almost burns my skin with cold.

A firm hand grips my shoulder. "Allow me. You'll get frostbite with those thin woolen mittens. Really, it's the least I can do." Rory pulls me to my feet and drops down on one knee to take over my search.

I want to blurt out that his stupid ring almost killed me. But I just can't seem to square the two things in my mind. A diabolical man giving me some kind of magically poisoned ring doesn't reconcile with the kind gentleman down on his knees in the dirty street snow digging for my phone. Especially not when I'm the one who wasn't paying attention because I was messing with my— Oh my gosh! Ledo's phone! That's it!

"Ah, here it is, Miss Moon." Rory stands, wipes off my phone on his pants, and hands it to me as though it were a priceless bottle of wine.

"Thanks. I gotta go, but thanks." I break into an

uncharacteristic jog and head down the alleyway to one of my garages. Next stop, Gunnison Avenue.

As I drive toward the veterinary clinic, I make a desperate plea to my mood ring.

"Look, I don't really understand how you work or even why you work, but I really need to find Toledo's phone and I really need your help. So, I'm going to get out there and dig my little fingers within an inch of their life and I need you to point them in the right direction. Deal?"

I hold my breath as I wait for the smallest flicker of a sign from my moody mood ring. The irony is not lost on me.

No sign is forthcoming.

I pull into the parking lot of the clinic and walk to the front door. Then I make a one-hundred-and-eighty-degree turn and walk slowly toward the street. As I approach Gunnison Avenue, I look for any signs that may possibly remain to indicate there was an accident.

I'm reasonably sure that the plow came down the road after Doc Ledo was struck. The prospect of digging through three or four feet of icy snowbank to try to find his phone does not entice.

I walk back and forth in front of the clinic, struggling to come up with a better plan.

A lovely young woman with a rambunctious Siberian husky approaches from the parking lot.

"Are you waiting for your fur baby?"

I suppose I do look like an anxious parent waiting to hear if I've had triplets or quadruplets. "No, thanks though." Inspiration strikes. "I slipped and my phone flew out of my hand and went into the snowbank. I was just trying to work up the courage to start digging for it.

She laughs uproariously and slaps her thigh.

I'm about to give her a piece of my mind concerning how rude it is to laugh at someone's misfortune when she drops some knowledge on me.

"Well today is your lucky day. Mistletoe is the best darn digger this side of the Arctic Circle. You point her in a direction and she'll dig clear to China."

I suppress the need to tell her that you can't actually dig to China, and pledge to let that childhood myth remain. Now, if I can just get a tiny bit of co-operation from my ring.

"Oh my gosh! That's the best news I've had all day. Let me retrace my steps and see if I can at least narrow down the area for little Mistletoe. And then we'll just let her dig, right?"

The lady nods her head. She hunkers down to give Mistletoe a pep talk, and I whisper some encouraging words to my ring.

Stepping off the curb, roughly where I imagine Toledo took his last step, I try to visualize the blue-

and-white truck impacting me on the left side. If Ledo was holding his phone— And then the vision hits me. I feel the impact. I see the phone fly out of my hand, so high in the air . . . I can feel my body hurtle through space and slam into the street. And my phone . . . My phone lands all the way in the opposing lane of traffic. I bend over and place my hands on my knees as I struggle to catch my breath. The imagery was so vivid, and the feelings so real, I'm a little bit dizzy.

"Hey, are you okay?"

"Oh yeah. I guess I'm probably coming down with something. I'm sorry. I think my phone is over there." I point across the street.

She looks at me like I might be a little crazy.

By my calculations, if Toledo's phone landed in the lane of oncoming traffic it's pretty likely that Artie plowed it into the snowbank across the street when she came up Gunnison from plowing the area around the park.

"All right. Come on, Mistletoe, let's go find this phone."

I have to admire this lady's belief in her puppers.

We check traffic and jog across the street.

My left ring finger tugs toward the embankment. Finally! Some help from my ring. My hand pulls toward the snowbank as I move it back and forth like a dowsing rod. I feel heat increase as I move to the right.

Mistletoe follows so closely I'm starting to wonder if she can sense the heat from the ring?

"Right here. I think this is where it landed."

To the lady's credit, she seems to believe me and not think that I'm completely insane. She let's Mistletoe off-leash. "Dig deep, Missy. Dig deep," she encourages the husky.

I cannot believe my eyes as I watch this Tasmanian devil-dog dig into the snowbank like it contains the juiciest pile of treats a dog could ever imagine. Mistletoe rears up on her back legs, pounces down with her two front paws together and digs like a mad dog. I stupidly reach for my actual phone in my pocket, because I really want to film this anomaly. Thankfully, a moment of lucidity stops me from pulling out the very phone she's supposedly digging for, and I instead join the chant. "Dig deep, Missy. Dig deep."

Less than thirty seconds later, that magnificent beast has nearly disappeared into the snowbank.

Mistletoe's owner looks at me and smiles. "She's amazing isn't she?"

I nod fervently. "She's incredible."

Suddenly the digging stops.

"What is it, Missy? You got that phone, Missy?"

Here's the moment of truth. Is this lady absolutely bonkers? Is her dog going to back out of that hole with nothing more than a cold muzzle?

Mistletoe reverses out of the snow-tunnel, and to my utter shock, is holding a cell phone gently in her mouth.

"Holy mackerel." I crouch down and hold out my hand. Mistletoe walks over and drops the phone in my hand like it's a tennis ball and we've been playing this game for hours.

Mistletoe's owner pulls some treats from the pocket of her winter coat and hands what looks like a delicious strip of beef jerky to the husky.

"Thank you so much! You have no idea—"

"Oh, think nothing of it. You made Mistletoe's day. She just loves to dig."

"Well, I can't thank you enough. But, if you wouldn't mind, I'd like to do a story on you and Mistletoe for the *Post*. I'm a freelance reporter and I just think it would make a great feel-good piece for this week's edition."

I lean down and pat Mistletoe profusely. "What do you say? A nice little human-interest story to lift everyone's holiday spirits?"

"Oh, what the heck."

I follow her inside the clinic to get a piece of paper and write down all of the particulars, because thank goodness the phone we recovered from the snowbank is dead, giving me the perfect excuse not to be able to tap out some notes on "my phone."

After we exchange the information, I give Mistletoe another pat of gratitude and make my escape before the receptionist asks the reason for my visit.

As I drive back to the bookstore, I call Silas. Where to begin . . .

CHAPTER 20

On my way back to the Bell, Book & Candle, I can't help but wonder if Silas will be able to get to Johan before Erick. I don't actually agree with Ledo's decision not to press charges, but I'm extremely curious to know why Mr. Olafsson moved the body. Part of me even worries that moving the body caused more serious injury than the initial impact. However, after the sensory overload of imagery that I was forced to relive in front of the veterinary clinic, I can't imagine anything worse than the impact.

Oh, *Little Rascals*. I missed my turn. With a quick check in the rearview, I back up, and slip down the alley.

After I close the garage door, but before I'm safely inside, Mr. Bombay appears in the alley.

"This is the second time today, Rory. I'm thinking it can't be an accident."

"You found me out. I was hoping you'd allow me to take you out for a slice of pie and some coffee this afternoon. I enjoyed our lunch together and I thought perhaps we needed one more engagement before you'd to agree to dinner."

I definitely want to confront him about the ring, but if he has an evil master plan I don't think I want to learn about it in this alley. A public place seems like a safer bet. And a public place where I know someone's got my back seems even safer. "I will agree on two conditions."

Rory bows. "Agreed. Name your conditions."

"First of all, you agree to answer any and all of my questions, honestly. Nothing is off limits. Nothing is placed on hold."

Rory's eyes darken, but he nods his agreement. "And the second condition?"

"That you admit here and now that you lied about the pin cherry pie at Myrtle's Diner. I want you to acknowledge that you repeated unverified gossip, because I know for a fact that Odell makes his own pie from a family recipe."

Rory chuckles warmly. "You got me. The owner of the patisserie is a bit of a gossip, and I took her at her word without bothering to check the facts. I acquiesce."

I grin smugly. “Good. Now let’s go to Myrtle’s Diner and have a slice of Pin Cherry Harbor’s best pin cherry pie.”

He offers me his elbow, which I take.

“Would you say it’s too cold for pie à la mode?”

I laugh openly. “Never.”

Tucked into a squeaky-clean booth at the diner, Rory orders us two slices of pin cherry pie à la mode and two cups of coffee.

“Would you excuse me for one moment?”

I nod, and he gets up and walks to the counter.

“Pardon me, Odell?”

Odell looks up without the characteristic warmth in his eyes and nods.

“I owe you an apology, sir. I unwittingly repeated some gossip and I apologize for impugning your reputation.” Rory nods.

Odell shrugs and mumbles his thanks.

Rory returns to the booth, sits down, and looks at me with an adorable plea in his green eyes. “Enough penance, Miss Moon?”

I try to ignore the warm tingle in my tummy. “For today.”

He slides his hand across the table and strokes the back of my hand.

Unfortunately, the gesture reminds me of what I really need to ask him about. I lean back and put both my hands in my lap. Resting the left on top so that a casual glance down will show me any message I might be lucky enough to get from my ring.

"You're not wearing the ring I gave you. Did you not like it?"

I toy with the idea of making up a story about being allergic to the metal, but that wouldn't give me the answers I need. On the other hand, I can hardly tell him the truth about my psychic powers, so I attempt to split the difference. "I had a strange reaction to the ring and Silas told me I shouldn't wear it."

Rory clenches his jaw, and I can see him weighing his own options. "What type of reaction?"

Touché. Perhaps he's better at this game than I am. "It's a little hard to describe. Maybe it was an allergy, but I definitely felt unwell." That's as near as I can come to the truth, and I hope it's enough to get me an answer.

"My apologies." He takes a deep breath and mumbles, "I should've known."

I lean forward. "Should've known what?"

He stares at me with a hint of intrigue lighting his gaze. "I suppose I wasn't entirely honest."

I knew it. Well, Silas knew it, but we knew it.

"I didn't get the ring at an estate sale. I fabricated that bit, because I didn't want you to refuse the gift. I assumed that if you knew I'd spent a tidy sum on it you would feel undue obligation. And I honestly thought it was a beautiful ring and didn't intend it to mean more than what it was—a friendly gift."

"All right. So what is it that you should've known?"

"The woman I bought it from has somewhat of a reputation in this town."

If he's about to tell me there's some version of *The Best Little Whorehouse in Texas* in Pin Cherry Harbor, I will eat my hat. And for only the second time in my life I'm actually wearing a hat, so the possibility is quite real. "A woman of ill repute?"

Rory laughs a little too long at my expense. "You are the most refreshing combination of brilliance and humor, and of course beauty. But let me get back to my story."

Odell sets our plates on the table with one hand and somehow manages to add two cups of coffee to the spread with the other. The man has skills.

"Thanks, Odell. I'm really looking forward to this." I wink.

He shrugs and heads back into the kitchen.

All right. He doesn't like Mr. Bombay. Is there a secret club I don't know about? Do they have jackets? I take a bite of golden, flaky crust, with delicious just-sweet-enough filling, and melty ice cream oozing over it all, and I forgive Odell all of his sins.

"You were right about the pie, Mitzy. It is the

best." Rory scoops a forkful of his own sinful slice and leans across the table to feed it to me.

My cheeks flush, but I'm no fool. I take the bite. "So tell me about this woman."

"Ah, yes. Ania Karina Nowak. A Polish gypsy who has a palm reading and tarot shop on the outskirts of town."

"How scandalous. That can't go over well with the locals."

"Indeed. It would appear that your grandmother was one of the leaders of the group that got the shop closed down, temporarily. I always heard about their decades-long feud, but I didn't think much of it, until today."

"What do you mean?"

"I bought the ring from Ania. I may have made the mistake of mentioning for whom the ring was intended. She no doubt made the connection between 'new owner of the bookshop' and the rumors about Isadora's heir."

Wow, seems like Grams really held some sway in this town. "What are you saying?"

"I know you're going to think it sounds crazy, but perhaps Ania put a gypsy curse on the ring. Terribly sorry. Perhaps I can take it back to her and convince her to remove the curse."

I swallow my delicious pie, but it feels a little like sand in my throat. Psychic powers. Alchemy.

Gypsy curses. Where does it end? And why does it sound like Rory believes that a Gypsy curse is real?

"I'm sure you're wondering why I would believe in a Gypsy curse." He chuckles. "My mother was very superstitious. I'm sure I grew up believing a lot of things that other people would find foolish. I throw salt over my left shoulder if I spill it. If I drop a knife, I know a man is coming to visit. If I see a penny, I pick it up. Mostly silly things that others ignore."

I take another bite of pie and toy with my next move. "Is Bombay your real name?"

He smiles a smile that could melt an igloo in two minutes flat.

I tear my eyes away and gulp down some coffee to cover my discomfort.

"It is. Happy to show you my driver's license, if that helps."

"No need. It's not like Mizithra is a common name. I get it." I lift my mug, but before I can take another sip of my coffee, he reaches across the table and wipes the tip of my chin with his thumb.

"You had a little ice cream there."

Oh boy, red flags, sirens, tingles. He's just too good to be true.

"Miss Moon, I'm afraid I need you to come down to the station. I had another conversation with Quince Knudsen and he let it slip that he'd met you before that day in my office." Erick raises a suspicious eyebrow and stares knowingly.

Wait? What? I didn't hear the door open. There was certainly no indication on Rory's face that Erick was approaching. This can't be happening. The man is immune to my advances and yet he seems to do everything in his power to make sure no one else accepts them either. I'm just about to unleash some choice words when Rory beats me to the punch.

"Tell you what, Sheriff Harper. As soon as Mitzy and I finish our pie, I'll escort her over to the station. I assume you're asking her to come in voluntarily and not officially, correct?"

Erick crosses his well-muscled arms over his broad chest and I blush a little. "Cooperation would be her best option at this point, Mr. Bombay."

"Very well, we'll see you shortly." The dismissive tone in Rory's voice is admirable.

Erick turns his baby blues on me and adds very officially, "See you shortly, Moon." He saunters out of the diner and it takes every ounce of self-control I possess not to turn and look over my shoulder.

Rory's hand reaches across the table and grasps my fingers. "Is there something I should know about you and Sheriff Harper?"

As far as I know, there's absolutely nothing he should know about Sheriff Harper and me. I suppose a humorous answer would be the best thing to diffuse the situation. “Only that he’s accused me of murder twice since I’ve moved to this town.”

Rory chuckles. “That’s not exactly what I meant, but it’s good to know.”

CHAPTER 21

I FEEL a little guilty about ducking out on Erick's summons and sneaking back to the Bell, Book & Candle, but there's no way I'm going into the station without Silas. Lucky for me, my alchemist-attorney is engaged in a pantomime game of charades with Grams.

"I am so glad to see the two of you," I exclaim as the bookcase slides closed. "I've had the weirdest day!"

Silas nods and Grams glares at me.

"Oh, sorry. Did you guys need an interpreter?"

"Well, what do you think, young lady?" Grams rests her ghostly fists on her hips. "Silas has just informed me that the emerald ring you accepted from Rory Bombay is cursed!" She shoots up to the ceiling like a phantom rocket and clucks her tongue with worry.

Silas straightens his faded green bowtie and harrumphs into his mustache. "I believe she was attempting to convince me to formulate some fashion of retaliation against Mr. Bombay."

Ghost-ma torpedoes from the ceiling, straight through me as she hollers, "You're darn tootin'!"

"Wow. You two really got into it while I was— away." Now seems like the wrong time to tell them that I was having pie and ice cream with— Oops, almost sold myself out.

"With who?" Grams floats in front of my face with a heap of otherworldly vengeance oozing from her aura.

"With whom," I correct.

"Why you little . . ."

Ignoring Grams' tantrum, I address the room. "I have several very interesting pieces of information to share, and if Grams can calm down for one second, I think I can clear up this whole mess."

Silas gazes through his enchanted spectacles and locates Grams. "Isadora, I believe we owe it to Mitzy to hear her side of things before we select a course of action."

Grams vanishes into the wall and I take that as further protest, but choose to shoulder on. By the time I'm halfway into the story of Mistletoe and the missing phone, Grams materializes behind Silas.

"Do you mean to tell me that you recovered Doctor Toledo's cellular phone from a snowbank on Gunnison Avenue?"

I nod triumphantly. "That is exactly what I'm telling you, and can you believe how my ring was working like a homing beacon?"

"I would postulate that your explanation would indicate that a dowsing rod is a more accurate description, but either way it is an impressive find. You will have to turn the cellular phone in to the sheriff and make a formal statement."

"Yeah, Erick came into the diner and asked me to stop by the station. Well, it was more like a demand, but I didn't want to go in until I brought you guys up to speed."

"I will place a call on your behalf and attempt to buy us a few days respite from the Sheriff's summons." Silas strokes his mustache and wags his head.

"Any luck getting a hold of Johan?"

"His daughter was house sitting for him, with her three offspring. She said he and Marguerite were in Canada."

"That seems sketchy. Did she say why?"

"She did not." Silas removes the wire-rimmed

glasses. "What does 'sketchy' have to do with travel?"

"Sketchy just means that it seems shady, like not on the up-and-up. I mean, do you think he's running from the law?"

"She agreed to pass along my message, so perhaps we will have a better understanding once we talk to Mr. Olafsson."

Grams can no longer keep silent. "And what does this phone recovery have to do with that wicked Mr. Bombay?"

"Oh, I forgot all about the Polish gypsy!"

Grams immediately avoids eye contact and Silas shakes his head. I share the story of the ring and make every effort to lift all blame from Rory's shoulders as I paint the picture of a vindictive, wronged gypsy.

"I was hoping to avoid this discussion, Mitzy. However, I fear I must be the one to inform you that your grandmother made her fair share of enemies in her lifetime. Not the least of which was the Polish gypsy woman who resides on the outskirts of town, Ania Karina Nowak."

My head is swimming with thoughts, ideas, and concerns. "And you think this Polish gypsy woman somehow knows about my gifts? Why else would she curse a ring in a specific way that would overload my psychic powers and make me sick?"

"Your grandmother and this woman didn't see eye to eye about all things clairvoyant. Isadora thought this woman to be a fraud and said as much, quite publicly."

"Meaning?"

"I believe the sheriff, at the time, took punitive action and the gypsy woman was forced to close her palm-reading shop, at least temporarily."

Grams materializes next to Silas. "She was bilking money from people who couldn't afford it. I'm telling you, I did this community a favor. Tell him what I said, Mitzy. Tell him."

I relay her message to Silas and he slips his magicked spectacles from his pocket and puts them on. "My dear Isadora, there are perhaps at least two sides to each tale. You can hardly expect your granddaughter to make a judicious choice with only half a story."

"Half a story! Half the story was all that Polish witch ever gave. It makes perfect sense that she would be selling half-baked curses! She's probably already opened another business and she's just looking for more ways to bamboozle hard-working citizens."

"So you don't think this has anything to do with me?"

Silas shakes his head slowly and his saggy jowls jostle back and forth. "I would suspect that this woman indeed knowingly cursed the ring before selling it to Mr. Bombay. She would have every reason to strike back at something Isadora holds dear."

"How would she—"

"If she has knowledge of your relation to Isadora, perhaps she merely suspects you possess a gift. Conceivably this cursed ring was merely a test. You must inform Rory to keep your reaction from the woman. The last thing we want to do is confirm her suspicions."

"The ring? Can you uncurse it or something?"

"I will endeavor to discern the mechanism of the curse and postulate a disruption. However, it is possible that you will not be able to wear the ring."

"You mean, ever?"

"Indeed." Silas's phone rings and interrupts our bizarre debate.

"Good afternoon. Silas Willoughby speaking. How may I be of assistance?"

Yikes, he really takes manners to the next level.

"You could learn a thing or two from him, young lady."

"Listen, Grams, I don't know what you've got against Rory, but once again he's innocent of your accusations. I really think you need to give him another chance. People change."

Grams rolls her eyes and dematerializes.

I open my mouth to scold her, but Silas interrupts.

"Mr. Olafsson has returned from Canada. I suggest we head over to the farm at once. It won't take long for Sheriff Harper to catch wind of their arrival."

CHAPTER 22

THE ONLY CONVERSATION on the way out to the Olafsson farm is the monotony of Silas giving me directions. When I pull up in front of an efficient, white, two-story farmhouse, Silas reaches over and places his hand on top of mine on the steering wheel.

"I should like to do most of the talking, do you understand?"

I really don't understand. But I do get the feeling that Silas has a subtlety that I lack. "All right. Whatever you say."

"Thank you." We trudge through the freshly shoveled path, climb the steps, and knock on the front door.

The man who answers looks decades older than

the man I remember seeing on the tractor driving down Main Street.

Silas extends his hand. "Thank you for seeing us, Johan."

Mr. Olafsson weakly shakes my attorney's outstretched hand and invites us into the living room. He offers us neither refreshment nor seats as he collapses into a recliner.

"May we sit down, Johan?"

The man in the chair looks up at us as though he's unsure how we got into his house. "What? Oh, of course. Yes, have a seat." He leans forward with his elbows on his knees and runs his hands through his hair, haphazardly attempting to smooth it into place.

"We're sorry to have bothered you so late in the day. How's Marguerite?"

The hollow-eyed stare that peers out at Silas and me is haunting and heartbreaking. My mood ring shifts to darkest blue and my stomach tightens in preparation for what I know is going to be horrible news.

"She's not well. She's not well at all. She's got six more of them radiation treatments before they can even tell us if they're working. We keep drivin' over to Montreal to that there proton beam machine. But all it seems to be doing so far is wearing her down.

It's almost like she's sicker now than before we started the treatments." He leans back in the chair and sighs heavily—the sound of a broken man who's holding his family together with a thread of hope stretched so thin, it could snap at any moment.

Silas nods and looks at me out of the corner of his eye.

"I'm so sorry to hear that, Johan. Marguerite has always been a kind woman and I do hope the very best for her, and your family. Is there anything we can do?"

Johan stares blankly at both of us. It's clear the weight of his wife's illness has pushed him near to breaking. He says nothing.

"I hesitate to put any more on your plate, but I feel you should know that the sheriff will most likely pay you a visit this evening or first thing in the morning."

The look in Johan's eyes speaks volumes. It's not the wild, panicked look of a cornered animal, it's the look of a man who's just one burden away from giving up.

Silas takes a deep breath and continues, "An eyewitness has come forward and identified the vehicle that struck down Doc Ledo."

Johan nods but doesn't speak or show any emotion.

"The story we heard is that the doctor was

struck by a blue-and-white 1980 Chevy pickup truck on Gunnison Avenue in front of the clinic."

This information does get a reaction from our host. He leans forward and swallows before his fingers grip the arms of the chair so hard his knuckles turn white.

"And believe it or not, the eyewitness says the driver of the vehicle then moved the doctor's body over to where it was actually discovered on Pin Cherry Lane."

I admire the way Silas seamlessly blends the actual eyewitness stuff with the "from Mitzy's psychic visions" stuff.

Johan slowly shakes his head and his shoulders slump forward.

"The driver must've had a good reason." Silas pauses, and the distant ticking of a clock resounds like a gong in the silence. "If there's any way I can help you, I will. Can you tell us what happened?"

The soft, encouraging timbre of Silas's voice nearly forces me to confess to a crime I didn't commit.

Johan wrings his hands two or three times as he stares fixedly at the floor. "I don't know how much the two of you know about getting old or about medical insurance, but neither one of them is anything like it's cracked up to be. Insurance don't seem to cover nothing, and gettin' old happens faster than you ever thought it would. When Marguerite got sick, we figured she'd take a few pills, maybe have to slow down a little, and that would be that. But when the tests came back, they told us she had some rare form of brain cancer that could only be treated with this special machine they got down at the Mayo Clinic. Well, we thought that was the worst news we'd ever heard."

"That must've been tough on both of you."

"That wasn't even the tough part. Tough part came when the insurance company said they wouldn't cover the proton therapy treatments because the provider was outside our network and somethin' about experimental treatments. You get the idea. Only one cure. Big expensive treatment. Insurance ain't gonna pay. So, seein' as how Marguerite is French-Canadian, with dual citizenship and what not, we figured we'd head up to Canada and take advantage of that socialist medicine. So, the treatments are every two weeks and it's an eighteen-hour drive, one way, to the only facility in Canada."

Silas nods. "That must be very difficult for her when she's feeling so ill."

I shake my head silently, unable to add anything meaningful to the conversation.

Johan takes a ragged breath and finally looks up from the floor. His eyes plead for understanding.

"He just stepped out right in front of me. You see, one minute he was standing on the curb looking at his phone, and the next—BAM! There was nothin' I coulda done."

"We know. We know." Silas waits a beat before asking, "But why didn't you call an ambulance?"

"Ah, you know me, Silas. I never know when to quit, always have one too many. Maybe I was driving too fast. Either way, you know they're gonna take my license. Then who's gonna drive Marguerite to her treatments?" His head falls into his hands and he mumbles, "Couldn't let 'em take my license. Couldn't let that happen." He wrings his hands and exhales long and slow. "I moved him over to Pin Cherry Lane so Artie would find him right away."

Despite Silas telling me to let him do all the talking, I can't take this any longer. I don't have the heart to tell Johan that Artie changed her route that night, but I have to do something. I kneel down next to Johan and place my hand on his knee. "Mr. Olafsson, I realize you don't really know me. But Doc Ledo is going to be paralyzed. And, in spite of that, he doesn't want to press charges. But if you sit here and wait for Erick to hunt you down, it's going to be bad. There's just no way out."

He sighs deeply.

"Johan, the best thing you can do is surrender

yourself to the sheriff. Get ahead of this thing, and let me help you. Like Mitzy said, the sheriff has the information about the vehicle. And if you wait for him to apprehend you, I'm afraid this whole thing could go sideways and then where will Marguerite be?"

"Maybe we just leave for Canada right now, and won't come back."

"Look, Mr. Olafsson, you seem like a good man. I don't see how you could live with yourself if you don't do the right thing. But I promise you, Silas will do everything he can to help you and—" I look at Silas and he nods for me to continue "—I will make sure that Marguerite doesn't miss a single treatment. All right?"

Silas mutters his agreement. "I recommend you call the sheriff before time runs out." He passes his phone to Johan.

The aging, brokenhearted farmer stares at the cell phone for a long time. And before he makes his decision, the soft shuffle of feet echoes from the hallway as Marguerite, head wrapped in a turban, dark circles under her eyes, enters the room.

Johan looks up with eyes full of love and admiration.

Marguerite smiles weakly. "My life—is not worth your soul. This too shall pass, my love."

He takes a hold of Silas's phone and presses "call."

I return to my place on the couch beside my amazing lawyer, and friend. Silas gives my knee a fatherly pat, and we both wait with bated breath while Mr. Olafsson tells his story to Sheriff Harper. By the time he's finished and hands the phone back to Silas, Marguerite has returned to bed, and the three of us are once again alone in the living room.

"He said if I come on down to the station tomorrow morning and turn myself in, it'll go a long way to making things right. He also said I should probably get a lawyer." Johan looks hopefully at Silas.

Silas chuckles lightly. "It goes without saying that you'll be well represented." He nods and rises from the couch.

I follow suit and Silas pats Johan firmly on the shoulder as we walk to the front door. "Shall we say 9:00 a.m. at the station?"

"Yes, sir."

As we're stepping out the front door, Johan calls meekly, "You'll tell Doc Ledo how sorry I am, won't you?"

I turn and nod. "Absolutely! I absolutely will."

CHAPTER 23

I AWAKEN to the silent predawn darkness and I know in my gut I won't be falling back asleep. I roll over to scratch Pyewacket, but his usual spot on the bed next to me is empty.

I whisper into the gloom, "Pye? Pyewacket, where are you?"

"Why are you whispering, dear?"

"*Robinson Crusoe!* Really, Grams, first thing in the morning? When I have a full bladder? You're not playing fair."

"Oh, Mitzy. You're too much."

I roll out of bed and stumble to the bathroom. I can't believe it, but there's absolutely no way I'm going to fall back asleep, and it's starting to feel like getting up early is becoming a habit. A terrible habit, which I intend breaking as soon as possible.

A ghostly chuckle drifts through the wall.

"You don't know me. I could become an early bird, you'll see."

"All right, whatever you say."

"So where's Pyewacket?"

"He went slinking out of here in the middle of the night and never returned. I didn't see any trouble, but he's been sitting by that back door like someone was paying him to be on watch duty."

My brain is far from its peak performance at this hour, but I know Pyewacket seldom does anything by accident. I dress quickly and rush downstairs. As promised, Pye is sitting in front of the back door on high alert.

"What are you up to?"

He turns and adds another row of claw marks to the well-scratched metal door.

I open it, thinking he means to take a morning run, but as soon as the frosty air hits his whiskers he bounds back into the bowels of the bookshop.

I'm about to slam the door against the cold when I notice an envelope wedged under a small box.

Opening the door a bit farther, I venture a peek up and down the alley.

Empty.

I snatch the box and envelope and hurry back

upstairs. I set both items on the coffee table and wait for Grams to appear.

"Who from?"

"I'm not sure. Pyewacket wasn't exactly forthcoming."

"What do you mean?"

"He scratched the back door, and when I opened it to let him out he ran back inside and I discovered this package."

"Is it from that horrible gypsy woman?" Grams arches a perfectly drawn brow.

"No idea. The envelope is blank and the box is pretty nondescript. Do you think I should open it?"

"I suppose . . ."

With my limited paranormal knowledge, I have a growing distrust for inexplicable items appearing out of thin air. I grab my phone, swipe up Silas's phone number, and instruct Grams, "If things go sideways when I open this up, you call Silas, all right?"

"I'll do my best, honey."

I start with the envelope, carefully sliding my finger under the flap, loosening the seal, and removing the note. "It looks like a man's handwriting."

"'Dearest Mitzy, I feel terrible about the cursed ring and I'd like to beg for your forgiveness. I would greatly appreciate an opportunity to make it up to you. Please allow me the pleasure of escorting you to dinner at Yves Bistro tomorrow night. The enclosed gift is yours to keep regardless of your answer, and it is most assuredly un-cursed! See you at breakfast, R.'"

Grams cracks off a long, low whistle. "That man is full of surprises and utterly relentless. I suppose you'll have to go to supper."

I set down the card and look at Grams with more shock than anything else. "Hold on a minute. Do you suddenly approve of Mr. Bombay? The terrible, horrible, no good, very bad man?"

Grams waves her bejeweled hand dismissively in my direction. "Never look a gift horse in the mouth, dear."

"I have no idea what that means, Grams. But it sounds to me like you're saying that your affections can be purchased."

I'm not sure if you've ever been chased by an angry ghost before, but they are very hard to out run. When I finally collapse onto the bed in a heap of giggles, Grams is laughing at least as hard as me.

She catches her breath first. Which I suppose is no surprise, since she's a ghost and really doesn't need the air. "Well, are you going to open that little box or not?"

"As you wish." I walk back to the coffee table, sit down in the scalloped-back chair, and carefully open the box. Inside, curled into a somehow perfect blooming rose, is a gorgeous pair of red, kidskin-leather winter gloves.

"The man has taste."

"And a flair for the romantic gesture."

I bring Grams up to speed on my horrible thin-wool-mittens-digging-through-the-snowbank incident and she fans herself with one hand. "Oh my, that is dashing."

"All right, Grams, enough girl talk. I gotta get some breakfast and get over to see Doc Ledo. I've decided that since Johan is turning himself in today, there's no reason for me to take Ledo's phone to the sheriff's station."

"Aren't you looking for an excuse to see Erick? Weighing your options?"

"Cut it out. In case you haven't noticed, there are no options to weigh. If we count all of the invitations to dinner I've received, the grand total is one."

"You know what they say, Mitzy, a bird in the hand is worth two in the bush."

"A stitch in time saves nine, don't cry over spilt milk, curiosity killed the cat?"

"REE-ow!" The sound of imminent retribution.

"Sorry, Pye! It was just a joke."

"Honestly! Just go to your breakfast." She chuckles under her breath.

"See you later, Grams. Love you." I glance over

my shoulder to give a wave and lo and behold ghost tears are pouring down my grandmother's face. "What is it? What did I say?"

"It's just—I love you too, sweetie."

Big girl emotions are not my strong suit, so I head out of the bookshop and over to the diner. The usual Friday morning crowd occupies the four-top by the front window and the booth in the back corner. My newspaper guy is sitting on one of the stools at the counter. I take a seat at the end of the counter and give Odell a nod. "I'll have the special, please"

He smiles and says, "What's the word?"

"Let's see . . . I solved the case—make that cases—I'm turning in my first story for the *Post* today, and, no big deal, but I have a date tomorrow night."

Odell chuckles heartily and jumps on the last car in my information train. "So Erick finally took the hint?"

A deep voice rumbles just behind me and sends a delicious tingle up my spine. "Actually, I'm hoping the honor will be all mine." Rory slips onto the stool next to me and grins expectantly.

"Yes, I'm accepting your invitation to dinner."

He smiles and nods pleasantly.

I'm happy to see he's not gloating. And when I glance up at Odell through the orders up window, his expression leans toward pleased. Which is probably the best I can hope for right now. I'm not sure how Rory got his reputation in this town, but opinions don't change overnight, especially not in almost-Canada. People seem pretty set in their ways up here.

"I only caught the tail end of that, which in my opinion was the best part, but what else is going on in your life besides a wonderful dinner tomorrow night?"

"I have a busy day, but I did solve the case."

Roy tilts his head with a little too much shock and says, "You don't say?"

I lean forward and nod meaningfully. "I do say. Maybe you haven't heard, but I have a pretty good track record." However, my shoulders droop when I think about Johan and Marguerite's situation. "To be honest, I'm actually not that happy I solved this one."

Tally slides a cup of coffee in front of me. "Nonsense. You did the right thing. And even if Ledo won't press charges, I'm certain the sheriff will."

"Well, I'm sure there's no point keeping it from you any longer. The driver's going to turn himself in this morning."

Tally steps back and swallows. "Who was it?"

I shake my head. "Unfortunately, it was Johan Olafsson. The worst part is—" I stop myself from joining the small-town gossip pool. It's one thing to tell everyone the name of the person who was driving the car; that information will be in the paper and the police report. Public knowledge. But it's not my place to share their personal business. No, my place will be to take care of setting up the rest of Marguerite's appointments. And making sure Johan's legal fees are covered by the Foundation.

Odell brings out my breakfast. "So what's this about an article for the *Post*? You writing about the case?"

I laugh a little too bitterly. "I've never been all that comfortable tooting my own horn. I'm actually writing a human-interest piece. I'm hoping Mr. Knudsen will run it on Sunday."

Odell wraps his knuckles twice on the silver-flecked white counter and says, "He'd be a fool not to," before returning to the kitchen.

Rory orders a cinnamon roll and coffee while I power through my breakfast.

Eager to get on with my day, I thank Odell, bus my dishes, and accept a hug from Tally. As I'm headed toward the door a gentle reminder reaches my ear.

"Shall I pick you up at four-thirty tomorrow?"

I turn and catch just a flicker of doubt in Rory's eyes, and I smile reassuringly. "Yes, four-thirty at the bookshop. Is there any dress code?"

"I'm wearing a suit, if that helps?"

"That definitely gives— me something to go on." Once again, I almost said Grams, and one of these days I'm definitely going to slip up. With a final wave to all, I head out the front door to the hospital to give Ledo his phone. The screen is cracked, but I imagine it'll still hold a charge.

CHAPTER 24

Breaking news Saturday morning is: "Johan Olafsson identified as hit-and-run driver that struck down Dr. Toledo Sikanen the night of the Yuletide Extravaganza."

I'm happy to report that between Doc Ledo's generosity and Erick's big heart, Johan is facing the minimum sentence of ninety days in county jail and a one-thousand-dollar fine—and we've already posted his bail. I've arranged transportation and payment for Marguerite to finish her proton-beam therapy treatments at the Mayo Clinic in Rochester. It's a shorter drive than Montreal, and should be quite a bit easier for her in the long run. Once again, I'm grateful for the Duncan-Moon Foundation.

The drive out to Stellen's house is longer than I remember, but the beauty of the snow-swept fields and ice-dusted pine trees fills the ride with splendid distractions.

Stellen chose Saturday rather than Sunday for our trip to Broken Rock, since his father spends all day in town delivering his taxidermy orders. Sunday is more of a family day, and Stellen said he's expected to be at home helping with chores. He's waiting outside when I pull up and he piles into the Jeep with an eager smile.

"Good morning, Miss Moon."

"Good morning, Stellen. And please call me Mitzy. We're friends, remember?"

He nods happily. "You don't have to buy me another statue. I mean, it's super nice and all, but I just want to say, you don't have to."

"I know. But, like I said, I really appreciated you telling me what you saw, and I know what it's like to lose your mom, you know?"

He swallows hard and nods.

The selection at the statuary center in Broken Rock is vaster than I would've imagined. As we walk down the first row, Stellen bends over and picks up a small heart-shaped stone, almost like a steppingstone.

"How about this one? This is good."

"Are you sure? I don't mean to brag, but I could

literally afford any statue in here. And, I've seen your meadow. I think it deserves a more memorable piece. Don't worry about the cost, okay? No strings attached, I promise. You already kept up your end of the deal."

He nods and sets the small stone heart back on the ground.

"Take your time. Walk up and down all the aisles and look at everything. You'll know when you find the right one."

He nods and trudges through the knee-deep snow toward the other end of the outdoor lot.

I guess it's pretty hard to shovel between all of this, or maybe they just haven't gotten around to it. As I glance up and down the rows of reindeer, moose, frogs, mushrooms, and pretty much all forms of flora and fauna, I have a warm little thought. I've never actually been to my grandmother's grave. Seeing as how she doesn't seem to be gone in my world, it never occurred to me to see where she's buried. Maybe I should find some little memento to place next to her headstone. At least it'll give me something to do while Stellen completes his search. By the time he tracks me down, most of the morning has disappeared, and despite the fact that I found a lovely marble cardinal inside the warm retail area, I've changed my mind about visiting the cemetery.

"Miss— Mitzy, I think I found something, but if it's too much, that's okay. I can find something else."

I set the little stone bird down on its shelf and whisper, "When I'm ready."

As I follow Stellen back to his discovery, I realize that no matter what he's chosen, I'll have to purchase it or I'll never have time to get back to Pin Cherry and get ready for my dinner date.

As we tramp down the row, I see various sculptures of elves, gnomes, and angels.

"Is this one okay?"

I don't even have to look at my mood ring to know that I would see an image of this statue in Stellen's memory meadow. It couldn't be more perfect. An angel crouched on one knee with his hand on the head of a beloved dog. The angel's wings are partially extended but the tips curve protectively around the dog, creating almost a heart shape from top to bottom. "I think it's perfect."

"Good. The angel's face kind of reminds me of my mom and . . . you know, the dog . . ."

"It's perfect, Stellen. A beautiful way to honor your mom and Chuckwalla. I'll tell them to load it up."

Back inside, the owner explains how I'll need a twenty-pound bag of sand to fill the base once we get it in position. I'm extremely pleased to hear that it's lighter than it looks and that the sand can be added separately, as I consider the distance from Stellen's driveway to his memory meadow. I hadn't really thought things through when I told him he could have any statue he wanted.

One thing I'm learning about my dearly departed grandmother is that she has more than a taste for finer things. Upon closer inspection, it appears that she replaced her addiction to alcohol with an addiction to wealth and haute couture. Her shoe collection aside, let me present her whole-hearted support of selecting the appropriate outfit for my date with the previously condemned Rory Bombay. Now that he's lavished me with gifts and invited me to an exclusive, upscale fine-dining establishment, all bets are off. Grams' change of heart appears to have a direct correlation to fabulous "un-cursed" emerald rings and buttery leather gloves.

"Have you finished your hair?" Grams hurtles through the wall from the closet into the bathroom and examines my attempt at a French twist.

"Oh no! Let me give it a shot." Her ability to affect material objects is definitely becoming stronger. As she pokes, prods, and smooths out my messy twisted hair, I can almost feel her touch.

"All right, dear, I've improved this as best I can and you'll have to stick one of those bobby pins right through me into this twist."

I do as I'm told, pretending not to feel the unsettling sensation of pushing my fingers through my grandmother's ghost. When I hold up the hand mirror to check my work, I have to admit Grams' magic touch—no pun intended—has improved the overall sophistication of the hairdo.

"Now, that's done. Did you use the green eye shadow pallet I pointed to earlier?"

"Yes, Grams."

"Let me look at you." She carefully inspects my makeup application and nods a hesitant approval. "That'll do. Now, into the closet." She blasts through the wall while I embrace my humanity and walk around to the actual doorway.

"Silas dropped off the ring earlier and he said it's perfectly safe for you to wear. He claims the hex was amateurish, and after some brief research he simply had to ground out the energy to release the endless loop that was trapping and intensifying your powers. But if I were you, I'd leave that mood ring in our jewelry box. I don't think it's worth the risk of wearing them both together."

"Agreed." I pick up the ring off the padded mahogany bench and slip it on my right hand. The delicate cat's-eye cut emerald absolutely sparkles in the exquisite closet lighting.

"It is a lovely ring, dear. That's why I chose the emerald-green silk-velvet cocktail number by Ceil Chapman, and the Jimmy Choo patent leather platform pumps."

I examine the curve-hugging cut of the tea-length emerald-green designer dress and smirk. "That should do the trick."

"There will be no trick doing, young lady. I still have my reservations about this man and I insist that this first date include supper only."

Oh boy. Hot tears well up in the corners of my eye and Ghost-ma rushes over, fanning her ethereal hands uselessly in front of my face.

"Don't cry, sweetie. Don't cry. You'll muss your makeup. And your eyeliner is absolutely perfect. Deep breaths. Look up at the ceiling and blink slowly."

I do as I'm told and somehow managed to hold the flood of teardrops at bay.

"What's wrong? I thought you wanted to go on this date."

"I absolutely do. It's just that . . . It's just . . . you were scolding me, and making rules. I really miss my mom."

"Deep breaths. Deep breaths. Your mom would

be so proud of the beautiful young woman that you've become. One of the greatest regrets of my life, besides leaving Odell, is not having the chance to meet your mother. But we have each other, dear. Now, you blink away those tears and slip into this gorgeous dress and let me see how you look."

I have to admire Grams' ability to plumb the depths of emotion and bounce right back to fashion in the space of sixty seconds.

Nodding, I attempt to exhale all the pent-up emotion in one go.

I slip into the perfect portrait of a well-to-do heiress and for the first time in my life, use something called a "zipper hook." "That's a very handy device."

"It's an absolute must for an empowered woman of means, living on her own."

I chuckle and turn back and forth in front of the full-length mirror.

"You look smashing, Mitzy. I wish I was going along."

I slip my feet into the rather high heels and groan.

"Don't you start. As I've told you before, I can easily think of ten women who would kill to wear those shoes for five minutes."

"They're gorgeous shoes, Grams. It's just that,

well, I don't know if you've noticed—I'm a little clumsy. And these heels just mean I have farther to fall." I gesture to the six or maybe seven inches of pointy-ness.

She laughs a little too long at my expense before she replies, "A lady of your caliber is worth waiting for. Just walk slowly and purposefully. If he tries to rush you, then he's not worth it."

Somewhere in the layers of those instructions, I feel she's not actually talking about shoes, but I'm too old to be having *that* discussion.

My phone gives a startlingly loud PING, and I stare at Grams. "He's here."

"All right, put on that cashmere overcoat and tell him you will be down when you're ready."

"Lessons from the expert!" I giggle while I text my version of that message to Rory.

Grams whizzes in front of me with her hands waving wildly. "The gloves! You have to wear the gloves. A man likes to see that his gift is appreciated."

"I'm wearing the ring, Grams. I don't want to come on too strong, all right?"

"Of course, the ring is perfect. Understated, plus it shows him that it wasn't cursed."

"But it was. Wasn't it?"

"Would you like to explain to him how your alchemist-lawyer used his arcane powers to banish the gypsy's curse?"

"Well, when you put it that way." I chuckle along with Grams and blow her a kiss goodbye.

Managing the circular staircase proves tricky in the Choos, so I wisely unhook the "No Admittance" chain before exiting out the side door. Twiggy is gone for the day, and I have no one to lock up behind me if I leave through the front door.

Rory's Land Rover is parked right outside the door and he's standing at the ready with the passenger side door open. "The interior temperature is a cozy 71°F and the seat warmer is on 'three.'" He grins and winks playfully as he takes my hand and helps me into the car.

Was that an *Elf* reference? This guy might have an unexplored humorous side. This idea intrigues me.

His hand lingers on mine for a moment. "You're wearing the ring." He rubs his thumb over the beautiful stone. "What about the curse?"

I attempt to look embarrassed as I lie. "No curse. I think I had a touch of the flu. Probably caught some nasty bug when I was swimming around in that Petri dish they call a high school."

"Hmmm." He gently lays my hand in my lap and pats it, but his face doesn't display the relief I'd hoped it would.

He keeps the conversation light and the banter flirty on the drive to Grand Falls.

Regardless of his assurances, I have my doubts about a Michelin star restaurant in almost-Canada, but as soon we pull into the circular drive in front of Yves Bistro, I have to catch my breath. The entire scene is lit with a plethora of tiny, white sparkling lights and the place oozes spectacular promise.

Rory notes my expression and tosses me a few details. "The staff all wear traditional Finnish costumes, and the homestead is covered in hand-hewn wood siding. Most of the structure is original, from the late 1800s, but the wine cellar is all new construction. The original settlers would only have had a small root cellar."

"You really do love antiquities." I grin.

"Do what you love and the money will follow. Isn't that what they say?"

"They do. Whoever 'they' are."

He stops his vehicle in front of the pristine sidewalk and a young man dressed in knee-length knickerbockers, a woolen waistcoat, large squat top hat, and buckled shoes jogs around to take the keys. His "twin" steps up to open my door but Rory calls to him, "I'll assist the lady. Thanks anyway."

He walks around the vehicle, opens my door and nearly scoops me out of the Rover.

His arm feels reassuring around my waist, and

I'm grateful for the added support as I navigate the narrow steps to the front door of the renovated homestead.

Once inside, a lovely coat-check girl in a skirt, cotton blouse, vest, apron, and beribboned head-dress takes our coats.

"The restrooms are down that hallway past the mahogany sideboard."

We nod our thanks, and Rory adds, "That's an exquisite piece."

The young girl smiles vacantly. I know that look. It's the "we all have to pool our tips, so I better not blow this for the team" look.

Rory guides me toward the stairs leading to the basement wine cellar and the pre-dinner pairings.

The stairs seem to be overly authentic. The treads are narrow and the run is steep. I have to turn my feet sideways to keep from tipping right out of my Jimmy Choos.

As soon as Rory hits the last step, a very hand-some Mediterranean-looking man glides over and grips his hand firmly. "Mr. Bombay! I was hoping you would return. And who is this breathtaking creature?"

I appreciate the breathtaking, but I'm not crazy about "creature."

Rory pats the man on the back with his left

hand as he draws me into the conversation. "This intelligent and fascinating woman is Mizithra Moon, of the Duncan-Moon Philanthropic Foundation."

The chef grips my right hand and raises the fingers to his lips. Before he releases his grip, he comments on my ring. "That is a stunning emerald, Miss Moon. But you truly wear *it*, not the other way around."

I'm not entirely sure I appreciate the way his eyes slide over my body like a greasy hand.

"What have you prepared for us tonight, Chef?" Rory casually inserts himself between my body and the chef's looming frame. But as soon as the topic of food is raised, the man is pure perfection. "Follow me, Mr. Bombay. Here we have a balsamic onion tartlet paired with a 1980 Samos Nectar."

After the third pairing of scrumptious bites with wines I can't pronounce, I excuse myself to use the restroom.

Two steps from the top of the stairs, a very recognizable set of broad shoulders darkens the doorway. And, true to form, my heel slips off the narrow tread, I wave my arms wildly and luckily fall forward, but unluckily smack my knee directly on the edge of the upper step.

The pain is excruciating, and it takes all my focus to keep from screaming or bawling like a baby.

Before I know what's happening, I've been scooped up as though I'm a damsel in distress, and Erick is giving orders like a medic on a battlefield.

The hostess is the first to be conscripted. "Move that arrangement off the sideboard."

A random server is next. "You, get me some ice from the kitchen. If you don't have plastic, wrap it in a dish towel." He sets me on the sideboard like a child's doll and lifts my legs up to rest parallel.

I was less embarrassed when I tripped and fell.

"Is there any chance you're here for some reason other than to rescue me?"

He takes the bag of ice from the kitchen staff and places it on my knee. "It's my mother's birthday. But let me check your ankle."

"Erick, I'm fine. Honestly. I just tripped. Nothing's broken. Seriously, this is very embarrassing."

He ignores my plea for leniency and continues his examination of my ankle. And I can't say that having his hands all over my leg is exactly a bad thing.

"I'm sure you'll have a nasty bruise on your knee, and I'm sorry about that. But I don't think you twisted your ankle." He holds up the Jimmy Choo like it's a tarantula and shakes his head as he sets it on the sideboard. "I imagine you'll be happy to know these deathtrap shoes appear to be unscathed."

His little triage center is starting to draw attention and the heat in my cheeks is from more than just his nearness.

He's right in the middle of taking one more "better safe than sorry" look at my ankle when things turn from bad to worse.

"Mitzy, what's going on?"

I'd like to say Rory's tone is all concern, but a great deal of it sounds like accusation or even resentment. Can I really blame him? I'm supposed to be on this very fancy dinner date, and somehow I've turned it into yet another opportunity for Sheriff Erick to rescue me.

"Rory, I'm so glad you're here. I tripped and fell. Extremely embarrassing. Yet not as embarrassing as all of this. Can you please get me down from here so we can continue our date?" I hope I've emphasized the word "date" enough for both of the boys to receive my meaning.

"Ah, Sheriff Harper. I suppose I should thank you for rescuing my dinner companion from a possible gangrenous infection."

Whoo, I do admire the sarcasm, although I'm sure Erick is simply acting on instinct and would much rather spend his mother's birthday with his mother.

"All part of the job, Mr. Bombay. I like to think that as sheriff, I'm never really off duty."

"You do seem to run a full-service department, Sheriff."

"I guess I'll have to get *myself* off this sideboard, eh boys?" I slip on my shoe, swing my legs down, and land gingerly on my feet, as Erick grabs my left elbow and Rory grabs the right. This evening shows no sign of improving. But at least now I feel confident in saying that things couldn't be worse.

"Ricky? Ricky, is this the lovely girl you're always talking about?"

I can practically feel the heat off Erick's face. But he doesn't even have a chance to respond before she tosses another one our way.

"My goodness! You're every bit as lovely as my Ricky says. That hair of yours! White as the driven snow!" She stares at me with a pleasant, motherly smile and adds, "And you in that dress! Breathtaking, dear. Breathtaking. Are you joining us for dinner?"

Clearly Rory is past the pleasantries and eager to restate his claim. "Good evening, Mrs. Harper, I'm Rory Bombay. I own the antiquities store in town, and Miss Moon is my dinner companion." He threads my arm through his elbow and nearly drags me downstairs.

I risk a backward glance and Erick shrugs in my general direction as he mouths the word, "Sorry."

I'd like to feel sorry, but I don't feel even a tiny bit apologetic. I'm not pleased that I tripped and fell, and made a spectacle of myself. But I've absolutely done worse this week, and it was worth it all to get the inside scoop on what "Ricky" really thinks of me. Breathtaking? That's something Erick's neglected to mention when he's telling me to mind my own business. I grin mischievously.

"Mitzy, are you actually all right? If you're injured, I'm happy to take you home and reschedule."

I better stop imagining what dating Erick could be like and start appreciating the date I'm already on. "Honestly, Rory, I'm fine. I think Erick just has a hero complex and overreacts at the slightest provocation. I tripped, which probably embarrassed him more than it hurt me, and he swooped in to save the day. I'm one hundred percent fine. I'm totally focused on enjoying my evening with my dinner companion." I smirk appropriately when I repeat his phrase and seal my promise with a little peck on his cheek.

I can assure you I do not need my mood ring to tell me how successful that gesture proves to be.

The worry evaporates from his sparkling green eyes and he smiles warmly as he scoops an arm around my waist. "I was hoping you'd say that, Miss

Moon. I'd like this to be the first of many dinners together."

I lower my eyelids demurely, but inside I'm wondering if I can successfully juggle my blossoming social life. I mean, I'm not that clumsy—right?

End of Book 3

~ A NOTE FROM TRIXIE

Another case solved! I'll keep writing them if you keep reading . . .

The best part of "living" in Pin Cherry Harbor has been the wonderful feedback from my early readers. Thank you to my alpha readers Angel and Michael. HUGE thanks to my fantastic beta readers who continue to give me extremely useful and honest feedback: Veronica McIntyre, Renee Arthur, and Nadine Peterse-Vrijhof. And big "small town" hugs to the world's best ARC Team – Trixie's Mystery ARC Detectives!

Much appreciation to my brilliant editor Philip Newey! Some author's dread edits, but it is always a pleasure to work with Philip, and I look forward to many more. Any errors are my own, as my outdated version of Word insists on showing me only what it likes and when it feels so moved.

Now I'm writing book four in the Mitzy Moon Mysteries series, and I think I may just live in Pin Cherry Harbor forever. Mitzy, Grams, and Pyewacket got into plenty of trouble in book one, *Fries and Alibis*. But I'd have to say that book three, *Wings and Broken Things*, is when most readers say the series becomes unputdownable.

I hope you'll continue to hang out with us.

Trixie Silvertale (December 2019)

SPARKS AND LANDMARKS

Mitzy Moon Mysteries 4

A suspicious fire. A Valentine's Day discovery. Will this psychic sleuth gamble—and lose?

Mitzy Moon's clairvoyant abilities are growing, but she never predicted arson. After waking to a towering inferno and loading her mentor into an ambulance, she thought things couldn't get worse. But when the sheriff links her father to the blaze, she's forced to take the case.

Coming up empty on love and leads pushes Mitzy to unnecessary risks. Now her otherworldly helpers, a nosy Ghost-ma and a fiendish feline, are the only ones who can save her bacon. But with break-ins, Bingo, and big storms stalling out her investigation, she may not be able to keep her dad out of jail.

Can Mitzy dig up the right clues, or will she fall for a sinister plot that puts her six feet under?

Sparks and Landmarks is the fourth book in the hilarious paranormal cozy mystery series, Mitzy Moon Mysteries. If you like snarky heroines, supernatural intrigue, and a dash of romance, then you'll love Trixie Silvertale's twisty whodunits.

Buy *Sparks and Landmarks* to light the fuse on a mystery today!

Grab yours here! https://readerlinks.com/l/884696

Or scan this QR Code with the camera on your phone.

SPECIAL INVITATION . . .

Come visit Pin Cherry Harbor!

Get access to the Exclusive Mitzy Moon Mysteries character quiz – free!

Find out which character you are in Pin Cherry Harbor and see if you have what it takes to be part of Mitzy's gang.

This quiz is only available to members of the Paranormal Cozy Club, Trixie Silvertale's reader group.

Click the link below to join the club and get access to the quiz:

Join Trixie's Club
http://trixiesilvertale.com/paranormal-cozy-club/

Once you're in the Club, you'll also be the first to receive updates from Pin Cherry Harbor and access to giveaways, new release announcements, behind-the-scenes secrets, and much more!

Scan this QR Code with the camera on your phone. You'll be taken right to the page to join the Club!

THANK YOU!

Trying out a new book is always a risk and I'm thankful that you rolled the dice with Mitzy Moon. If you loved the book, the sweetest thing you can do (*even sweeter than pin cherry pie à la mode*) is to leave a review so that other readers will take a chance on Mitzy and the gang.

Don't feel you have to write a book report. A brief comment like, "Can't wait to read the next book in this series!" will help potential readers make their choice.

★★★★★

Leave a quick review HERE

https://readerlinks.com/l/1562453

★★★★★

Thank you, and I'll see you in Pin Cherry Harbor!

Scan this QR Code with the camera on your phone. You'll be taken right to the page to leave a review for this Mitzy Moon Mysteries series Books 1 - 3!

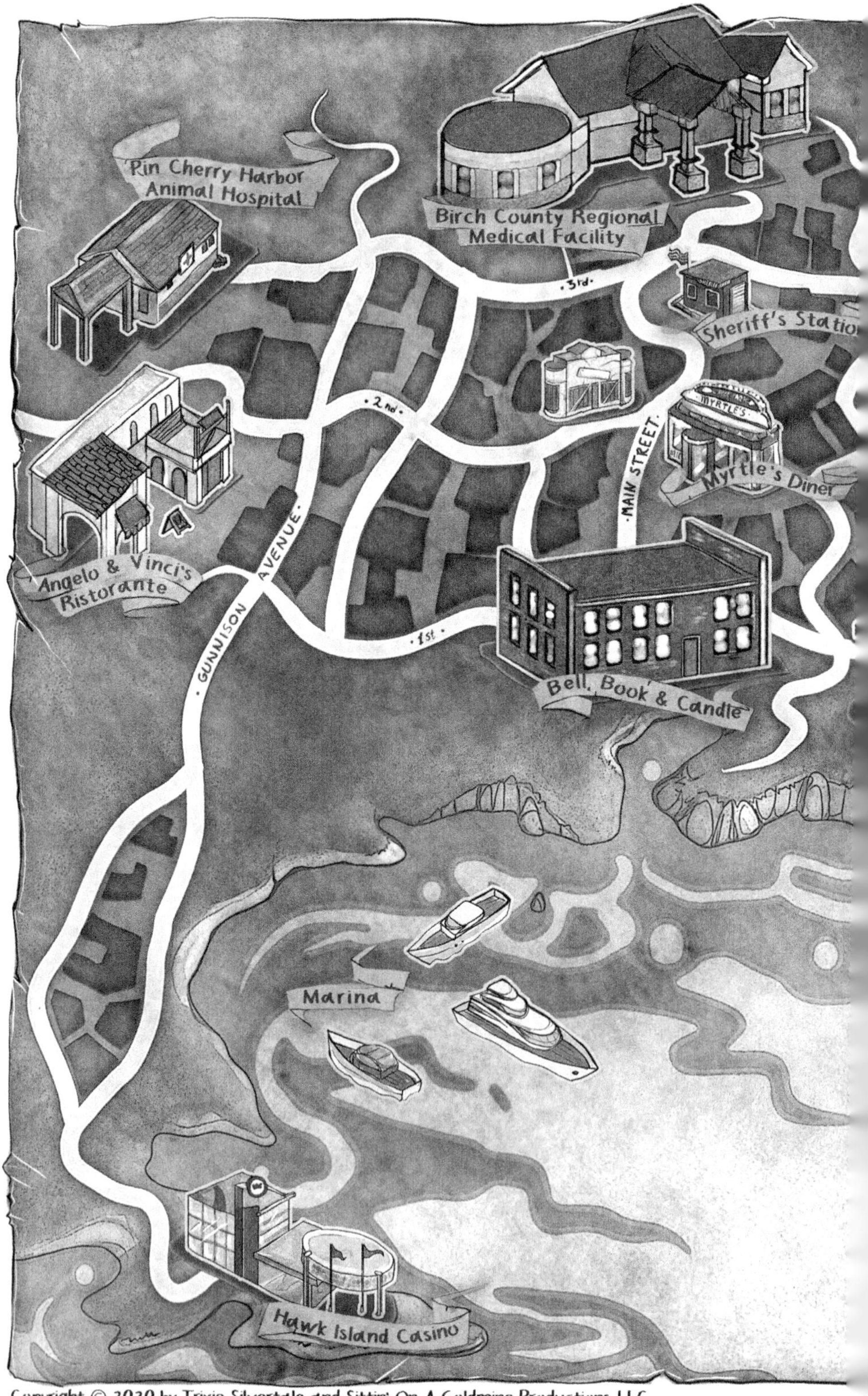
Pin Cherry Harbor Animal Hospital
Birch County Regional Medical Facility
3rd
Sheriff's Station
2nd
MAIN STREET
MYRTLE'S
Myrtle's Diner
GUNNISON AVENUE
Angelo & Vinci's Ristorante
1st
Bell, Book & Candle
Marina
Hawk Island Casino

iggly Wiggly
WIGGLY
Pin Cherry Harbor High School
City Hall
3rd.
TRAIN
Train Depot
3rd.
oux
PATISSERIE
Pin Cherry Harbor Library
2nd.
1st.
Final Destination
an Restorative Justice
Pin Cherry Harbor
est. 1894
Chez Osprey
Lighthouse
REN

ALSO BY TRIXIE SILVERTALE

MITZY MOON MYSTERIES

Fries and Alibis: Paranormal Cozy Mystery

Tattoos and Clues: Paranormal Cozy Mystery

Wings and Broken Things: Paranormal Cozy Mystery

Sparks and Landmarks: Paranormal Cozy Mystery

Charms and Firearms: Paranormal Cozy Mystery

Bars and Boxcars: Paranormal Cozy Mystery

Swords and Fallen Lords: Paranormal Cozy Mystery

Wakes and High Stakes: Paranormal Cozy Mystery

Tracks and Flashbacks: Paranormal Cozy Mystery

Lies and Pumpkin Pies: Paranormal Cozy Mystery

Hopes and Slippery Slopes: Paranormal Cozy Mystery

Hearts and Dark Arts: Paranormal Cozy Mystery

Dames and Deadly Games: Paranormal Cozy Mystery

Castaways and Longer Days: Paranormal Cozy Mystery

Schemes and Bad Dreams: Paranormal Cozy Mystery

Carols and Yule Perils: Paranormal Cozy Mystery

Dangers and Empty Mangers: Paranormal Cozy Mystery

Heists and Poltergeists: Paranormal Cozy Mystery

Blades and Bridesmaids: Paranormal Cozy Mystery

More to come!

ABOUT THE AUTHOR

Trixie Silvertale grew up reading an endless supply of Lilian Jackson Braun, Hardy Boys, and Nancy Drew novels. She loves the amateur sleuths in cozy mysteries and obsesses about all things paranormal. Those two passions unite in her Mitzy Moon Mysteries, and she's thrilled to write them and share them with you.

When she's not consumed by writing, she bakes to fuel her creative engine and pulls weeds in her herb garden to clear her head (*and sometimes she pulls out her hair, but mostly weeds*).

Greetings are welcome:
trixie@trixiesilvertale.com

BB bookbub.com/authors/trixie-silvertale

facebook.com/TrixieSilvertale

instagram.com/trixiesilvertale

Printed in Great Britain
by Amazon

26276537R00463